FRANCIS PLUG
Writer in Residence

PAUL EWEN

Leabharlanna Poiblí Chathair Baile Átha Cliath
Dublin City Public Libraries

GALLEY BEGGAR PRESS

First published in 2018
by Galley Beggar Press Limited
37 Dover Street, Norwich NR2 3LG

A CIP for this book is available from the British Library

Paperback ISBN: 978-1-910296-92-9
Limited edition ISBN: 978-1-910296-93-6

Text design by Alex Billington at Tetragon, London
Printed and bound in Great Britain by Clays Ltd and TJ International

For Violet & Vincent

'That I have not got a thousand friends, and a place in England among the esteemed, is entirely my own fault. The door to "success" has been held open to me. The social ladder has been put ready for me to climb… Yet here I am, nowhere, as it were, and infinitely an outsider. And of my own choice.'

D.H. LAWRENCE

'Drunk and with dreams I'm lost out at sea.'

ANGEL OLSEN,
'Drunk and with dreams'

To David Attenborough,

Wow, what should I write? Thinking, thinking. I can't think! I'm supposed to be a proper writer, but I can't even think, let alone write. I can't even pen the most Lower Paleolithic of greetings. Perhaps I have an Early Stone Age skull. You would know, right? My hands haven't evolved either.

Francis Plug

Today **How To Be A Public Author**

they seem more like flipper hands. You should use me in one of your documentaries, David Attenborough. Except I'd probably run away from you, or hide, in a hole, or release a pungent spray. But I'm not dangerous. I'm actually quite docile, like a sub-species of tortoise, upended on my shell, arms + legs kicking. The sun's too bright! It's burning my tender feet and tummy! I'll probably be savaged by... what eats tortoises? Hyenas? Buzzards? Komodo dragons? Termites? Drop bears? You're the expert, David Attenborough. I need to get back to the shelter of my cave. Do tortoises live in caves? Well I do. I'm a cave tortoise, with white, dead eyes. Please, you have to

help me!

Best wishes!

Francis Plug.

GALLEY BEGGAR BRITAIN

The entrance doors to the BBC's Broadcasting House open inwards, like in scary children's stories. The two receptionists are men, one of whom is speaking into a phone, like a Telethon volunteer. I inform his colleague that I'm here to see Sarah Johnson.

Receptionist: Francis Plug?
FP: Yes. Do you know me?
Receptionist: No.
FP: Darn.
Receptionist: You're very early.
FP: Ah, yes. The thing is, I need a bit of time, you see. To sober up.

My visitor's pass is encased within a plastic pouch. All passes are to be displayed prominently, so I pin mine to the middle of my chest, like a circuit board on a *Doctor Who* character. A foyer sign declares that staff and visitors may have their bags and persons searched upon exiting the building. They should get someone from *The Bill* to do that, or perhaps Noddy's friend, Mr Plod. But it looks like they've signed up unknowns for the task. What a shame. They've really missed a trick there.

My reception seat faces the entrance doors. Despite many comings and goings, there's no sign of any famous people. A woman sits nearby reading her phone. She doesn't ring any bells, but maybe she's a star in the making.

FP: Are you here for the *Sherlock* job?

Woman: Sorry?

FP: Are you here for the *Sherlock* job?

Woman: No.

FP: *Monty Python*?

Woman: No.

FP: *Teletubbies*?

Woman: No.

FP: *Some Mothers Do 'Ave 'Em*?

Woman: No.

FP: *Morph*?

Woman: No.

FP: *Crimewatch*?

Woman: Sorry, I need to do something, okay?

The drinks are already wearing off, even though I've come directly from the Yorkshire Grey. Being a Samuel Smith's pub, the Yorkshire Grey has no TVs or radios blaring out. There's also a policy of no advertising or promotional material in-house, so the refined surroundings lack the shouty-ness of other pubs. The BBC appeals for similar reasons. Of course, that'll all change when I'm on air, wanging on about my book.

If you're being broadcast to the nation, and beyond, it's best that you balance your alcohol intake in the run-up. Doing an 'Oliver Reed' is not ideal, but nor is the other extreme: arriving in tatters, a nervous quivering wreck. It's all about calculating the equilibrium. Too wonky either side and you'll end up skew-whiff. My pre-interview drinks had to be methodically thought through, therefore, like a Formula One team considering the track surface and weather conditions. I didn't want to ram full-tilt into a fence, but nor did I wish to stall the engine on the starting grid.

It's easy to see how overnight success and fame can be overwhelming. Unable to cope, many are steered off the straight and narrow path, turning to drugs or drink. Of course, some of us new arrivals are off this path already, so we kind of bump back on briefly, careering wildly, before veering off the opposite side.

Samira Ahmed is interviewing me on Radio 4, for the *Front Row* arts programme. It's a pretty big deal. As an emerging author, it's important to grasp any such prospect with both hands. Given nearly 200,000 books are published each year in the UK alone, there's a lot of pressure to stand out. To squander a chance, such as a BBC interview, due to some ill-thought action or behaviour, would be most careless. All those other authors out there wouldn't thank me. If I encounter them later, at some literary event or such-like, they may prove less than cordial.

Fellow Author: Francis Plug? What a prick.

Sarah Johnson is a producer for Radio 4. She called me the other day with some questions which, I gathered, were to help Samira Ahmed ask *her* questions. But I suspect it was also an opportunity to assess my broadcast abilities, to get a heads up, prior to the recording, in case I spoke like Sasquatch. However, just because I didn't snort and gibber down the phone doesn't mean I'm fit for broadcast. Desperation isn't always something you can hear. Without visual cues, like twitching, fidgety eyes, soiled clothing, or a subservient, demeaning posture, such a judgment is ultimately uninformed. Rancid, petrol-smoked breath and sour, unwashed skin can only present themselves in person.

Although I didn't swear on the phone, I'll have to mind that too. Coarse language is something I used to keep in check, but now, as a result of my circumstances, I've let it slip. This unpicked thread of beery words can be traced back to a letter of eviction for my flat, and the subsequent repossessing of my van and gardening tools, which stripped me of my livelihood and primary means of income. There have also been some unrelated legal issues and threats to contend with, and the small matter of living under fir trees for a time, or hiding overnight inside pubs. Perhaps any screw-ups can be bleeped out, or replaced with another audio bite from the BBC's extensive archive, such as a Big Ben toll, or a Thunderbirds launch, or a howler monkey.

When Sarah Johnson arrives to collect me, I'm ticking off a list of things that I hope to see, for real, during my BBC visit.

FP: Weather presenting stick. Zippy's zip-mouth earring. *Songs of Praise* candle...

Sarah Johnson: Hi Francis, I'm Sarah.

FP: Hi Sarah.

Sarah Johnson: Have you come far?

FP: No, I'm in West Hampstead at the moment.

Sarah Johnson: Oh yes.

FP: As opposed to Hampstead Village. I haven't caught the gravy train just yet. I haven't started wearing a suit jacket without a tie.

Sarah Johnson: No, sure. West Hampstead's a quick trip on the Tube, isn't it? Jubilee line to Bond Street?

FP: Actually, I got the bus. The 139. It heads straight down Abbey Road, over the zebra crossing outside the studios.

Sarah Johnson: Of course, *the* zebra crossing.

FP: Yes. I always imagine the 139's brakes failing, and we career down Abbey Road, taking out all of the Beatles. Splat! And that would be the end of all that.

Sarah Johnson: Mm. Well, thankfully you're a few decades late.

FP: There's still Paul and Ringo. The worst ones.

A set of revolving doors leads from the foyer into the depths of the building itself. These are patrolled by a security guard, but, disappointingly, it's not Ronnie Barker in his *Porridge* uniform. Sarah Johnson beeps a turnstile with her staff pass so we can progress further, before beeping the lift into action. Inside, important people are talking earnestly, but they aren't famous important people. Sarah chats separately with me as we journey upwards. Most of the TV studios, she says, are based in the newer U-shaped wing of the building, whereas I'll be in the old bit, with the radio crowd. That's a shame, I think. What could possibly be worth seeing for real in a radio studio? Soundproofing foam? Hollowed-out coconut shells used for making clippity-clop horse noises? I begin ticking a new list off on my fingers. The lift is very slow.

Sarah Johnson: Have you done any radio work before, Francis?

FP: No. But when I was little I used to listen to Spike Milligan's story *Badjelly the Witch*. That was on the radio all the time.

Sarah Johnson: Was it? I don't think I know that one.

FP: It's when Tim and Rose go looking for their cow Lucy, who's been kidnapped by a witch, called Badjelly. She tries to poke God's eyes out.

Sarah Johnson: The witch does?

FP: Correct.

The other people in the lift have stopped talking and are now looking at the ceiling.

FP: And Badjelly the witch is always screaming KNICKERS, KNICKERS! STINKY-POO, STINKY-POO!

Sarah Johnson: Ah, here we are.

There are more pass-operated doors to beep, and a myriad of hallways and turns as we delve deeper into the BBC's house. They have plenty of spare bedrooms by the look of it, many of which have soundproofing on the walls, which would be good insulation in winter.

FP: How many toilets are there in this house?
Sarah Johnson: In Broadcasting House? I really couldn't tell you.
FP: More than Buckingham Palace?
Sarah Johnson: Probably...
FP: They have seventy-eight. Seventy-eight throne rooms.
Sarah Johnson: Do you need the toilet, before we start?
FP: Better safe than sorry, right?

When I'm done, hands washed and dried, we proceed into another long corridor. Two women wait further ahead. One of these, I learn, is a sound engineer called Jeneal, and the other is my interviewer, Samira Ahmed. Like Sarah Johnson, they are most welcoming and do their best to put me at ease. No doubt they're used to dealing with famous authors, and since my novel is a thinly veiled self-help guide, alluding to fears of public speaking and social encounters in general, they are extra vigilant. Sarah Johnson magics up a plastic cup of water before directing me to my seat in the studio. She and Jeneal adjourn to the control room next door, where they're visible through a large window. It's like looking at them in space, from the deck of the *Enterprise*, except they're the ones behind the controls, and I'm the floating one, lacking oxygen. Samira Ahmed and myself are on either side of a large round table. From it sprout a dozen or so protruding microphones, each with a different coloured foam top. Mine is green.

FP: Ha! It's like Zoot's nose!

Samira Ahmed: Zoot?

FP: The saxophone player in *The Muppets*. Even though he's blue, he has a green foamy nose.

Samira Ahmed: I see.

FP: Fozzie Bear has brown hairy fur, but his nose is pink. And Floyd Pepper, the bass player, is purple but his nose is orange.

Samira Ahmed: Interesting. *The Muppets* crop up in your book, don't they? When you're at the Arundhati Roy event and you're wondering which Muppet says 'Five seconds till curtain'.

FP: How did you know that?

Samira Ahmed: It's in your book.

FP: What, you've actually read my book?

Samira Ahmed: Yes, of course.

FP: Shit a brick!

Jeneal, it transpires, has used our Muppet chat to do a sound level check. Samira Ahmed suggests I read a passage from my book, and we can use this as a conversation starter. A pre-selected passage has already been typed up and printed onto a single sheet of paper. Some authors recommend reading your own work aloud as part of the writing process. This, they believe, helps with the rhythm and flow of the text. Personally, I feel a bit silly reciting my written words aloud, particularly since I tend to write in the sort of pubs where spoken word verse hasn't really caught on. Attempting to voice it now, into Zoot's nose, is friggin' embarrassing. It's like getting up in front of the class to read what you did in the holidays, except the class has 60 million people in it, not even counting BBC World Service, which probably runs into the billions. On top of that, I certainly don't remember my holiday journals being so confusing and poorly written.

FP: Whoah. This must have been closing time stuff. Seriously.

Samira Ahmed: Do you want to try again, from the top?

FP: Okay. But maybe you should all just turn away. Talk amongst yourselves…

While I attempt to read my own book, three members of BBC personnel must wait, their time funded from the pockets of the unsuspecting British public. Through my headphones comes Sarah Johnson's voice. Because, on top of everything else, I have to wear blimmin' great headphones.

Sarah Johnson: Francis? Listen, it's fine. Don't worry, we can get an actor in to record that, not a problem. We do that a lot.

FP: I can hear the sea. Can you? Can anyone else hear the sea?

Front Row is an arts magazine show that aims to enlighten listeners by probing those in the arts world about their work. Unfortunately, I don't have any answers. My book, and the processes behind it, are every bit as baffling to me as they are to the next guy. My responses therefore begin as guesses, before inflating into minor untruths, and ultimately elements of fiction themselves. That is, when I remember what the question was.

Samira Ahmed: Sorry, you were talking to George Orwell?

FP: Yes, at the bar of the Boston Arms, in Tufnell Park. And he said, 'Wow, you so have to write that. You'll totally smash it.'

Samira Ahmed: But… didn't he die in back in the 1950s?

FP: [*Pause.*] Maybe it wasn't the Boston Arms. He used to work here at the BBC, didn't he? Not the Boston Arms. No, it was the Yorkshire Grey…

My fidgeting doesn't help. Apparently I've been tapping my nails on my visitor's badge, squeezing my plastic cup in and out, and kicking the metal legs of my chair. In a sensitive audio environment like this, it's not just your sweary words you need to mind. Simple physical movements can end up sounding like a hand dryer in a cuckoo clock factory during the Blitz. Just as well that control room window is soundproofed. They're probably calling me all manner of oaths.

When Ian McEwan was on *Front Row* a few weeks ago, I tuned in, to try and learn from his mistakes. But he had everything buttoned down and sewn up. In fact, he was even correcting his interviewer, and laying down the law. He's clearly an old hand at these things, with fourteen novels under his belt, and his work has even been adapted by the BBC itself. In comparison, as a debut novelist, I'm hardly in any position to throw my weight around. Although possibly sitting in the same chair as Ian McEwan, it's hard enough for me simply not to break noisy wind as a result of my poor diet.

Samira Ahmed: … isn't it? How do you feel about that, in relation to your own work?
FP: Um… I think… it would make a ripper show on the BBC, wouldn't it? Who would I talk to about that…?

Fortunately, this isn't going out live. So all the stuff-ups and the really stupid stuff can be edited out later, sifted from the minor stuff-ups and less stupid stuff. At least it's only radio. At least I'll only *sound* like a complete tool.

Samira Ahmed: Let's stop there, shall we?

Removing the foamy green microphone cover, I affix it to my nose.

FP: What a friggin' Muppet.

As Sarah Johnson escorts me back through the maze of Broadcasting House, every beeped door represents a certain goal reached, like a new stage in a Super Mario game. My interview, Sarah Johnson explains, will be broadcast later this evening, some six hours from now. Enough time, I say, to dig a decent hole, and to sit in that hole, with grass fronds and flax as covering.

Sarah Johnson: I suppose. If you get a hurry on.

As we turnstile back into the reception area, David Attenborough makes a low-key entrance through the main doors. As BBC stars go, he's top of the crop. His career, spanning over sixty years, has been legendary. He is, in fact, the legendary man. He's also a longtime supporter of the BBC, recently praising them and their support of the Natural History Department. The key to the BBC's success, he claims, is its public ownership, which forces it to maintain the highest of standards. Although a national institution, the BBC has been under threat from the present government, who want to slash its budgets as part of their controversial austerity measures. If they had their way, the BBC's two male receptionists would be replaced by one woman, in a pretty frock. And instead of self-opening entrance doors, there would be heavy, old-fashioned ones that you'd have to open yourself, even if you had no arms or legs.

FP: Hello, David Attenborough.
David Attenborough: Hello.

FP: I've just been in for an interview, on Radio 4. About my new book.
David Attenborough: Oh.
FP: Here, I've got a spare copy, let me sign it for you.
David Attenborough: Sorry, what was your name?
FP: Francis Plug. 'To David Attenborough' okay?
David Attenborough: Okay, I am in a bit of a rush…
FP: To David Attenborough…

The book-signing task, I'm finding, is a task indeed. Especially the personal dedications. Straight signature copies, for bookshops, is a blind, impersonal job carried out at pace, as if one were a seismograph during a short, violent earthquake. But personal dedications are different. They require real human contact between myself and a poised, living person, with specific expectations. Even process-driven remarks, such as 'All the best' or 'Best wishes', are potential traps, as I found out at my own book launch.

Man: 'With worm regards'?
FP: Sorry?
Man: You wrote 'With worm regards'.
FP: Ah, yes.
Man: Could you maybe just correct it? Turn the 'o' into an 'a'?
FP: You don't want my worm regards?
Man: Um…?
FP: Lovely worms. With their soil fertilizing. Worm regards to you, sir.

Signing a book for a man who has communicated with forest tribes, gorillas, and members of the royal family obviously requires some special acknowledgement. David Attenborough is standing right there, and he's in a hurry, so I have to think fast on my feet. But I can't. I can't think. I've just had my brain fried, and now I'm pulling into the pits with no petrol, four flat tyres, and billowing smoke.

FP: Sorry, this is embarrassing…

David Attenborough: It's all right, don't worry about it.

FP: No, I am a writer, I know how to write things. I just don't know… I'm not used to writing with other people around. It's a bit like getting undressed at the beach, beneath your wet towel…

David Attenborough: Honestly, you needn't worry.

FP: No, no, no. I've started so I'll finish. That's from a BBC programme, isn't it?

THE
COUNTRY
GIRLS

EDNA O'BRIEN

To Francis Plug

Edna O'Brien.

HUTCHINSON OF LONDON

I live by myself in a garage designed for one car. As a residence, it doesn't quite equate with certain perceived ideas regarding my new literary standing. There's the overriding dampness for one thing, mixed with the ingrained whiff of car oil. The insulation is very poor, the natural light non-existent. And the nightly run of skittery rats really doesn't measure up to the success that my BBC interview might suggest. The garage door isn't even automatic.

My lodging is one of thirty-four conjoined garages, laid out like beach huts behind a stretch of West Hampstead shops. Access is via an alleyway off the high street, allowing vehicle passage, including one man's noisy Porsche, which lives next door. All the wooden doors are painted green, though the shades vary greatly, depending on their upkeep. At night they can't be left open even a smidgen due to bleeding thieves. Having no exterior padlock, my door is a regular target, appearing easy prey. But at the first sound of these light-fingered tinkerers, I am quick to lay down the law.

FP: [*Shouting.*] FEE FI FO FUM!!

West Hampstead doesn't have the literary glamour of its more famous villagey neighbour, but it's nice enough. And although living in a garage, I have actually been published. It might not pay that well, but I'm not eating the rats. Free rent certainly helps. My former gardening clients, the Hargreaves, too old to drive their Bentley and being privy to my literary aspirations, offered me their garage as a writing studio. Given I was between homes at the time, the 'writing studio' became a lodging instead. As a home, it obviously lacks many of the usual comforts. Upon awakening, for instance, I am forced to wee at length into a peach tin. The heating isn't brilliant either. At present, in late October, it's like a breeze-block fridge. Holes in the doors, as well as being rat paths, also enable nippy drafts. A fan heater wouldn't go amiss. Perhaps I'll put the word out at my next author event.

It's mid-morning and although shut inside my garage, I'm in no danger of being asphyxiated by the enveloping fumes. Because the fumes in question contain malt and barley and are presently being expelled, rather than inhaled. Unusually, my phone rings, surprising me with its distinctive *Hit Me with Your Rhythm Stick* ringtone. It's Sam, my co-publisher. He has a couple of 'interesting prospects' to discuss. Firstly, Waterstones' Piccadilly bookshop would like me to attend their Christmas signing event, as a featured author. There'll be free mulled wine. All I have to do is sit around and maybe sign some books.

FP: Let me just see if I'm free that evening yes I'm free.

Also, more importantly, Sam wishes to discuss a prospective job. An actual means of regular employment. The University of Greenwich are looking for an inaugural Writer in Residence.

Sam: It's a paid position. Not much, but... Elly and I thought you might be interested?
FP: A paid job? As a writer?

Sam: Yes. We're not sure exactly what the role would entail, but essentially you'd need to start producing a significant work, such as another novel.

FP: You mean write? They would actually pay me to write?

Sam: Yes.

FP: Ha, ha! When do I start? I can move in today if need be.

Sam: Well, you wouldn't actually *live* there, at the university. But you'd probably get a desk, maybe even an office. Of course, you'd need to apply for the role first, Francis. And if you're lucky, get interviewed…

FP: I can start whenever, I'm really flexible. Tomorrow? If it helps, I can start tomorrow. Just a little desk is fine. It doesn't need to be made from arbutus wood, like Edna O'Brien's.

As small independent publishers, Sam and Elly can't afford to pay me much. But they've tried their best to find me money from other outlets, such as editorial pieces, or online stuff. When my novel first arrived at their Norwich house from the printers, they paid for me to come up on the train and fed me lunch, and drinks, as I signed 100 copies at their dining table.

FP: Wow. I could stay here forever.

Sam: Ha, ha! You better not miss that train!

Thanks to Elly and Sam, copies of my book found their way to reviewers, and it met with some minor acclaim. It didn't win the Booker Prize though, which was an absolute travesty. *I* think it was. Still, as I say, it has had some success. This has bewildered many of the local pub regulars. As one chap noted, they were surprised I could even read. But having seen the reviews I waved about unabashedly, they now think I'm minted. On the day of my BBC interview, I stupidly told all the pub staff and patrons to tune in. As it happened, no one 'could be arsed'. But they still insisted I purchase drinks for the entire pub. In retrospect, I should have applied the Little Red Hen's 'loaf of bread' model to my drinks round, because I still haven't paid that tab back, and probably never will. Since then I've been less vocal about my writerly status, although I haven't been able to shake my nickname.

Pub Patron 1: There he is. It's Gideon.
Pub Patron 2: Gideon? Why do you call him that?
Pub Patron 1: Because his book is everywhere, supposedly, but no one with any fucking sense wants to read it.

The copy I presented to the pub, to be displayed behind the bar, quickly disappeared. When I enquired after it, Ed the landlord said they'd used the cover to start the fire, and the inside pages were being used for arse wiping in the staff toilets.

FP: Mind you don't block your pipes. It's good quality paper.
Ed: No, you're wrong. Chapters one to ten are disintegrating in Beckton sewerage treatment works as we speak.
FP: I hope you didn't wipe your poo on the title page. I wrote a special dedication on that, remember?
Ed: Did you? I added my own signature to it, I'm afraid.

Upon publication, I received ten complimentary copies of my book. It was tempting to sell them all on the Internet, signed first editions, to the highest bidders. But I ended up giving them away, to people I was anxious to impress. My parents, for one, and also my sister Claire. For Anna, my niece, I added a personalized hand-drawn etching of Julian Barnes' severed head. A copy was set aside for the Hargreaves, with thanks for my 'studio', and copy number five was posted to Mr Stapleton, another former gardening client who's involved with the

Booker Prize (what a waste of postage *that* was). A further copy was chewed by rats, so I dropped that into a St Vincent de Paul shop, explaining to the volunteer that despite its condition, it was signed by the author and therefore immensely valuable. A dedicated copy was sacrificed to the pub, as mentioned, and I drunkenly gave another away to someone in the Czech & Slovak Bar & Restaurant, because they looked a bit like Kafka. David Attenborough secured my final spare copy, which leaves just the one edition for any future author events, despite its obvious signs of damp.

If I'd had my sensible shoes on, I would have invested my publishing advance in gardening equipment, to further my primary career. Instead, it all went on drink and cartons of cigarettes. Still, pubs make good offices, being warm, full of desks, and offering soap and mirror facilities. Tidy hair and hygiene are givens for the respected public figure, so I also pay occasional visits to Swiss Cottage Leisure Centre, making use of left-behind shampoos. Seeing my ungainly wet flesh could be traumatic for my readers, but if they're anything like the average author event attendees, they probably swim in deeper waters than me.

Besides aiding cleanliness, pubs are where I write, honing my craft. At present, this involves formulating ideas for the next book. One thought I'm currently chucking about concerns a family who live in a shoe. But it's not the latest trainer, so they're sad. The drinks themselves, while not of a fruit variant, help to get the juices flowing. They're also very useful, as discussed, for surviving the public side of the job.

Novels aren't the only things I write in pubs. I also write ads, for myself, to put on the pub noticeboard.

Experienced residential gardener for hire.
Currently without tools or van.
If you have the tools, he's the gardener.
Competitive rates.

When I last checked, none of the little tear-offs at the bottom of the page were taken, although someone had written across the top:

THIS GUY DOESN'T NEED TOOLS. HE IS ONE!

Replacing the notice, I include an additional contact number, for my agent.

My agent has an office on the edge of Bloomsbury with impressive views across London. It's a very desirable address. Not that she lives there. She may sleep in a one-car garage for all I know, but somehow I really don't think so. As I pace around the reception area waiting for my agent's assistant to collect me, coins fall out of my trouser pockets, spilling onto the floor.

Agent's Assistant: What are you doing down there, Francis?
FP: I've got holes in my pockets.
Agent's Assistant: Oh dear. Can I get you a drink?
FP: Yes, please. Two glasses of sherry, any kind.

My agent's office has various books displayed on stands, like in a bookshop. These represent her victories, the manuscripts she has sold on for publication. It took quite a while for my own book to find success. None of the big publishers would touch it with a barge pole.

Agent: The general comment seems to be: 'We just don't know what to do with it.'
FP: Perhaps they could publish it, as a book, and sell it?

There was another problem. Many of the publishers remembered a particular Booker Prize ceremony, which I, as an unpublished author, had attended. According to some of those present, I'd made a bad impression. It wasn't *that* bad. Okay, so I nearly died, but no one else did.

Eventually a very small publisher took a punt. Small, as in two people. Although a newish venture, Elly and Sam had already garnered acclaim by publishing certain top-notch books that the large, established publishers had chosen to disregard. Perversely, the huge, corporate publishers with the deepest pockets tend to be the tightest and most risk-averse, while for small publishers like mine, each book is literally sink or swim. Still, at least the little folk retain their integrity. Despite suffering sleepless nights fraught with financial worries, at least they can sleep well at night.

FP: … At least they're not morally bankrupt, greedy-guts…

Agent: Now, now Francis. You don't want to burn any *more* bridges. So… what was all this about David Beckham?

On West Hampstead High Street, I noticed a bus shelter advert for a whisky brand, which was fronted by the footballer David Beckham.

FP: David Beckham? Fronting whisky? Come on! He's the golden boy of healthy sports. The nice lad with heaps of kids and charity training camps and really straight royal family mates. The pretty face, the safe pair of hands. If anyone should be advertising whisky, it's me. Whisky and I have a genuine, honest association. That whisky brand needs to sign me up, quick smart.

Agent: Yes, but David Beckham's a football star. A fashion model. You're a minor, first-time novelist. Who, to be fair, doesn't photograph well.

FP: But… but he probably drinks protein shakes. I drink whisky. I should be the face of whisky, even if it's not a pretty one. And there might be freebies. How do we get the ball rolling on this?

Agent: Uh, Francis…

FP: Also, how do *I* get an assistant, who brings people drinks?

After reaching a stalemate on my global whisky ambassador prospects, I stand and prepare to leave. As I do, coins run out of my pockets, down my legs, onto the plush carpet.

FP: Not again!

Agent: You want to get yourself a coin pouch.

FP: A what?

Agent: A coin pouch. A small leather wallet thing you keep your coins in.

FP: That sounds like just the ticket. Do they have them at the Pound Shop?

Agent: The Pound Shop? I wouldn't know. Try Liberty's.

Being an author isn't all it's cracked up to be. Most emerging writers, like myself, need a second trade, unless they're inheritors of significant wealth. Even established mid-list authors are struggling these days, competing against the latest literary trend or 'hit'. Books may be perceived as important in England, home of Eliot, Austen, Shakespeare and Dickens, but as the author of one, I don't feel all that special. Unlike other professions, there's no pension plan or health benefits. Most festivals and appearance slots are unpaid, even though the majority of attendees probably park their cars in the sort of place I live. Perhaps we're expected to be paid in adulation and glory, should any come our way. But if that's the only carrot, we may end up very poor indeed.

Successful authors may have a different view on the writerly life than mine. It would make sense to connect with some of them, to seek out their advice and support. Edna O'Brien might be helpful in this regard. Given her extensive oeuvre, and the many book launches and events under her belt, she must be well equipped to deal with the pressures of author life. Philip Roth once called her the greatest living woman writing in English. As far as I know, he has yet to pass comment on my own abilities. Perhaps he's still poring over the wording. He obviously doesn't need any help in that regard, but I'd be happy to offer suggestions. For instance:

> On the strength of his first book, Francis Plug may well be the greatest writer that ever lived. Which is why, when I die, I'm setting aside a portion of my will for his future development. I encourage all other ageing authors of standing to do the same.

Edna O'Brien is being interviewed by Professor John Mullan as part of a live Book Club event. There'll be a book signing after, so it's a good chance to 'touch base'.

FP: I can really identify with your *Country Girls* characters at the moment.

Edna O'Brien: Oh yes?

FP: Yes. Especially when they go from the countryside to the big city. Because I was a gardener, working in gardens, and now I'm a glitzy published author.

Edna O'Brien: Is that right?

FP: Yes. My photo was in the *Sunday Times*. And I've been interviewed on the BBC. But I'm completely out of my depth. Truth be told, I feel like a lumping eejit.

Edna O'Brien: It can take a bit of getting used to.

FP: I'll be kissing babies next. Do you have to do that?

Edna O'Brien: Kiss babies? Other people's babies?

FP: Obviously I'd put my hand on their mouth and kiss that.

Edna O'Brien: Oh. What did you say your name was?

FP: Francis Plug.

Edna O'Brien: Francis Plug?

FP: Yes, have you heard of me?

Edna O'Brien: I haven't, no.

FP: Darn. Oh, I like that bit in *The Country Girls* when Caithleen says, 'I decided to drink, and drink, and drink, until I was very drunk.'

Edna O'Brien: Did you. What's your book called?

FP: *How to Be a Public Author*.

Edna O'Brien: I must look out for it.

FP: Hilary Mantel has written a blurb for the cover.

Edna O'Brien: Has she? Really? What did she write?

FP: Well, she compared me to Goethe and Shelley...

Edna O'Brien: Gosh.

FP: And then she finished by saying I probably should be chained up.

Edna O'Brien: Chained up?

FP: Yes. I didn't get that bit either.

*To Francis Plug,
with best wishes*

ANONYMITY

A Secret History of English Literature

JOHN MULLAN

John [signature]

London

faber and faber

While Edna O'Brien signs books, Professor John Mullan stands around awkwardly, looking a bit lost. He's the Head of English Literature at the University of London, and it turns out, like Edna O'Brien, he's written books too. Nabbing a copy of one from the desk, I use it as a foil for making conversation.

Professor John Mullan: Francis Plug? The author?

FP: Yes! You've read my book?

Professor John Mullan: No. But apparently I'm *in* it.

FP: Oh… right…

Professor John Mullan: I understand you make fun of my tight black top. And you accuse me of being a 'microphone hog'.

FP: I think you're reading too much into the text, Professor. It's just a novel. And you can't believe everything you read.

Professor John Mullan: How very profound.

FP: I didn't know you'd written a book. Maybe I could interview *you*, on stage. That would be much better than *me* being interviewed by *you*. I wouldn't have to answer all your befuddling literary questions.

Professor John Mullan: Befuddling?

FP: Yes, sir.

Professor John Mullan: But that's rather the point of a book club, isn't it? Asking befuddling literary questions?

FP: I guess. But if you're an author it's a total nightmare scenario.

Professor John Mullan: I think most authors actually relish the opportunity to delve deeper into their work.

FP: Doubt it. They just want to move on to the next thing, don't they? All this critical analysis, it makes you go cross-eyed. Like this. [*Cross-eyed expression.*]

Professor John Mullan: Really. Well, if you'll excuse me, I best circulate.

FP: Wait, I wondered if I might ask you something.

Professor John Mullan: Yes?

FP: The thing is, I've been put forward for a Writer in Residence position, at the University of Greenwich.

Professor John Mullan: You? A Writer in Residence? Good lord.

FP: Thanks. The thing is, I'm not particularly 'academic'. I haven't been blessed with a Cambridge education like yourself, so I don't have loads of chums I can call on for a nod-nod, wink-wink, who's-your-father, quick ascension up the ladder, as it were.

Professor John Mullan: I think you'll find it doesn't operate quite like that…

FP: Yes it does! [*Laughing.*] God! Everyone knows that!

Professor John Mullan: Really.

FP: The thing is, my gardening background doesn't open many doors in the literary/academic worlds, so could you possibly put in a good word for me in Greenwich?

Professor John Mullan: Based on what, exactly?

FP: Um, well… this nice chat? And here, see… I have a copy of your book…

Professor John Mullan's hardback book is rather expensive, and that's one of the problems with drinking. You can make irrational, impulsive purchases. Not on this occasion fortunately, because theft is another problem brought on by drinking, especially when you're hard up, due to the fact that you write books and aren't paid to wang on about them as well.

Liberty department store is one of Britain's most famous shops, first trading in 1875. It is contained within a Tudor revival building, and borders nearby Carnaby Street. This is all news to me too. I've never been near the place. As well as fancy, unusual items, Liberty also sells normal things, like plates. Except they cost a packet.

Salesperson: Do you like that one, sir?
FP: Well, it's a pretty picture and all that. But seriously, you won't even see it when it's covered in gravy.

There are a number of coin pouches on offer. The leather ones are the most expensive, while the cheapest option is made of fabric and comes with a 'fresh Art Nouveau-style finish'. It's £65.
Finding the nearest pub, I spend a stupid sum on drinks instead.

It would be nice to have someone to share my writerly life with. But this of course is the author's conundrum. You can't become a big literary success if you're out with your mates all the time, or having dinner with a prospective partner. You need to be sat down writing, by yourself. Fortunately, us authors are blessed with wonderful imaginations, so good friends and other halves can simply be conjured up. Sometimes, in my West Hampstead haunts, I'll pretend I'm out with my nearest and dearest. If someone starts dragging a chair away, I might protest.

FP: Oi! You just tipped my mate on his arse!

Or, if they attempt to share my table:

FP: Hey! Get your big fat bum off my friend's head!

In Edna O'Brien's *The Country Girls*, one of the nuns runs away with the gardener. Even with my gardening pedigree, I've had no advances from nuns. Having a garage for a home probably doesn't help. After many drinks in the pub, following Liberty's, I end up talking to two women, because of the many drinks.

FP: I've had a few drinks, yes. In fact, I can confidently say that I'm in no state to attend to a dying heifer, for instance.
Woman 1: What?
FP: I s'pose I better get myself back to the garage.
Woman 2: The garage?
FP: Yes, I live in a garage.
Woman 2: You live in a garage?
FP: Yes, a garage. Like the person who invented the Silicon Valley... that all started out of a garage, didn't it? And those bands?
Woman 1: Maybe. But those garages probably had houses attached to them. They didn't *live* in the garages.
FP: Did I tell you I was on the BBC?
Woman 2: Yes!
Woman 1: Jesus, he's blotto, let's run.

Francis!
plug

PORCELAIN

West Hampstead is in north-west London, while Greenwich is in southeast, so getting between the two is a right faff. Logistically, it can be done in two bus journeys, the 139 and the 188, but this takes over two hours each way. A bus could start growing a beard in that time. Bus journeys also cost money, especially twenty of them a week, and every week I'd end up spending almost an entire day on a bus. Over time, an evolutionary period, I'd start growing wheels for legs. Or a fabric seat for a bottom. Of course, the very idea of my landing the Greenwich post is demented. As Captain Ahab might say, it's madness maddened.

In profile, my 188 bus resembles a breed of whale known as a right whale, especially its head. This differs from the head of a sperm whale, which is more like a modern Routemaster bus. The sperm whale's head, according to Ishmael, 'may be compared to a Roman war-chariot (especially in front, where it is so broadly rounded)'. The prominence of the forehead is its key feature. Same with the modern Routemaster. The right whale's head however, like the 188 or Alexander Dennis bus style, has a less rounded, more squarish head. These details are especially noticeable when you're reading *Moby Dick*, like I am. Moby Dick is a sperm whale, and if you picture him, not as a whale but as a bus, he actually becomes quite simple to catch.

FP: 'There's hogsheads of sperm ahead, Mr Stubb, and that's what ye came for. Sperm, sperm's the play!'
Bus Passenger: I beg your pardon?

Like whales, buses can be temperamental, especially when provoked. After swimming along placidly with the smaller fish, all it takes is a few passenger bell rings, all for the same stop, and the bus's mood will change. As if struck by a harpoon, it will lurch ahead, swing impatiently around other buses, run through lights. That's how this 188 is behaving. Although a red right whale, its characteristics are more like that of a white sperm whale, angrily blowing out of its horn hole. It's being tormented by folk wearing headphones, who can't hear the sound of previous bells, with their ears.

When I met Moby, the famous musician, he seemed altogether fascinated by my bus-as-whale findings.

Moby: I'm sorry? You think London buses are whales?
FP: Yes, have you found that too?
Moby: I haven't, no. No, I really can't say I have.

As well as having a name like a sperm whale, Moby is actually a direct descendant of author Herman Melville. At his own book event however, he admitted he'd never finished *Moby Dick*, citing its out-of-date descriptions. It's certainly true that Melville's characters have a habit of saying 'thar' instead of 'there', and of calling trousers 'trowsers'. But I suspect Moby may have been put off by the rather graphic whale-hunting depictions, and the methods for breaking those magnificent mammals down into useable, human-friendly chunks. Despite being known for his multi-selling albums, Moby refers to music as a hobby that makes him happy. But animal rights activism is his real job. As for writing a book, that's a whole new field, and he was open about its difficulties versus writing music.

Moby: If you write a really good chorus, you can repeat it in the same track. But if you write a great paragraph, you can't just repeat it three times.

Moby claimed to have no intention of further touring, but he was on the book tour circuit, which is surely much worse. Although a confident speaker, he seemed somewhat apprehensive when awaiting questions, lacking the arrogance of many big-shot authors.

FP: Writing, I suppose, is what makes me happy. Gardening is my primary job, although I'm presently out of work.
Moby: That's too bad.
FP: 'Squeeze! squeeze! squeeze! all the morning long; I squeezed that sperm…'
Moby: Um…
FP: Your ancestor wrote that.
Moby: Oh. Right.
FP: *And*, weirdly, you're a product of *his* sperm. Fancy that.
Moby: I see. Yes. Kind of…
FP: '… would that I could keep squeezing that sperm forever!'
Moby: Yes. Nice to meet you.

Greenwich is a famed maritime port set on the River Thames, and according to Ishmael, it once served as a base for English whaling ships. Until recently, the Royal Navy was lodged here too, although the crew-cut crowd have been replaced by long-haired, late-rising types, commonly known as students. The University of Greenwich has three campuses, spread over London and Kent, but the main one is here in Greenwich itself, occupying three of the four Old Royal Naval College buildings. The Creative Writing department is based in this picturesque riverside site, set amongst the historic pillars, domes and carved monuments. Having arrived unfashionably early, I decide to seek out a drink and take in the local scene.

Although rich with seafaring connections, there are no bawdy oaths to be heard on the Greenwich streets today. With its proximity to the banking world of Canary Wharf, and its large influx of tourists, Greenwich is altogether scrubbed and polished. But that needn't be a barrier. As a residential gardener, I'm used to working in well-to-do areas well above my station. Even minted areas tend to have budget drinks on offer somewhere. If I am successful with the residency, I'm sure I could find someone with an anchor tattoo. I might even get one myself. Tattoos are very popular with the young folks these days. So if things got awkward in class, and the students started mentioning authors I hadn't heard of, or discussing highbrow criticism or literary theory, I could just roll up my sleeve like the Fonz.

FP: Heyyyy!!!!

Greenwich has UN World Heritage Site status, and due to a thousand years of links with the monarchy, is an official Royal Borough. On the grounds of Greenwich Park is a former palace called the Queen's House, and the present campus grounds were also the site of Greenwich Palace, birthplace of Elizabeth I, Mary I, and Henry VIII. Of course, if Henry were alive today, I daresay he'd reside in the Chicken Palace.

The most famous thing about Greenwich is its Mean Time. This was formerly the global time standard, set at the Royal Observatory, also in Greenwich Park. Pubs don't seem to be short on the ground either, which is useful when you get barred from them a lot. The first two I inspect seem rather pricey, so I'll need to do a proper scout around if I end up dropping anchor. It will be interesting to see, when they call time at the end of an evening, whether it's Greenwich Mean Time, or its superseder, Coordinated Universal Time.

Some of the overseas tourists have cameras protruding out of their chests, like Daleks, which just goes to show the breadth and depth of the BBC's influence.

FP: Excuse me, just so you know, this isn't some futuristic space world. This is historic Greenwich, England. You're supposed to go backwards, not forwards.
Overseas Tourists: [*To each other.*] What did he say?

Greenwich Market dates all the way back to the 1300s. I stop in to a nearby charity shop for muscular dystrophy.

FP: I don't suppose you have any coin pouches?
Charity Shop Woman: Coin pouches? Hmm. I don't think so. Only this sort of thing, for children.
FP: 'Hello Kitty'?
Charity Shop Woman: Yes.
FP: What does that mean?
Charity Shop Woman: I think it's just like... a friendly cat.
FP: Sounds perfect. What's the damage?
Charity Shop Woman: You want it?
FP: You bet.
Charity Shop Woman: Ah, let's see... that's £1.
FP: £1? Wow, it pays to shop around. I nearly paid £65 for one at Liberty's. And that was their *cheapest* model.
Charity Shop Woman: I suppose that was a finer example.
FP: Not really. Not sixty-four times better. It was a pouch you kept coins in. Same as this one.
Charity Shop Woman: Yes.

FP: Still, it's a shame I have to give you a £1 coin, which I could have kept in my new Hello Kitty coin pouch.

Charity Shop Woman: Well, you could buy something else and I could give you change for that, which you could then put in your coin pouch.

FP: No, you're taking the piss now.

Taking pride of place in the central square of Greenwich is the *Cutty Sark*, an original nineteenth-century clipper ship that once sailed the world's seas, collecting wool from Australia and tea from China. These days it rides a glass wave of tourist museum and gift shop, and due to some unfortunate fires, the most recent caused by a faulty vacuum cleaner, possibly isn't quite as 'original' as it was. But to keep the area's maritime history alive, it has been painstakingly reconstructed, offering the outward appearance of authenticity, or 'the real deal'. That's the angle I'll be gunning for myself, quite soon, in my interview.

I'm meeting the Programme Leader of the University's Creative Writing department, Dr Alex Pheby. My guess is he's not a real doctor, but one of those pretend doctors who rush to the assistance of ailing persons on commuter trains, without having a friggin' clue what they're doing. Dr Alex initiated the new Writer in Residence role, and will be overseeing the successful candidate. We'll be discussing the position and my own suitability for that position. The university site is hard to miss; you can count all the buildings on one hand. But I'm hopelessly lost.

FP: Excuse me, do you know where the King William building is?

Security Guard: Yes, it's that building just there. The entrance faces the road, around the back.

FP: So it's kind of on the outer edges of the university, far, far away.

Security Guard: No. It's just there.
FP: There?
Security Guard: Yes, there.
FP: Thar?
Security Guard: Right there.
FP: Thar she blows!
Security Guard:

The King William building, like the others, has a rigid white pallor, reminding one of death, horror, and things that truly appal. The entrance is currently draped with tarpaulin and scaffolding, and builders mingle with students in the entranceway, like worker bees coming and going from a hive. Except some are physical worker bees and the others are probably writing essays about dead authors worker bees. One of the builders has his green worker gloves in his white, upturned hard hat.

FP: Ha! It looks like you're carrying a bowl of salad!
Builder: What the fuck?

With seven minutes to kill, I stand around outside, beside a fence railing, smoking my tomahawk pipe to windward. Students hunch about in groups, their lectures having just finished, or preparing to commence. Some, like me, are smoking, but without the same level of keenness, or focused desperation. Most are staring at phones, no doubt touching base with their social media worlds, checking on new 'posts' and 'updates'. The old whalemen didn't have to worry about that. According to Ishmael, they were completely isolated from the news of the day, often cast out at sea for three years at a time. When living a life on the waves, he reported, 'a sublime uneventfulness invests you'.

FP: A whaleship was Ishmael's Yale and Harvard.

Students: What?

FP: I said, don't forget to smell the bracing sea air, you scruffy young tearaways.

A frazzled guard sits at a post inside. Flurries of students flash their passes at him, each of which he attempts to scrutinize, as if tracing the path of a single, fast-moving fly. Explaining my meeting with Dr Alex, I furnish him with the relevant telephone extension. His conversation with Dr Alex is brief.

Guard: You better come and collect him.

The guard disappears with one of the builders, jingling keys. When Dr Alex Pheby arrives, he's a bit puzzled.

Dr Alex Pheby: I don't understand why he didn't just let you come up to the office.

FP: It is a mystery. Maybe he thought I was one of those gun-toting, homicidal maniacs who murder people on university campuses, like this one.

Dr Alex Pheby: Possibly.

Dr Pheby looks a little bit like a doctor, and a lot like a mad professor. He has a short and distinguished ginger beard, and his eyes are intense and lively, as if engaged in a never-ending public fireworks display. He is moderate in height, and can't be much over forty.

Dr Alex Pheby: Shall we go for a drink? I take it you're not a raging alcoholic, like the character in your book.

FP: Sorry, which character?

As we walk across the college grounds, I ask if he's heard anything from Professor John Mullan, at the University of London.

Dr Alex Pheby: No… in what regard?

FP: Oh, it's just he was going to put in a good word for me. He mentioned it when we were out with Edna O'Brien.

Dr Alex Pheby: I see. Well no, I haven't heard from him. I'm sure he's very busy.

FP: Yes, of course, of course. [*Pause.*] Still, I'll give him a right kick up the arse next time I see him.

Like its Greenwich surroundings, the Old Royal Naval College is popular with sightseers. On the edge of the college grounds is the Discover Greenwich Centre, with information about the site and local area. Adjoining this is a restaurant and bar called the Old Brewery. Large vats are visible through glass-partitioned walls.

FP: Sorry, is that like a proper brewery?

Dr Alex Pheby: Yes, it's part of a local Greenwich brewery. They're doing quite well, I believe.

FP: Wait, you're saying there's an actual *brewery… on-campus*?

Dr Alex Pheby: Yes, shall we talk about the position?

Dr Pheby has a head cold, so he orders a coffee.

FP: You can't beat a spot of gin and molasses to clear the sinuses.

Dr Alex Pheby: Is that so? I'll have to try it. But I'm teaching a class at twelve.

FP: Maybe just a hot rum toddy then, Dr Alex?

Dr Alex Pheby: Call me Alex.

FP: Alex. Or, what about Ishmael? Call you Ishmael?

Dr Alex Pheby: Alex is fine.

Dr Alex reiterates some of the details that Sam had initially discussed. Because it's a new position, the exact duties are yet to be buttoned down, offering the successful applicant the opportunity to help shape the role. Yes. Sure. Fine. I'm simply nodding at everything Dr Alex says. It's a struggle not to laugh. Things are going brilliantly. But I have to stay in check. It's important to show keen interest, and humility.

FP: I'm not one for bells and whistles. I don't need twenty-four-hour secret service police protection, like Salman Rushdie.
Dr Alex Pheby: Okay, good to know.

Dr Alex heard my interview on the BBC. So did his senior colleagues, he tells me.

Dr Alex Pheby: Your book is certainly getting lots of coverage. You must be very pleased.
FP: Yes, I'm amazed. Better to be talked about, and all that. But my interview skills still need work, as you can probably tell, from this one.
Dr Alex Pheby: You came across okay on the radio.
FP: Thanks. Apart from that bit where I was shouting, KNICKERS, KNICKERS! STINKY POO, STINKY POO!
Dr Alex Pheby: Really? They must have edited that bit out.
FP: You are joking me.

Dr Alex is drinking his coffee very slowly. Both of my pint glasses have been empty for ages.

Dr Alex Pheby: Have you started a new book yet?

FP: Yes I have. I've got a title and everything.

Dr Alex Pheby: Oh, what's that?

FP: *Moby Dick.*

Dr Alex Pheby: *Moby Dick*? That's been used before, hasn't it?

FP: Yes, but…

Dr Alex Pheby: We tend to get a bit iffy about plagiarism in the academic world, you see.

FP: Sure, sure. But my interpretation differs from the more famous version. It concerns a man's worldly quest to hunt down a bus. A bus that won't wait for him, even when he runs after it, shouting.

Dr Alex: Ah. That's quite different, isn't it…

FP: Oh yes.

Dr Alex Pheby: Did you say you caught up with Edna O'Brien recently?

FP: Yes, I did.

Dr Alex Pheby: You know her?

FP: Yes, we get on famously. And Philip Roth, I know him too.

Dr Alex Pheby: Really?

FP: Yes. But trying to get a few lines out of him, honestly. It's like trying to get blood out of a stone. You wouldn't think so, would you?

Dr Alex looks at his watch.

Dr Alex Pheby: Um, so do you have any questions for me?

FP: Yes. Do you ever dress up in togas?

Dr Alex Pheby: Togas?

FP: Yes, to keep in theme with all those Roman pillars on campus.

Dr Alex Pheby: No, we don't tend to wear togas. They're not actually Roman, those columns. They're Grecian, I believe.

FP: Okay, good.

Dr Alex Pheby: There aren't any orgies either, as far as I'm aware. At least none that I've been invited to.

FP: Well, if I hear about any I'll be sure to let you know.

Dr Alex Pheby: Thanks.

Dr Alex has to go to his lecture, so I bid him farewell, hoping to hear from him soon. I remain seated in the Old Brewery, attempting to gather my thoughts. It wasn't as stressful as my other interview, the BBC one. At least it wasn't being broadcast to millions. It helped that I could see a brewery, and that I was able to drink from its wares, during the interview process. Although not an accomplished academic, I have published a book, and it turns out certain people go nuts for that. And if whaling ships can have carpenters and blacksmiths, surely a university can have a gardener? Anyway, it seemed to go well, all considering. Or at least I think it did. It's hard to gauge for sure. I am rather drunk.

The Discover Greenwich Centre, adjacent to the brewery, merges museum with info kiosk, offering a concise overview of the Royal Naval College site. Perhaps this will prove useful one day, but for now I'm more interested in the 'hands-on' section, where you can dress up as a sailor or a pirate.

FP: Ah-harrgh!

Woman: Can my son have a turn now?

FP: Ah-harrgh!

The Trafalgar Tavern is a majestic riverside pub, positioned due east of the uni. Majestic riverside pubs, of course, tend to attract tourists and other well-coined folk, so I attempt to use my seafaring knowledge to cut a deal.

FP: Say, do you know the Cape Horn measure?
Bartender: The Cape Horn measure?
FP: Yes. You fill a glass to a certain point and that's a penny. Then a bit more and that's a penny more. Then a bit further and that's a penny more. Then…
Bartender: No, we don't operate that system here. We're not bloody stupid.

It's low tide on the Thames, and a man is slowly sweeping a metal detector about the stony sand. He's wrapped up to the nines, with kneepads strapped over waterproof trowsers. It's a very monotonous task, not helped, I presume, by his headphones playing static, intermingled with the occasional beep. Let's really hope he's not sitting next to me on the bus home. After removing a patch of wet, stinky earth with a trowel, he looks up and I catch his eye. Rubbing my fingers together to indicate money, lots and lots of money, I point towards another area of the bank, on the lee-beam. Throwing invisible money into the air, showering myself in the riches, I urgently point again to the treasure source.

When leaving the Trafalgar, I am shrouded by an overhanging vapour, as if I've just blown all my drinks from my spout. It's very cold, but fortunately I have a thick whisky coat of blubber.

RUTH RENDELL

A NEW LEASE
OF DEATH

To Francis Plug,

Ruth Rendell

PUBLISHED FOR THE CRIME CLUB BY
DOUBLEDAY & COMPANY, INC.
GARDEN CITY, NEW YORK
1967

A larger-than-life snowman is lumbering around just inside the doors to Waterstones Piccadilly. It's not that unusual, being winter time and close to Christmas. You see them all the time, out and about. But this one is a notable example, given he's the hero of Raymond Briggs' famous book. A smiling, enthusiastic woman halts him and poses alongside while another woman takes a photo. *The Snowman* is a children's book, but the posing woman is a grown-up. No one rushes up to me as I proceed further inside, or even offers a nod.

There's no sign of Raymond Briggs, the creative brain. He's not stupid. He's probably at home, lying on a sunbed, with goggles made from walnut shells. Why lump yourself with the public and all that photo nonsense when your characters can do it for you? He's a smart cookie, Raymond Briggs. He's laughing his toasty head off. But how can I emulate his very clever thinking? Although a novel, my book features me for the most part, and I'm real. Perhaps I need a Francis Plug costume that some enthusiastic nobody can wear. They can meet my public while I drink wine in the shadows. Yes, it's definitely worth bringing up with Elly and Sam. Maybe they could cut some sort of deal with Madame Tussauds.

Ruth Rendell, the star attraction for this special Christmas evening, is supposedly on this prestigious ground floor level, but I'll believe that when I see it. I've brought a book along for her to sign, even though I'm convinced she's actually dead. Either way, I'll need to top up with some mulled wine before I find out. Not being in the same league as her or the Snowman, I traipse up to the first floor, to take my place among the lesser scribes.

As it turns out however, I'm sharing a table with spy/thriller writer Mick Herron, winner of the prestigious Golden Dagger Award. He's written a raft of books and, judging by all his signature requests, has quite a following. It's useful to observe a seasoned professional at work. Mick has a very personable manner with the customers, and, like me, is making good use of the free mulled wine being dished out gung-ho by the staff. Unlike myself, however, he's also indulging in the complimentary Christmas mince pies, and therefore leaving many crumbs scattered over our table. It would be harsh to blame the poor interest in my book entirely on Mick's many pie crumbs, but when faced with tens of thousands of books in Waterstones' flagship store, the discerning shopper may well be dissuaded by a messy surface that encourages rats.

We've been provided with two black Sharpie pens for our signings, but I brought along a less shouty biro.

FP: Do you have one of those fancy cross-continent signing pens, Mick, like Margaret Atwood?
Mick Herron: Her LongPen, you mean?
FP: Yes, that.
Mick Herron: I haven't, no.
FP: Not that anyone on this continent seems interested in my signature, let alone in Quebec.

The LongPen is a pen attached to a robotic hand, which allows a person to sign a book in one country while in another. It was conceived of by Margaret Atwood, who most likely thought it would be a good way to avoid signing queues, and also admirers with pissy breath.

Mick Herron: What sort of stuff do you write?

FP: Novels, like you. Are any of your characters here tonight, like the Snowman downstairs?

Mick Herron: Oh no. No, they're far more discreet.

FP: Sure, sure. And I suppose they're mostly dead too. Which'll make it harder for posed photos, with the public.

Mick Herron: Right.

FP: Speaking of dead people, I'm just going to pop down and see Ruth Rendell.

The busy foot traffic on the ground floor ensures greater interest in the authors situated there, enhancing the popularity of already popular authors and cute fictional constructs with seasonal relevance. Ruth Rendell's hair is as well coiffured as ever, and I recognize her perfume from a previous encounter at Paddington Station.

FP: I thought you were dead.

Ruth Rendell: Did you? Well, it would appear not.

FP: But I saw your ghost in Richard Booth's bookshop, in Hay-on-Wye. You slimed me.

Ruth Rendell: Slimed you? Meaning what, exactly?

FP: You know. It was you all right. Absolutely. There can be no doubt.

Ruth Rendell: [*Waving hand in front of her face.*] Have you been drinking petrol?

FP: Not exactly. I had a few whiskys earlier, but now I'm on the free mulled wine. I'm signing books too, upstairs. Because I'm a published author. Of repute.

Ruth Rendell: 'To Francis Plug'. Is that you?

FP: Yes. Have you read my work?

Ruth Rendell: Never heard of you.

FP: I was on the BBC… oh, would you mind adding a doodle… of that body bludgeoned by the axe…

Ruther Rendell: Next please.

No one has enquired after my book in my absence. Mick needs to visit the loo, so I offer to mind his diminishing stock. A middle-aged pair approach the table.

Woman: Are you Mick Herron?

FP: Yes, that's me. These are my spy books.

Woman: Wonderful. Would you mind signing one for me? This one.

FP: Sure.

Man: Where do you get your ideas from?

FP: My spy ideas?

Man: Yes.

FP: Well, I am a spy. So I just take notes as I go.

Woman: You're actually a spy?

FP: Yes, I'm a spy. But for God's sake, don't tell anyone. You'll get me killed.

Man: Oh, no, we won't tell anyone.

FP: Do you know what they do to us spies when they 'out' us?

Man: No.

FP: Electrodes on the bollocks. Like jumper leads, on the wrinkly old balls. Can you imagine?

Woman: Oh my word. That's just awful.

FP: [*Demonstrating.*] Bzzz, bzzz! Brrmm, brrmm. Start you up like a frosty engine. That's what'll happen to me, if you breathe a word of this.

Man: We won't, honest.

FP: Who should I sign it to?

Woman: To Dorothy, please.

FP: To Dorothy.

As she walks away, Dorothy begins flicking through her purchase, revealing the author blurb inside the back cover, and the photo of Mick Herron, with glasses and a clean-shaven face.

Mick Herron: Back again.
FP: I sold one of your books.

The free drinks keep arriving, despite sales on my side of the table being totally dead. I begin to wonder if the mulled wine is leaving me with a dripping red mouth, like one of Mick's victims. An older woman approaches, lowering her glasses and raising her eyebrows, like a teacher's mother, who was also once a teacher. She leans onto the table, resting her knuckles on the cover of my book, leaving indentations.

Older Woman: Francis Plug?
FP: Yes.
Older Woman: I think I heard you on Radio 4.
FP: Right! Yes! I was on Radio 4, yes! STINKY-POO, STINKY-POO! KNICKERS, KNICKERS!
Older Woman: I beg your pardon?

From her shoulder bag she produces a stack of small printed sheets containing tiny rectangular boxes. Peeling two off, she passes them to me.

FP: What are these?
Older Woman: Bookplates. Would you mind signing them?
FP: Bookplates? What are bookplates?
Older Woman: Oh, they're just for adding signatures to books, at a later date.

FP: But my books are right here, right now. There they are.
Older Woman: Are they first impression copies?
FP: I imagine so. I have no idea.

She picks up one of my books and flicks to the publishing page, with the small print.

Older Woman: No, they're not. They're reprints. Look.
FP: Reprints? Wow. That's good news.

Putting the book down, she takes her free signed boxes and prepares to leave.

FP: Wait, don't you want a book? Even one?
Older Woman: No. They're not *first impressions*, are they?
FP: Yes, but… It's the same book, apart from one little number.
Older Woman: No thank you.

She departs with my signature, times four, leaving me performing dagger-stabbing actions, for Mick Herron's benefit.

Mick is originally from Newcastle, but he now lives in Oxford. He's a very nice chap, and we're in the middle of a most cordial authorly chat when a member of the public interrupts us. How annoying! It's an old gent, dressed in a rather dapper grey suit with a blue trim. He speaks in a very plummy, Pathé-style voice, as if narrating a black and white film about dangerous electrical fuses.

Old Gent: In the old days, there was only a very small number of authors writing books. Very good books they were. Proper, well-written books. But now, everyone's an author.

As he says this, he looks rather severely at us, especially me. Browsing our books, he asks Mick if he is a detective writer.

Mick Herron: I'm more in the spy thriller realm.
Old Gent: Oh well, you see, that's me. A spy, yes, those are the circles that I move in.
Mick Herron: Well.
FP: [*Cough.*] Bullshit.

The word 'bullshit' was supposed to be cloaked within my cough, as if it were *part* of my cough. Instead, it emerged separately, *after* the cough. The old gent exhales deeply before leaving in a huff.

FP: Oh dear. I bet authors didn't behave like that in the old days. I'm really not flying the flag for us modern literary folk, am I Mick?
Mick Herron: You probably want to test that cough thing of yours before putting it into practice.
FP: It's the public interaction that's the problem. I might be getting paid, in mulled wine, but that doesn't make me qualified for the job.

Mick raises a glass.

Mick Herron: Here's to your unqualified success.
FP: Cheers!

Eventually I sign a book for a young woman lugging a huge pile of books inside a black shopping basket. Her male friend/partner has his own brimming basket too. I didn't even know bookshops *had* shopping baskets. My precious first customer doesn't seem particularly interested in my book. It's as if she were ticking off a grocery list, and my novel is something less essential, like corn flour. She asks for a dedication, so at least she isn't intending to immediately flog it, online, for a minor profit. Unfortunately, I make a hash of it. Instead of writing 'Thanks for being my precious first customer', I write: 'Thank you my precious, must have the precious, so bright, so sparkling, my precious.' When I realize my error, I attempt to correct it, adding directional arrows to highlight which word should have gone where. It's a friggin' mess. The first book I've signed all night. Have I learned nothing from Mick? The young woman doesn't seem to notice, or care. So I quickly shut the book and pass it across, before corralling the pie crumbs like sheep in pens.

A very pregnant woman asks me to sign my second book of the evening. She's not a customer, but a fellow author, Niki Segnit, who is signing books herself, at a different table. Her publisher is expecting her new book in two days' time, she tells me, but Niki's expecting twins, at any moment.

Niki Segnit: That deadline is just not going to happen. Who knows when it'll be finished?
FP: I'll finish it for you, if you like.
Niki Segnit: Ha, ha. Good one!

Mick has to catch his train back to Oxford. Wishing him a fond farewell, I settle in for a final stretch at the square desk alone. Only a few people now roam the first floor, some of whom have been wandering around since I arrived, some three hours before. They look nervously towards us, the remaining authors, as if plucking up the courage to approach. That was me, less than a year ago. Although full of warm wine, I stare nervously back at them. They might be standing and I might be sitting, but we're very much in the same boat.

The ever-friendly staff continue to set me up with drinks.

Cheerful Wine Provider: How've you been getting on?
FP: Well, I've got these. [*Pointing to crumbs.*]

No doubt aware of my undiminishing pile, he politely requests that I sign my second impression books, to give the store a fighting chance of future sales success. Rather than signing at my leisure, he stands alongside, clutching a sheet of stickers that trumpet: SIGNED BY THE AUTHOR. As soon as I've finished a copy, he immediately seizes it, affixes a sticker and progresses it to a pile. It might sound relatively simple, signing your own name and writing the date, but under time pressure, after many drinks, it can all go askew.

FP: What was the date again?
Cheerful Wine Provider: Sixteenth.

A short time later:

FP: Sorry, what was the date again?
Cheerful Wine Provider: The sixteenth.

Soon afterwards:

FP: I know this is really annoying…

A bit later, unable to find the loos, I wander through a door marked STAFF ONLY. Inside is a storeroom of sorts, with a toilet leading off to one side. Resting on the toilet, I nod off.

When I awaken, the lights have all been switched off, leaving me completely disorientated. Finding a switch outside the toilet, I'm able to recognize the door back to the bookshop. Approaching it, I'm startled to see the Snowman, standing very close by, alongside a sidewall. Although unmelted, he is clearly lifeless, a mere costume, suspended from a hanger. Retrieving him, I put him on.

The bookshop is in darkness too. Wandering about inside the oversized costume, I try and think how a snowman might behave. They're quite boring when you think about it, although Raymond Briggs made his one sneeze and drive a motorbike and fly. But I want to claw people, so I growl and bellow, pretending to be a polar bear instead.

There aren't any people to claw or chase. Not a soul. The shop, it seems, is deserted. Even the doors to the street, as I discover, are firmly locked. I'm stuck inside Waterstones Piccadilly for the night.

Polar Bear: Ha, ha!

It's brilliant, of course. Much warmer than my chilly old garage. There's carpet for one thing, and I'm wrapped in thick, snuggly layers of polar bear hide.

After finding some stray red wine bottles in the basement level, I remember that Waterstones Piccadilly has its own bar, up on the fifth floor. Off I go, like a polar bear searching for seals around the ice floes, before they melt. But I'm also a magical snowman flying in the air.

FP: [*Screaming, in falsetto.*] I'M FLYING IN THE AIR!

THE
SECRET AGENT

A Simple Tale

by

JOSEPH CONRAD

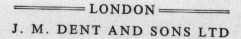

=LONDON=
J. M. DENT AND SONS LTD

A day or so after my Christmas event, there's a call from Elly. She's just got off the phone to Waterstones. The good news, she says, is that I'm currently a hit on social media: *Author locked in Waterstones Piccadilly overnight! Drinks his way through!*

Elly: They're now thinking of having an official public sleepover, in-store.

Unfortunately, the Snowman is in a right state. When discovered, with myself inside, he was spread-eagled on his back, his white chest riddled with red wine splotches. It looked like a drive-by shooting. A photo of this was circulating online also.

Elly: We haven't actually been asked to pay for the costume yet. Or the carpet stains. Or the drinks. Or the broken glasses…
FP: Ah…
Elly: We'll just hold our breath and see. But, the other reason I'm calling…

The University of Greenwich has appointed me as their Writer in Residence. I'm in shock.

It's a cause for celebration, of course. Parading through the streets of West Hampstead, I feel like I'm in that Björk video where the post boxes start dancing, and the rubbish bins too. Although bursting with the news, I'm wary of making a pub announcement, given the likelihood of a large round, combined with a large round of indifference. Instead, I buy a bottle of Cutty Sark and jump on a right whale.

The 188 conveniently stops outside a pub, on the western approach to Greenwich. The Gate Clock is a Wetherspoons establishment, which means it's more suited to my ongoing celebrations budget. Sir Christopher Wren, if alive today, would probably be less enamoured with the place than I. Having designed the Royal Observatory, and also the Old Royal Naval College, home to the University of Greenwich, it's likely he would find it drab, and a tad crude. Architecturally, it is a bit of a stinker. From the outside it resembles a bunker hideout made from a cereal box. It would probably make Sir Christopher turn in his grave, which, incidentally, is situated inside St Paul's Cathedral, which he also designed. But given he was born into a wealthy family and was best mates with the King, he probably wouldn't appreciate a pub that serves food and drinks at a fair price to good honest folk. As nice as it may be to drink all day in fancy historical pubs, frequented by Charles Dickens and his ilk, us modern, contemporary writers lack such means. Weathered timber snugs, or high seas-inspired art prints in a riverside setting don't come cheap. Whereas gambling machines featuring Noel Edmonds, while not in the spirit of nautical, Royal Greenwich, are more my lot. The carpet design in here *is* quite special, though. It resembles small clusters of people talking, inside sacks. Having landed a job up the road, I imagine I'll be seeing a lot more of this particular pub floor.

The Gate Clock's namesake is to be found just outside the Royal Greenwich Observatory, where it's recognized as the official instrument to depict Greenwich Mean Time. The Observatory features in Joseph Conrad's *The Secret Agent,* which, since my last visit, is one of the few novels I've found with any relevance to Greenwich. According to one short sentence: 'The whole civilized world has heard of Greenwich.' And yet it's clearly never been a hotbed for authors or their fictional works. Charles Dickens gave it the odd, brief mention in *Our Mutual Friend*. In *Great Expectations* Pip rows down to Greenwich, and in the opening chapter of *Bleak House* the ubiquitous fog is 'in the eyes and throats of ancient Greenwich pensioners, wheezing by the firesides of their wards'. Still, it's no Bloomsbury or Fitzrovia. Even *The Secret Agent*, first published over a hundred years ago, is predominantly set elsewhere, in the likes of Kensington. What makes Greenwich key to Conrad's story is an attempted bombing of the Observatory. This act of terrorism was based on a real event. On 15th February 1894, French anarchist Martial Bourdin was blown up with his own bomb close to the Observatory site. Some theorists, such as curator David Rooney, have suggested he may have actually been planning to target the gate clock, a symbol of the British Government's attempt to standardize international time and therefore exercise control over the lives of ordinary folk. Conrad himself called Bourdin's act 'a blood-stained inanity of so fatuous a kind that it is impossible to fathom its origin by any reasonable or even unreasonable process of thought'.

From the cheap and informal surroundings of the Gate Clock pub, I head towards the austere, foreboding grounds of the university. In John Williams' campus novel *Stoner*, hero William Stoner goes from hoeing corn and mucking in on the farm to the serious world of academia. When he first observes his new university, it's with some trepidation:

> *Stoner stood unmoving, staring at the complex of buildings. He had never seen anything so imposing... he walked for many minutes around the edges of the campus, only looking, as if he had no right to enter.*

Of course, Stoner hadn't come straight from the pub, hot on the heels of a *Fear and Loathing*-type bus journey across London. When I look afresh at the white stone buildings of the Old Naval College, in the knowledge that I am now its Writer in Residence, I have to laugh. Laugh and point, holding sides. Do I actually have the qualifications for such a post? Have I gone in over my head? No! And yes! Like William Stoner, I'm much better suited to more humble quarters, tilling the land. But don't tell anyone.

FP: [*Fingers to lips.*] Sshh! Sshh!

It's probably worth reading more of those campus novels, to get me up to speed with university life. I've already read A.S. Byatt's *Possession*, and J.M. Coetzee's *Disgrace*, both cornerstones of the genre. J.M. Coetzee, a Distinguished Professor of Literature, holds a senior position at the University of Adelaide. A.S. Byatt went to Cambridge and Oxford, and was a university lecturer. As an academic-in-waiting, perhaps I could pen a campus novel too. It might help me escape the 'silly' tag that has dogged my reviews. Being a campus novelist may well present me in a different light, as a more serious author. It might just afford me, by association, the respectability that I deserve. Or, that I could really, really use. Surely, with a campus novel under my belt, joining the ranks of A.S. Byatt and J.M. Coetzee will be a mere formality. But perhaps, like them, I need to initialize my first two names. Maybe I should be F.V. Plug from now on.

Social Commentator: What does the 'V' stand for?
FVP: Um… Volcatron? [*Laughs.*]

In *Possession*, there is an infatuation with a long-dead writer, while in *Disgrace*, a lecturer is obsessed with a young and modern student. Perhaps my Greenwich campus novel could be based around an academic who falls in love with a very old ship, which has been rebuilt after a fire, so is therefore very young. And maybe he kisses it a lot.

The college has gardeners of its own, and when I smile broadly at one, he nods in a slow, forced manner, as if he was dead and his head was being tilted forward by a pathologist's two hands on a forensics table. After William Stoner arrives on campus at the University of Missouri, he quickly progresses from student to associate professor. Perhaps, if I play my cards right, I could be on for a career trajectory also. Maybe I could end up like Hagrid in Hogwarts University of Witchcraft and Wizardry, with my own hut, and a wood fire.

FP: Wicked!

After lording over the university grounds, which I am to survey, I head across the road to Greenwich Park and clamber up the hill. It's a chance to see the Observatory up close, and to view all of Greenwich, my wider remit.

The December sun is pleasant, but like a 40-watt bulb, offers adequate lighting rather than any notion of heat. In truth, it's blimmin' freezing. Still, there's an admirable view, with St Paul's clearly visible, along with the distant heaths of Hampstead and Highgate. Below are the college grounds, and it's possible to see the Water Gate to the Thames Path, and the brown river water, framed on either side by Wren's domes, as if one were a hot tap, the other cold.

The original Gate Clock is an actual clock, on an actual gate, attached to the side of the Observatory. Although presently correct, I've caught it on a good day. Being permanently fixed on Greenwich Mean Time, it is actually an hour out throughout the UK summer period.

FP: *Then*, I suppose, it's behind the mean times. Get it?
Tourist: Are you talking to me?

Christopher Wren's Royal Observatory building now houses a museum, because the official English Royal Observatory has moved to Cambridge University. Hardly surprising really, with all those glaring lights from Canary Wharf. You'd be lucky to see the moon at all, let alone a small boy sitting on the end of it with a fishing rod. There aren't any nervous fellows in suspicious vests lurking around. Given the English Royal Observatory has moved out, it's probably less of a target. Their explosives probably wouldn't ignite anyway, in this cold. Or maybe they were supposed to blast to kingdom come half an hour ago, but their watches are out.

It's interesting that the fictional high point of Greenwich centres around a terrorist act, given the current spate of attacks in Europe and beyond. A supposed religious organization has claimed responsibility for these, with many of its members meeting similar ends to Martial Bourdin. *The Secret Agent* portrays the perpetrators as victims, exploited by a higher order. In *Moby Dick*, a book about a whale, Ishmael has his own thoughts on religious extremism:

> *Now, as I before hinted, I have no objection to any person's religion, be it what it may, so long as that person does not kill or insult any other person, because that other person don't believe it also. But when a man's religion becomes really frantic; when it is a positive torment to him; and, in fine, makes this earth of ours an uncomfortable inn to lodge in; then I think it high time to take that individual aside and argue the point with him.*

Holding strong views on modern life is a peculiar demand of public figures. Writers in particular are often singled out for answers. But just because *I'm* an author, doesn't mean I'm a qualified one. It's not like

I've been entrusted with the nuclear codes. Approaching important matters with a hazy head is more my bag. Joseph Conrad, usefully, backs me up in this regard:

It is not the clear-sighted who lead the world. Great achievements are accomplished in a blessed, warm mental fog.

Payment is required in order to enter the warm Observatory. I'm sure it's very interesting, but I'm supposed to be celebrating my new kick-arse job, not visiting the museum! All that boring informative stuff will come soon enough, when I start at the university. Right now it's time to party! Running down Greenwich Park hill, I lose my balance and fall, face first, into the rich, blessed earth.

Back at the Gate Clock, in its pub form, it probably looks like I've just stepped out for a game of rugby with the lads. But rugby gives you ears like melted plastic supermarket packaging. Everyone knows that.

I remain at the Gate Clock until last orders.

Bartender: Time at the bar, please.
FP: Is that Greenwich Mean Time?
Bartender: Piss off.

CHANGING PLACES

A Tale of Two Campuses

David Lodge

For Francis Plug
who is writing a campus novel
with best wishes

David Lodge

SECKER &
WARBURG
LONDON

NICE WORK

A Novel

David Lodge

For Francis Plug
with best wishes

David Lodge

SECKER &
WARBURG
LONDON

SMALL WORLD

An Academic Romance

David Lodge

To Francis Plug
with best wishes

David Lodge

SECKER &
WARBURG
LONDON

I'm kicking off my campus novel campaign with David Lodge's trilogy, followed by Malcolm Bradbury's novel *The History Man*. All four books were written and set between the late 1960s and the 1980s, although I can't imagine universities have moved on much, especially since they choose to reside in buildings where Dracula might live. In more recent years, American writers have dominated the campus novel genre, where it's almost seen as a rite of passage. There have been some British exceptions, including Zadie Smith's *On Beauty*, and Linda Grant's *Upstairs at the Party*. Spanish author Javier Marías has written a fictional account of Oxford life in *All Souls*, and Haruki Murakami covered student uprisings in *Norwegian Wood*. It's exciting to think what my own interpretation might cover. Not silly stuff, that's for sure!

Dr Alex appears surprised when I arrive for the informal induction bearing all my worldly goods. He nervously reiterates the 'no accommodation' proviso, even though 'In Residence' is clearly spelled out in my title. Dismissing the items with a wave, I seek to allay his suspicions.

FP: These old things? No! They're just a few office trinkets, for my desk.
Dr Alex: A fold-out bed?

FP: Um, it's not a bed. It's… just a… a yoga prayer mat.
Dr Alex: A yoga prayer mat?
FP: Ha-ha!

Not wishing to stoke his anxieties further, I omit my intention to answer all office telephones in the manner of a TV butler:

FP: Hello, Writer in Residence?

According to the papers, Greenwich house prices rose by a quarter last year, the highest rate for all of London. This, the reporter claimed, was due to its close proximity to Canary Wharf. No wonder there's no great literature written here. Not only is the place overrun with kings and queens, it's full of minted bankers too. All the writers have run a mile. But not me. I have a secret plan, to secretly live, in secret, in residence. The income offered by the university, Dr Alex has hinted, will be somewhere around the minimum wage mark. Making use of these buildings as they were originally intended, therefore, to house the infirm and damaged, makes all the sense in the world. Of course, this will require a degree of discretion. Not a university degree of discretion, but something in that sort of ballpark.

As Dr Alex walks me through the different levels of King William, I surreptitiously list any abandoned offices or alcoves that could perform as bedrooms.

Dr Alex: You're taking a lot of notes…
FP: Oh. It's just… description. For my campus novel.
Dr Alex: You're writing a campus novel? Is this the one about the sperm whale? That's actually a bus?
FP: There may be sperm in it. I haven't decided yet. David Lodge and Malcolm Bradbury certainly have lots of sperm in *their* campus

books. Or copulation at least. In *The History Man*, Dr Howard sleeps with his students, his colleagues, and his colleague's wives.

Dr Alex: Yes, I'm not sure we're quite as sexually charged here. It's not exactly the swinging sixties or seventies.

FP: No, but these days we have Gangnam style, which is kind of a sexy horse dance.

Dr Alex: Yes, again, not here so much...

According to David Lodge's characters, writing a good book can fast-forward your academic career, so I'm keen to crack on with mine. They also claim it's impossible to be excessive in flattering one's academic peers.

FP: Nice shirt.

Dr Alex: Thanks. I read about your stay at Waterstones. That certainly got a lot of attention.

FP: Yes. Was it a factor in your decision-making process, for the position?

Dr Alex: No, I can confidently say that particular news came to light *after* the Vice Chancellor's approval.

FP: Ah.

Dr Alex: That reminds me, our PR officer wants to talk to you about a press release, to announce your appointment. I've forwarded her your email.

FP: Sure.

Dr Alex: Probably best if you don't mention the Waterstones thing. Especially the Snowman massacre.

FP: Got it. Will I need one of those creepy author photos, smoking a pipe or something? I have a pipe, obviously.

Dr Alex: Do you smoke?

FP: Yes. Especially when people set me on fire.

Smoking, it turns out, is prohibited in the building. Even for staff.

FP: Really? But in *Changing Places*, Maurice Zapp, the English Lit professor, smokes cigars in his office. Even during tutorials.

Dr Alex: Yes, but that's set in the 1970s. As I say, things have moved on.

FP: No sex, no smoking. What's left, skittles?

Dr Alex: Funny you should mention that...

Dr Alex suggests King William's cobblestoned courtyard as a smoking zone of sorts.

FP: Other smokers don't go there, do they? I hate that.

Dr Alex: What is it you hate?

FP: Chatting. With other people.

The King William building really is a confusing myriad of corridors and hallways. The third floor is particularly strange as the corridor doesn't run in a complete, continuous circuit around the building. Instead, at certain points, it simply ends abruptly, forcing you to descend a set of stairs, before popping up again, like a plastic arcade rabbit, ready to be bashed with a mallet. It has to be said, for all his plaudits, Christopher Wren's head wasn't exactly screwed on too tight.

At the far end of the muddled third floor, towards the famous Painted Hall, is Dr Alex's office. He gestures to a desk, just inside the door.

Dr Alex: So, the plan is to put you here. Cherry Smyth, a poetry lecturer, also uses it, but she's currently on leave.

The desk sits at the edge of a short thoroughfare between Dr Alex's office and a larger room. This, I'm told, is allocated to members of the Drama faculty. Despite empty offices on other floors, the Humanities department seems quite staffed up. My new desk faces a plaster wall. On this is a poster for a Modernism exhibition, and various artsy postcards, including one of Sarah Lucas with two outer eggy breasts. Cups hold pens, and a ceramic dish holds many silver paperclips. The message icon on the desk phone is flashing red, and the black computer screen is dead.

FP: I think the computer's broken.
Dr Alex: Broken? No, it's just switched off.
FP: Okay, gotcha.

There are no medical certifications on the walls. The desks and shelving are modern in design, made from light, cheap-looking wood, with grey, alloy legs, like toy parts. Dr Alex's desktop, I conclude, is rather messy. Piles of papers and piles of books, and piles of papers with books inserted at varying points between the papers. More books are crammed onto bookshelves, on either side of his desk. His desk faces away from the third floor window, through which both of Wren's domes loom up, very close behind, each catching the low winter sun. Just inside the office entrance, the brown carpet has been aggressively scraped and scuffed into a harsh fan shape by the continuous opening of the door. The carpet isn't especially thick, so the door is most certainly at fault. But you can't blame a door, so, rolling my eyes, I attribute yet another design flaw to that cowboy Wren.

Next to our office is a uni-sex toilet boasting even better views of the domes. Opposite the toilet is a small kitchen area, with a fridge and tea- and coffee-making facilities.

FP: Are there showers anywhere?

Dr Alex: Showers? I didn't pick you for a fitness type…

FP: Oh yes, I am. I'm a runner. One of those runners. Like Haruki Murakami. I run and run. Like the blazes.

The showers are in a completely different building, so that's going to be interesting. Where will I dry my towel? Perhaps I could affix it to the mast of the *Cutty Sark*.

There's still paperwork to be signed and completed before I can receive an official ID card, allowing uninterrupted passage throughout the campus. In the meantime, Dr Alex offers me a spare access card, which should open most doors, he thinks. It's rather an emotional moment, as if I were taking possession of the keys to a new house. Which, of course, I am.

Dr Alex: Oh, a couple of things before I forget. Firstly, I'm putting together a literary festival, based here on campus, and it would be great to get you involved. It's not until later on next year, but these things need to be organized in advance.

FP: Oh yes. Absolutely. You can count on me.

Dr Alex: Great. Do you think you could rope in some other authors too? Use your connections?

FP: Sure, sure. I'm very well connected.

Dr Alex: That would be a huge help. You'd have a slot yourself, of course. In fact, if you wanted to, you could do a combined event, with another campus novelist, say.

FP: Good idea. Maybe Philip Roth.

Dr Alex: Probably not that famous, to be honest. We're quite a small operation. With a limited budget, unfortunately.

FP: Leave it with me. I'll make some calls, to some big-hitters, and we'll get this thing happening.

Dr Alex: Well, great. The Vice Chancellor will be most impressed.

FP: Not just the Vice Chancellor. I think the actual, proper Chancellor will be really pumped too. You bet.

Who is this Chancellor person? I have no clue at all. But according to Dr Alex, it was their green light, from the upper echelons of the university, that gave the all-clear for my position. I suppose I should identify them, in order to appease them. Like most writers, I probably look good on paper, but being personable is important too. Particularly when other people are involved. Like boss people. And fellow authors, at literary festivals. Such as the one I've just committed myself to. The phrase 'digging one's own grave' comes to mind, and I'm reminded of those helpful folk working in supermarkets who encourage you to use the self-checkout machines, which will ultimately replace them.

Dr Alex: Also, you're invited to our end-of-year dinner. It'll be a chance for you to meet Zoë, the Head of Department, and all the other staff.

FP: Dinner?

Dr Alex: It's nothing formal. Just an office Christmas party thing, in a local pub.

FP: Phew. For a minute there I thought I might have to eat something.

In David Lodge's *Small World*, the academics go 'on the lash at conferences, recovering their youth sacrificed to learning, proving to themselves that they're not dryasdust swots after all'. I wonder if the Greenwich lot will apply the same principle to their Christmas drinks? Will they go ballistic as well? I really, really hope so.

Dr Alex excuses himself, saying he's going to get some work done at home.

FP: Watch out for that frozen urine. Falling from aeroplanes.
Dr Alex: I... will.

Sitting behind my new desk, I stretch and move my limbs about, as if getting used to another person's car. The gilded domes continue to shine against the grey, levelling sky, a scene criss-crossed by the intersecting leaded windows, as though viewed through a tennis racket. In the distance, beyond the roof of the adjacent Queen Mary building, a single chimneystack is visible. This is fashioned in a dark-brown brick, reinforced with black struts, giving it the appearance of a burnt toasted soldier against the pure egg-white of the campus. Below is King William courtyard, formed of thousands of uneven brick-sized tiles. The Grecian pillars hold up a triangular plaster frieze depicting horses, angels, gods and soldiers. I must pop down soon, for a Gauloises cigarette

But for now, with straightened back, eyes straight ahead, I pat the desk with flat palms. The prospect of sharing an office makes me anxious, not just in terms of chat, but also in respect to my absences. My last book was written down the pub, and I expect the campus novel might be too. In David Lodge's *Changing Places* there is a brief mention of Garth Robinson, the resident novelist of Euphoric State University who, it is claimed, 'was very rarely resident'. Unlike Garth, I'll certainly be putting in the campus hours, even if, for most of them, I'll be asleep.

My desk patting, meanwhile, has built into a kind of drumming, before escalating further, into a wild, frenzied, thumping/pounding exercise, with loud moans. A man comes through from the adjacent Drama room. I didn't even know he was in there.

Drama Man: Everything okay?

FP: Oh. Yes. Sorry about that. There was a, what do you call them, woodlouse. Yes, a woodlouse. It was running all over this desk here, spraying out little bits of… they were like little kinds of woodchip things, sharp, splintery daggers, all over this area here. Dangerous wooden splintery daggers.

Drama Man: Really?

FP: Yes. And obviously I was trying to curtail that, the spraying of the wood, with the sides of my fists.

Drama Man: I see. Well, it seems to have gone.

FP: Yes. It's gone now.

Drama Man: I'm Harry, by the way.

FP: Hi, I'm Francis. I've just arrived.

Harry: You're the Writer in Residence, aren't you?

FP: Yes, that's it.

Harry: Welcome. I must read some of your work.

FP: Thanks. Yes. So… drama. Have you seen *Puss in Boots*, the stage version? I hear that's very good.

Harry: Is it? I must look out for it. Do you know where it's showing?

FP: Um, Willesden, I think, near West Hampstead. A primary school there.

Harry: Okay…

FP: I expect you'll be very busy with Shakespeare's four-hundredth anniversary thing?

The whole world is set to celebrate the four-hundredth anniversary of Shakespeare's death. Shakespeare himself won't be here to celebrate it, which is a shame. It really won't be the same without him. I might be a fully qualified gardener, but I don't dig up graves. Apart from dog ones, by accident. I suppose, during this anniversary period, everyone will be considering Shakespeare's work, instead of mine. Even though my book needs much more of a push than all his stuff. Especially his sonnets, with the very lazy titles. Shakespeare didn't do the literary festival circuit, or the bookshop events, but he's still famous. He even has his own epithet, or adjective. If something relates to, or is characteristic of, his plays, it is described as Shakespearian. Just as something oppressive is deemed to be Orwellian, or something marked by surreal weirdness might be Kafkaesque. To date, I haven't been handed such a title, because unlike those authors, I'm much harder to pigeonhole. Although, the *Times Literary Supplement* did say my novel was 'pure silliness'. Maybe I could be associated with silly things. Another review, written by an Amazon customer, read:

> *I just don't get it! If it had not been that I was reading this for a book club, there is no way I would have continued to the end. It is such a load of drivel. I certainly did not find one line funny. A huge disappointment. One star.*

I suppose this could be built upon, in relation to my epithet. I could be associated with things that really, really aren't funny.

> *Oh no. The lava from that volcano has buried the entire village, in their beds. They never saw it coming, not even the little innocent children. How very Pluggian.*

> *Oh my word. Did you see that giant sinkhole? The one that opened up directly beneath Great Ormond Street Hospital, tipping all the poorly children out of their hospital beds into the sewers? That's most Pluggian.*

Before Harry can reply, a desk phone rings, very, very loudly from back in the Drama Department. It's like a blinkin' fire alarm.

Harry: Ah, that's mine. Excuse me.

The bedroom I have earmarked is on a different section of the third floor. After some trial and error, fighting against the building's inept structural weirdness, I successfully retrace my earlier footsteps. The darkened room, while not favoured with old charm or pretty octagonal windows, is, thankfully, unlocked. Like Dr Alex's office, it too faces towards the King William courtyard. Small and bare, its carpet indents speak of former desks and filing cabinets. Unlike my garage, a large, wall-mounted heater is at hand. Turning this on, full tilt, I return with my possessions, carefully storing them beyond the view of the windowed door. Some decorations or knick-knacks could be in order. Perhaps a miniature laser light, shining the steady path of the Meridian timeline, before striking a host of strategically placed mirrors, whizzing off in every which direction. Discretion however, is key. Officially, my home is still a West Hampstead garage, with rats. Unofficially, I live in a palatial, listed building designed by Sir Christopher Wren.

David Lodge, nearly eighty, is promoting his latest book at a King's Cross event. After starting out as a temporary assistant lecturer, he rose to become a professor at Birmingham University, where he worked with his friend Malcolm Bradbury. He retired in 1987 and he admits he's really out of touch with today's students. The campus novel genre, he believes, is currently more focused around creative writing classes, given that many writers are teaching these to earn money. David Lodge wears glasses, and as well as being very deaf and needing two hearing aids, he's also chronically anxious.

David Lodge: Anxiety is a very big part of my life. It seems to get worse as I grow older.

Considering the pressure on authors to also function as public figures, that's a brave thing to admit. Especially in a large public auditorium, like this one. It's also refreshing to hear of another fallible author. Not that David Lodge has been held back. He's a big name, both in the UK and also in France, where he's reached the top of the charts. It's not like his anxiety is affecting his performance this evening either. He gives two readings, and in one of them he even sings. Given his popularity in France, perhaps he could be Britain's representative in the Eurovision song contest.

David Lodge's hearing aids have difficulty picking up far-away sounds, so at question time he enlists help from his interviewer, Mark Lawson. Someone asks if his old campus novel characters could be revived, but Lodge claims that, as they are a good ten years older than himself, they'd be too old now. Another question pertains to the name of his hearing aid brand, because, the audience member explains, they seem very good. The author replies, somewhat hesitantly:

David Lodge: Phonak. But they're for professional use, so they're very expensive.

Perhaps that could be the title of my campus novel. *Phonak*. Sounds a bit like *Kojak*. Maybe, instead of smoking cigars, my hero licks lollipops. Sugar-free ones, with reclaimed timber for sticks.

New York Times **Literary Editor**: Our Book of the Year, unreservedly, is *Phonak* by Francis Plug.
FP: Yay!

At signing time, I notice David Lodge has a very red nose, which may relate to the bad hay fever he also mentioned suffering from. Still, in spite of his various ailments, he's retained a thick head of hair, not to mention a most impressive moustache.

FP: I'm writing a campus novel myself.

David Lodge: Are you?

FP: Yes, it's set at the University of Greenwich.

David Lodge: Oh. I grew up around there.

FP: Did you? I feel like I'm growing up there myself. I'm the Writer in Residence, but between you and me, I've got no friggin' clue what I'm doing.

David Lodge: So... you...

FP: I feel like a pretend ship's captain, steering the ship through dangerous seas. I'm waving my hands, willing the sharp rocks and icebergs to part.

David Lodge: Well, you obviously know how to write, so just focus on that.

FP: Yes, but most of the reviews for my last book talked about how silly it was.

David Lodge: Oh. What's the angle on your campus novel?

FP: It's all a bit vague at this point. I've been thinking about talking animals, whales as buses, lollipops and sperm. But not sexy-time stuff. You and Malcolm Bradbury covered all that already.

David Lodge: Did we?

FP: You *so* did. You even likened the act of reading to a Soho strip-tease act.

David Lodge: Well...

FP: Hey, maybe I should write a *Moby Dick* type book, but on land, set in the *Cutty Sark*. It won't be chasing anything because it's grounded, above a gift shop. But when students and academic staff walk past, the ship's captain tries to spear them. That's what today's readers want.

David Lodge: Do they?

FP: Search me.

David Lodge: Okay, well…

FP: Is it true you're a CBE, a Commander of the Most Excellent Order of the British Empire?

David Lodge: Um, yes, I'm…

FP: How do you score one of those? Because I really need to ditch this 'silly author' tag.

David Lodge: To be honest…

FP: Can you get us into a royal wedding? Or just the after party…?

The university's PR woman has dropped me a line. As well as providing her with information about my life, she would also like me to promote my appointment myself, via my social media connections. That might be difficult, I explain, because I don't have any. My publisher however, is very good at connecting with the world on my behalf. A bit like publishers used to do, before they hired marketing departments, who then instructed the authors to market themselves.

My photo-booth photo is less than ideal. In retrospect, it was a mistake to light the pipe inside the booth because it looks like I'm posing, fully clothed, in a sauna.

Returning late to my new home, I don't count on the guards patrolling both the west and east gates. David Lodge is right to describe the university as 'a small city-state, an academic Vatican'. The grounds are closed, and because I have no official staff ID, I'm turned away. Contemplating a cold night in Greenwich Park, I first circumnavigate the college, deciding to chance it over the precarious spiked fence facing the Thames. My hands indented by iron points, I tumble over, falling on the grass, on my arse. Using my temporary electronic card, I access a discreet side door from King William Court, ascending an old staircase within, seeking out my new bedroom amongst the hodgepodge network of darkened corridors.

A blustery gale blows outside on my first night in my new home. In my head, over the course of the night, are thoughts of classrooms filled to the brim with water. I'm trying to write something serious and sensible on the blackboard, but the chalk is smudging, and the students are blowing large bubbles with all their laughter.

THE
BOTTLE
FACTORY
OUTING

BERYL BAINBRIDGE

To Francis Plug

best wishes

Beryl Bainbridge

DUCKWORTH

It's dark when I awaken, in need of a wee. My peach tin's not in its normal place, and the garage floor feels soft and furry. It takes a moment for my new reality to register. There's no urine receptacle because this is a university, with proper toilet access. That's one problem solved. But where *are* the toilets? My office may have adjacent facilities, but my new bedroom doesn't come with an en suite. My stream is set to fire. Shuffling out into the darkened corridor, I look left, then right. Which way? There's nothing but offices. Perhaps through the double doors, by the stairwell. But there're no conveniences to speak of. Curses. It's like one of those large pubs with poor signage, except there's no one to even ask. The pressure is now immense. It can't wait. All I can do is minimize the carnage, point and contain. That shelf unit, with the course handouts. Behind that.

The thin hallway carpet takes the brunt, blasting the silence with a coarse, industrial noise, like the sound of thick cardboard being torn. As a child, I was curious to hear what my wee sounded like, so I placed the round sensor component of my toy stethoscope against the end of my doodle. The wee shot up the tubes and into my ears. It's a similar sensation now, this noisy cascade, like a never-ending tap, a magic porridge pot filling the entire university with hot musty wee. Stop little pot, stop!

Later, I'm awakened again, this time by the clunking of the hallway doors.

Disorientation also returns, but the light of day offers some clarity through the muggy haze. The sound of floorboards creaking and stretching provides an impetus for action. My fellow academics are starting their days, and my bedroom door has see-through glass. In the corner, out of sight, are my stored possessions, but centrally placed, in clear view, is an army bed and one sprawled, ungainly mass. Scrambling up, patting down hair, I poke my head cautiously into the corridor. All clear, I move with the stealth of a wounded bison bearing a protruding tranquillizer dart. The hallway carpet is too thin to be absorbent, and the wee, having followed short rivulet channels, has pooled. Fortunately, the heating hasn't kicked in properly, so hovering flies are thus far dissuaded. The light and dark tones of brown thread also help disguise my shame, and that faint tang, I decide, is just a university smell, which, as a recent arrival, I'm as yet unaccustomed to.

The toilets, in the filtered, blinking light of day, are very close. Attempting to dampen down my bed hair with tap water, without success, I pull out reams of toilet roll, which I bunch, returning to surreptitiously mop up my puddle disgrace. Perhaps, with the aid of chalk, I can mark out some directional arrows, for future big nights. Or, as part of my Writer in Residence legacy, I could leave some neon toilet signs.

Dr Alex mentioned shower facilities in the Dreadnaught building, near the west gates. To defer attention from my wild hair, I exit the King William building with both hands on my head, like a Guantanamo Bay detainee, being marched to my wash-down by an invisible guard.

My shared office, when I find it, is locked. My electronic card, while good for external beeper access, doesn't work in keyholes. Even my attempts to shimmy the lock with it are foiled. Still, I don't *need* an office. At this stage of my campus novel development, I can simply write notes by hand. Dr Alex's designated office hours are stated on the door. All other times are by appointment. You have to make an appointment to see the doctor. He doesn't seem to be here much himself. Of course, he's no doubt in lecture rooms for the most part, passing on wisdom. Whether I'm expected to remain in residence remains unclear. James Kelman once wrote: *In my early thirties I landed a job as a writer in residence, but discovered the one thing a writer in residence doesn't do is write in residence.* Worryingly, he would set his alarm early, in order to write first thing. His residential duties, it was implied, were required for 'other things'.

FP: [*Biting finger.*]

Some blue seats sit quietly at the end of the corridor, alongside the kitchen area. Perching on one, I attempt to dry my showered hair with a tea towel. A woman arrives to make a cup of tea, even though her brown mug reads 'Keep Calm and Drink Coffee'.

Woman: Hi, it's Francis, isn't it? Are you locked out?
FP: Yes, but I think I can remove the door from its hinges. With a bit of argy-bargy.
Woman: What do you mean?
FP: Well, if I use my shoulder as a battering ram, I'm hoping I can bust the door down and gain entry that way.
Woman: I wouldn't do that, actually. This is a listed building, which includes the doors and the doorframes. I've got a key, if it helps.

One of the dome clocks tolls the dolorous hour of 11 a.m. Dr Alex's wall clock is one hour fast, perhaps willing the summer holidays to arrive. But this is the very dead of winter. When the uni breaks up for Christmas tomorrow, I'll be able to roam the corridors alone, in peace. Let's hope there aren't any ghosts.

Where are the light switches? I have no idea. They're neither in by the door nor out in the hallway, so I sit in the darkened room, pondering my new life as an academic scholar and novelist, to which I draw no conclusions. A different woman walks past in the corridor, stopping at the open door.

Woman: Oh. Hello. I didn't know anyone was in there.

FP: I am. I'm in here.

Woman: Why haven't you got any lights on?

FP: I'm playing Murder in the Dark.

Woman: Murder in the Dark?

FP: Yes.

Woman: By yourself?

FP: Yes.

Woman: How does that work?

FP: Well, you just sit here in the dark, shaking with fear, petrified that someone is going to come along and murder you.

Woman: God. That doesn't sound like a very fun game.

FP: No, it's not very fun at all.

Woman: Did you think I was coming to murder you just now?

FP: Yes, I did. I thought maybe you were going to give me the old one-two, then dump my limp body into a sherry hogshead barrel, nail it shut and roll me into the Thames.

Woman: Really? God. Well, if I were you, I'd hide under that desk next time, or behind those filing cabinets. Rather than just sitting there out in the open like that.

FP: [*Nodding.*] Right.

Woman: You do know where the light switch is, don't you?

FP: Oh yes.
Woman: Okay. Well, I'll leave you to your game.
FP: Bye.

I wonder who that was?

The department dinner takes place this evening, and even with the promise of free drinks, I'll need a few early ones, because first impressions count. With my temporary pass in tow, I head first thing to the Student Union bar, in order to benefit from their heavily discounted drinks. The Student Union lies beyond the college grounds, in a separate building near the main gates of Greenwich Park. A sign points the way to the bar, through a side door. Taking the initiative, hoping to reach it without human contact, my passage is halted by a young man behind a reception counter, who pulls me up sharply.

Young Man: Excuse me! You can't wander past here without ID.
FP: Ah, it's here. Here it is.
Young Man: No, I need photo ID.
FP: But. But I'm the Writer in Residence.
Young Man: Sorry. You need proper photo ID.

Unbelievable. I've only been here five minutes and already the students are giving me grief. It's too early in the day for a witty retort, so I simply hobble off like an injured sportsman, reluctant to leave the field despite obtaining brain damage.

This setback has cost me precious drinking time. Fortunately, the staff dinner doesn't start until 7 p.m., so if I head to the Gate Clock now, I may still be in with a fighting chance.

Barman: Morning, sir.

FP: Yes, yes. Time is of the essence, young man.

It's difficult to know what to wear to these dinner engagement things. The teaching staff, I imagine, will all be dressed in black skivvies with roll-necks, like Ernest Hemingway, or the Milk Tray man. In this sense, I should blend in fine. Polo sweaters are charity shop favourites, and black wool more easily conceals spilled food and drink. It's also an overcast day in winter, so my sweater might come in handy later on, if I'm sleeping out of doors.

For the department staff, I imagine Christmas drinks would be quite a break from the ordinary. A special occasion to mix with their colleagues in a slightly inebriated state, and spout off whatever's on their mind. It's a good opportunity for them to meet me for the first time too. Although, in this respect, I suppose it'll be more a case of what you see is what you get.

Four hours have passed at the Gate Clock, and my department outing doesn't start for another four more. It probably makes sense to stretch my legs and get some fresh air. One old boy just put on his coat and headed out the door, before coming straight back in and ascending the stairs to the loos.

Old Boy: [*Aloud, to no one in particular.*] Better safe than sorry.

The Yacht, like its close neighbour the Trafalgar Tavern, is a riverside pub, accessed via a narrow, alley-like path. The department has tables booked at the back, which faces directly onto the Thames. Everyone seems to be here already, making the most of the free drinks. Although somewhat tanked up, my anxiety neurons aren't yet fully quashed. Dr Alex provides a welcome sight therefore, given he's saved a spare seat for me at his table.

FP: Here I am, fashionably late.
Dr Alex: Fashionably? I don't know about that. You look like a fisherman!

Meals have already been ordered, so a menu is thrust my way, and a small fuss made. But there are bottles of wine on the table, and they're full ones. Christmas is almost here, and since I'll be on my own, on an army-issue fold-out bed, I may as well celebrate now.

Dr Alex is to my right, and to my left are a woman and also a man. They have names, which I'm told, but don't exactly clock. Other people sit at the table too, mainly women, and another man. The man and woman to my left confide with me directly, and most often. At some point in the future I hope to ascertain their names and understand their place in the scheme of things, but for now I concentrate on making sure our glasses are filled, especially the one gripped by my other hand.

Woman: Alex tells us you're writing a campus novel. You're not going to implicate *us*, are you?
FP: *Dr* Alex, you mean? He's a doctor, you know. But can he fix a cough? I really don't think so. He thinks I look like a fisherman. Do you think I look like a fisherman? Do you want more of this wine? Does anyone want more of this wine? What about this wine? Or this one? I'll look after them, there they are.

Some soup and bread has been ordered on my behalf, and I dispense with it out of politeness, despite seeing it as a hurdle to what should have been a straight 100 m race.

Man: What are you reading at the moment, Francis?

FP: What am I reading? I've just been reading *The Bottle Factory Outing* by Beryl Bainbridge. In preparation for tonight, for this department outing.

Man: She never actually won the Booker Prize, did she? Like all the authors you mention in your book.

Dr Alex chips in.

Dr Alex: Not in her lifetime. But she was posthumously awarded it, for *Master Georgie*.

FP: I met her, at a *Guardian* event. In *The Bottle Factory Outing*, she writes about gibbons screaming. In Richard Flanagan's Booker Prize-winning book, he writes about screaming monkeys too. Monkeys, monkeys! Screaming, screaming!

Woman: So… it's good, her *Bottle Factory* book?

FP: Yes, it is. There's a bit where Brenda sees a cat sharpening its claws on a tree and she thinks, you shouldn't do that, you cat. Wonderful, I told Beryl Bainbridge.

Woman: And what did she say?

FP: She laughed. But I don't know why she laughed. And now I never will. Look at those awful buildings.

Across the river, in the near distance, are the towering towers of Canary Wharf. Their after-hours lighting is so bright, it reflects all the way over here, on the passing waters of the Thames. How do the good honest folk in the Isle of Dogs get any sleep with that intense friggin' light blasting out? No wonder bankers always look so tanned.

There are four separate tables with around forty staff in all, but we don't mingle, except for Dr Zoë, the department head, who pops over to say hello.

Dr Zoë: Welcome, Francis.

FP: Thank you. Would you care for some wine?

Dr Zoë: I'm all right, thanks.

FP: Okay, I'll care for it.

Dr Zoë is chief of the entire Humanities department. She is very warm and bright, and nothing like the fusty, tweed-jacketed university head I'd expected. Perhaps they're different in the Humanities. Or maybe she's just let her short black hair down for the Christmas do. As we exchange cheerful pleasantries, a pesky little bar fly hovers between us. I start slashing at it with my pen, which is possibly not the most humanitarian thing to do.

Dr Zoë: Did you get fed?

FP: I did. Die, you little bastard!

After Dr Zoë moves on, there's a bit of a lull in the conversation. Then the man near me pipes up.

Man: Did you hear about the nuclear reactor on campus?

FP: The nuclear reactor?

Woman: Oh yes, the nuclear reactor. On the campus.

FP: A nuclear reactor? On campus?

Everyone nods.

FP: Holy fuck!

It turns out that an actual nuclear reactor was, until quite recently, housed on campus. It was in our own King William building, left over from the Royal Navy's occupation of the college. Everyone knew about it. I'm desperate to know more, but my colleagues begin pulling Christmas crackers, creating lesser explosions of a different kind within controlled cardboard wrappings. Producing a pen from my pocket, I scrawl in large letters across my hand: NUCLEAR REACTOR!

My party hat slips over my face, indicating that my head is not as large, or as filled, as those of my colleagues.

Colleague: Did you know if you hold a cracker and don't pull, you'll always come away with the larger section?

These academics know their stuff. They even work out the cracker jokes.

FP: Why does Father Christmas have three gardens?
Colleague: Um, let's see… oh, hoe, hoe, hoe.

Determined to extoll my own breadth of knowledge, I ask the table if they can name two popular songs that mention mashed potato. A woman on the far side correctly identifies 'Do You Love Me' by the Contours, but a second eludes them. Triumphantly, I reveal the Beastie Boys track 'B-Boys Makin with the Freak Freak'.

FP: You know! [*Reciting.*] 'Shit, If this is gonna be that kind of party, I'm gonna stick my dick in the mashed potatoes!'

Upending another wine bottle in its plastic cooler, I notice everyone else has shed their party hats, But I keep mine on regardless, even if it's now more of a frilled neck collar, like that worn by a queen casualty of Henry VIII.

FP: Ah, stuff it.

Standing up, I announce to the table that I really have to go to Tarzan's.

Woman: Tarzan's?
FP: The Gents. Me go to Tarzan's, you go to Jane's.

The department, of which I am part, begin to abandon the Yacht. Dr Alex, to his great credit, stays on, like a musician on the *Titanic*, defiantly playing as the whole scene begins to lilt.

Dr Alex: Caught any fish?
FP: No. But I've drunk like one.
Dr Alex: That's the general idea, I would hope.
FP: You're right. Yes, let's literally drink the bar dry. I'm not joking.

Dr Alex soon calls it a night too, leaving me as the sole representative of the University of Greenwich party. After attempting to order two fresh bottles of brandy, for Dr Zoë, I'm told the tab has been paid and wound up. Instead, I'm left to finish off all the unfinished prepaid drinks, on all the four tables, racing against the bar staff who are attempting to clear them.

Rather than turning right towards my new university home, I stumble left, following the Thames Path in the direction of the Millennium Dome. A wooden sherry hogshead barrel floats past on the Thames, and although quite steaming, I'm sure I can hear shouting coming from inside it. A short distance away is yet another pub, entitled, surprise, surprise, the Cutty Sark. Outside is a massive black anchor, and on this, in white paint, someone has painted:

DAVID CAMERON IS A WANCHOR.

People have started to spill out of the Cutty Sark pub, but the barmaid assures me they're still open.

FP: Woo-hoo!

The couple sitting on the sofa opposite mine continue to talk and laugh, despite my presence. The man is reclining like a king, crossing his left knee with a light suede shoe. Producing my notebook, I attempt to write a campus novel to beat all campus novels. But I've almost passed the threshold where alcohol can unlock the creative juices. Instead, it appears to have overwhelmed them, forcing their retreat to my testes, waiting to be whizzed out. After a particularly uproarious spell of laughter from the life-loving couple opposite, I jump in.

FP: Hello!
Woman: Hi.
FP: We've got great seats, haven't we? Right here by the window.
Man: Yes, they're good.
FP: Thanks for letting me sit here.
Man: Not a problem.
FP: What a view!
Woman: It's lovely isn't it?
FP: It certainly is. Apart from those awful buildings over there.
Woman: Canary Wharf?
FP: Yes. Look at their lights on the Thames, polluting it, like waste from a factory. All that lurid colour, like a friggin' circus.
Woman: That's your building, Richard. Causing that nasty light pollution.
FP: Really? Do you work there?
Man: Yes. I'm one of the circus clowns.
FP: Why don't you turn the lights off when you leave?

Man: It's not me, is it? I just work there.

FP: Maybe you could put a notice up on your noticeboard. 'Last to leave? Don't forget to turn the lights out.'

Woman: [*Laughs.*] Yes, do that, Richard!

Man: It's the cleaners. Blame the cleaners.

FP: Huh? The cleaners?

Woman: Cheers!

FP: Cheers!

Woman: Are you from around here?

FP: Yes, I live in Greenwich.

Woman: We live here too.

FP: Nice and handy for your work, Edward.

Man: Richard.

FP: I'm Francis.

Woman: Hi Francis, I'm Sally, and you've met Richard.

FP: Hi Sally, hello again, Richard.

Woman: We're up on Royal Hill.

FP: Royal Hill, a royal hill. D'ya have a good view, then?

Man: Yes.

FP: I used to live in Primrose Hill, at a banker's house.

Woman: We thought about Primrose Hill, didn't we?

Man: What was this guy's name?

FP: *His* name, because you rightly guessed it was a 'his', was Mr Stapleton. Leonard Stapleton.

Man: No, don't know him.

Woman: Where are you, Francis?

FP: Me? Oh, I'm in this Christopher Wren-designed place, just near the waterfront, right in the centre of the village.

Man: Christopher Wren?

FP: Yes. He also designed Greenwich Observatory and St Paul's Cathedral. Is your place a Christopher Wren?

Woman: St Paul's Cathedral?

Man: Where are you exactly?

FP: The Old Naval College. Do you know it? Next to the *Cutty Sark*, the ship version, on the riverside.

Woman: Wow, you live there?

FP: Yes.

Man: Is it an apartment?

FP: It's just this listed place, with a dome. So Marcus, your view is basically of your work, then?

Man: Richard.

Woman: Yes. It is, come to think of it.

Man: Oh come on, you *love* the view…

They begin arguing, causing Harry to lean forwards. He should be careful with his red wine, given his suede shoes. It's really hard to concentrate on writing my campus novel with all this arguing, so I quietly excuse myself, finding some peace and quiet in a cubicle in the Tarzans.

There is a knocking, and shortly after a pounding on the door.

Angry Man: Hurry up, will you?

FP: All right, hold your horses.

Angry Man: What the hell are you doing in there?

FP: I'm writing a novel! Mr Impatient!

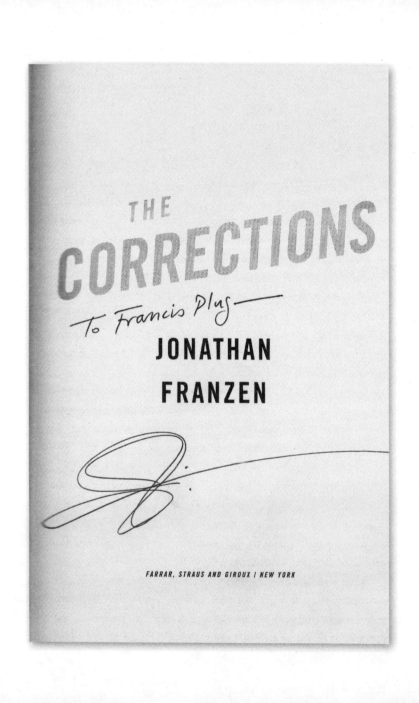

THE CORRECTIONS

To Francis Plug——

JONATHAN
FRANZEN

FARRAR, STRAUS AND GIROUX | NEW YORK

It's very late when I awaken. There are no heavy footsteps in the hallway, although it feels like big old boots are stomping on my head. Raising an arm to clap over my eyes, I'm aware of some stain or blemish on my palm. Two large smudged words appear in wavering focus, written in black pen. NUCLEAR REACTOR!

A sign above the sink in the department kitchen also uses large words. NOTICE TO ALL STAFF. PLEASE MAKE SURE YOU CLEAN THIS SINK AFTER USE. THANK YOU. It's important to abide by the rules, so after bringing my entire guts up in it, I set about getting that sink all ship-shape.

A tray on the bench spills over with upturned mugs. Some hold simple abstract patterns, while others feature Scrabble letters, flower designs, or ten-year anniversary motifs for the Royal Literary Fund. They've been washed and dried for use, but perhaps they all have owners. Maybe the one I've chosen is someone's special mug. Although plain blue and nondescript, like a pale-blue egg, perhaps it once anointed a cherished baby with christening water. Or maybe it was the sole personal effect to survive a *Titanic* voyage. Anyway, it's in safe hands now. Even if those hands are jittery and trembling like hell, emblazoned with the words NUCLEAR REACTOR!

Some authors, like Orhan Pamuk, swear by coffee. Caffeine certainly helps keep the mind alert, and may be beneficial when developing new thoughts. For me, it's greater use is as a breath freshener, scalding all traces of that sour alcohol tang, or acidic bile. Given it's free in this kitchen, I should make full use, drinking quickly in order to clean and replace the cup, before its academic owner discovers its absence. I don't want to have to defend myself pub-style, with swinging, windmill arms.

There are no intoxicants of any kind in the kitchen area, not even a bottle of *halbtrocken* Austrian champagne. So, after pouring boiling water down the sink, to annihilate the sick, I head outside for a wretched, breath-corroding cig. Smoking on campus grounds isn't the best example to set for the impressionable young students, and the prospect of burning down these listed buildings is also worrisome. In 1779, the chapel in the Queen Mary building was razed by fire, supposedly attributed to the drunk tailors working in their office upstairs. In Jonathan Franzen's novel *The Corrections*, cigarettes are extinguished on palms, tongues, and on the tender skin behind the ear, but I stub my Dunhill out on a flagpole. At that moment, the dome clock tolls, even though nothing foreboding or momentous has just happened.

FP: What? *What?* Stupid clock!

There's still no sign of any department staff inside, so my off-licence drinks are drunk in peace. In *The Corrections*, a game is mentioned which strikes me as good fun. The objective is to kick an item, such as a package, up a staircase using 'only genuine sharp kicks', as opposed to 'any sort of pushing or lofting action'. A book sent to me, out of the blue, by another publisher, may suit this game well. It's a proof copy, which the publisher thought, having heard me on Radio 4, I 'might enjoy very much'. But I don't like the look of it, not one bit. And because the words NOT FOR RESALE are printed on the back, it appears I'm stuck with it. So, having taped it back into its envelope, I attempt to punt the packaged book up the third floor staircase. The envelope is quick to rip, and after tearing completely, the book itself, which

I continue to boot, starts to look rather tatty. A distinguished older man, who I'm certain I haven't met, passes through my field of play.

Distinguished Older Man: Are you kicking that book?
FP: Yes. It was Jonathan Franzen's idea.

After he's gone, I sit silently on the stairs, unmoving, as if on the naughty step.

On a windowpane behind Dr Alex's desk is a messy, streaky bird poo. It's very distracting. Particularly when you're trying to think of high literary matters. Jonathan Franzen has a twitcher hobby, and I become distracted with that thought. At one of his London events, an audience member asked him which birds he hoped to spot in Britain. Jonathan Franzen was sitting back in his upholstered chair, with his arm slung over the top, as if he were cruising in a big American car. Except, given the direction of his arm, it seemed like he was driving a large British car instead. An Austin Westminster, perhaps.

Jonathan Franzen: Actually, I've already spotted a pink-footed goose. Which really did have pink feet.

He wasn't so good, it transpired, at spotting audience members.

Jonathan Franzen: Let's go with the young man there.
Audience Member: Actually, I'm a woman.
Jonathan Franzen: Sorry, sorry. It's these stage lights…

When I met Jonathan Franzen afterwards, at the signing, I was keen to follow up on his twitchering.

FP: I think you've confused the pink-footed goose with the Ruffle-Necked Sala-ma-goox.

Jonathan Franzen: The Ruffle-Necked Sala-ma-goox?

FP: Oh yes. You must have spotted one of those. Very common they are, the Ruffle-Necked Sala-ma-goox.

Jonathan Franzen: No, I don't think so. That sounds like a Dr Seuss bird to me.

FP: They're everywhere in this country, the Ruffle-Necked Sala-ma-goox. I can't believe you haven't seen one. Maybe you should get your eyes tested.

It really is very difficult to concentrate on my campus novel with that blimmin' great poo on the window. All I can think about is Jonathan Franzen, running through a field with a huge net. He's wearing those googly-eyed glasses with the eyeballs popping out, on springs.

The Corrections isn't strictly a campus novel, but it does have certain sections set around a Connecticut campus, and a character, Chip Lambert, who happens to be an assistant professor in Textual Artifacts. For someone new to the academic world, it also offers many useful insights in regards to appropriate behaviour and conduct. Chip Lambert is an example of how not to behave. Particularly his liaison with a first year undergraduate student. Already, in my brief foray into campus novels, this is becoming an ongoing theme. In Alison Lurie's *The War Between the Tates,* Brian Tate, a political science professor, begins an affair with a female student, fracturing the relationship with his academic wife, Erica. And in Francine Prose's *Blue Angel*, a creative writing lecturer follows a road equally rocky. It is a strong theme in Susan Choi's *My Education*, Nell Zink's *Mislaid*, and plays a role in David Lodge's campus trilogy and Malcolm Bradbury's *The History Man*. At least in

The Corrections the sexual references are funny. 'The jismic grunting butt-oink', for instance, and 'The jiggling frantic nut-swing'. Jonathan Franzen also writes about a talking turd. And he's acclaimed as one of America's most respected authors. It really gives me hope.

Other useful tips from *The Corrections*: avoid fraud, breach of contract, kidnap, sexual harassment, serving liquor to underage students, possession of controlled substances, stalking, making 'obscene' and 'threatening' and 'abusive' telephone calls, and trespassing with intent to violate a young woman's privacy. Nothing about trespassing on a campus after hours, weeing in historic, stately corridors, or vomiting in kitchen sinks. So far so good!

A family of children have commandeered the dress-up area in the Old Naval College's Discovery Centre, so I sign up for a guided walking tour instead. Due to the inclement December weather, demand for outdoor walks is tanking, to the point where our 'group' consists of myself and the guide. It's a first-rate result, because people on tours always look like plonkers, whereas I'll just look like I'm out strolling with my mum. Maureen is a former Greenwich resident who now lives in neighbouring Blackheath. Our tour begins in the Discovery Centre itself, beside a model of the Palace of Placentia. This was on the site of the current college, and was designed in a Tudor style, similar to its contemporary, Hampton Court, which still exists today, in Richmond. After being born and raised here in Greenwich, Henry VIII inherited the palace, expanding it out to include recreational facilities, such as jousting. A replica jousting lance is displayed within the centre, and visitors are encouraged to lift it. But it's housed in an encasement, because if it was loose, you may turn around and whack someone with it. And then turn the other way and whack someone else. And so on.

FP: I suppose this was the phallic equivalent of a big expensive car. And they were riding on a horse, which had a massive big nob already.

Maureen: Um… possibly.

FP: Have you read *Doubtful It Stood: Anxieties of the Phallus in Tudor Drama*?

Maureen: I can't say I have.

FP: It's very good.

Greenwich Park, now separated from the college by a road thoroughfare, is where Henry VIII did his hunting. Some think the Isle of Dogs, across the Thames, is where he kept his hunting dogs. In 1660, after the Reformation, the unwanted palace was demolished. Queen Mary II later commissioned a hospital to be built for the wounded naval heroes, many of whom were missing body parts, or had syphilis, or suffered from mental health problems. In a very short time, the grounds went from housing the royal elite to harbouring riff-raff. My own arrival, I fear, is heralding a similar transition.

Maureen and I set off along the riverside end of the grounds. As she talks, her warm words become visible in the cold wintry air. They are difficult to hear, however, due to the chopping rotor blades of a hovering helicopter. This seems to be an ongoing scourge above Greenwich, as if we were under constant overhead surveillance. Either that or they're forever updating the *EastEnders* opening titles.

Maureen: This is King Charles Court, currently home to the Trinity Laban Conservatoire of Music and Dance. They often rehearse and perform in the chapel, which we'll visit shortly. The other three buildings are all occupied by the University of Greenwich.

FP: Do the university people gang up on the Trinity Laban people and fight them?

Maureen: No, no, no. They're young adults, not school children.

FP: Yeah, but three against one. That's good odds in a fighting situation.

Maureen: There aren't any fights. It's very civilized.

FP: I bet there are.

It turns out Samuel Pepys (pronounced 'Peeps', as in curtain twitcher), the famous diarist, was briefly lodged in the Admiral's House, right here in King Charles Court. He was writing about these surrounds in the seventeenth century. Some 350 years later, based in the adjacent King William Court, I'll be aiming to do the same. But I won't be wearing a wig, or well-heeled shoes with buckles. My words, if I can write them, probably won't be read in ten years, let alone centuries. But at least I don't have a silly surname beginning with 'P'.

Between King Charles Court and Queen Anne Court is a statue wrapped in plastic.

FP: Who's in the bin liner?

Maureen: That's George II. His statue was carved out of a single piece of marble. But it's seen better days, to be honest.

FP: The ageing process. Happens to all of us. Look at my eyebrows. Like broom ends.

Maureen: It's a bit more complicated. When the navy were here, they painted him. But the chemicals used later, to remove that paint, ate away at the marble. So now he must be wrapped up during the winter months, to prevent further deterioration.

FP: They should have just buried the man instead of trying to embalm him. Let nature take its course. Right? It's not like he's Ho Chi Minh.

It took years to build the four central buildings, and many navy pensioners were basically living in a building site. Today, much scaffolding remains, for upgrades. The infirm and the elderly were housed in the upper quarters of the buildings, without elevator access. They were also drunk on gin most of the time because the water was putrid. As a result, they would often misbehave. To install a sense of discipline, the naughtiest residents were made to wear their coats inside out, revealing their yellow trim. The 'yellow coats' were thus outed as drunken troublemakers.

FP: My coat's black.
Maureen: Yes…?
FP: Just saying.

The architectural centrepieces are the twin baroque domes. One sits atop the eighteenth-century chapel in Queen Mary Court, and the other above the famous Painted Hall in King William. Approaching these, Maureen draws my attention to the weathervanes on top.

Maureen: Each of those weathervanes is covered in over 200 sheets of gold leaf.
FP: Does Quasimodo live inside the turrets, ringing the bells?
Maureen: No, he doesn't. There are no bells, but the Queen Mary dome has a working clock inside.
FP: The bells, the bells!
Maureen: In 2000, the roof and dome of the Painted Hall were completely replaced. The scaffolding had to be free-standing so as not to damage the building, which is a Scheduled Ancient Monument, the highest order of protection for a historic building in Britain.
FP: Why aren't there any signs saying 'No Ball Games'?

Maureen: Well, because…

FP: That's an oversight. Even decrepit old housing estates have those.

A soprano and piano accompanist from Trinity College are rehearsing in the College Chapel. Maureen speaks quietly, so as not to kill their vibe.

Maureen: The Old Naval College has always been run as a charity, so its grandness has been sourced on a budget. The floorboards beneath the pews, for instance, are wooden planks taken from decommissioned ships. Many of the chapel pillars aren't real marble, and some of those 'carved' reliefs are actually painted on. Similarly, many of the statues and edifices around the college are made from cheap Coade stone.

Like the *Cutty Sark*, the college looks the part without being entirely authentic. Fingers crossed I can pull off a similar trick myself.

Near the doors to the chapel is an inner stairwell leading to a secret underground passageway. This, Maureen explains, is the Ripley Tunnel, or Chalk Walk, linking the Queen Mary building with King William. Just off this, behind two locked doors, is a basement room containing a very old skittle alley. This was specifically built to keep the old pensioner reprobates occupied. Switching on various lights, Maureen directs me in for a nosy. Only last year, she says, an historic fireplace was discovered behind one of the plaster walls. In 1972, a modest archaeological dig in the central square outside unearthed 200 Tudor items. There are many, many hidden things beneath these grounds, Maureen believes. She has heard rumours of tunnels that go all the way under the road to Greenwich Park, but no one seems to know for sure.

She invites me to have a 'bowl' in the skittle alley using wooden practice cannonballs, which are very heavy. There are no holes to put your fingers in, so I do my best to line it up with fumbling, hungover hands.

Maureen: If you could please roll the ball, rather than throw it. We don't want to create any new excavation sites…

I shunt it forwards with an obvious lack of oomph. It manages to rumble off on a bumpy, wayward path, very slowly making its way to the far end of the lane where it knocks down all the wooden pins.

Maureen: Oh my word. You actually knocked them all down, first time. That's very unusual. No one ever does that.
FP: Thanks, Maureen. Usually when I knock things down like that there's loads of glass to clean up.

Today in the famous Painted Hall, a class of nursery children are lying on the floor, in a circle, gazing up at the richly decorated ceiling. Off to one side, a huge scaffold has been erected, reaching all the way to the artistic centrepiece. Major restoration work is set to begin, and Maureen says there may be opportunities to climb to the top of the scaffolding this year, on tours, with hard hats. Queen Mary, who features with King William in the centre of the painted ceiling fresco, is said to have designed the gardens at Hampton Court Palace. She was, it seems, very well recognized as a gardener. If I had the Hampton Court gardens on my CV, I'm sure I could find work in a flash, even without a van or any gardening tools to speak of.

Although Mary and William were major benefactors of the Naval College buildings and the Painted Hall, the ceiling centrepiece wasn't finished in their lifetimes. Still, not only are they most prominently featured in the final work, but the artist they were bankrolling, Sir James Thornhill, depicted them in heaven.

FP: That's very presumptuous, don't you think, Maureen? Maybe if they'd shared all their riches with the poor, instead of living in a palace and feasting on whales in small balls. No, they went straight to hell really, didn't they, Maureen?

Maureen: Bit harsh.

After this commission, James Thornhill also painted a dome in St Paul's Cathedral. He was the first British artist to be knighted, but this had nothing to do with the fact that he depicted the King and Queen, his employers, residing in heaven.

We emerge onto the outside steps between the domes and royal courts. In front is the Thames with the Isle of Dogs and Canary Wharf beyond. Behind is Greenwich Park and the Queen's House, another royal residence built between 1616 and 1635. On the hill above that is the Royal Observatory.

Maureen: The Royal Observatory is the home of Greenwich Mean Time and the dividing point between the eastern and western hemispheres.

FP: Yes, I know. It all sounds so important, doesn't it? And yet, apart from Joseph Conrad, novelists just can't be arsed with Greenwich. Even Conrad sees it as minor description fodder. What's that all about?

Maureen: I beg your pardon?

FP: I'm going to fix all that, Maureen. I'm going to put Greenwich back on the map, in my book. You'll be in it too.

Maureen: In your *book*? Oh, God. Really?

A large group of visiting students and teaching staff are standing near us by the steps. They're all staring back towards the park.

Maureen: Ah, the timeball is set to drop.

FP: Eh?

Maureen: You see the red ball on top of the observatory? It was originally installed in 1831, and it drops every day at 1 p.m. to signal the correct time for ships passing down the Thames. It's a bit of an attraction.

As we watch, the ball drops in stuttered stops and starts before easing down the final stretch of its short rod. As an 'experience', it is completely underwhelming. But the gathered crowd begin cheering, whistling and whooping as the dome clock strikes one.

FP: That's it? That's a tourist attraction? Oh dear me. You've got to be joking.

The group have turned inwards and are laughing. Sometimes I'll get excited and silly about very minor things too. But only after I've spent all day in the pub.

FP: What's your excuse? Grow up!

ALL
ABOUT
DRINKING

FIONA FOSTER

ALEXANDER McCALL SMITH

ILLUSTRATIONS BY
IAIN McINTOSH

for Francis Plm

[signature]

MACDONALD PUBLISHERS · EDINBURGH
Loanhead, Midlothian, Scotland

In order to progress my study of campus novels, it is necessary to secure the texts. As a fully fledged academic, this should be possible, and effortless, via the university library. But without an official designated pass, my access to higher knowledge, beyond the electronic turnstiles, is denied. Successful writers have researchers working for them, collating and distilling piles of relevant texts. Nelson Mandela managed to source important books, on an island, in jail. Yet I can't even read a campus novel, in a library, on a campus.

To track down *The Secret History* by Donna Tartt, therefore, I must resort to the other library, used by the public. West Greenwich Public Library has, thus far, managed to escape the government's rampant austerity cuts. Although priding itself on its bigwig authors, Britain is currently wiping out grassroots access to books and knowledge. The UK's economy suffered a battering after the 2008 financial crisis created by the banks. Now, many years later, it would be really helpful if they, and the other responsible financial institutions, could act to stop libraries closing. Instead, they're investing their money in literary tents at the Hay Festival, and sponsoring the Booker Prize and its slap-up Guildhall dinner. I suppose Doxford Park Library in Sunderland, now closed, wouldn't generate the same PR as a high-end literary gathering, or a posh prize-giving event in the City of London. Rather than promoting and safeguarding tomorrow's readers, writers and thinkers, the financial industry is merely adding their logos to corporate events, rubbing shoulders with the literary establishment and their own kind.

Perhaps a clever spider, housed inside a financial institution, needs to spin a message in its web, to draw attention to the plight of the good honest folk whose libraries face the chop. Maybe its silken threaded message could read:

SAVE THE LIBRARIES, YOU SHITS.

Fortunately for me, West Greenwich Library is yet to be boarded up, squatted inside, or razed to the ground. A free copy of Donna Tartt's campus novel awaits on the designated shelf, although the checkout area is largely inhabited by robot machines. I may be socially awkward, but I still find people easier to communicate with than beeping metal contraptions. The young librarian in attendance has a keen desire to help, but there is a further stumbling block. My library card is only valid for the Borough of Camden, and this library, and my new posting, are in the wider remit of Lewisham. To get a Lewisham card, I must provide a permanent address, in Lewisham.

FP: The thing is, I now work here in Greenwich, at the university. In a senior literary role, involving books. Like this one here, which I desire.

Librarian: It's your home address we need. Do you have a utility bill? We need some proof of residence, before we can proceed with your registration.

FP: *We?* Are you a Siamese twin?

Librarian: Sorry?

FP: Is there another head tucked down your jumper there?

Librarian: I mean the library, collectively.

FP: Ah. Well, given I am currently unable to provide residential details, how will I borrow this book, in the interim period?

Librarian: You'll have to wait until you're registered, I'm afraid. Or you can read it here, in the library.

FP: Are alcoholic drinks permitted?

Librarian: No, they're not.

FP: Hmm. How's that going to work?

Librarian: Well, if you're with the university, perhaps you could access *their* library.

FP: Yes, that would be ideal. But I haven't been officially processed yet, so I can't even get beyond the turnstiles.

Librarian: Oh dear.

FP: If I just run off with this Donna Tartt book, very fast, would that set the bleepers off?

Librarian: Yes, it would. You'd find yourself in hot water if you did that.

FP: Hmm. Have you read *Curious George Visits the Library*?

Librarian: The children's book? No, I haven't.

FP: *He* gets issued a library card. And he's just a little monkey.

I vow to return to West Greenwich Library with a long straw and two cans of high-strength beer embedded in my deep coat pockets.

A shop in Greenwich is offering sunbed use for 70p a minute. I must say, I'm tempted. Over the Christmas/New Year break, the college heating is completely switched off. This makes perfect sense, of course. Why waste precious energy when no one in their right mind will be here to benefit? As a result however, King William has a ghostly chill, even in the middle of the day. At night, my fold-out bed emits no ultraviolet radiation, and my room is a veritable icebox. You can imagine what it was like in the old days, for the navy pensioners. They must have been popping their clogs like mad.

My daytime hours, therefore, are largely spent in the pub. Occasionally, adorned in a tight woollen hat like a sailor on land, I brave the low-tide beach, combing for clay pipe fragments discarded by early London smokers. At other times, I face the inside cold, exploring the multi-layered corridors and stairwells of King William, or, via the Chalk Walk passage, the nooks of Queen Mary, tapping the walls, looking for naval treasure. Most offices are locked, but not all. On the black, dead computer screens, I affix cryptic Post-it note messages, to be discovered in the New Year:

- DONUT MAKE ME ANGRY.

- 'DON'T THROW FRUIT AT A COMPUTER.' — MICHAEL ROSEN

- I MIGHT BE A DEAD PENSIONER FROM THE 18TH CENTURY, BUT I CAN STILL ACCESS MICROSOFT OFFICE.

It's a bit *Scooby-Doo*, creeping through this dark and freezing place, aware that it once housed unbalanced, wild-eyed sailors. The chill is comparable to my garage existence, except now, I'm the rat, scuttling about.

On Christmas Eve, a faculty member suddenly appears out of the gloom, just as I happen to be racing an office chair along the corridor, very, very fast. The male colleague, I'm fairly certain, is someone I've never met.

FP: Oh my word! You scared the living crap out of me! I thought you were a dead ordinary crewman!

Male Colleague: Well, I wasn't exactly expecting a speeding chair racer either. Haven't you got some place to be, on the eve of Christmas?

FP: No. The big day comes quicker if you keep yourself occupied. Rather than hanging around the chimney.

Male Colleague: I see.

FP: Should I be worried about ghosts in this place?

Male Colleague: No, I haven't heard of any.

FP: No ghouls prowling the old decks?

Male Colleague: Not ghouls, but… there was a report of a prowler, who urinated in the corridor. A very recent report.

FP: Oh. That's, ah, folklore… surely?

Male Colleague: Not yet. But it probably will be.

FP: Um, I encountered an apparition myself once, in a bookshop, in Hay-on-Wye. I thought it was the ghost of Ruth Rendell, but I've actually met her since then, and she was very much alive. At least, I think I did.

Male Colleague: You believe in ghosts, do you?

FP: Oh yes. How else to account for the slime?

Male Colleague: Hmm. I noticed that many reviews of your book discussed how silly it was.

FP: Right, but… I don't think they understood its real depth. The depth of its… water.

Male Colleague: Hmm. I must say, I think its 'depth' escaped me also. 'Silly' is an apt description in my view.

FP: That's one interpretation. Shared by many, granted.

Male Colleague: I'm sure your posting here will attract a certain publicity for the university, and the department. But personally, I would have preferred someone with more clout. With a proven track record, so to speak.

FP: You mean a firework who's not a fizzer.

Male Colleague: Yes, exactly that.

FP: But who? I'm setting the bar very high, don't you think? [*Nervous laugh.*]

Male Colleague: Well, let's see. Someone established, articulate, mature... oh, I know: Alexander McCall Smith. Yes, he has a very respectable oeuvre, and a strong following to boot. His books have been universally translated and adapted for the screen. And he's funny of course, without being silly...

FP: [*Sigh.*]

Male Colleague: He's also a doctor, and a very scholarly gent. He's a popular draw for the big literary festivals, and he's a confident, well-presented, entertaining fellow. Yes, Alexander McCall Smith. He ticks all the boxes, really.

FP: But what about his 'evils of drinking' book? That's not entertaining at all. It's depressing is what it is.

Male Colleague: Sorry, which book is this?

FP: You haven't read it? I thought you were familiar with his oeuvre. It's some terribly dry thing where he declares that drinking alcohol is bad, bad, bad. Personally, I think he'd go down like a shit balloon at Greenwich, with all the young students of today.

Male Colleague: Well, I wasn't aware...

FP: Not everyone regards me as a banger without the fizz. It's only certain people, the ones who are properly informed about books and have read mine and judged it poorly.

Male Colleague: Right. And also the people who have encountered you in person. At the department dinner, for instance. Something about inserting your penis into mashed potato?

FP: That was a riddle, a clever riddle. None of your esteemed fellows could solve it. Only I knew the answer, even though I'd basically spent all that day in the pub. With drinks. Yes, drinks, Dr McCall Smith! Alcoholic ones! Doctor and the Medics!

Male Colleague: Oh dear.

FP: I may not have all the qualities of your Dr Smith, but you can't junk a set of Christmas lights just because a couple of bulbs aren't working. Jonathan Franzen wrote that.

Male Colleague: Yes, but…

FP: That's what I need: some merry Christmas lights. For Christmas. Merry Christmas!

THE RACHEL PAPERS

Martin Amis

To Francis Plug

Martin Amis

Jonathan Cape Thirty Bedford Square London

The New Year has materialized through the gloom, and as university personnel emerge in ever-increasing clusters, it dawns on me that my role has officially begun. For the first time in my life, I actually have a paid job as a writer. A contract is yet to be finalized, however, so my specific position requirements are still unclear, as is, more importantly, when I will be paid.

I'm the first to make it into the office, on account of living the closest. The messy, streaky bird poo remains on the windowpane behind Dr Alex's desk. Attempting to ignore this, I switch on the computer. A new message has arrived, inviting me to 'process'. Apparently I now have official clearance and can get my ID card sorted. Hopefully it can be used in cash machines, and to settle bar tabs.

When the office door opens suddenly and Dr Alex enters, I sit up straight in my chair and look alert.

Dr Alex: Hi, Francis. Happy New Year.

FP: Yes, just so you know, that wasn't me.

Dr Alex: Sorry?

FP: On the window there. That white, messy streak.

Dr Alex: What, the bird shit?

FP: Yes, I believe it was a bird. A bird was responsible for it. Not me.

Dr Alex: Right.

FP: Because… I don't want you thinking, these authors, coming in here, doing shits everywhere.

Dr Alex puts his bag on a spare seat near his desk. He takes a good long stare at the poo.

Dr Alex: Okay, good to know.

My head lowers to my Martin Amis book, which I open to some random point in the middle, my eyes darting side to side, without reading.

Dr Alex: Good Christmas?
FP: Yes, thank you. Very quiet. Stayed at home, for the most part.
Dr Alex: In West Hampstead?
FP: Oh yes.
Dr Alex: Nice. So… I was thinking it would be good if you could meet up with the students. Help critique their creative writing projects.
FP: God! Oh my God! Yes, sure.
Dr Alex: They haven't met you yet, so it would be a chance to introduce you, for them to put a face to the name. And obviously, to get some tutorage from a working writer.
FP: [*Head in hands.*] Of course!

Oh my word. He expects me to actually engage with the students. How's that going to work? Quick, think of a foil, a spanner in the works…

FP: But… but you need a Phd to actually teach though, right?
Dr Alex: A fid?
FP: Yes. A Phd.
Dr Alex: Oh, you mean a PhD?
FP: See? I can't even pronounce them, let alone, you know, use one. Which is a shame. Darn.

Dr Alex: Yes, but you're classed as a 'visiting lecturer'. So you don't need one.

FP: No. Right. No. No, no, no, no, no, no, no, no, no.

There's a scene in Jane Campion's film *An Angel at My Table* where the novelist Janet Frame is nervously teaching in front of a class when a school inspector arrives to observe her. Although biographical, it's like some sort of horror show. Janet Frame excuses herself, exiting the classroom, before walking at pace down the corridor, and then off, away, away, into the countryside. So it has a happy ending. When I was noting potential bedrooms in the building before Christmas, I was also keeping track of all the designated EXITS.

Also, what if the students are better writers than I am? What would the Chancellor and department heads say then? I could end up looking like a total dick. Or, in accordance with the university's equality guidelines, a complete tit.

Dr Alex: Before I forget, Auriol and Patty want to catch up. They're helping to organize our book festival.

FP: Oh.

Dr Alex: I don't suppose you've managed to interest anyone yet? Edna O'Brien, say?

FP: Um… apparently she's… she's got a hen-do that weekend. With blue alco-pop drinks and those clip-on angel wings. But Martin Amis is keen, I believe.

Dr Alex: Really?

FP: Oh yes. He's like totally chomping at the bit for the Greenwich Book Festival.

As I slip out of the office, one of the cleaners is making a big show of all the empty beer cans in the designated recycling bin, widening her eyes and tutting.

A haircut, that's what I need. Contrary to popular perception, universities are not populated by long-haired, big-bearded Allen Ginsberg types. Most of my male colleagues appear to maintain their hair at a sensible length, while observing a regular washing routine. This is something I should aim for also. If I can fit in with the grooming habits of academia, hopefully my inappropriateness in other areas, such as writing, will be less stark. Given I'll need a photo for my ID card, I head off to find a barber.

Usefulness to society is a theme considered in Jonathan Franzen's *The Corrections*, and also in David Lodge's campus novel *Nice Work*. Philip Swallow, one of Lodge's characters, wonders if anyone would even notice if university staff were to go on strike. However, in the same book, Robyn Penrose argues that her students are not in the business of studying something 'useful' like mechanical engineering. 'Because they're more interested in ideas, in feelings, than in the way machines work.' In *The Corrections*, Chip Lambert's father Alfred believes very strongly in doing work that is useful to society. His wife Enid believes Chip, as an academic, is only helping himself. Teachers *are* of great use to society, of course, encouraging their charges to think for themselves, to question and challenge perceived norms, and to try and understand alternative viewpoints, therefore fostering tolerance. But writers in residence? Hmm. Perhaps less so. Residing in a closed office, presiding over words for an ultimately silly book? About as useful as lips on a woodpecker. Or a one-armed trapeze artist with an itchy bum. No, if I want to be useful to society, I probably have to teach. Even if the chances of the students actually benefiting is most questionable. Maybe I'd be more useful marking papers. If so, I'll be sure to add exclamation marks and smiley faces, like Chip Lambert, so they don't hate me.

Barbers, unlike writers in residence, are very useful. They solve a practical need, contributing directly to all facets of society. Fan Barbershop is situated to the east of the tourists' Greenwich, away from the bankers' hilltop homes, where the normal folk live. As a business proposition, Fan Barbershop seems cheap and cheerful, boasting a countertop busy with scissors, clipper attachments and brushes. The sole resident barber politely directs me towards the window-side chair, using my head to advertise his small business to passers-by, as a real concern, where actual hair is cut. Alongside the scissors and brushes are an array of powders, lotions and sprays.

FP: That's quite an ensemble of hair products you have.
Barber: Yes, yes. But nothing for the breath, sorry.
FP: Eh?

When asked for the service that I seek, I enquire of the hairstyles favoured by the modern young students of today.

Barber: Ah, the young men, they like the 'quo vadis'.
FP: Quo vadis?
Barber: Yes, the close-cut style, with the cropped fringe.
FP: Right, I think I know. Like the 'Cut Here' directions for a brain surgeon.
Barber: Like Barack Obama. He has the 'quo vadis'.
FP: Yes, that's what I need. More respect.
Barber: Yes, yes. Yes.

A gown is tied around my neck, extra tight.

FP: Sorry about my hair, in its present state. I've let myself go a bit. But at least I don't wear leather trousers. Chip Lambert, an assistant professor in *The Corrections*, wears leather trousers. But he calls them 'pants', because he's American. Leather pants! Weirdly, Howard Kirk, a British sociology lecturer in *The History Man*, wears leather trousers too. No wonder society questions the academic's role in the world. On top of that, they both have grossly inappropriate sexual relationships with their female students. They're giving us a bad name. Of course, they're purely works of fiction. I mean, what young woman in her right mind would go for an aged man in leather trousers? Leather pants!

Barber: Do you want your eyebrows trimmed too?

FP: Dear me.

My hairs fall to the floor, ungracefully, in clumps. My forehead begins to resemble a designated parking spot.

FP: I'm thinking about getting a tattoo also. They're very 'in' with the young folk, right? Do you have any?

Barber: Tattoos? Me? No.

FP: Sure, fine.

Barber: What sort of tattoo do you like?

FP: Well, I was thinking of getting an anchor, to tie in with naval Greenwich. But perhaps I could get a tattoo of Tattoo, from *Fantasy Island*.

Barber: Huh?

FP: Too intellectual, right? Thought as much. I don't want to wear my academic head on my sleeve. On my upper arm.

Barber: There's a tattooist just up the road. Here, I've got a card.

FP: Thanks. I'll probably need a few drinks in me first.
Barber: *More* drinks?

I'm not even in my coat when the barber takes a broom to my dead hair. People are always sweeping up after me. Usually it's broken glass.

To get my ID processed involves sitting before a tiny camera affixed to a computer. While waiting for the software to crank up, I read the many informational posters on the Student Centre wall. Greenwich Sexual Health offers tests for HIV and other STIs in the comfort of your own home. Plagiarism is BAD. All additional sources in one's work must be quoted and referenced. If not, you will be CAUGHT. There's a Domestic Violence helpline, and the Samaritans are represented too. The Student Union also offers drop-in times for free student advice. The Student Union, as I understand, is a pub. Bartenders are great for advice. Although they can sometimes flip their lid and frogmarch you out, giving you a shove, pulling the door to.

Administration Guy: Right, if you could just look straight into the camera there.

Loose hairs from my haircut have found their way down my back, creating an impossible-to-scratch itch. This causes me to grimace, as if attempting to pull the lower half of my body out of quicksand. My clenched teeth are grinding, and I feel like a horse getting used to its bit. The man tilts the little camera, trying to line it up with my snorting head rattling the bridle.

A plastic card embedded with my name and photo is presented. The stricken horse-in-quicksand pose has been well realized. Now officially processed, I cut a fast path to the Student Union. The receptionist today is less curt, and beeps my pass as if I were a grocery item, like a Flake.

FP: My title is AFFILIATE, apparently. I don't even know what that is. More like a SILLYATE. A SILLY IDIOT.
Receptionist: Pardon?
FP: What do you think of the haircut? Are we liking the haircut?

The Student Union is actually called Bar Latitude, which immediately causes warning bells to clang. The bar design is based on the hull of a ship, and a spiral staircase behind represents a mast of sorts, with a rainbow flag as a sail. There's a free cash machine, and three TVs tuned to different channels, which must be distracting if you're trying to get your homework done.

FP: Beer, please. A lot of it.

Two further warning flares are subsequently fired, in quick succession. The first, which I have spectacularly failed to foresee, concerns the student contingent. With all thoughts on rock-bottom prices, it never occurred to me that the general student populace might be privy to my refreshment regime. That they may, indeed, bear witness to my great thirst, and any subsequent actions resulting from this. The phrase 'dirtying one's own doorstep' springs to mind.

The second issue concerns the rock-bottom prices. A pint of local Greenwich lager in Bar Latitude is almost double that of a lager in the Gate Clock. How can that be? Aren't students in enough debt as it is? Honestly. Anyone would think they don't want them to drink. A poster announces that the water is free.

FP: Yay!

There's only one other patron, and he's eating a sandwich, which he's washing down with water. Drinking my expensive beer like water, I return my glass to the bar with a clonk and depart for the Gate Clock, moulting hairs, pondering a massive infusion of cheap gin.

Kingsley Amis died in 1995, leaving behind a campus novel classic (*Lucky Jim*), a Booker Prize winner (*The Old Devils*), and a son who has also written some books. When I first met Martin Amis, at the Hay Festival, he seemed a bit 'off'. But as he's scheduled to do an event in London's Southbank Centre, I'm hoping we can 'reconnect'. More specifically, I want to sign him up for the Greenwich Book Festival and prove I'm not a firecracker without the fizz. Although our last meeting went badly, I was just a nobody gardener at the time, and now I'm a writer in residence. Also, Martin Amis has interesting ties with academia, so that's something else we have in common. Maybe, when we meet this time, we can exchange one of those special handshakes, with the twiddling fingers.

In 2007, Martin Amis was appointed the Professor of Creative Writing at Manchester University. His posting made the headlines because he was paid around £3,000 an hour for his contractual teaching, the same hourly rate, it was reported, as a Premiership footballer. In comparison, most visiting lecturers were paid between £20 and £50 an hour. I hope his students didn't assume their author–teacher's salary was a standard benchmark. As someone who reputedly dresses like a fisherman, at least I can offer the Greenwich students a more grounded view of their prospective authorly lives to come.

Like his father, Martin Amis has also touched on academia in his writing. In his first novel, *The Rachel Papers*, Charles Highway is a cocksure young man who is contemplating entrance to Oxford. Martin Amis himself attended Oxford, although he doesn't give the city the best of write-ups. According to Charles Highway, he'd 'never known a place so full of itself'.

Martin Amis: Francis Plug? I know that name, don't I?

FP: [*Holding out hand, twiddling fingers.*] We have met before, but I don't think I left much of an impression. Nothing positive, at least.

Martin Amis: Remind me?

FP: Can I first just say that I'm now Writer in Residence, at the University of Greenwich.

Martin Amis: Nice part of the world.

FP: Yes, it is. I'm actually setting my new novel there, on campus. It's a campus novel, as it happens. Like that written by your distinguished father.

Martin Amis:

FP: *The Rachel Papers* wasn't really a campus novel, was it? Not a proper one. And it didn't win the Booker Prize…

Martin Amis: Right. I remember you. You're that piece of shit from, where was it… Hay, the fucking Hay Festival.

FP: You seemed a bit unhappy then, at that time. But I s'pose even £3,000 an hour can't buy…

Martin Amis: No, you can fuck right off, actually.

FP: Sure, but… you don't happen to be free later this year, do you? For the Greenwich Book Festival? You and me, on stage, having a chat, sharing some light moments? That would be lovely, wouldn't it, Martin Amis?

Martin Amis: [*To an assistant.*] Get this prick out of here.

Darn. He would have been a good catch. I bet even the Chancellor's heard of Martin Amis.

Chancellor: Who snared Martin Amis?

Dr Alex: Francis Plug, Chancellor. Our Writer in Residence. He's such an asset to the university.

Chancellor: Francis Plug. He sounds like an absolute ripper.

Dr Alex: You bet. He's off the bleedin' scale. Well done you, for signing off his appointment.

Chancellor: Let's crack open the drinks fridge!

Martin Amis, it's suggested, didn't even spend much time on campus. It's not like he needed the student discounts, or lack thereof. In *Lucky Jim*, his dad's campus novel, Jim Dixon is presented as a junior lecturer who's well out of his depth. He drinks a great deal, sets fire to his bedding, and has an uneasy relationship with his superiors. This heady combination causes him to habitually pull strange and disturbing facial expressions. It doesn't make the most comfortable of reading. To be honest, it all sounds a bit close to home.

DORIS LESSING

A fű dalol

francis Plurq

Doris Lessing

MAGVETŐ KIADÓ · BUDAPEST

There's been some good news from the Continent. My book, Elly informs me, is to be published in Germany, in German. *Wunderbar!* First Greenwich, now Germany. It's all the Gs! What's next? Gin? Why not? Yes, I think I'll have a gin.

FP: Gin, please. In a short glass. Glass!

Who's German? Hans Fallada. He wrote a book called *The Drinker*, and in it there is a passage that reads: 'My whole body was so full of drunkenness, it seemed to hum like a swarm of bees.' Robert Walser was a German-speaking Swiss writer who wrote a lot about Berlin, in Germany. One of Robert Walser's prose pieces contains this: 'Once you have your fist around your second or third glass of beer, you're generally driven to engage in all matters of observations.' He also wrote: 'People who have no success with people have no business with people.'

There's been no word from Hungary, although it's still early doors. Doris Lessing had *her* books translated into Hungarian. Mind you, her body of work was recognized as outstanding by the Nobel committee, whereas my oeuvre is yet to fully mature. I was fortunate enough to meet Doris Lessing before her death, and she signed a copy of her acclaimed novel *The Grass Is Singing*, in the Hungarian translation. It wasn't supposed to be a Hungarian edition. Seriously, that's the last time I buy a second-hand book on the World Wide Web. Assuming, of course, that at some hour of the day or night, using my payment details, I did so.

When the journalists camping outside her home informed her of her Nobel Prize win, Doris Lessing, stepping out of a cab, said: 'Oh Christ.'

FP: When I win the Nobel Prize for Literature, I'm going to say, 'Shit a brick!'

Doris Lessing: Good for you!

FP: Or, 'Are you shaking my shit?'

Doris Lessing: That's a new one to me…

FP: Or, 'Oh my God, that there is some crazy shit you spouting outta your mouth!'

Doris Lessing: Okay. Yes.

FP: Or, 'What the shitty shit?'

Doris Lessing: Yes.

FP: Or… or…

Doris Lessing: Shall I sign these other peoples' books, while you keep thinking?

There's further news from the EU. Another interview, it transpires, is in the offing. This time however, the setting is Paris, in a most distinguished bookshop. Shakespeare & Company. They're even offering to put me up, inside the store, where the likes of Jack Kerouac and Allen Ginsberg have stayed. It's an exciting prospect, but obviously a bit terrifying too. On top of the cultured Parisian crowd, there's also the sleepover element. What if I can't find the loo? The invite also follows closely on the heels of the *Charlie Hebdo* attack. Paris remains on high alert. In *The Secret Agent*, science was the intended target. Now it's journalism. If you write or draw something we don't agree with, we're going to kill you. Still, you can't hide behind the curtains, or in a cupboard. I better brush up on some French.

As well as singing grass, Doris Lessing also wrote, like Joseph Conrad, about terrorism. Her novel *The Good Terrorist* is set in early-eighties Britain, when terrorist incidents in London were commonplace, due to the ongoing conflict with the IRA. At the time, Thatcher and her Tory ministers were also being targeted, with fruit and eggs. Throwing eggs at politicians continues to be popular. In 2010, Tony Blair was pelted with eggs in Dublin, at a book signing. However, these days, it's worth first considering how much exercise the eggs' mothers had.

The Good Terrorist follows a group of protest movement characters who envisage the end of capitalism. In the garden of their occupied Camden house, a large hole is dug to bury many buckets of human shit, left to fester after the council filled their toilets with concrete. The shit isn't singing, but it's certainly humming. For Alice, the central character, Thatcher isn't the only villain. To her, universities represent 'the visible embodiment of evil, something that wished to crush and diminish her. The enemy. If I could put a bomb under that lot, she was thinking. If I could… well, one of these days…' Fine. But at least wait for my stint to finish.

Doris Lessing didn't shy away from coarse language in her novels either. In the English edition of *The Good Terrorist*, she writes: 'The filthy, shitty swine, the shitty fucking fascist swine.' And then, on page 31: 'You filthy bloody cuntish Itlers, you fascist scum.' Although I respect her right to write whatever she wants, you won't find that sort of language in my book.

Shakespeare & Company is positioned by the river Seine. Today in Greenwich, down by the river Thames, the low tide beach has been commandeered. It looks like police forensics. With their high-vis coats and boots and waterproofs, they pore over the silt, as if combing the scene of a murder. Brilliant! A riverside crime scene in Greenwich. A bloated corpse, yay! But no, it turns out they're just a bunch of museum types picking through old stuff. A team of expert archaeologists, to be precise, having a sniff around. They're part of the Thames Discovery Programme, based at the Museum of London Archaeology (MOLA). As I watch, measuring tapes are laid, metal detectors hovered. When an item of interest is found, a small spade is produced, and a portion of earth is lifted, craned to one side, and dropped into a sealed bag. A display table up on the Thames Path features all manner of ceramic fragments, shoes, mobile phones, and many clay pipes in various states of repair. An older woman holds court behind this as I browse the spread-out contents.

FP: I found a clay pipe myself, just down there.
Older Woman: Oh yes? Was it a Prick?
FP: You what?
Older Woman: A Henry Prick. His pipes are very common round here.
FP: Henry Prick? Sorry, is this *The Kenny Everett Show*?
Older Woman: Henry Prick made many clay pipes in the early 1700s. This is one of his here. See the initials? 'HP'.
FP: Wow. I might use him as a character in my book. Except, the twist will be, he's actually a really nice guy.
Older Woman: I don't follow.

The archaeologists have amassed many buckets on the foreshore. One is simply filled with scrubbing brushes, as if they were planning to drain the river entirely and give it a really good clean. Already they've revealed the wooden planks of a former boat launch, previously hidden from view. Descending the steps with care, I creep gingerly over sections of measuring tape, and around the many bags and buckets. A woman in a colourful scarf is digging around the unearthed boat ramp.

FP: Do you win a prize, if you find something in the sand?

Woman: Sorry?

FP: We used to do that with ice lolly sticks. Find a block in the sand and choose a prize.

Woman: Well, if we find something good, I suppose that *is* the prize.

FP: Yes, that makes sense. If you find a jewelled Gothic sword, you shouldn't also receive a jelly snake.

Woman: No.

FP: I've done a bit of digging myself, in my time. I'm a gardener, you see. Or was. Now I work at the university, just there.

Woman: Which department?

FP: Creative Writing. Once, in my previous job, I dug up this putrid, stinking dog. But the thing was, I'd buried it there myself. I just forgot.

Woman: You forgot you'd buried a dead dog?

FP: Yes. What a pong.

Another archaeologist comes over. He is an older man with a white cap and beard.

Older Man: Hello.

FP: Hello. We were just talking about dead, putrid dogs.

Older Man: Oh.

FP: Have either of you read *The Good Terrorist* by Doris Lessing?

Woman: I've read Doris Lessing, but not that one, I think.

Older Man: No.

FP: Alice and her comrades bury bucket after bucket of human poo in the garden. And then the police dig it up.

Older Man: Where did all the poo come from?

FP: From people's bottoms.

Older Man: Yes, but why was there so many buckets of it?

FP: I'm not going to dish you up a spoiler. Read it yourself, diggy.

to Francis-Plug —
Joyce Carol Oates

The Accursed

JOYCE CAROL OATES

FOURTH ESTATE • *London*

There's a catch-up for the Book Festival in the Queen Mary Undercroft. As well as meeting Auriol and Patty, I'm introduced to Maureen, Olivia and Cindy. Dr Zoë and Dr Alex have both put in apologies. I wish I'd done that. Because it turns out it's a proper *meeting* meeting. Was I supposed to come prepared, with hand-outs? I've no idea. But anyway, what's to hand out? There's nothing to report. Vladimir Nabokov is still pending.

Auriol: Nabokov? He's dead, isn't he? As in, *long* dead?

Maureen: Died in the seventies, I think.

FP: Good. Great. That makes things *much* easier. Let's strike *him* off the list, then. Now, Martin Amis.

Maureen: Martin Amis?

FP: Martin Amis *is* alive, I can report. As it happens, I caught up with him in person, for a chat, on the South Bank. But unfortunately, he's a 'no'. He was literally face in hands, moaning at the prospect of missing our fine festival, which he ranks right up there with Hay, Glastonbury, Burning Man, Woodstock...

Patty: Wow. Not bad for an inaugural event.

Olivia: Which hasn't even happened yet...

FP: Right, right. Um... so... Elena Ferrante. So she/he told me she/he is prepared to be interviewed, for the first time, on stage in Greenwich, as long as her/his face is in a creepy haunted house shadow, and her/his voice is distorted, so it sounds like the start of that song 'Let's Go Silly'.

Olivia: Huh?

FP: You know, that seminal eighties pop track, 'Let's Go Silly'.

Cindy: 'Let's Go Silly'?

FP: Yeah. Why not? Let's go silly. Where? Gate Clock?

With nothing concrete on the glitzy 'talent' side of proceedings, the meeting moves into more logical concerns, such as pricing, weather contingents, and face painting. In these areas at least, progress has been made. I'm the one dragging the chain. Yes, I have some big-name connections, especially in Booker Prize circles. But *I'm* not a big name. And it's not like I can sell the festival on the strength of my personality. Perhaps I need to be bolstered further by blue alco-pop drinks, to emphasize the fun times and good cheer to be had by all, even the authors, at the Greenwich Book Festival.

Turkish morocco cigs are packed in their box like a group of friends at a party in my garage. Lighting one with a tiny, gilt-trimmed match, I inhale deeply, as if I were an opened door, creating a powerful vacuum effect that is further enhanced by another open door somewhere out back. Maureen, my tour guide, happens by, walking along the King William balustrade. Rushing up to her, I shout:

FP: NUCLEAR REACTOR!

Maureen: Nuclear reactor? Oh, you mean JASON?

FP: Jason?

Maureen: The nuclear reactor based here in the college?

FP: It's true, then?

Maureen: Yes. JASON was the code name they used, an acronym for the months it took to install it: July, August, September, October,

November. It was housed just over there, on the ground floor of the King William building.

FP: There?

Maureen: Yes, literally just there, in one of those rooms by the court-yard. When the navy moved out in 1998, some Ministry of Defence staff remained guarding the college entrances, which everyone thought was a bit strange. Turns out it was to safeguard JASON. And then, some time later, it was secretly removed in the dead of night. Ironically, Greenwich declared itself a nuclear-free zone while a nuclear reactor was installed in one of its most prominent public buildings.

FP: Goosey!

A nuclear reactor on campus. It's definitely a step up from an amateur bomb in Greenwich Park. Perhaps, in *my* novel, I could take out the observatory properly, along with every other Wren building, and then some. Thanking Maureen, I wander slowly over to the Thames. The tide is out and the scummy froth and debris resemble some kind of bog kingdom. A dog is barking at the water's edge.

FP: [*To the dog's owners.*] Ahoy there. Watch those lion mane jellyfish and their potent toxin. Mind you and your dog there don't suffer a paralysis of the heart muscles and die.

Dog Owner: Lion mane jellyfish? In the Thames?

FP: Strange things are afoot, kind sir. Please keep alert.

A steamboat passes by, skippered by an old man with a bushy white moustache. A wake is caused, rattling the dirty stones on the shore of the bog kingdom.

FP: [*Shouting.*] Beware the rattling stones! Of the bog kingdom!

Dog Owner: Yes, all right. Calm yourself.

One of the campus gardeners is edging out the upper lawn, near the domes. I approach with the offer of a Turkish cigarette, which he refuses.

FP: I used to be a gardener, you know. Now I'm Writer in Residence here at the university.
Gardener: Oh yeah?
FP: I don't suppose you're growing any angel's trumpet flowers? Cousin of the jimson weed?
Gardener: Are you joking? That's totally lethal, that stuff.
FP: Yes, I know. It's just they're my little niece's favourite.
Gardener: [*Shaking head.*] No chance of that stuff here.
FP: What a shame. I'll have to find something else to affix to her postcard. Yes, some of us still write postcards. Say, here's something that transcends both the writing *and* the gardening disciplines: [*Clears throat.*] 'And then my heart with pleasure fills, and dances with daffodils'.
Gardener:
FP: It's just a short piece.
Gardener:
FP: I'll let you get on.

Up on the white stone balcony of Queen Mary, high above the balustrade, a young teenage girl in a white gown tears up white flower petals, letting them fall slowly to the grass edge below.

FP: Here, you'll have your work cut out for you, tidying up all that.
Gardener: What?
FP: All those flower petals that girl up there is dropping.

Gardener: What girl?

FP: That one.

Gardener: Dunno what you're talking about, mate.

Like the University of Greenwich, Princeton University has Grecian pillars. That is, if Joyce Carol Oates is to be believed. Her campus novel *The Accursed* is set around 1905/1906, and concerns the supposed arrival of the Devil on campus, and the terror he unleashes. My arrival in Greenwich was, I hope, more low-key. Yes, there's been wee in the corridor and sick in the sink, but it's not like my breath's as 'hard and dry as ashes', or my skin 'flaccid, and fish-belly-white'. Not as a general rule of thumb.

Unlike the college gardeners, my immunity to the February cold is diminishing. Writing in residence doesn't exactly get the blood circulating. As an author, I'm becoming more reptilian in manner. There are no sun-drenched rocks to lie on, so I seek out warmth in the college chapel.

In Princeton's campus chapel, there is a most disturbing incident when a minister is attacked by a 'shimmering phantom', a ghoulish serpent snake, which binds his thrashing body and chokes him to death in front of a terrified congregation. Although I pray for something similar, my chapel visit is all rather ho-hum. Apart from the ORNC staff, offering guided talks or info, there is no congregation at all. Instead, there's just a massive organ, floorboards from ships, and lots of fancy decorative features, no doubt documented, in full, by writers of fact.

FP: Excuse me. Have you heard any whispered voices, inciting rude, unchristian words?

ORNC Guide: No?

FP: What about talking cherubs, firing real darts?

ORNC Guide: No?

FP: Okay, well if you do, I'll be sitting just over there.

ORNC Guide: Over there?

FP: Yes. I'll be trying to think of something that could set off a nuclear reactor.

Joyce Carol Oates features real people in her campus novel, which is something I've been dabbling with myself. US President Woodrow Wilson was formerly the President of Princeton University, and in *The Accursed* he muses on his undergraduate years there, recalling 'a claustrophobic little world of privilege and anxiety in which one was made to *care too much about too little*'. Before his time, however, back at the start of the 1800s, some Princeton students cared enough to raise hell, setting off charges of gunpowder in the building. Others kidnapped unsavoury teachers, tarring and feathering them. Perhaps the teaching aspect of my role is something I need to discuss more fully with Dr Alex.

Another real person featured in her novel is writer Upton Sinclair, most famous for his protest book *The Jungle*. In *The Accursed*, he accesses Princeton's historical archives for his research purposes, despite feeling estranged from the campus, aware that its grand architecture and society wealth first sprung from the labour of others. It was an idyllic setting, he observed, yet so much a bastion of privilege it could make him physically ill if he allowed himself to dwell upon it.

Compared to others on campus, Upton Sinclair felt like a scarecrow. And yet, as a result of writing one book, he suddenly became a worldwide celebrity, and was read by Winston Churchill and invited to dine at the White House with President Roosevelt. On the strength of my book, I've just been invited to talk in Crystal Palace. It sounds like one of the Queen's many homes, and that's the sort of gravitas I'm lending the event, without actually dressing for the occasion.

Dr Alex: You're reading to the Queen?

FP: Kind of.

When Upton Sinclair is in a bustling tavern, he bemuses the waitress by ordering a glass of milk. In Crystal Palace, I bemuse the bartender by ordering two glasses of oversweet, cloying sherry, followed by a double Old Grand-Dad whiskey.

Bartender: The party starts here, does it?

FP: It's for my voice box, for later. Ahem. La, la, la, la, la, la...

Bartender: Yeah, all right. Right, got it.

A narrow one-way street divides the Postal Order pub from the Bookseller Crow, the venue for my talk. Sitting at a table by the window, I stare intently across, staking it out. Flanking the shop on either side are cafés, and two doors along is the Crystal Palace Aquarium, which, judging by its window display, seems to be selling tree branches. A cigarette break is a good excuse to spy further, like one of Mick Herron's characters. My smoke drifts up through the foliage of the pub's overhanging flower baskets, and a light rain trickles steadily down my sunglass lenses. Let's hope my disguise holds up. Otherwise, as we all know, it's jumper leads on the bollocks for me.

An automated pedestrian crossing makes an almighty peeping racket right outside the Crystal Palace Aquarium. You really have to feel for those poor little fishes' ears. It can't help the serenity of the bookshop either, which has its front door open, in the rain. There are no tree branches in the Bookseller Crow's window, although they do have T-shirts, on hangers, possibly drying. What they need is something to lure in this captive pub crowd directly over the way. Maybe some signs, with words:

BOOKS CAN ALSO HELP YOU
ESCAPE REALITY, PUB PATRONS.

Or:

WHY NOT STARE AT A BOOK FOR HOURS,
PUB PATRONS? INSTEAD OF A WALL?

The signage above the shop window includes a phone number.

Bookseller Crow: Bookseller Crow.
FP: Is that the Bookseller Crow?
Bookseller Crow: Yes, this is the Bookseller Crow.

I know! I know it is! I just saw you answer the phone!

FP: Is Francis Plug doing a talk in your shop tonight?
Bookseller Crow: He is. Starts around seven o'clock.
FP: Great. Cos he's my favourite author.
Bookseller Crow: Really? Okay. Well, come along. Should be an
    interesting evening.
FP: I will. Is it true that members of the royal family are attending also?
Bookseller Crow: The royal family? Not to my knowledge, no. No,
    I can't imagine that happening. Not at all.
FP: You never know, right? Make sure your entranceway doesn't get
    damp with all this rain, because the Queen is used to smelling fresh
    paint, not mouldy books.

Being a Wetherspoons pub, there's no piped music or television coverage in the Postal Order, so it could almost pass as a bookshop. Except for
the sharp clicks of joints seizing, and the cistern-like noise of bladders

filling to their brims. If any of the patrons are attending my book event, they don't let on. Like Upton Sinclair, I may as well be a scarecrow. Which isn't ideal, given my Bookseller Crow appearance. Who's going to buy my book if I scare the bookshop away? Perhaps the punters just don't recognize me. When an author photo was mooted for the back flap of my book, I opposed the motion. The flap is technically part of the cover, and as I explained to Elly and Sam, it's best if readers don't judge my book by its cover.

My noisy phone rings in the dead calm of the pub.

FP: Hello?

Woman: Hi, is that Francis Plug?

FP: Yes?

Helen: Hi, it's Helen here from the Inland Revenue. Is now a good time to talk?

FP: No, I'm actually in the Palace at the moment. For an engagement.

Helen: The palace?

FP: Yes, *thee* Palace. It's all very dignified, so I'd rather not talk just now, on a phone, about little people problems.

Helen: Should we arrange another...?

Beep, beep, beep.

Not wishing to be sloshed for my public engagement, I switch to strong beer. After wrapping my hands around the glass, the warmed pint comes to life, as an owl.

FP: Oh my word. My pint's turned into an owl.

The owl's sharp talons dig into my palm. Even with the relative hush of the pub, it's a nervy bird, reluctant to leave the coop. But all it needs is a little encouragement. Heaving it up into the air, I bid it fond adieu.

FP: Fly away! Fly away!

Rather than taking flight, the owl turns back into a pint of strong beer and smashes all over the floor. Unlike other Wetherspoons carpets, the Postal Order's design is nothing special: red squares with blue borders and standard flower motifs. The smashed and spilled pint adds a certain something, I tell the patrons, who, unlike my owl, are flapping. The duty manager doesn't buy the new carpet design either, or the owl story. Instead, I'm publicly disgraced, turfed out, on my ear. Seconds later, I'm welcomed at the Bookseller Crow, as an acclaimed author, with open arms.

Jonathan Main: Francis, welcome. I'm Jonathan.
Justine Crow: I'm Justine. Great to have you here, etc.
FP: Ha, ha! Brilliant!

A number of people are milling around inside the shop.

Justine: It's not a bad turnout.
FP: Any sign of Her Majesty yet?
Jonathan: No. Are you expecting her?
FP: Possibly. Whatever you do, don't tell her you accept cards. She hates those. Because her face isn't on them.
Jonathan/Justine: ?
FP: Wait, I forgot to smoke.

The punters outside the Postal Order point at me, blowing their smoke upwards, as if launching missiles across the narrow road divide. It's like *West Side Story*, except this is South East London.

Another real life author in *The Accursed* is Jack London. Unlike Upton Sinclair, who despairs at the besiegement of his privacy, Jack London welcomes the glare. For his talk at Carnegie Hall, he guarantees 'a juggernaut of a performance'. His consummate confidence and 'astonishing charisma' are helped along by frequent swigs from a silver flask, causing him to shout, 'Revolution now! Revolution now!' His audience erupt in applause, stomping their feet and cheering. The Bookseller Crow isn't Carnegie Hall, but like Jack London, I am primed with drink. His appeal was 'to the downtrodden, exploited working-man of America and of the world', while I'm aiming to connect with anyone who turns up.

FP: Revolution now! Revolution now! Ha, ha!
Audience: [*Looking at each other.*]

Despite being a small business, constantly pummelled by Internet giants, the Bookseller Crow has provided the audience, and myself, with free wine. It's a very nice gesture, although, on top of the oversweet cloying sherry, the whiskey and the strong beer, it makes the words in my book even harder to read than normal.

FP: Sorry about this. It's just… my book is a bit mouldy and starting to pong. I didn't buy it in this shop. The damp wasn't caused by rainwater. It's from my old house, which was actually a garage. Not like you folk, living in a palace.

Winding up the botched reading, I open up the floor for questions.

FP: Yes, you sir.
Audience Member: Hi. Where does the factual world finish and the fictional world begin in your novel?

In the distance is a very sharp *peep, peep, peep*.

FP: Sorry, I think someone's crossing the road.

There is a pause while we all wait for the person, or persons, to cross the road.

FP: Were there any other questions?
Audience Member: You didn't answer my one.
FP: Are you quite sure?
Audience Member: Yes.
FP: What was it again, your question?
Audience Member: Where does the factual world finish and the fictional world begin in your novel?
FP: Perhaps I can explain it this way. On either side of this bookshop are cafés. Presumably, they both sell sandwiches. But in fact, they themselves are the bread slices, and the Bookseller Crow is the interesting sandwich filling. Don't you think?
Audience:
FP: Were there any other questions?

Afterwards I'm asked to sign some books. It's lucky I have gum, because my breath is heavy with hops, ash, camphor, and ambergris.

Audience Member: Hi, I enjoyed your book.
FP: Really? Serious? Wow. Thanks. Did you enjoy tonight's talk also?
Audience Member: Less than the book, to be honest. The book, at least, made some sort of sense. Sort of.
FP: Well, I really appreciate you turning up. You could be at home watching a TV programme about people watching TV.

Audience Member: That's not on tonight, is it?

Justine and Jonathan invite me to join them and the bookshop staff for a drink in Crystal Palace.

FP: Not that place opposite, though. Their carpet's boring and it's strewn with glass.

As we pass the Crystal Palace Aquarium, I note that the tree branches range from £20 up to £32.95. For tree branches.

FP: See that? Instead of selling books, made from trees, you should just sell trees, in their raw form.
Jonathan: Yes, I imagine the margins on branches are quite favourable.
FP: You could even perch a crow on one. Here, you can have that for nothing.

It seems like everyone in Crystal Palace knows the Bookseller Crow crew, but their author in tow isn't ringing any bells. Even when bright people are handed really big hints, on a plate.

FP: Rhymes with Grancis Blug?
Crystal Palace Person: No. Sorry.
FP: What about my voice? On Radio 4?
Crystal Palace Person: I can't place it.
FP: Maybe you recognize this quote of mine: 'The Hay Festival is a blank field filled with words.'
Crystal Palace Person: No.
FP: They still haven't paid me for that line. Or given me a slot, in a friggin' tent. Not even one of their small tents. Or a really small

two-person tent, for camping. No, nothing. I'd be happy to stand on the grass, outside, if it was a nice day, but they haven't offered. Their loss, right?

Jonathan and Justine ask about my book sales.

FP: They're good, I hope. Now I'm living in pricey Greenwich.
Justine: Where in Greenwich are you?
FP: I'm in the Old Royal Naval College.
Justine: What, you're actually *living* there?
FP: Yes, but it's kind of hush-hush. And, it's Christopher Wren-designed, so it's altogether substandard. Did I tell you I saw a flying reptile, of the Jurassic period…?

It's suggested I visit Crystal Palace Park, where there are reputedly many dinosaurs. Perhaps, I say, we could collect some tree branches, to sell for blimmin' heaps.

FP: Yeah, let's go.
Bookseller Crow: Bye, then.

Walking through the park in the pitch dark is like walking through the Valley of the Shadow of Death. But I fear no evil, because after my sherry, wine, whiskey, beer, and shots of Kentucky bourbon, I'm mashed. Even when an inner demonic voice implores me to return to Greenwich and climb the *Cutty Sark* mast, in the nuddy, I simply bat it off, laughing.

THE RULES OF

ATTRACTION

To Francis Plug

best wish

Bret Easton Ellis

BRET
EASTON
ELLIS

I awaken outside, in Crystal Palace, straddling an iguanodon. Fortunately it's not a teleosaurus, because I could have found myself submerged in pond water, and it's very, very cold.

The day of my first student induction quickly rolls around. It's a terrifying prospect, like an author event horror show, set to play out over and over.

In the introduction to Richard Fariña's campus novel *Been Down So Long It Looks Like Up to Me*, Thomas Pynchon writes of the situation at Cornell University in the spring of 1958, when both he and Fariña were students there. Not only was drug-taking prevalent, but student protesters were storming the home of the university president, deploying rocks, eggs and smoke bombs. This was in 1958, way back in the good old days.

The Rules of Attraction, by Bret Easton Ellis, opens in fall, 1985. The students are now taking every drug known to humankind: heroin, cocaine, acid, crystal meth, methadone, ecstasy, morphine, and wheelbarrows of weed. Not only are they taking drugs, but they're dealing them too. And having abortions, committing suicide, writing graffiti on toilet doors, using explicit language, and listening to Black Flag and Twisted Sister. This was over thirty years ago, way back in the good old days. Which makes you wonder just what the students of today must be like. God only knows. Maybe they drink their own wee.

In preparation for meeting them, I therefore take full advantage of the Gate Clock's early opening hours.

Bartender: All ready for the seminar?

FP: I beg your pardon?

Bartender: You're the Writer in Residence aren't you?

FP: Ahh…

Bartender: The Creative Projects seminar, at eleven? I'll see you there. I'm in the Creative Writing BA course.

FP: But… you're a bartender.

Bartender: Got to earn money somehow. I'm full-time at the uni. You're assessing my work today, I think.

FP: Oh my god!

Seizing my drink, I shove it up the inside of my jumper.

FP: This isn't alcohol. It's just… raspberry cordial.

Bartender: What, that Metaxa Greek brandy I just poured you?

FP: And I'm not the Writer in Residence. I'm… I'm the Lord High Admiral Chief Naval Officer Commander.

Bartender: Oh. Okay. [*Saluting.*] Aye, aye, sir.

Dr Alex is leading the session. It's his class, I'm just participating in a support capacity, as a supposed authority on creative writing.

FP: [*Biting finger.*]

In *The Rules of Attraction*, a student raises her hand and says: 'This class is a total mindfuck.' Today, I can't help but think that the shoe will be on the other foot.

Creative Projects can be any genre of writing the student chooses, be it fiction, poetry, performance writing, playwriting or screen-writing. Today's session is a critique. We, the teachers and students, are expected to offer feedback on selected works-in-progress. The students are waiting outside the room, some sitting on the thin carpet, leaning on walls. They appear friendly, especially the bartender, who, big-smiled, salutes me.

QM202 is a normal, one-level room, rather than a vast tiered lecture theatre. Dr Alex sits on the end of a horizontal bench containing computer monitors, and the students position their chairs before him, forming a circle. I remain on the periphery, like a broken off tail from a Q. Dr Alex introduces me, as the Writer in Residence. The bartender is probably still smiling, but I wouldn't know because I'm blanking her. Another student, whose work we are to critique first, has done a no-show. Dr Alex can't even recall her, suggesting unacceptable attendance rates. I wonder where she might be, and wish myself there too.

Because the abstainer isn't here to defend herself, the group starts off by piling into her piece. It concerns a mystery fog that causes entire countries to disappear. But as the group determines, there are plausibility issues. Russia is the first to mysteriously vanish. But what about the neighbouring countries? What about the fuel that Russia supplies to the other countries? Surely that would be immediately cut off too? Wouldn't it have been better to start with a small island that disappears first, before moving on to the big nations?

Dr Alex: What do you think, Francis?

FP: Um… well, I'm worried this is actually real.

Dr Alex: Real?

FP: Yes. Entire countries being swallowed by fog, and the young woman who exposes the story mysteriously disappears.

There are some embarrassed half-laughs.

Dr Alex: I wouldn't worry. It seems she's missed classes before. And then turned up again.
FP: We could be next. In Britain.
Dr Alex: Let's move on, shall we?

Annoyingly, the piece from the bartender is particularly well realized. It's a historical fantasy extract that has apparently progressed since its last outing with the group. Most of the students struggle to find fault with it, choosing to highlight the positives, of which there are many. But there is also a small contingent of nit-pickers, desperate to criticize. One young fellow seems determined to find problems with the piece, despite its promise. He cites his historical knowledge at every possible opportunity.

Nit-Picker: A blacksmith drinking rum? As if! A blacksmith would be drinking mead!

The bartender, who is taking note of the comments, appears somewhat exasperated.

Bartender: Fine, I'll change the drink. Whatever.
Dr Alex: So, apart from the nit-picks…?

The next piece has also been presented before, and the initial comments suggest it hasn't moved on much. A romantic novel extract, it concerns an adulterous wife and her lover who have a bad car accident while engaged in sexual acts. The author of this piece is sitting in the circle staring at her fingers. As the group presents feedback, she bites her nails. One of the critique rules is that the authors must remain silent.

It is an opportunity to instead listen and absorb feedback. Given the unfavourable comments however, the author pipes up, attempting to defend herself and her work.

Student: But I cut out a chunk at the end, which I wasn't happy with, and I still need to replace it...

Dr Alex: No, come on, you know the rules.

The negative feedback persists. The tone of voice doesn't work. It's unoriginal. It's clichéd. Oh dear. The author looks as if she might cry. However, Dr Alex is careful to handle the feedback sensitively, moderating the group, balancing the criticism with positives where applicable.

It's like a scene directly out of Francine Prose's campus novel *Blue Angel*. Professor Ted Swenson's Creative Writing class follows the same structure, although he acknowledges the 'ritual sadism' of silencing the students. 'What maniac invented this torture, this punishment for young writers? Imagine a group of established authors subjecting themselves to this! It's not an academic discipline, it's fraternity hazing. And the most appalling part is that it's supposed to be helpful. The bound and gagged sacrificial lamb is supposed to be grateful.'

Dr Alex: Francis? Anything to add?

FP: Um... I crashed my van once. When I had a van, for gardening purposes. It was nothing to do with sexy times. I believe it was more a case of avoiding a sleeping policeman, by driving on the pavement.

Student: You didn't crash into a person, did you?

FP: No, I didn't, thanks for asking. But I did crash into a grit container, containing grit. And then a public rubbish bin, and then...

Dr Alex: Okay, well...

FP: Actually, there's a scene in Philip Roth's campus novel *The Human*

Stain where a car crashes due to sexy time action. So if a big-name like him can write that stuff, why can't she?

Dr Alex: Yes indeed. See? You could be the next Philip Roth!

FP: Maybe you'll meet him, at the Greenwich Book Festival.

Dr Alex: Who, Philip Roth?

FP: Yes. Sure, I just need to make a few more phone calls…

Dr Alex: Seriously?

FP: You bet. Can you cover his flights from America and hotel and appearance fee and stuff?

Dr Alex: Hmm, no, I don't think our budget will stretch that far. That would probably end up costing more than we pay you for an entire year.

FP: Really? Stuff that for a joke. No, let's totally ditch him. I'll try Agatha Christie. Or Spike Milligan…

The students hastily depart, in varying degrees of mental trauma. At least they'll be prepared for lives as public authors, particularly the review component. Dr Alex has a meeting to attend, and I really need the loo, so we arrange to catch up later.

A series of different tugs plough the Thames, bearing the collective titles *Reclaim*, *Recovery*, *Resource* and *Redoubt*. My own states of being, I've found, can be linked with these tugs. Right now, smoking a Parliament, having survived the student induction, I'm feeling the first signs of Recovery.

The huge old dining tables in the Painted Hall make good writing desks, given the austere, cultured surroundings. Unfortunately, it seems the significance of the ceiling and painted walls isn't quite significant enough for some visitors, who'd rather stop and natter.

Tourist: Do you work here?

FP: Yes, I'm working here right now. I'm not eating my breakfast, in my PJs.

Tourist: What is it you're writing?

FP: I'm writing a fictional piece of great significance. Trying to.

Tourist: Ah. You're immortalizing yourself on the page. Like these figures here, immortalized in paint.

FP: Yes, except King William and Queen Mary paid someone else to immortalize them, in allegorical heaven. Which is like buying an ad for yourself during the Superbowl.

Tourist: I suppose.

FP: There's another way to get immortalized on that ceiling though.

Tourist: Oh yes?

FP: It involves a catapult device, which projects you at a catastrophic pace straight up into the ceiling. Splat!

Tourist: Goodness me!

FP: There must be some smart cookie here at the university who could engineer the thing. Then you too could enter heaven and be proper royalty.

Tourist: So… obtain immortality… by way of an early death?

FP: What? No, of course not. It would just be a bit of fun. God!

Another tourist, an American, also stops to yak. It's starting to get a bit boring. I make a point of mentioning Victor, his fellow countryman, from *The Rules of Attraction*.

FP: He came to London too, like you. But he was especially rude.

American Tourist: Was he?

FP: Yes, he was. He ate a grapefruit next to the Thames, and was reminded of a Pink Floyd album cover. But then he said that despite everyone speaking the same language as him, they were all arseholes.

American Tourist: Did he?

FP: Yes, he did. Except he said 'assholes'. He couldn't even spell it correctly. And he complained about the rain and how expensive it was, and then he left.

American Tourist: Well…

FP: Good riddance, I say. And people complain about how whiney and moany British people are.

American Tourist: But… they are, surely?

FP: Well, yes. I suppose. Yes, fair point, well made.

It's impossible to think in the Painted Hall, let alone write. Having been outed in the Gate Clock, I head east, via the Thames Path, in search of a discreet drink.

On the massive black anchor outside the Cutty Sark pub, it now reads:

BORIS JOHNSON IS A WANCHOR.

In *Been Down So Long It Looks Like Up to Me*, Gnossos Pappadopoulis finds a bottle of Cutty Sark Scotch inside a cupboard he's hiding in. 'He opened it up, tipped it against his lips, and poured. It was altogether glorious.' But the Cutty Sark pub, I fear, with its riverside spot, is all too prominent for my needs, not to mention pricy. Instead, it might be worth investigating some of these less-trodden back streets.

Hidden from sight on a small, quiet corner is the Star and Garter. It even has moulded windows, as an extra precaution. Just across the road is a huge four-chimneyed building bearing the brown stack that is visible from our office. It's like some sort of factory, possibly producing laser guns. Although not billowing smoke, I don't loiter, not wishing to be sterilized by gamma rays.

The Star and Garter is old-fashioned but it's not historic, thus proving more financially viable. Apart from myself and the bartender, there's just a couple of old boys in for lunch. It's a good place to work on my new book, although not the private university office I'd once imagined, with oak furniture, mountains of leather-bound books, and a stained-glass desk lamp. That fabled environment is already becoming a staple scene in my campus novel readings, and the English professors all seem to have really big houses. Rather than the reverent hush of timeless academia, the Star and Garter offers televised horseracing from Newbury, competing with the hits of the 80s on Magic FM.

Joyce Carol Oates used a real campus in her novel, and I'm going to too. There's no need to make anything up in Greenwich. It's quite unbelievable already. Birthplace of time, site of a former palace, home to Henry VIII, maritime hub, nuclear reactor. Not to mention Henry Prick. Still, even the most interesting of settings can use a good kick up the pants. The addition of an outside danger, a present threat. Off the top of my head, I'm thinking a secret nuclear bomb factory, with four chimneys.

FP: Do you know what that large, threatening building next door is? With the chimneys?

Bartender: It's the Greenwich Power Station, love.

FP: A power station? Wow. Does it actually work?

Bartender: Yeah, it still works. Powers some of the London Underground. They're talking about doing more with it, more green stuff an' that.

FP: What, you mean like toxic green sludge, with steam rising off it?

Bartender: No, like eco stuff.

FP: Ah. But aren't you worried it's going to blow sky-high?

Bartender: No...

FP: One of those big old chimneys, shooting up in the air, then around, like this, before plummeting, straight down onto your pub. SPLAT!

Bartender: You're a cheery one, aren't you? [*Shaking head.*] Honestly.

Oh my word. A power station. Almost within a stone's throw of a nuclear reactor. It's literary gold. Forget Greenwich the pleasant riverside village with gilded royal trimmings. It's actually a modern-day ticking time bomb.

FP: BOOMPHA!

Bartender: Jesus!

FP: Flames, burning on the Thames! J.M.W. Turner, eat your heart out!

Old Boy: He's a bit excited, isn't he?

Bartender: Hmm. Sounds like he wants to blow up the power station.

FP: [*Clapping with glee.*] Ha, ha!

Outside, smoking a Camel, it's possible to get a better grasp of the power station and its imposing structure. The dark-brown chimney struts are supported by tens of thousands of lighter-brown bricks. The few windows, set far from ground level, are shielded from sunlight, or prying eyes. An entrance door features death warning signs, and the foreboding perimeter wall hosts all manner of barriers and security cameras to dissuade unauthorized entry. Maybe tights over the head, in the dead of night? I make a mental note to ask the bartender if she has any spare tights.

Back at my pub desk, I start considering the new possibilities for my campus novel. Rather than recounting yet another lecturer–student relationship, I should look to broaden the field, to encapsulate nuclear explosions and major disasters. A working power station, in my mind, provides a perfect setting for this, especially one in close proximity to a campus. The potential is there, I believe, to turn this Royal Borough into a right royal mess.

I'm consolidating the most violent of explosions, on paper, when I hear the bartender conferring with a new patron, at the bar.

Bartender: Here, you'll want to watch that chap over there. He wants to blow up that power station of yours.
Pub Patron: Is that a fact?
FP: [*Calling out.*] Ha, ha. Not really, kind sir.

This new mystery man, it transpires, is a manager at the power station. Explaining my own position, and my fictional interest in his station, for my forthcoming book, he seems impressed. It's like a VIP pass, this Writer in Residence gig. Even if, on closer inspection, my photo ID would encourage caution.

FP: Of course, I can only imagine what it's like inside.
Power Station Manager: Tell you what, send us an email and we'll see what we can arrange.
FP: Great! Just as well I didn't stay cooped up in the office today. You don't meet overlords of nuclear power plants when you're stuck, head down, at a desk.

INVISIBLE

———

PAUL AUSTER

Francis Plug

A Frances Coady Book

HENRY HOLT AND COMPANY

NEW YORK

An email arrives from the power station chap. My credibility has been verified and a visit has been duly arranged.

FP: Serious? That's blimmin' mental.

This title of mine can really open doors, even large metal ones, with death warnings. Not that I wish to use my position for social advantage. It's all in the name of research, this. It won't be a nice jolly, or some fun meander through a nuclear power plant. No sir, no madam. This is proper graft, serious stuff. I might even have to wear a boiler suit, like MC Hammer.

Paul Auster's novel *Invisible*, while including a brief, mandatory mention of a professor–student liaison, also explores a new take on the campus genre. Rudolf Burn, a Columbia professor, has a supposed double life, with alleged links to secret intelligence and espionage. Rather than your average dullard professor, it's suggested that Burn may be a special undercover agent. When asked what he teaches, he even cites 'disaster', and it's said he 'advanced ideas that made him sound like a bomb-throwing anarchist'. That's the sort of character I'm keen to progress myself, possibly based on Dr Alex. With gentle prods, I try to find out about his own subterfuge leanings.

FP: I don't suppose you were an informer, back in Algeria?

Dr Alex: Algeria? You mean the independence war, against France? In the early sixties? A decade or so before I was born?

FP: Um, actually, I meant the end of the Cold War. Was that your doing? Are you a spy, working for the government, the military and the police?

Dr Alex: Hmm. I don't think I could fit all that in, to be honest. Given the hundreds of thousands of words I have to read, correct and grade.

FP: Or not.

Dr Alex: Pardon?

FP: Nothing.

Adam Walker, the central character in *Invisible*, is a student, briefly depicted on the ground here in London, but not, surprise, surprise, in Greenwich. Like Victor Ward in *The Rules of Attraction*, he is dismissive of the city and of England in general. Unlike Victor, however, he stays for four years, albeit in 'a shithole flat in Hammersmith'. Back in Columbia, he and his sister are described polishing off a bottle of Cutty Sark Scotch. That's the closest Greenwich ever seems to get to literary mentions: via a Glaswegian whisky and a Glaswegian ship. My novel will feature Cutty Sark whisky too. It's a much better fit than that brand David Beckham pushes. Male glamour and coolness don't really sit well with me. Cutty Sark, however, is bang-on. I even dress like a fisherman.

Like Joyce Carol Oates and myself, Paul Auster has set his fictional work around a real university. If his novel *Invisible* is accurate, Columbia University has a most impressive library, and also a statue of Rodin's *The Thinker*, denoting wisdom and deep knowledge. Here on the university grounds of Greenwich, we have a decrepit statue of a fusty old monarch who is covered in bin bags. Instead of wisdom, he represents old privilege and modern decay.

Paul Auster is visiting London to promote his latest book. He's being interviewed in Beveridge Hall, Senate House, which is part of University College London. Senate House provided the model for George Orwell's Ministry of Truth building in *1984*. There are no free beverages in Beveridge Hall tonight, which is a sad truth indeed. Still, I'm equipped with drinks of my own, and there are some interesting design features to take in. The round suspended lights look like something you might stand beneath to get 'energized', and the wooden wall panels behind the stage resemble a slightly dated American garage door.

FP: [*To person alongside.*] But are we inside the garage, or parked outside, on the driveway?
Person Alongside: I have no idea what you're talking about.
FP: Your loss, kind sir.

Due to the unusual seating arrangements, I find myself sitting almost side-on to Paul Auster, at the same raised level as the stage. Sitting forward, with legs tucked beneath his chair, his side profile resembles the reddy-orange zig-zag on Ziggy Stardust's face. He's a surprisingly tall man, Paul Auster, and although he's just turned seventy, there's a sense of Buzz Lightyear about him, helped by a similar physical stature and bold, determined eyes. He normally steers clear of these events, he says, but is embracing his current tour, and enjoying it. At his signing, I say I'm sorry, but I find that very hard to believe.

Paul Auster: Why's that?
FP: Are you kidding? Look at all these people. What a friggin' nightmare.
Paul Auster: Well, yes. But it's not something I'm pushed to do very often.

FP: What about pushing buttons on your chest? Do you do that?

Paul Auster: What do you mean?

FP: Like Buzz Lightyear does. Do you know him? You bear a strong resemblance.

Paul Auster: Name rings a bell.

FP: He has wings attached to his arms.

Paul Auster: Has he?

FP: Yes, he has. And his sights are ultimately set on the universal good of humankind.

Paul Auster: Well. I suppose there are worse doppelgängers.

FP: Did you notice the garage door behind you, during your talk?

Paul Auster: Garage door?

FP: Yes. It was like you were being interviewed in my old house. Or just outside it.

Paul Auster: [*Pause.*] I see. Well, thanks for coming.

FP: Oh! Speaking of my garage: would you be okay staying in it? For the Greenwich Book Festival?

Paul Auster: Sorry?

FP: The Greenwich Book Festival. You've been specially handpicked to attend.

Paul Auster: I hadn't heard about that.

FP: Don't worry, it's all been sorted. Out of interest, how many air miles do you have?

A few days after visiting Senate House, I find reason to visit an even grander house. With time to spare before my nuclear power station tour, and needing to sober up, I wander across to the Queen's House in Greenwich Park. Entry is free, which adds to its attraction, and if my power station guide asks how I've passed my day, visiting the Queen's House sounds preferable to necking drinks in the Star and Garter.

When James I commissioned the Queen's House 400 years ago, it was an apology gift for his wife, for swearing in front of her.

FP: You have got to be shitting me.

Situated near the Maritime Museum, it holds an unimpeded river view through the Old Naval College, a stipulation from Queen Mary to Christopher Wren when drawing up his plans for the Naval Hospital. The spiral Tulip staircase, which I ascend to the Great Hall, is the scene of Greenwich's most famous haunting. In 1966, a visiting Canadian reverend, R.W. Hardy, photographed a ghostly figure supposedly wisping up it.

FP: Have *you* ever seen the Tulip staircase ghost?
Guard: I haven't, no.
FP: No rattling chains?
Guard: No.
FP: Well, I suppose it gets the punters in. Even though it's free anyway.

The perfectly square hall provides the centrepiece for the house, and its chequered black and white floor tiles use white Italian marble and black Belgian marble.

FP: It's a shame these black and white tiles aren't in a zig-zag pattern. You could put red velvet curtains on that wall, a few sofa chairs around here, a tall lamp, and hey presto, you've got the Red Room, from *Twin Peaks*.
Guard: Um...
FP: Get a dwarf, someone floating through the air on wires, and you'd have a proposition that people might actually want to pay for.

The hall acoustics perfectly accentuate my 'Someone Left the Cake Out in the Rain' ringtone.

FP: Yes?

Man: Hello, is that Francis Plug?

FP: Yes.

Man: Hi, my name is Rick. I'm calling from the Inland Revenue. Is now a good time to talk?

FP: No, I'm actually in the Queen's House at the minute.

Man: The Queen's house?

FP: Yes.

Man: I see. You mean Buckingham Palace?

FP: No, the other one.

Man: Windsor Castle?

FP: No, the other one.

Man: Balmoral Castle?

FP: No, the other one.

Man: Sandringham House?

FP: No, the other one.

Man: Hillsborough Castle?

FP: No, the other one.

Man: Craigowan Lodge?

FP: No, I'm in the other one, in Greenwich. I'm in the Queen's House in Greenwich. With the Hans Holbein paintings, and the J.M.W. Turners, and the William Hodgeses. I'm trying to avoid a sliming in the Tulip staircase.

Man: When would be...

[*Beep, beep, beep.*]

After stopping back in at the Star and Garter, I press the power station buzzer, no doubt unleashing a cacophony of dulcet bells, reminiscent of a haunted house chime, with huge spiders dropping from hidden ceiling compartments, and skull sockets in stairwell nooks glowing an unholy red. While waiting for the butler and his bulging forehead, I step back to once again take in the scale. The Queen's House may be grander than Senate House, but neither compare, in my estimation, with Greenwich Power Station. There's no pomp or ceremony here. Brown Victorian brick totally trumps white stone, and unlike that other four-chimneyed power station in Battersea, presently being converted into luxury apartments and corporate offices, the Greenwich Power Station is still a proper workhorse. There's plenty of room for an inflatable pig, Pink Floyd. But you better get in quick, before it's all blown sky-high.

A normal fellow called Chris has been assigned to my tour. He greets me at the death-sign door, pointing at my cig.

Chris: Ah, you'll have to extinguish that, sorry.
FP: Really? Oh yes, of course, of course. Don't want to blow the place up prematurely. Let me put it back in its tin. It's a Schimmelpenninck, you know. They're Dutch.
Chris: Do you have any other inflammable items on you? Lighter, matches?
FP: Sorry, yes, here. This place will be a fireball before I'm even in my jumpsuit!
Chris: No, no. We have plenty of security checks in place, don't worry.
FP: Of course. But say you were a mad professor who wanted to blow it all sky-high. A mad *university* professor. Of English, say. With eyes like a fireworks display. What's step one?
Chris: You're an author, right?
FP: Yes, I am.
Chris: So is that what your book's about? Blowing this place up?

FP: I really can't divulge the inner workings of my conceptual process. All I can say is that what you have just suggested may well be an avenue that I'm exploring very, very closely.

Safety might be important, but the required uniform is a total let down.

FP: What, just a hard hat?
Chris: Were you expecting something else?
FP: Yes! I was hoping to look like a rapper, on a music video shoot.
Chris: Oh.
FP: Instead, I'm going to look like a Conservative Chancellor, on a PR visit!

The 1906 Greenwich Power Station is one of the oldest operational power stations in the world. It was originally built to generate steam power for London's former tram network, but gas turbines replaced the steam units in the late 1960s. Today its modest output supplements the requirements of the London Underground, which, in itself, uses about the same amount of power as Leeds.

Chris leads me, via designated yellow floor strips, to the building's grand old turbine hall. It is here, he explains, that six new gas engines are set to be installed, further bolstering London Underground with low-carbon energy, and generating cheaper heat for local residents. Looking up at the cathedral-like arched ceiling, spanned by a giant gantry, I imagine the aforementioned gas, loose and ignited, blasting all this to kingdom come.

FP: So, this is it. The epicentre for utter carnage.
Chris: Sorry?

FP: Just imagine. Those clanky old metal staircases melting like candlewax.

Chris: Are you planning a film adaptation for this book of yours?

FP: Hey, yes. There's a thought. Absolutely. Say, maybe you could play the hapless station manager, who proves grossly inept in halting the mad professor, and thus averting disaster on an unprecedented scale.

Chris: [*Whistling without noise.*] Right, cheers for that.

The current turbines are an industrial submarine blue, and like most things in here, they've been riveted to heck. Their protruding ends resemble stubby keys, or the short trunks of futuristic robotic elephants. Beyond these is the Control Room, where many wall-mounted buttons are shielded with protective metal covers. This, I suspect, is in case one of the engineers falls asleep, their beaky nose slumping forward, initiating catastrophe.

FP: What's with the 'Danger Risk Of Death' signs?

Chris: Well, this is a working power station. We have to err on the side of caution, for our staff and visitors.

FP: And not just them, right? I mean Greenwich village is a UNESCO Heritage Site. You don't want to raze that, utterly, to the ground.

Chris: Just to be clear, we generate gas power in a very limited capacity. We're a small, low-key operation. Not some massive nuclear power plant. We're nothing like that.

FP: Sure, sure. But we could pretend you are, couldn't we?

Chris: Well, that wouldn't be accurate, or... DON'T TOUCH THAT!

FP: 'Can't touch this!'

Chris: Seriously, you mustn't touch anything.

FP: 'Break it down!'

The day after my power station visit, I return to the Star and Garter where I'm met with a frosty reception.

Bartender: No, I'm not serving you. No. I've heard all about your 'visit' next door. We have a good relationship with those lads, and I'm not having you wreck it.

FP: But...

Bartender: No, sorry. You'll have to drink elsewhere.

There are many different ways to structure a novel, although most authors stick with the tried and tested, centuries-old linear model. Unlike art and music, novels don't move on every generation. By and large, they just keep getting written the same way they've always been written. Of course, as part of my campus novel revamp, I intend to change all that. To plot my new book, I'm using a stick in the sand of Greenwich beach. The first stage involves etching out a rough map of Greenwich, highlighting the square and *Cutty Sark*, the Old Royal Naval College grounds, the park behind, and the power station to the east. The incoming tide is incorporated, as a plotting device, steering the narrative by way of its unpredictable whims, adding a sense of dread, and panic and fear. Although gently lapping, it represents a fifty-foot tidal wave, and where it hits first will prove pivotal to my story. Stricken students and academic staff run manically around, some in flames from the nuclear fallout, unaware that they're about to be extinguished. Where will the wave strike first? Will it flood the campus, trapping people una-wares in the basement level café and skittle alley? Or will it overwhelm the molten furnace of the power station, triggering electrical surges, flying sparks, and further explosions of ungodly proportions? Or will the Thames breach the Greenwich Square as a priority, submerging the museum area beneath the *Cutty Sark*, drowning the foreign school parties, the tourists and the aged, before the tea clipper itself casts off, careering away on a twenty-first-century journey down the Thames? It could go any which way, my novel, depending on today's incoming tide and my stick-etched map of Greenwich.

As I wait for my story's climatic peak, a voice calls out from above.

Voice: Hello.

A few of the Creative Projects students have stopped on the river path above in order to observe the workings of an actual novelist in full flow.

FP: Oh. Hi-ya.
Student: What are you doing?
FP: I'm turning a world of sand and river water into the very fabric of literature.
Student: Really? How?
FP: By harnessing imaginative forces through the manipulation of nature.
Student: Which translates as?
FP: I'm speaking in plain English. Now it's up to you to process that information and formulate your own interpretation.
Student: Oh. Okay.
FP: What I could really do with is some ex-Royal Navy cordite explosives, for the after-shocks.
Student: Sorry?
FP: And some black metal piping, to stuff the cordite into, in order to torpedo Royal Hill and blow Greenwich sky-high.
Student: You want to blow Greenwich sky-high?
FP: Yes, I want to blow it to kingdom come. Say, you youngsters haven't seen any German bombs washed up on the shore, have you?

Student: Huh?

FP: Those large 500 kilogram ones, preferably unexploded? No?

Students: [*Shrugging, shaking heads.*]

FP: Keep an eye out, won't you?

The conclusion of my scene is very interesting, thanks in no small part to the heavy swash from a passing tug, aptly named *Reclaim*. As well as my own shoes becoming engulfed, certain swathes of Greenwich are turned into Atlantis-like settings. And, soon afterwards, BOOMPHA!

My experimental approach to the campus novel has borne much fruit. But although constructing vivid settings, rich with detail, less is still definitely more in my book. In my new book. After all, it's a novel, not a David Attenborough documentary. When reading a book myself, I like to have the freedom to imagine that the walrus was pink and smoking a pipe.

TO FRANCIS PLUG

ORANGES ARE NOT
THE ONLY FRUIT

—————————— ❧ ——————————

JEANETTE WINTERSON

[signature]

P A N D O R A   P R E S S

London, Boston, Melbourne and Henley

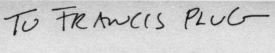

Jeanette Winterson has called Shakespeare & Company 'the most famous bookshop in the world'. In 1919, Sylvia Beach, from Princeton, New Jersey, opened the original store in Paris. It would attract the likes of Ernest Hemingway, Gertrude Stein, T.S. Eliot and Scott Fitzgerald. After the war, another American, George Whitman, opened a separate Parisian bookstore at 37 rue de la Bûcherie. In 1958, Sylvia Beach gave George her shop name and blessing. Shakespeare & Company has continued at no. 37 to this day, providing a bed for weary and skint writers.

George Whitman's daughter, another Sylvia, has since taken over the running of the shop with her husband David. George died in December 2011. The store is located on Paris' Left Bank. London, by contrast, is known for its South Bank. What I really need is money freely dispensing from a hole-in-the-wall bank.

In preparation for my French trip, I visit a Marie Curie charity shop, picking up a copy of George Orwell's *Down and Out in Paris and London*.

Marie Curie Person: Are you a British taxpayer?
FP: I certainly am. I drink and I also smoke, so, by way of my personal vices, I'm basically keeping this nation afloat.
Marie Curie Person: Good for you. You'll be on the Queen's Honours list before you know it.

FP: Thanks, but I'm not so sure. The Queen was supposed to come and see me read in Crystal Palace, but she did a no-show. Possibly because I once ruined a literary ceremony attended by Camilla, the Duchess of Cornwall. I think they hate my guts now, that family.

Marie Curie Person: Oh, well. You'll just have to be one of those unsung heroes.

FP: I have a lovely singing voice. Do you know 'I Love My Leather Jacket' by the Chills?

Marie Curie Person: I can't say I do.

FP: [*Singing.*] 'I love my leather jacket. I love my leather jacket. I love my leather jacket. I love my leather jacket...'

An email arrives from Adam at Shakespeare & Company, checking to see I'm all set. It's worth staying on in Paris a few days, he writes, because Don DeLillo, the lauded American author, is appearing in the shop two nights later. Apparently a Parisian university is carrying out a symposium of his work, which might be worth a look also. Whatever the heck that is.

DON DeLILLO

To Francis Plug

Don DeLillo

White Noise

Elisabeth Sifton Books
Viking

My Eurostar train connects London St Pancras with Paris Gare du Nord. A terrorist event was foiled on a French train recently, thanks to the quick actions of some off-duty US Navy SEALs who overpowered a heavily armed man of bad persuasion. Although not military trained, I have two large books for clobbering and bullet absorption, and one smallish one to throw like a ninja star. The latter is the George Orwell, the formers are *The Hunchback of Notre-Dame* by Victor Hugo, and *White Noise* by Don DeLillo. No major threats have presented themselves thus far, which is just as well because I'm travelling backwards.

To get to the Left Bank, I must descend to the Métro and board a train to Saint-Michel Notre-Dame. Before this, however, at a cost of 70 euro cents, I need to spend a penny. A cleaner ushers me towards a cubicle. When my task is complete, I look in vain for a flush device.

FP: Flusher, flusher. Where are you, ya blimmin' flusher?

All set to give up, I spy a foot pedal at floor level. When I press it, the toilet flushes. Dear me. You flush the toilets in France with your foot!

FP: VROOM-VROOM! VROOM-VROOM!
Person In Adjoining Cubicle: [*In French.*] Hey! Slow down! You wanna get someone killed?!

Paris remains on high terrorist alert, and there's a notable presence of heavily armed police. Hemingway didn't write about counter-terrorism during his time in Paris, nor does it come up in the numerous campus novels that mention the city, such as *The Marriage Plot*, *The Rules of Attraction*, *Old School* or Paul Auster's *Innocent*. Paris is supposed to be a city of love and romance, not ultra-violence. Of course, Victor Hugo, France's most famous writing son, didn't skimp on the bloodshed. Even *The Hunchback of Notre-Dame* has its share of wanton death and demise. Today, however, I find it easier and more comforting to equate the heightened security and sub-machine guns with my own visit, as an international author of repute.

Shakespeare & Company is directly across the Seine from Notre-Dame cathedral, where Hugo crushed many people with falling beams, or had them perish from melting metal. The bookshop, made from rickety old wood, is not on fire. Portable shelves are arranged outside, and the public idly browse these, without fear of death. I rub my hands with excitement, and also for warmth. Although a cloudless day, it is most bitterly cold.

Inside is cluttered, rustic and warm. Books are piled, almost to ceiling height, on wonky weathered boards. My own novel is displayed just inside the door, and I murmur my approval, catching the eyes of customers, nodding a good deal and pointing. The cashier's desk is like something you might have purchased castor sugar from in yester times. Awkwardly, I ask the young, English-speaking grocer for Adam, who is chairing my evening talk. In this role, Adam has interviewed John Berger, Naomi Klein and Ethan Hawke, and in two days time will be taking Don DeLillo's measure. But when he arrives, he doesn't strike me as some foreboding David Frost figure. Instead, he is a young, quietly spoken Englishman, tall and bespectacled, without pretensions or uplifted fighting fists. He escorts me out of the shop, back in through a secret adjacent door, and up a spiralling, concrete-strewn staircase.

Adam: Sorry about the mess. We're getting a lift put in.

A third-floor door is marked with a hand-written sign announcing: THE HOUSE OF GEORGE. This, Adam explains, is where George Whitman, the original proprietor, lived until his death, aged ninety-eight. Now, for my three nights in Paris, it will house me. I feel like I'm stepping into some massive shoes, possibly suede, hand-sewn overnight by little French elves.

At the back of an entranceway piled haphazardly with books, is a round wooden table offering magnificent window-side views of Notre-Dame. Wow. It's literally right there. An old typewriter sits silently on a side desk, and a passageway leads past a small kitchen to the rear. Adam directs me through to George's former bedroom, with its oak beam ceiling, writing desk, and more books shelved from floor to ceiling. There are towels, toothpaste, and even an in-house cat. Agatha, a stray, was discovered down in the shop's Crime section, before being named after its most famous practitioner.

Adam: Are you okay with cats?
FP: *For dogs we kings should have lions, and for cats, tigers.*
Adam: Sorry?
FP: Just messing. I'm not Louis XI. A little cat is fine.

My inaugural French event takes place in less than two hours. Adam leaves me to settle in and get my head together. In English, this translates as downing some fast ones. Sitting at the round table, I watch the lowering sun turn Notre-Dame the same colour as my whisky. The old cathedral was bombed and bullet-holed during WWII, and until the 1990s, was apparently black, covered in old soot. But tonight it gleams wonderfully golden. Agatha's purr sounds like the rotating blades of a hovering helicopter. She is sprawled across my midriff, literally hosing my black jumper with tortoiseshell fur. What will my fashionable Parisian audience have to say about this?

FP: Bad cat!

Prior to show time, Adam, and Octavia, a fellow worker in Shakespeare & Company, join me at the table for red wine and a chat. Their demeanours are relaxed and friendly, but I suspect, like the BBC team, they're ascertaining my suitability for public display; in this case, within their famous shop. When Adam mentions that the audio of my event will be piped around every floor, later appearing as a podcast on their website and related social media, I begin a quiet chant.

FP: *Non timebo millia populi circumdantis me: exsurge, Domine; salvum me fac, Deus!*
Adam: Sorry, what's that you're saying?
FP: It's from *The Hunchback of Notre-Dame*. It means, *I will not fear the thousands of the people gathered together about me: arise, O Lord; save me O my God!* Something along those lines.

We descend the pocked and dust-strewn staircase, stopping at a side door.

Adam: You go first because you're sitting on the far side.

On the other side of the door, unbelievably, is a stage. A small modest stage, granted, but a stage nonetheless. In front of it is a packed house of people, seated, standing and staring. It's like we've just emerged through some kind of portal. It's also like that dream where you're standing before your entire school in the nuddy.

FP: Shit a brick!

When Charles Bukowski visited Paris, he drank openly from wine bottles on live French TV. This was beamed out to 60 million viewers. He didn't talk at Shakespeare & Company, but his European escapades were collected in a book entitled *Shakespeare Never Did This*. I didn't bring my whisky bottle downstairs because I'm not Charles Bukowski, although, like him, I do enjoy frequenting pubs. In truth, I forgot it because I'd been offered the red wine, which I finished. Now, instead of whisky, there are many French faces, staring, staring. Cat hairs!

In *The Hunchback of Notre-Dame*, Quasimodo is honoured in the annual Festival of Fools. Tonight, I too have been given a platform and a stage. Just as a hunchback, hidden away in his bell tower, can produce the most exquisite sounds, so too may a writer, from their solitary room, produce a work that stirs the soul. Yet when the hunchback, or the writer, appears before the public, they are nothing short of grotesque.

Adam gets the interview underway by introducing me and suggesting I stand before a plastic lectern to read from my book. With my jumper temporarily obscured, I take the opportunity to give it a vigorous rub-down. The light and cheerful section I've chosen to read is therefore delivered in a manner befitting my physical exertions, which could be misconstrued as abject fury, or an uncontrollable form of mental illness. Bloody cat!

Returning to my seat, I continue to pick at the hairs, pretending they are logs, and my thumb and forefinger are steel claws, connected to a shore-based crane. It gives my fingers something to do, in lieu of a drink.

Adam: Thanks, Francis. In your book you allude to writers being woefully unprepared for their new public realities. You were determined not to be one of these writers yourself. How successful have you been in this regard, do you think?

FP: Not terribly. I wasn't prepared for that door over there, straight onto the stage. And I forgot to bring a drink with me, which doesn't show much foresight either. Actually, I probably should have read my book again, to get up to speed. It's supposed to be very good.

A chirpy siren belonging to a French emergency vehicle can be heard passing outside. This causes me to sit forward on my seat, in case I need to make a run for it.

Adam: It's not just stage pressure, is it? There's also the pressure of maintaining a social media presence.

FP: No, I stay well clear of that carry-on. Otherwise, you know, I'll just end up writing stuff like, 'Mick down the pub is a flaming dickhead'. Or: 'Graham down the pub is', I don't know, 'a big-eared nob'. Or: 'Bill down the pub is a stupid arse…'

Adam: Right.

I feel like James in his giant peach, except my peach is much, much smaller, and the pecking seagulls are really, really hungry. Another siren can be heard, and this time I get up and move towards the stage door.

Adam: Oh… Francis?

FP: It's all right, Adam. I'm just going to get a drink.

Adam: I'm sure we can ask someone…

FP: No, no, no.

As well as my whisky, I return with a glass, so I'm not openly drinking from the bottle.

FP: There. Next question?

At some point, the questions and answers begin blurring into each other and I find myself asking questions, having run out of answers. Or, I simply make statements, hoping these may suffice as answers to other people's questions. God knows what I'm spurting out, on stage, in the world's most famous bookshop. God knows, and also the billions of people around the world who'll have access to the podcast.

Afterwards, I sign a few books, although the state of my signature probably won't be of use to those wishing to engage in identity fraud, for instance.

Adam and friends whisk me off to a nearby bistro where I use hand gestures, unsuccessfully, to depict the very large drink I desire. We progress to some outer Paris pubs, and after more drinks, I tell Adam I'm ready to be interviewed on live French television. Nothing has been pre-arranged in this regard, and even with Adam's phone calls, and my background interjections, citing the BBC and David Attenborough, there are no available slots. More drinks are consumed, and I find myself outside, in a large square. Here victims of terrorism are remembered with candles, peace banners, and graffiti. The cold no longer affects me, but seeing this is all rather sobering.

The Hunchback of Notre-Dame opens with Parisians being awakened by the noisy peal of bells. Although bedding down directly opposite those peals, I sleep like a log. A real log, not an imaginary cat hair log, at the dockyards. Quasimodo was deaf too.

When I finally awake, Agatha is sound asleep on my legs. If there have been any murders in the night, she has no interest in solving them.

The windows must be triple-glazed. Despite the busy traffic out on Quai de Montebello, very little filters in. French sirens, I've noticed, are chirpier than English ones. They're more up for a laugh. The bells are more cheerful too. Compared to Big Ben, the toll of Notre-Dame is proper fun times. Big Ben's peal, when you actually listen to it, closely, is basically saying, 'Kill yourself.'

Insects have bored holes in the ceiling beams. Unlike George Orwell's Parisian room, however, no ants are visible, marching in formation. As rooms go, in this most famous of cities, George Whitman's must rate as the very finest. This isn't an exclusive, opulent, exorbitant hotel. The richest billionaire in the world can't stay here. This room, with its much-loved predecessor, its unique, personalized book collection, and its very special fur-hosing cat, is by invitation only, for bookish types. For once, the struggling, lowly writer wins. Any greedy, billionaire shits staying over in Paris, you totally lose.

There's a knock at the door. A woman, in her mid-fifties perhaps, stands in the stairwell outside. She looks like she's just stolen 101 Dalmatians. Still unbathed, I am showered with words of the French language.

FP: Lordy! Brakes on, madame!

Woman: Sylvia?

FP: Non, non! Back, back! Moi? Lion tamer! Seigfried and Roy? Oui? Oui, moi!

Woman: [*In perfect English.*] Ah, yes, I see. You are Roy. Yes, definitely Roy.

FP: Whoah, madame. Roy? Non, non…

Woman: You think I'm a beast you can tame, Roy?

FP: Non, non. I cannot even tame your little French cats, with all the hairs.

Woman: Pardon?

FP: Look, I have to shower. I have the sweaty pong, oui?

Woman: Cheap whisky, that is what I smell. Listen Roy, you must pass this message to Sylvia… [*A veritable stream of unintelligible French.*]

FP: Ha, ha! You bet!

It's nearly lunchtime when I'm finally in a state to face France. The stairwell is crowded with strong French workmen excavating the lift shaft. I nod politely, keen to hide my ignorance of their language and construction matters. In spite of this, the void between us is all too apparent. While they are covered in plaster and general building debris, I remain blanketed in friendly cat fur.

For 800 years, until the Eiffel Tower's construction, Notre-Dame was the tallest building in France. By the early nineteenth century, it was in total disrepair. Hugo's novel is widely credited with attracting positive attention for the cathedral, which ultimately helped save it. My novel, I fear, may send the Old Naval College the other way.

It's possible to ascend the massive towers, although if you're terribly hungover, I wouldn't recommend it. You have to queue outside, for one thing, and if you stand in the freezing cold for well over an hour, you end up resembling the gargoyles protruding from the exterior walls and edifices. Still, if you're lucky, you may see French policemen race past, on rollerblades!

FP: [*Singing.*] Hands up! Baby, hands up!

The cathedral steps very nearly did me in, for real. I actually thought I might die. There are 387 steps in all, and after the first twenty, it felt like I was shouldering a massive barrel-shaped hunch, containing sherry.

FP: Mercy! *Domine; salvum me fac, Deus!*
Tourist: Is he all right?

Hugo lets us imagine a view from the cathedral's lofty heights in 1482.

> *The spectator, on arriving, out of breath, upon this summit, was first of all struck by a dazzling confusion of roofs, chimneys, streets, bridges, squares, spires, steeples. All burst upon the eye at once.*

Little has changed in that sense. Especially the 'out of breath' part. As well as seeing gargoyles up close, and the Eiffel Tower in the distance, Notre-Dame offers a bird's-eye view of Shakespeare & Company. It's possible to see the third floor window to the House of George, where Agatha, from this height, would best resemble a fur ball. While it's wonderful to take in the broad expanse of Paris, without threat of the cathedral being stormed by an angry mob, that warm bookshop room does beckon.

The kitchen and table area in the House of George is also used, I discover, by employees of the shop. Collectively known as 'Tumbleweeds', they tend to be visitors to Paris from all parts of the world, who receive free board in exchange for two hours' work a day. Before and after their shifts, they congregate in here, at the window-side table, to eat and to chat. Although exhausted from my epic cathedral climb, an Austrian woman, who attended my talk, is keen to pick my brain.

Austrian Woman: It was interesting, your interview, but sometimes a bit confusing.

FP: What do you mean?

Austrian Woman: Well, Adam would ask you a question, and then you would talk about something else, not relevant to the question.

FP: Hmm. I think I was *expanding* on his questions. Taking them to the next level.

Austrian Woman: No. I don't think so. Like he asked about your attendance at the Booker Prize ceremony, and you started talking about the foot-flushing system of French toilets.

FP: I was really, really tired. Have you ever travelled all the way from London to Paris? Oh my word. It's such a demanding journey. Exhausting.

Austrian Woman: You were shouting, 'VROOM-VROOM!'

FP: I suppose they'll be wanting you downstairs now, won't they? At the coalface…?

Sylvia drops by with her young son Gabriel. Given the worldwide fame of her bookshop, with its illustrious past, Sylvia is arguably more of a celebrity than many of the authors she stocks. So it's like having a celebrity turn up at your house, out of the blue, to say hi. Except, of course, this house is hers.

Gabriel is two, and he's a bit tired and grizzly. To keep him entertained, I do a repetitive dance, in a German techno style, with piston-like hands. It doesn't seem to cheer him up at all, so I do it faster.

Sylvia: Anyway, I better get this one home.

FP: Oh, before I forget… a woman dropped by, at the door there. She had a message for you. Something about killing all the Dalmatians? I think a ransom was required…

As they leave, I pretend to shoot Agatha dead, blam, blam, blam, and Gabriel is briefly appeased.

On Rue Descartes, not far from the Pantheon, I pass La Maison de Verlaine, a restaurant dedicated to Paul Verlaine. It was in this building that Verlaine died of alcoholism and misery. A plaque on the same building denotes that Ernest Hemingway was also resident between 1921 and 1925. A bar nearby serves drinks, and all that talk of death and alcoholism and misery has made me thirsty. The bartender resembles the young woman who stares out from the bar in Manet's *The Bar at the Folies-Bergère*, except there's fewer mirrors and bottles, and she's actually looking down, at her phone.

When I awake, it's the middle of the night. I'm slumped against a wall, on the side of a cobblestone street. After much squinting and refocusing, the street reveals itself as Rue Mouffetard, which kind of rings a bell. A pigeon lies splattered on the road. Like me, it was given wings for flight, but has ended up sprawled on the ground, wedged in the cobbled ruts. Just around the corner is George Orwell's street, Rue du Pot-de-Fer. It's a very sing-songy name, something you appreciate more when you sing it aloud, to the tune of 'Chanson D'Amour'. As I walk slowly back towards the Seine, I sing that street, passing through other Parisian streets, which may be songs also.

FP: RUE. DU POT. DE FERRR. LAT DE DAT DE DAT!

When I awake, it's an overcast morning. When I awake again, as in now, it's a bright and sunny afternoon. The cold, however, prevails. Most of those braving the outdoors stand stiffly, arms pulled down, as if preparing to jump into a swimming pool fully clothed. In desperate need of sustenance, I surrender to a café near my bookshop home, requesting an English breakfast. When served, it is completely foreign to me. The waitress, who isn't English, or French, speaks English.

Waitress: Everything okay?
FP: Wonderful. I must say, I'm very impressed with all the driver-less cars zipping around out there. Compared to England, France is so advanced, such a high-tech country.
Waitress: Driver-less cars? Really? I have not noticed any.
FP: You must have. Every single car, virtually. Only front passengers.
Waitress: Ah. You see, here in France, the steering wheels are on the left side.
FP: [*Pause.*] I work at a university.

Don DeLillo's symposium is being held, in part, at the Sorbonne, a famous university just down the road. One of the Sorbonne's most infamous alumni is the Japanese student Issei Sagawa, who, in the early 1980s, killed a fellow student and ate various parts of her body. Japan still hunts and kills whales, and you have to wonder if this is actually just Issei Sagawa, serving his own voracious appetite.

Although not registered for the symposium, I'm hoping I can blag my way in by capitalizing on my language difficulties. Besides, as a scholar presently reading *White Noise*, perhaps I can actually bring something to the party. If nothing else, it's a good chance to find out what happens at these conference things. If David Lodge's *Small World* is anything to go by, academics deliver papers on the subject in question, and then they drink loads and everyone makes out. But are the drinks free? I'm going to find out.

No I'm not. At the Sorbonne's main entrance, on Rue Saint-Jacques, uniformed guards are demanding ID, and even patting down selected entrants. On the pavement opposite, two police officers wield huge sub-machine guns. Walking around the block, to the reception entrance on Rue de la Sorbonne, I encounter further security types in blue uniforms and peaked hats. Back on Rue Saint-Jacques, I try to reason with the guards.

FP: Eh… I am… how you say… 'Writer' [*scribbling on air*] in 'Residence' [*hands pressed in air like roof gable*] at the University of Greenwich [*undulating hand, like ship on waves*], England, Angleterre [*Benny Hill peace sign, cross eyes, tongue out*].
Guard: [*Shrugging shoulders.*]
FP: Eh… I… don't eat… people. I… eat… English breakfasts. Or… I would, if… you… knew how… to make them.

The guard, out of patience, steers me on my way.

FP: Eh… *my* university has *two* domes, two [*two fingers*]. Yours, only one [*one finger*].

Don DeLillo is not staying in the House of George, although I bet he wishes it were so. The organizers of his symposium, at which he is scheduled to talk, as a 'living writer', have probably lumbered him with some swanky hotel, in a room previously occupied by a retired couple dipping into an immense pension accrued from a shameful company for which they performed boring, soul-destroying work. Tonight however, Don DeLillo is meeting interviewer Adam around the third floor table. Agatha is probably welcome, but I've been asked to stay scarce.

It's my final night in Paris, and I'm going to see Don DeLillo in the world's most famous bookshop. As a visiting author myself, I've even been reserved a special seat. Turns out I'll need it. A queue starts forming outside at least two hours beforehand, and once the sun departs, it's blinking cold. Leaving the event attendees to form into ice sculptures, I go off in search of a hot-stuff pub.

Dear Anna,

Bonjour from gay Paree!
The other night, I performed live on stage here in France, to a crowd of people. A a bit like Jay Z. There was even a special artists' entrance door, and when I came through it, there they were, my waiting crowd. Yay, it's Francis! They weren't screaming with excitement, although at one point I did have a sort of encore, in the sense that I went off the stage and then came back on again.
Paris is the city of lovers, and also a place to die of alcoholism and misery, or to be shot dead for trying to be funny, or where a 'friend' might eat you.
Did you know that French drivers drive on the right? Of course you did. Everyone knows that!

Love, Uncle Francis.

Shakespeare & Company has wonderfully rickety features, but it's somewhat lacking in space. Books are the priority, creating walls of their own, while the airy bits for people compete with wooden beams, jutting shelves, and tourist bags. When needed as a venue, it must squeeze the punters around the nooks, seating the chosen, accommodating the lucky. Returning from the pub, I am ushered past the shivering folk still queuing outside, and in through the ram-packed crowd. As opposed to my minor interest talk upstairs, Don DeLillo is appearing on the ground floor, in the very heart of the shop. Unlike George Orwell's grim experiences in Paris, I am being personally escorted like a star, to my own reserved seat. Yet again I'm counting my blessings. It's best, in such situations, to act cool, and maintain a sense of humility. But arriving directly from the pub, I can't help smiling broadly at my good fortune, giving thumbs up to strangers, and also laughing lightly.

My reserved bench seat is against a right wall, in the thick of it. Others are stuck behind supporting posts, or in back rooms, or even, I suspect, listening in from upstairs. Two modest chairs await, like theatre props, on a stage that's the height of a hand. The stage backdrop, being bookshelves, is a mass of colourful covers and spines. The same plastic lectern I used is going to serve for Don DeLillo. But I can't say I spoke at the same lectern as him, because when I did he hadn't. Although technically Don DeLillo could claim to have talked at the same plinth as me. I really hope he does. I'm yet to break America. Let's hope he's not allergic to cats.

Kristin Scott Thomas, the actress, has just sat down, right next to me. With her, to her right, is Bella Freud, the fashion designer. They were both personally escorted to their seats by Sylvia, who's also famous. Check me out! Kristin Scott Thomas has recently finished a run at the Old Vic, but tonight an author's on stage, and she's in the audience, watching the show.

FP: Hi, Francis Plug.
Kristin Scott Thomas: Hello.
FP: I didn't see either of you at my event a couple of nights back.
Kristin Scott Thomas: No.
FP: Were you stuck in the queue, outside?
Kristin Scott Thomas: No, we weren't.

An announcement on the tannoy asks us to avoid any photography and filming, and to switch off our phones.

FP: It's like being at the cinema, isn't it? At one of your films.

Kristin Scott Thomas shudders, even though she's in here, where it's warm.

Don DeLillo, seventy-nine, is about the same height and build as me, so premium-sized, as opposed to bulk-buy/economy pack. He explores death a great deal in his work, and tonight, both he and Adam are wearing grey, like the skin of dead people. Adam says he is honoured to welcome Don DeLillo, one of the most important and influential writers of recent decades. Don DeLillo stands to read an extract from his novel *Falling Man*, which is printed on A4 pages. The passage concerns events immediately following the attack on the World Trade Center towers.

Don DeLillo's turtleneck jumper is grey. Adam wears an open grey cardigan with a lighter grey shirt beneath. 'Everything is grey,' Don DeLillo reads.

FP: Oh my word!

Nudging Kristin Scott Thomas, I point at the grey clothing, mouthing the words, 'Everything is grey.' When she displays both perplexity and annoyance, I don't think it's an act.

The shop is incredibly quiet during the reading, given the mass of people and the proximity to the roary road by the splashy Seine. The odd scrape of a stool, one cough. An old boy to my left is wearing a black leather jacket, and this rubs and squeaks purely on account of his breathing.

FP: [*Whispering.*] You sir, need an oiling.
Old Boy: [*Whispering.*] Pardon me?
FP: [*Whispering.*] You need an oiling.

Before sitting down, Don DeLillo passes his reading glasses to a woman in the front row, who is of a similar age. Perhaps it's his wife. Or maybe that was the author equivalent of throwing your underwear into the crowd.

Adam asks about the 9/11-related reading. Don DeLillo mentions that his book *Underworld* had the twin towers on the cover, four years before they went down. He also covered the subject of terrorism in his novel *Mao II* back in 1991. A character in this book remarks: 'Years ago I used to think it was possible for a novelist to alter the inner life of a culture. Now bomb-makers and gunmen have that territory.'

Don DeLillo: Terrorism has become a major element in our lives. It sometimes seems as though terror and war are covering much of the planet. And in fact, it is that way, isn't it?

It's reassuring to hear that when he first began, he didn't have loads of author mates either.

Don DeLillo: When I started I didn't know any writers. I knew no one in the publishing industry and I didn't have any writer friends.

We're in the same boat there. If Don DeLillo comes to the Greenwich Book Festival, he'll be my friend for life. He also found enormous beauty and power in James Joyce's *Ulysses*. He points out that both Joyce and Hemingway had close associations with Shakespeare & Company. James Joyce used the original shop as an office, and owner Sylvia Beach first published *Ulysses* in its entirety in 1922.

After the event's conclusion, Don DeLillo is set up at a book-signing table out back, near the children's section. As we wait in the queue, one of the 'tumbleweeds' comes around with free glasses of red wine. They know, I assume, that meeting one of the most important and influential writers of recent decades demands courage.

FP: Two, please.

Don DeLillo gets me to confirm the spelling of Plug, in relation to the number of 'u's.

FP: Just the one. Although when my work is translated into Hungarian, who knows?

Don DeLillo: Are you a writer?

FP: Yes, I am. In fact, I did an event here myself, just two nights back. Although it was less an 'author' event and more a toxic airborne event.

Don DeLillo: I see.

FP: I tried to visit your symposium, at the university, but they stopped me, with sub-machine guns.

Don DeLillo: Is that a fact?

FP: Yes. I thought about bursting through the guards, sprinting, darting, weaving, to the symposium. But then I thought, what if this symposium thing's actually just really boring? So I thought, stuff it, and went and found a pub/bistro place.

Don DeLillo: I think you made a wise decision.

FP: Of course, when you arrive at the University of Greenwich, for your Book Festival engagement, there won't be any sub-machine guns at all. No way. Just a proper English cooked breakfast. I suppose you'll be wanting crispy bacon. Hash browns?

Don DeLillo: Sorry, what was this? A book festival in Greenwich?

FP: Yes, not your New York Greenwich, obviously. With all that neon lighting and mirrored sunglasses and graffiti. No, this is the royal one, in London. With the nuclear power station. And Henry Prick...

The two chairs remain on the little stage. Don DeLillo's, seat, alas, is no longer warm. After grabbing a copy of my book from the shelf near the door, I begin reading from the same plastic lectern as Don DeLillo, to empty stools.

To Francis Plug—

W O N D E R

B O Y S

Michael Chabon

Villard Books
New York
1995

Back in London, the optimistic chimes of Notre-Dame seem like a far-off dream. There's no sign of those German royalties, so I can't exactly live like royalty myself. And the bottles of duty free Cutty Sark, and the packs of Old Gold have been consumed and inhaled, like that [*clicks fingers*].

Greenwich hasn't changed much. The river still runs one way, and then, a bit later, the other. Beneath its sullen, murky waters lies the Greenwich Foot Tunnel, an underground pedestrian passage. Now well over a hundred years old, it connects Greenwich with the Isle of Dogs and Canary Wharf. Although, for my money, it better resembles a tunnel to the afterlife. Like the path to heaven, there are many rules for entry. A bold red sign lays down the law: *NO Cycling, Busking, Animal Fouling, Littering, Loitering, Skateboarding, Skating, Spitting, Smoking. Dogs to be kept on leads. KEEP LEFT.* As I journey northwards, on a pub-finding mission, two of those rules are being broken before my eyes. Sporty types in Lycra clothing are whizzing past on bikes, some sounding shrill bells like swear words.

FP: It's a foot tunnel, you thicko! Maybe you should use some brain-power, instead of… your stupid legs!

Further along, encamped at the base of the tunnel's curved wall, a young man in a black duffel coat plays a doleful, melancholy piece on a cello. Although the tune escapes me, here in this cavern, with its grimy, toilet-like tiles, and all the pressure of the entire Thames pressing from above, such a mournful ode can't help but move. Upon the cello's canvas case rests the barest scattering of coins. The young musician is performing his art for the love, without expectation of great reward, or approval. Judging by his coinage, he'll be lucky to have a garage roof over his head. A few yards on, I find myself weeping big tears. Crying is a bit over-exposed these days, particularly on talent shows, to encourage phone-in votes. But sometimes it can't be helped. Britain is currently in a sad state, especially for the financially challenged. Many students fall into that camp. Their mental health has reached crisis point, according to experts in the field.

Hangovers, from my experience, really don't help. Approaching the northern end of the Foot Tunnel, still immersed in the wafting, sorrowful melodies of the cello, the glass elevator doors close in my face. Inside are a couple with a pushchair and a man with a bicycle. All stare out at my streaming tears as they ascend, angel-like, to the Isle of Dogs. I stumble up the spiral steps, and none of those people are waiting for me, at street level, to see if I'm all right.

The university, viewed from the other side of the river, becomes a complete mirror image of itself. Not from the waters of the Thames, which are brown and choppy, but through its basic structural alignment. If you put a line down the centre of the grounds, the buildings appear like replicas of themselves, facing either side of an open courtyard. Queen Anne reflects King Charles, Queen Mary's dome reflects King William's. The Queen's House appears behind, with its unobstructed view, and George II's statue, just visible, is like Laura Palmer's wrapped body, except vertical.

Somewhere in Greenwich, a clock strikes eleven. Its chime serves as a reminder. In two hours from now, I must host a class, on my own, without crying. Like the cellist's piece, the tone is doleful.

A black iron bench cools my bottom. On it a plaque reads: 'In Memory of Walter Albert Broom 1913–2007.' He did well to fend off the long white tunnel. A cold wind chills my wet face. The wind is attracted by the river's lack of large protruding objects, known as buildings. Seagulls sit atop the Thames water, drifting backwards, towards the sea. Although stationary, I feel like I'm moving again, in the same direction.

The King William dome, which looms large through the staff toilet window, commands a presence here too, on the opposing bank. Behind it, in my shared office, Dr Alex is likely sitting at his desk, his bottom cushioned and warm while mine freezes, turning black. Perhaps he's looking at my chair, wondering if that supposed Writer in Residence is taking the piss. Perhaps he thinks of that other applicant, who now, with the passing of time, appears ideal. Still, at least he has the office all to himself.

Dr Alex professes strong views on many things, and unlike most people I come across, he doesn't even need to be pissed up. There are times when he appears to resemble a Trotskyite revolutionary. Particularly when he's talking like one.

Dr Alex: Universities attract their share of leftwingers, so the conservative powers are always imposing restrictions on what we can and can't say. They don't want us inflicting the student populace with liberal thinking. It's got to the point where, legally, we're not even allowed to teach Marx. It's absurd. Some courses, such as Lit Theory, have a grounding in Marxism, so understanding it is key. Universities are here to offer alternative viewpoints, to open eyes. If you can't get an alternative view of the world from universities, where can you get one from?

FP: Pubs?

Dr Alex: Yes, pubs. Actually, quite a few places. Libraries, bookshops, community halls. But universities offer some very good signposting.

Standing up, I give my freezing bottom a series of warming bats, as if each cheek were a drum in the percussion section of the Isle of Dogs Symphony Orchestra. Dr Alex's bottom could probably use a stretch, from that comfy chair. Texting him, I offer a suggested route for a pleasant stroll.

> *Across KW courtyard. Turn left. Down central steps. Straight past mutilated George II, through Water Gate, top of Royal Steps. Look across the river!*

He appears about five minutes later, spying me on the other side, waving manically. Cautiously, he waves back, before bending over his phone.

> *Everything all right?*

It's like the future, communicating across vast waters, without even speaking.

> *Yes, all good thanks!*

He raises a hand, without waving it, and turns back towards the office. With real-time, interactive encounters like this, I'm really going to turn the whole literary novel genre upside down. On its head!

There's no reason why the Isle of Dogs can't feature in my Greenwich campus story. In Michael Chabon's *Wonder Boys*, the actual Pittsburgh campus barely features at all. The novel centres around the life of Grady Tripp, a drug-smoking English professor, who fantasizes about his students, gets stoned with them, and dishes them up codeine pills with whiskey. Although occasionally making it into the uni, he's more often in his car, on a farm, in a glasshouse, or in some dive bar. Joseph Conrad pops up too, with a quote in the epigraph.

> *Let them think what they like, but I didn't mean to drown myself. I meant to swim till I sank – but that's not the same thing.*

Can two campus novels have the same epigraph? Maybe I'll save that one for my memoirs.

Chabon is pronounced Shay-bon, not Char-bon. When being interviewed in the British Library's Conference Centre, Michael Chabon spoke of London's unique smell, which he always recognized.

Michael Chabon: After a couple of minutes the smell is lost, but I definitely register it. Perhaps it's the river?

Try as I might, I can't smell anything, and the Thames is right there. Perhaps Michael Chabon, like Grady Tripp, smokes Afghan Butthair. At one point, halfway through a question, he paused and said:

Michael Chabon: Excuse me, I'm gonna sneeze.

We the audience held our breaths, preparing for the inevitable gale-force blast into the microphone. But in fact, no sneeze was forthcoming.

Michael Chabon: Okay, I'm not gonna sneeze.

At the book signing, I should have asked him if his nose, like Jonathan Franzen's eyes, was malfunctioning. Instead, I attempted a more personalized pitch for the festival.

FP: Please say yes. Lovely Greenwich. On the Thames. [*Inhales.*] Mmm! Afghan Butthair. Wafting, billowing. From the power station. Four chimneys! What say you?
Michael Chabon: You smell funny.

There don't appear to be any early-doors pubs on the Isle of Dogs, at least not at its southern point. Having a secret hideaway, beyond the Royal Borough, would have been useful. Still, I suppose I only would have burnt more bridges, or, more correctly, severed an underground foot tunnel. Returning to the bench of Walter Albert Broom, I swig from a bottle of cheap whisky, given no exclusivity rights have been signed with Cutty Sark at this point.

On my return journey through the passage, I spy an Emergency Help Point, consisting of a round plastic object affixed to the wall with a central red button. Those in need of assistance are requested to press this 'just the once'. What happens next? Well, in a distant room somewhere, a buzzer will buzz-buzz-buzz, and someone will throw their Chicken Palace box into the air, before scrabbling about for another button, or perhaps a lever, which, when activated, will set into play a repetitive air raid-type siren, and a red flashing light, and maybe a sprinkler system, dousing from above. Is possible? According to the small print, Help Points like this are connected to the Royal Greenwich control room, on standby twenty-four hours a day. Really? Where is this mysterious control room, the Royal one? Perhaps, in my book, they can sound the alarm when the power station starts melting, causing explosions in the sky, which result in nuclear waste flowing down Greenwich Hill like lava. Breaking a third tunnel rule, I begin smoking a Chan Mei Chong cigarette, from Korea.

The tide is out on the Greenwich shore, revealing stones and much detritus. With just over an hour till I meet my students, I consider a river-edge stroll, in order to benefit from that fresh, invigorating breeze. The Royal Steps are wet, mossy and treacherous. An ominous sign at the approach warns: DANGEROUS STEPS! DESCEND AT YOUR OWN RISK. It's mostly a caution for the elderly and infirm, or for the very young and carefree. As someone who falls between those brackets, I should be more than capable of navigating a few wet stones sensibly. Except I'm liquored up to my neck. The bracing wind really isn't helping. Overall, the experience is akin to walking down a steep, open-top hydro slide. Patience and positive thinking serve me well, however, and reaching the shore without incident, I make for an old tyre embedded in the sand. That could make for an interesting prop later, in my class. Hoisting it free from its deep berth, however, is hardly plain sailing. It's like removing a half-buried Cadillac from Amarillo earth. A slab of wet timber serves as a digging and levering instrument. After considerable reserves of strain and energy have been applied, the soggy old tyre is unearthed. Such exertions conflict with the calm, relaxing stupor of the whisky sups, and in need of a sit-down, I rest against the river wall, beyond the sight of pedestrian traffic above.

When I awake, the encroaching waters have fully breached my outstretched legs, and are lapping at my crotch. My crown jewels have been infiltrated with mucky brown river water. The Thames, these days, is known to house abundant life, including pretty sea horses. But it also still strains pig bones, dead ducks, and putrid shoe-sole innards in the bargain.

FP: Mercy!

My third year Creative Writing students are shelling out £9,000 a pop, for a single year. Their resident writer, employed for a single one-year term, has sodden, stinking trousers, and a dripping, heavy jumper. Grasping the tyre, now filled with water, I walk like an abandoned mattress towards the wet, moss-covered steps. My ascent can be likened to pulling heavy sacks of grain to the top of a barn, except my pulley system uses eels for ropes. Upon reaching the summit, in shoes sloshing like brown, muddy mouthwash, I hear the timeball drop on the roof of the Royal Observatory. One o'clock!

FP: Shit a brick!

My students await.

FP: Hello everyone.
Students: What the...?
FP: Read any good books lately?

The dripping, mucky tyre is a bit whiffy. Me too.

Student: What happened to you?
FP: Sorry I'm late. Just been collecting some additional items for today's class. Going the extra distance, to help you make the most of your financial investment in your own educations.
Student: What's with the stinky tyre?

FP: This tyre is from the past. It's embedded with stones. See? They represent the passing of time. I have reunited it with solid, dry land.

Students: ?

FP: But it's also from a car. And cars take you off in new directions. Like... to Wallsend-upon-Tyne. Or to the shops. Or to the bottom of an old mucky river.

There is a noticeable silence while this concept is absorbed.

Student: And the point of that is...?

FP: It's a metaphor. You see? Yes? You're going to need to know what metaphors are if you want to be a successful author, like me.

Student: We know what metaphors are. But what is the metaphor in this case? And what is its relevance to this lesson?

FP: Look, didn't you ever read *The Wombles*?

Student: *The Wombles*?

FP: *The Wombles* take something, like an abandoned tyre, and they turn it into something else, something useful.

Student: So...?

FP: Well, I've turned this tyre into something, haven't I?

Student: Have you?

FP: Yes! I've turned it into a metaphor!

Student: A metaphor for what? Driving to the shops? That's not a metaphor. What exactly *are* you talking about?

FP: You really need to open your minds, some of you.

Even though I was late, the shortened class seems very, very long. The students keep asking lots of questions that really won't help them write a book. Standing here, in my damp, clinging clothes, I feel like my head and hands are locked in stocks. The students keep throwing questions at me, like wet sponges, and I can't bat them away so they splat in my face.

Student: Wasn't this lecture supposed to be about characterization?
FP: Was it? Oh. [*Pause.*] Hey look, when you bounce up and down on this tyre, it's like a see-saw landing pad.

Some water squirts out and a few of the students actually laugh, albeit briefly.

FP: Ha, ha. Yes!

Compared to Grady Tripp, I think I did all right. Except his students seemed to like him, and enjoyed his classes. But you don't just suddenly become very popular and articulate, witty, charming. These things take time to master. Small steps, like those on the wet, moss-ridden slabs leading to the Greenwich shoreline. Otherwise you'll fall on your arse!

Dr Zoë's official title is the Head of Department of Literature, Language and Theatre. She's working late, and I bump into her in the corridor after swaggering back from the pub.

FP: Uh oh.
Dr Zoë: Hi, Francis. Burning the midnight oil?
FP: Yes. Yes I am. Writing. Writing, writing, writing. I'm writing like silly, like stupid…
Dr Zoë: Good. How was Paris?
FP: Yes, great thanks, great. Really great. Have you sat on that toilet, in that toilet room, in there?
Dr Zoë: Have I sat on the toilet? Yes, I have sat on the toilet.

FP: What a view! Isn't it? The domes? They're right there!

Dr Zoë: Yes...

FP: It must have one of the greatest views of any toilet in the world.

Dr Zoë: You think so? I tend to pull the screen down on the window. It's a bit more private...

FP: Hoist it up! Experience the vista!

Dr Zoë: Well, perhaps...

FP: Front row seats! For the vista!

Dr Zoë: Okay.

FP: Of course, I usually stand up, facing the other way...

Dr Zoë: Right. Got you.

As I meander off, like a tyre being prodded with a stick, Dr Zoë calls out.

Dr Zoë: Oh, Francis, I forgot to say. We're having our department meeting in the coming weeks. I hope you can join us. It'll be a good chance to find out what's going on, see how we operate.

FP: Ahh.

Dr Zoë: I'll make sure you're included on the emails.

JANE SMILEY

MOO

To Francis Plug—

Jane Smiley

Flamingo
An Imprint of HarperCollinsPublishers

My agent hasn't got back to me about the Cutty Sark brand partnership idea. Or about anything at all. It's probably for the best. At least I don't have to start wearing sponsored clothing. A writer in residence decked out in an emblazoned cap or, God forbid, a polo shirt, might raise a few eyebrows. To win respect, I'm probably better off in drenched fisherman clothes, which smell of the webbed feet of dead ducks.

Jane Smiley's campus novel, *Moo*, explores the subject of commercial interests in universities. A corporation called Trans National offers money to Moo University to research their own commercial projects. A McDonald's restaurant is also planned for the campus. Corporate interests don't appear to have a foothold in the University of Greenwich, so as brand ambassador for a whisky company, even a maritime one, I would be setting a bad precedent. However, the major publishers are corporations, and from what I understand, some of these have been afforded audiences with the Creative Writing students here. One publishing rep is said to have told the students to avoid writing comedy, because it doesn't sell. Other British universities have banned commercial publishers entirely after claims they were attempting to steer the students towards certain genres which suited their own business interests. There is an argument that students need to be aware of market conditions, if they intend to forge a living from their work. But the market changes very fast, and the writing process is very slow. J.K. Rowling didn't wait until wizard books were 'in'. Surely it's better to write whatever comes naturally and forget the market entirely. Perhaps that would have been a better subject to cover in my inaugural student lecture than 'Tyres in Rivers?'

A memo has been circulated specifying that, as part of a cost-saving measure, the cleaning staff will no longer be emptying individual office bins. Staff will be required to dispose of litter, waste and recyclable materials in communal bins located in the corridors. No skin off my nose. That's where I've been putting my empties anyway, to avoid detection. What's interesting though is that a very similar decree is issued in Jane Smiley's fictional campus novel.

'... furthermore, faculty offices will no longer be cleaned by the janitorial staff.'

The cutbacks in *Moo* are attributed to the state governor's distrust of the university, which he perceives to be loaded with cash, bank-rolling highly paid faculty staff, who are secretly Marxists. Rather than paying for the university out of state funds, or, in his words, 'robbing from widows and children', the state governor is keen instead to let corporations and the private sector pick up the financial tab. Knowledge, therefore, is given a commercial value, and the students become known as 'customers'.

Although paying £9,000 a year, students at the University of Greenwich haven't purchased a future ticket to success. It's understand-able that they'd want to get their money's worth, especially in terms of quality teaching, which may or may not involve study items that smell of sea horse manes. But the university doesn't run like a business. Students are required to think and to work, while the university, for its part, provides the environment and expertise to set them on the right path. Members of staff are still subject to rigid assessments from the paying students, and one of these students has assessed that my class, involving 'metaphors', wasn't up to scratch, expressing customer dissatisfaction.

FP: Okay, maybe the tyre was a bit pongy, but there was a very serious point behind it, to do with, I think... tread.

Dr Alex: It was more the smell of your breath that was of concern.

FP: Ah. Perhaps that was the... the fumes, the methane... from the bottoms of the sturgeon fish...

Dr Alex: [*Shaking head.*]

FP: Fair enough. The thing is... I don't think I'm cut out to be a teacher, Dr Alex.

Dr Alex: Alex. Call me Alex.

FP: Call you Alex.

For the time being at least, I'm being relieved of my teaching duties. Which, obviously, I'm quite relieved about.

The Painted Hall is touted as 'probably the finest banqueting hall in Europe', even though Admiral Lord Nelson's decomposing body lay in state here for three days. It was originally intended as a dining room for naval pensioners, but when it was decorated, the pensioners considered it too grand and began eating their meals in the basement croft instead. The serving navy were happy to eat in here, however, with the higher commanding officers dining in the elevated section at the back. When the rear area was last conserved, it's said the repairers found traces of gravy on the walls. Today's Greenwich pensioners either live in multi-million pound houses, or off tins of beans. They're all welcome to visit the Painted Hall, for free, and view Sir James Thornhill's masterpiece. But political messages about monarchy, religion and naval power, delivered in allegorical form, aren't everyone's cup of tea. And although accessible to all, it's no longer the eating space it was. Dining is now restricted to special private occasions, for those with the very deepest pockets.

Overcast skies are prevailing, and electric candles have been lit, glowing eerily on the banquet tables. It's as if Dracula were lying here, in a relaxing, scented bath. Dr Alex mentioned that many of the students are infatuated with writing fantasy sequels, so they should work in here too, although I really hope they don't.

The scaffolding has moved. A set of wheels makes this feasible, although the expanse of its supports must necessitate a lot of table shifting, along with the eighteen chairs for each. Even with this mobility, however, the art restorers haven't progressed much on the ceiling. All they have to do is colour in what's already there. Try filling in hundreds of blank pages with thousands of words that actually make some sort of sense. Nightmare.

Although racking my fagged brain, I still haven't managed to move my campus novel beyond the basic theme of explosions. But it does have a new working title: *Green*, as in Greenwich, as in naïve, unknowledgeable, clueless. The band REM used it as a very successful album title, and it's also been used by a political party and a giant. Plagiarism is clearly an issue, but what about *Moo*? Old McDonald's estate must have been all over that.

The scaffold resembles a huge metallic grasshopper, but none of the culture tourists seem interested in this, nor its two female occupants, who cause it to wobble like heck with every step. Dressed like cavers, their torch beams are aimed towards the ceiling, indicating areas of repair. White-gloved hands gently dab at the paint, perhaps extracting samples. According to Maureen, the Painted Hall was last cleaned in 1963, having since been exposed to pipe smoke from the navy staff, the coal fires of south London, and also chimney smoke from the power station. The scaffold is currently positioned beneath the ceiling's central oval frame, where Queen Mary II and King William III are showboated.

Standing at the base, I call out to the conservers, as opposed to the conservatoires, which are schools of fine music.

FP: How's it going up there?

Art Restorer: Not bad, thanks.

FP: You're very high.

Art Restorer: Yes. We've got a good head for heights fortunately.

FP: One head? Between you?

Art Restorer: A good pair of heads, then.

FP: Are you not worried by the ghost of Lord Nelson?

Art Restorer: The ghost of Lord Nelson? No. Is there one?

FP: Yes. You really should get up to speed. His dead body lay in state here, you know.

Art Restorer: Yes, we knew that. Have you seen his ghost yourself?

FP: Yes, I saw him just now. He was tinkering with your scaffold there.

Art Restorer: Was he really?

FP: Yes, he was messing with the wheel locks. You better watch that.

Art Restorer: I suppose we should. Thanks.

FP: Especially if you're adding some colour to Queen Mary's cheeks, for instance. Because next minute… whee! You're off! He's sent you careering over there somewhere. And poor old Queen Mary's left with a pink moustache. Nightmare.

Art Restorer: That would be unfortunate.

FP: Or he might just shake the living heck out of your tubular grasshopper structure. He's not actually living himself, you see. He's a very angry man.

Art Restorer: Is he a man? Or is he a ghost?

FP: Um…

Art Restorer: What about you? Are you an angry man?

FP: Me? No, not at all. I'm just a simple soul, minding my own beeswax.

Jane Smiley is late for her bookshop event. Her interviewer, Alex Clark, has been waiting patiently in her interviewer's chair, but after a distant London clock chimes seven, she sensibly shuffles off to the wine table. Jane Smiley is conducting a UK tour and is presently in transit from Leeds, a city which, I understand, uses the same amount of power as the London Underground.

When Jane Smiley arrives, she is coughing and blowing her nose. As well as Leeds today, she was somewhere else last night, and Cheltenham the day before. No wonder she's under the weather. Fatboy Slim might tour around the Mediterranean islands, but the rock stars of the literary world must contend with drizzly English towns, and city folk who smell of nuclear power plant emissions. Like Paul Auster, Jane Smiley is noticeably tall. But her appearance this evening is dominated by her multi-coloured, open-fronted jumper. The crocheted sleeves, when raised for the purpose of hand gestures, drape down in huge loops, like those on a magician's cloak. The blend of wools feature a lively mix of blues, greens and purples, and the unbuttoned buttons, like the pointy collars, are massive. Jane Smiley is left-handed, or so I deduce from a modest digital watch affixed to her right wrist with a red strap. She talks with Alex Clark about the Nordic Sagas and about her Pulitzer Prize-winning novel, *A Thousand Acres*. But it's very hard to focus on these things when caught up in the world of the crocheted jumper.

Alex Clark announces that Jane Smiley will be signing books. Jane Smiley, even with her English cold, seems animated and enthusiastic at the prospect.

Jane Smiley: I'm a really good book signer. Fast and lovely. I once signed 1,100 copies in one hour and fifteen minutes. My full name.

In her signing queue, I read aloud the title of the book I am holding.

FP: *Moo.* [*Pause.*] *Moo…*

Moo is set in the late 1980s, in a state university in the American Midwest. Jane Smiley received a PhD from the University of Iowa, and currently teaches at Iowa State University.

FP: Hello, Jane Smiley.
Jane Smiley: Hello.
FP: Are you a bit snuffly, there?
Jane Smiley: Oh yes. Nothing serious.
FP: It's not that noticeable. With your accent and all.
Jane Smiley: Good. I *think* that's good…
FP: I had this dream during your talk that I was walking up the inside sleeve of your magician's jumper, and it was like some cavernous, multi-coloured tunnel with refracted light beams bursting through the crochet holes, like lasers.
Jane Smiley: Well.
FP: It was a cross between a tunnel and a dance floor, and I was dancing with a robotic 'hands-as-pistons' action.
Jane Smiley: What were you dancing to?
FP: It was a Fatboy Slim track.
Jane Smiley: Which one?
FP: Um, 'Star 69'.
Jane Smiley: Interesting. What do you think inspired this dream?
FP: Um, apart from the jumper in question, I'm not completely sure.

Although, in your absence earlier, I did spend some extra time at the drinks table.

Jane Smiley: I see.

FP: By the way, I've heard that absinthe can be a good cure for the common cold.

Jane Smiley: Is that so? Was this from a competent medical source?

FP: No. It wasn't from Dr Alexander McCall Smith, or anyone like that. It was just some bloke down the pub.

Jane Smiley: Sounds good enough to me. Thanks, Francis Plug.

FP: No worries. After all, you'll want to be fit as a fiddle for the Greenwich Book Festival.

Jane Smiley: Pardon me?

FP: When you headline at the Greenwich Book Festival, in Greenwich, with Fatboy Slim. You won't want to be sneezy.

Jane Smiley: I don't think…

FP: I'll make sure there's plenty of absinthe on hand too, just in case…

Warmer weather has started to establish itself. As a result, the black tarpaulin has been removed from George II's statue, like plastic surgery bandages. But he hasn't been enhanced, or even mildly preserved. Instead, he's a total mess. He's like a badly decomposed murder victim, discovered after many weeks, at the water's edge, beneath a bridge. So much for respected royalty. He's covered in lichen. And his face appears gnawed, as if by rats. To be honest, he looks like I feel.

Just up the path from George II, at the 'Water Gate' entrance to the river, a photographic shoot is taking place. A woman with long blonde hair is holding two immaculately groomed Afghan Hounds, both long-haired blondes also. Three moody male models mope around the woman and the dogs. They are wearing suits, and one of them is sitting on a spotlessly clean motorbike. The woman, and the dogs, and the moody men are facing the river. Behind them, as a backdrop, are the twin domes. Is this how they fund the upkeep of the Old Naval College? By selling motorbikes to dogs? What *are* they trying to sell? The university? Greenwich? Clothes? Motorbikes? Suits? Shampoo? Dogs? Flea collars? Domes? Grass? Encyclopaedias? Vegemite? For some reason, it makes me want to buy whisky.

A number of different bars are mentioned in *Moo*. One, called the Black Hole, is frequented by students who perceive beer as food. Down But Not Out is an undergraduate hangout, and Drakes is described as the only non-student bar that hasn't been 'designed at corporate head-quarters to evoke some kind of brand of alcoholic nostalgia'. Leaving the photographic shoot, I return to the serious business of the real world and begin canvassing Greenwich bars for a new Greenwich bar.

Cupping my hands to my face like floppy transplanted ears, I peer through the windows of various prospectives. In a place on Nevada Street, the barman has small studs inserted into the back of his neck. As pubs go, it's not bad, quite pubby. But it's just up the road from the uni library, and its windows are a bit too see-through for my liking. Also, a pint is a good deal more than the Gate Clock's. 'Like us on Facebook', says the pub. No, I won't do that. But perhaps I'll like you in the real world if you halve your prices and pull your curtains.

Just over the road, at the base of Crooms Hill, is the Fan Museum. Although a detour from my designated task, it's a Greenwich insti-tution, and maybe they could direct me towards an inexpensive pub, ideally hidden deep within Crooms Hill itself, in a bunker, with a secret password.

The Fan Museum charges an admission fee, which I'm reluctant to pay. While dithering, I find myself engaged in small talk.

FP: Is the Fan Museum any good?
Woman: I can certainly recommend it.

FP: The Duchess of Cornwall has visited, I see.

Woman: Yes. She bought a number of items in the gift shop.

FP: Did she? How nice. I think she hates my guts, the Duchess.

Woman: Really? Why?

FP: It's a long story. I've got a fan in my office, as it happens. A very interesting one. Over at the university.

Woman: Oh yes?

FP: Yes, it was made there, at the university. Every day I look at it, for free.

Woman: Do you know what it's made out of?

FP: Carpet. Do you know any good cheap pubs nearby, where someone could lie low?

Woman: Hmm.

FP: Not terrorist folk. Or bomb makers, or committers of atrocities. Just normal, simple, cheerful types. Who want to avoid like-minded normal, simple, cheerful types.

Woman: Well, the pubs on Royal Hill are sort of out of the way...

FP: Thanks, I'll give them a try. Bye then.

Woman: You're not going to visit us today?

FP: No, I need a drink after that big long chat.

Woman: Oh. Well, maybe another time then.

FP: Doubt it.

A number of dog walkers are out around Royal Hill, some with multiple dogs in tow. A young grey-haired man approaches, carrying a King Charles Spaniel in an upholstered basket. The basket has shoulder straps like a backpack, but is slung forward, like a baby carrier. Hopefully, his well-groomed dog is somehow incapable of walking, even with its four legs visible and intact. Hopefully the man himself is just a caring fellow who, in lieu of dog wheelchairs being invented, is shouldering that burden upon himself. But a dog named after a king, on Royal Hill, in an upholstered basket; it certainly does raise suspicions.

The first Royal Hill pub I find is a greatly modernized and smartened-up place boasting a rounded bay window frontage. To be honest, it looks like it's seen better days. Back when it was shabby and genuine and real.

Chalked on a blackboard near the bar are the words:

'A man who lies about beer makes enemies.' —Stephen King.

Wow, how did Stephen King get that gig? Working for a small, tucked away little English pub? How can I do that? There must be a catch. You probably have to be a king.

A framed photograph depicts the Queen Mother behind a bar, pouring a pint of bitter. She's just helping herself, which is why they've put her photo up, to appeal for witnesses. She won't get away with this, even in death.

FP: Excuse me, I know the culprit, in the CCTV image. It's the Queen Mother.
Bartender: Sorry?
FP: Just there. But you're out of luck. She died some years back. Still, it's worth keeping an eye out for her grandson, Charles. You can't be too careful with that family.

Jammed right next door is another pub. It manages to lack even more in the character department, having opted for an ultra-modern, strip-everything-back approach. So why is this drink more expensive than next door, where there are more things? What exactly is the extra cost for? Possibly the quarry bill, for the slate flooring. In the old days, pub floors were basic wood scattered with sawdust, but the well-heeled locals around here clearly expect something finer to touch the bottom of their shoes.

A dog walker is sitting at the next table, with three dogs lying on the slate floor beneath. It must pay really well because he's onto another pint and has just ordered a steak lunch. There was an uproar recently when it was reported that many dog walkers were earning more than nurse and ambulance staff. For walking on their own two legs. When the steak arrives, the dogs all scramble up and stare longingly towards the plate with big, sad dog eyes. Their walker meanwhile, looks like a dog when it appears to be laughing. Before tucking into his steak meal, he orders yet another pint. What will he do when he needs a wee? There's a treacherous staircase down to the loos, which will be difficult enough to navigate, let alone with three dogs. If his descent is successful, will he force the dogs to smell his strange human wee, and others? What if they start drinking it, out of the urinal? A safer bet perhaps is to hold it in, like the dogs, and whizz against a lamp post down the street.

Rather than heading further up the hill, I turn into Circus Street, which sounds like a lot more fun. There's much to be said for clowns and clowning. Unfortunately, in this day and age, clowns are getting barred from hospitals because some people believe their honking noses scare children. Sharp pointy needles and leukaemia are perhaps more frightening. The Morden Arms sits on the corner of Circus Street and Brand Street. Outside benches welcome the smoking classes, and a small A-frame blackboard reads:

The Best Atmosphere in Greenwich:
MOR-DEN-A-PUB

Inside is small, interesting and rather quiet. A log burner is fitted into a fireplace, and on the mantelpiece above is a personally inscribed photo of Henry Winkler patting a dog. Further up the wall is a young Johnny Cash, giving the citizens of Royal Greenwich the 'birdy'. Microphones, speakers and a P.A. system are set up in a corner, and a small blackboard lists the 'Gigs in March'. There is also, I notice, an 'Open Mic Night' every Tuesday at 8:00 p.m.

Hosted by Charley. 10 acts plus a sing-song.

Pints are most reasonable, and because the pub is tucked away down a back street, away from the village centre, there's no sign of any students. An older man, who the bartender refers to as Ray, is discussing his little black book.

Ray: I tried ringing them all recently, but no. They were all dead.

Unlike the preceding pubs, the Morden is a bit shabby. Unlike Jane Smiley's pubs, it hasn't been 'designed at corporate headquarters'. Instead, with its hotch-potch of furniture, murals and newspapers, it has a genuine 'lived in' feel. There's no slate floor or fancy restaurant. The only meals they appear to serve are crisps. It has all the signs of a regular haunt, this.

Samuel Pepys and Joseph Conrad both wrote of the Cheshire Cheese pub in London's Fleet Street, so perhaps I could incorporate the Morden into my balls-of-fire campus novel. Perhaps a chimney from the exploding power station could fly across Greenwich and crash right through the roof. Maybe that Ray chap could walk in with a glowing head. Ray sits at the end of a long pew, while I'm stationed at the opposing end. As I ready myself to exchange greetings, there's a huge whump behind the bar. It shakes the entire pub, possibly dislodging dog poo from the surrounding pavements.

Ray: It's all right. The world hasn't ended. Just some deliveries of beer.

The whump is from the trapdoor leading to the basement. The bartender is an older woman called Judith. She and her husband David run the place, Ray informs me. I'm at the university, I tell him, in Creative Writing. Over the next couple of drinks, I share some initial thoughts on scenes for my new book, set in the Morden Arms.

Ray: A flaming Sambuca, that sets a customer's entire body alight?

Ray: The microphone stand is mysteriously rooted with 11,000 vaults?

Ray: Someone's head is peering into the cellar when the trapdoor falls?

Another bartender arrives for her shift, and I order a drink for myself because Ray won't take my money.

Bartender: Oh, a Hello Kitty purse.
FP: Yes, it's normally very full. But I stopped into some more expensive pubs on the way.
Bartender: We don't get many Hello Kitty purses in here.
FP: It's a coin pouch, actually. With a friendly cat.
Bartender: Oh, I see. That's quite different. [*Smiling.*]
FP: Is there a problem?

The bartender's name is Emma. Ray brings her up to speed with my big ideas.

Ray: He says it'll be like the Queen Vic, in *EastEnders*, except with Henry Winkler, and nuclear fallout.
FP: And saloon-type brawls.

Emma: Saloon-type brawls? Hmm. I *think* these chairs are made of balsa wood. Why don't you stand just there, Francis? No, face *that* way.

After workshopping some Morden Arms scenes, my campus novel has moved on significantly. The knowledge that I now have a safe hideout has certainly helped. Filled with confidence and numerous drinks, I farewell Ray and Emma, and march briskly towards my friendly local tattoo parlour.

On the way I drop by a cashpoint machine. A homeless man sits alongside, reading a book. It's not my book, but still, feeling happy and generous, I offer him the key and address to my garage, seeing as I'm no longer using it.

FP: It's not one of those empty palatial homes in the Royal Borough of Chelsea, but it does have a roof and four walls, if you're interested.

The tattooist is a tall strapping fellow with an abundance of black hair. He laughs when I explain my anchor design concept.

FP: It's quite a poignant piece, actually.
Tattooist: Sure, sure.
FP: On my upper arm here. Like the sailors.
Tattooist: [*Laughing.*]

The tattooist's arms are as big as my legs, and feature many different tattoos, all fighting for space.

FP: You know what your arms remind me of? The sleeves of a cub scout's jumper. Those are all your badges.

Tattooist: [*Not laughing.*]

FP: You keep earning new ones.

Tattooist: [*Not laughing.*]

FP: Ow!

Hoisting myself over the university fence is more difficult than normal because, even with the drink anaesthetic, my bandaged arm really hurts.

On Beauty

A NOVEL BY ZADIE SMITH

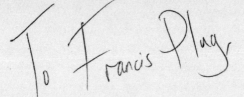

THE PENGUIN PRESS

New York

2005

Elly has forwarded me an email from the executive producer of Literary Death Match. This, I understand, is a live literary event, combining author readings with a gameshow-style format. Four different authors go head-to-head reading seven minutes or less of their own work in front of three all-star judges. The judges grade the readers on Literary Merit, Performance and Intangibles, before choosing two authors to advance to the finale. The finale is, in their own words, 'a silly game', such as a literary spelling bee, or Pin the Moustache on Hemingway. It sounds truly awful, but I'm led to believe Jeffrey Eugenides is a former participant, and he's written a campus novel of repute. Rather than replying straight away, I fester on it.

Before reading Jeffrey Eugenides' book, Zadie Smith's campus novel awaits. The library has a copy and I can withdraw it now. But Zadie Smith is doing a gig in town, and asking her to sign a library book may be crossing a threshold of frugality, even for an author. Zadie Smith has been an outspoken supporter of libraries, particularly in light of the government's cuts. When her local came under the axe, she and many others campaigned rigorously for its life. Their case was given greater impetus by the fact that Kensal Rise Library was officially opened, over 100 years ago, by Mark Twain. But even with this illustrious connection, and despite being championed by its famous card holders, Kensal Rise Library was closed down. What's the bet, somewhere in that library, there is, or was, a book that emphatically explained why closing it down was a really bad idea. But, of course, the politicians and councillors were too busy looking for their own names in the newspapers, or tweeting lines taken directly from sympathy cards, to be arsed to try and find it.

Although British, Zadie Smith has chosen an American campus as the setting for her story. Wellington College is a fictional campus, somewhere near Boston. In real life, Wellington is the capital of New Zealand, and if the Big Friendly Giant is to be believed, people from there taste of old boots. Like me, Zadie Smith has proper university credentials, having been a Fellow at Harvard University and a tenured professor of fiction at New York University. But while her novel is based in New England, mine is slowly coming to life in very old Greenwich.

Zadie Smith's event is at a bookshop called Crockatt and Powell, not far from Waterloo Station.

FP: Would you mind also signing this?

Zadie Smith: What is it?

FP: Um, it's like a petition, to keep the libraries open…

Zadie Smith: Sure. Wait. Hang on. No it isn't. This says: 'By signing this document, you are legally bound to appear at the Greenwich Book Festival…'

FP: Ah. Yes. I must have mixed the papers up…

Zadie Smith: '… on stage with Francis Plug.' Is that you?

FP: Or, you can just, y'know, appear on stage yourself.

Zadie Smith: Is this for real?

FP: Look, it's a very fluid situation, we'll keep you updated on specific details as they come to hand…

Unfortunately, Crockatt and Powell, the independent bookshop, like Kensal Rise Library, has now closed down. I did think of inviting Zadie Smith to visit Greenwich prior to the festival, in order to woo her with the local charms. But having only recently discovered the Morden Arms, the last thing I want is for that to close down too. Let alone the university, the *Cutty Sark*, the Greenwich Foot Tunnel...

On Beauty is a loose reinterpretation of *Howards End* by E.M. Forster. Zadie Smith admits to using that book as 'scaffolding' for her own novel. In a way, all artists are reliant on the work of their predecessors, to inspire them and give them a leg-up. It's certainly a model I have followed, finding titbits in Booker Prize novels for my previous book, and, more recently, in campus novels too. Scaffolds are all the rage in Greenwich, where the focus, like with *On Beauty*, is on giving history a modern gloss. The Painted Hall is getting a new coat, and the *Cutty Sark* ship, having being razed twice, now looks, literally, ship-shape. It has to. There's an entire whisky brand banking on it, not to mention a fancy riverside pub. But why? It didn't chase the great white whale, or plunder chest-loads of solid gold sovereigns. All it did was ship boring old tea.

FP: Yo-ho-hum.

The staff in the Painted Hall are starting to recognize me. One of them approaches, looking grim-faced. On her name badge is the word 'Judy'.

FP: Afternoon, Judy.
Judy: You're at the university, aren't you? The resident writer?
FP: Yes, that's it. Francis Plug.

249

Judy: Well your behaviour in here yesterday was completely unacceptable.

FP: Yesterday? I was in here yesterday?

Judy: You were clearly very drunk. And your language was… utterly base. And crude.

FP: That sounds *very* out of character.

Judy: This is not some rowdy public bar.

FP: No, of course, of course. Although there is that info screen over there, with the guy rabbiting on and on.

Judy: At least he has something informative to say. Unlike you. Pointing at the cherubs with 'their widdlers out'. Honestly. We have visitors from all over the world. They were shocked. This is a historical site. They, *we*, expect some decorum.

FP: Yes, but the Australian visitors…

Judy: And you call yourself the 'resident writer'. What sort of example do you think you're setting to the students?

FP: I understand. The thing is, I'm wrestling with a new work of literature at present, which demands an outpouring of uncontrollable passions and feelings.

Judy: Well, Rimbaud, we're volunteering our time for free, and we don't need your 'uncontrollable feelings' to contend with. It's not acceptable, and we won't put up with it.

FP: But…

Judy: If there's a repeat of yesterday, the Vice Chancellor will be informed. Are we clear?

FP: Yes, Judge Judy.

Blimey. I've never been barred from an early eighteenth-century Painted Hall before. Feeling completely flat and lifeless, like Eeyore, without tail, I slump dejectedly off to the off-licence. An hour or so later, now a hive of bees, I make my way to my first faculty meeting.

FP: Lordy! Ha, ha!

Faculty staff meetings feature in Zadie Smith's *On Beauty*, offering potential insights as to what I might expect. For instance, the central Howard character rues not arriving early to nab some 'escape route seating', instead finding himself 'forced right up to the front...' Determined to benefit from this sterling advice, I arrive promptly at Queen Anne's Edinburgh room. Unfortunately, there isn't a 'back' as such. The seats slot beneath tables, which are arranged in a conjoining rectangle, facing inwards. The 'back' of the formation is furthest from the two possible exit doors, while the chairs nearest the doors, where I sit, are where Dr Zoë and other important people end up sitting. The Chancellor, from what I understand, actually lives somewhere in this Queen Anne building. Perhaps he or she beds directly above this room. That might explain why the light fitting overhanging our table arrangement is swaying slightly, without any obvious provocation. Nudging a colleague alongside, I raise my eyes to the light fitting.

FP: If it's rockin', don't bother knockin'.

Given my limited efforts to meet and socialize with my colleagues thus far, many of them are regarding me for the first time. It's possible my appearance is unsatisfactory, as a result of my shabby clothes, and my need for a further haircut. The initial bees begin dropping, with X's for eyes, as if due to some mysterious pesticide mist. I imagine my fellows inspecting the cut of my cloth, like members of Rembrandt's Draper's Guild in *The Staalmeesters*. Perhaps my breath stinks too. Dipping into my pocket, I retrieve not one but three gum capsules and begin chewing on all of them.

Dr Zoë, who is chairing the meeting, makes a point of introducing me from the off and thanking me for my attendance.

Dr Zoë: And I believe, Francis, you're currently procuring some big-name authors for our book festival?
FP: Hnurr.

My mouth feels like it's full of rubber bands. Although shrinking into my seat, the woman to my left addresses me directly.

Female Colleague: Is your arm okay, there?
FP: Hnur? Yurr.
Female Colleague: It looks painful. Did you burn it?

Removing the wet gummy blob, I add it to the underside of the table, before stammering out a response.

FP: No. It's not burnt. I believe it was... a lion's mane jellyfish. Swimming off the coast of... Greenwich... coastline...

A younger male staff member, to my right, piles in.

Male Colleague: That looks like a tattoo to me.
FP: I'm pretty sure it was the harmful toxins of... the stinging tendrils...
Female Colleague: A tattoo! Oo, let's see!
FP: Honestly, it's nothing, honestly...

The first item on the agenda is my new tattoo. Succumbing to group pressure, I awkwardly reveal my reddened and tender arm.

Male Colleague: An anchor! A swashbuckling anchor, by heck!
FP: [*Muttering.*] It's a symbol of maritime...
Male Colleague: Greenwich! It even says Greenwich!

Female Colleague: That's dedication for you. That's commitment to the post.

FP: It's just… they're very popular with the young ones, aren't they. With the students.

Another Female Colleague: Hmm. I'm not quite sure *anchors* are in though, are they? That's more an old Popeye thing. Or Captain Pugwash.

Male Colleague: Or, in Francis's case, Captain *Plug*wash.

Random Colleague: Captain *Plug*wash! Ha, ha! Captain *Plug*wash!

Other Colleagues: Ha ha ha, ha ha ha!

FP: Yes, I see. Yes, very funny. Oh yes. Yes.

The department meeting that follows isn't as contentious as those in *On Beauty*. In fact, it seems to be very administration-focused, and not particularly relevant to my role. To be honest, I don't really take much in, focusing more on the swinging light fitting and Captain Pugwash, and whether my face is as red and blistered as my arm. To quote Zadie Smith, I wonder if it resembles 'a smacked arse'. At the first hint of a conclusion, I make the most of my seat position and bolt for the exit.

Female Colleague: Thanks, Captain *Plug*wash!

FP: Yes…

Male Colleague: Aye, aye, Captain!

FP: Okay, great!

In my former life as a gardener, my nickname at the Covent Garden flower market was 'Peat Man'. Apparently using a pen and paper to write, which I did, over breakfast, was a custom that died out many, many centuries ago. Although the lads insisted that my nickname was also related to my 'smelly, trampy' appearance.

As I puff furiously on a Dutch Drum, I take some consolation from the fact that I now have a public house retreat to flee to.

The Morden Arms is quiet when I arrive, and so am I.

Ray: Are you all right there, Francis? You seem a bit forlorn.
FP: Oh, I've just been stuck in a really tedious meeting over at the university. Boring!

A mobility scooter belonging to Gus, one of the old-timer regulars, is jammed inside, next to three baby buggies. Some mums have descended on the bar, two of them getting pints, with another opting for a large red wine. One of them lifts her baby up, outwardly facing, and sniffs its bottom.

FP: Gus forget his scooter?
Ray: In a manner of speaking…

Gus, it transpires, fell over in the Gents last night and was taken to hospital. Apparently it's the second time in as many months. Gus has been barred from numerous Greenwich pubs, due to his temper and very colourful language. But he's tolerated here. It's nice not to be the only pub 'character' for a change. Gus was involved in the war in Cyprus, experiencing a ruptured stomach from a land mine. Which might explain his anger with the world. Last night's accident sounds serious. Fortunately, Ray, a former ambulance paramedic, was on-hand, assisting with initial aid.

Ray: Blood everywhere. But today… babies.

When Ray laughs, it's like the beginnings of a bad cough, wrapped inside a cocoon, that blossoms into a beautiful butterfly, with wings that look like eyes. As well as zipping about in ambulances, Ray also worked as a tree surgeon, before undertaking a role at the Maritime Museum. He is a practising Buddhist and is outwardly very calm, although he still has a sense of flashing siren about him.

FP: Do you know if an ambulance and a police car and a fire engine have ever crashed into each other, at the same time, with their different sirens blaring?
Ray: I expect so.

Apart from the occasional trip abroad, Ray is seeing out his retirement in pubs, which, as an ex-paramedic, he well deserves. His surname, it turns out, is 'Chipps'. Ray Chipps.

FP: You could be in a novel, with a name like that.
Ray Chipps: Not one of yours, I hope. I'm liable to be strapped to a wind turbine, or wrung through a washing machine wringer.

Tonight is Open Mic night. I'm not really in the mood for it, but if I'm going to do a Literary Death Match, I'll need all the practice I can get.

By early evening, the Morden is rammed. The mic stand is in position, and the mic has been turned to 'ON'.

FP: Hello everyone, thanks for clapping. Um, I'm Francis Plug, the Writer in Residence down there at the University of Greenwich.
Everyone:
FP: So… I was just going to read a short extract from my novel.
Everyone: [*Muttering, mumbling.*]

FP: Sorry, am I popping? The last time I talked through a mic was on BBC Radio 4, and they told me my 'p's' were popping.

Everyone: [*Muttering, mumbling.*]

FP: And the time before that, on a mic, was probably in the Guildhall, at the Booker Prize ceremony.

Everyone: [*Muttering, mumbling.*]

FP: I didn't win the Booker Prize, by the way. I wasn't even nominated. But the drinks were free. [*Two thumbs up.*] Hey, look over there. It's Henry Winkler, the Fonz! Heyyy!! [*Two thumbs up.*] Heyy!!

Everyone: [*Muttering, mumbling.*]

FP: Anyway. Who wants to hear a novel extract?

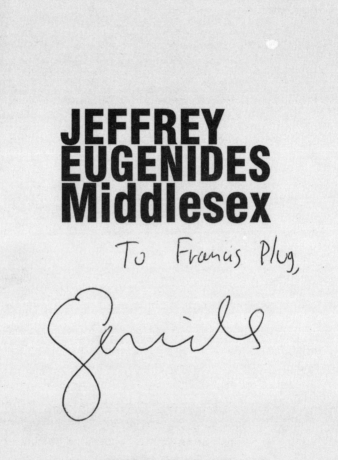

JEFFREY EUGENIDES Middlesex

To Francis Plug,

[signature]

BLOOMSBURY

Jeffrey Eugenides is not to be sniffed at. He's a Pulitzer Prize-winning author, and two-time finalist for the National Book Critics Circle Award. In the lead-up to my Literary Death Match appearance, which Jeffrey Eugenides was purportedly involved with, these accolades have been playing on my mind. My apprehension and need for a guiding voice is perhaps understandable. Even with a BBC appearance under my belt, and an official academic post, I fear I'm still regarded as a 'silly' author. So a gameshow event, where my writerly talents may well be debased further, is not ideal.

Jeffrey Eugenides' *The Marriage Plot* is a well-respected inclusion in the bastion of campus novels. His most acclaimed work is *Middlesex*, and his first novel, *The Virgin Suicides*, was adapted for the screen by Sofia Coppola. And yet such credentials have been tested, it would seem, by his participation in a trivial contest. His literary worth supposedly judged upon attributes of showmanship and performance. Even though he's since been named a fellow of the American Academy of Arts and Sciences. He's also been awarded an honorary Doctorate of Letters from Brown University. Perhaps, like the campus novel genre, this Death Match is a right of passage, a necessary tour of duty for the progressing author. Maybe, after a few drinks, it's a right laugh. If there was some sort of payment offered, to pay for those drinks, it would help soften the blow, but there's been no mention of any.

After Elly forwarded me the details, I emailed the producer:

> *Hello,*
> *Thanks for considering me for your Death Match.*
> *Are you quite sure Jeffrey Eugenides has done this?*
> *Will I get paid?*
> *Best wishes,*
> *Francis Plug.*

A reply wasn't immediately forthcoming. Eventually I received a much shorter email than the original one:

> *Hi Francis,*
> *Yes, Jeffrey Eugenides was involved with one of our events.*
> *We can offer a fee of £40.*
> *Best, Bonnie.*

£40. It won't pay for the hours of anxiety. But it should all be over in an hour. Maybe two, with the faffing about. It's not the same hourly rate that Martin Amis enjoyed, but £40 is £40, and I could certainly use the money. Who knows, perhaps I'll sell some books. And if it all goes terribly wrong and I am publicly shamed, my literary career ruined, my university standing compromised, my life no longer worth living, well, I'll simply lay the blame entirely at the feet of Jeffrey Eugenides.

Replying to the executive producer in the affirmative, I shut down my university computer with my heavy head, which I continue to butt on the keyboard.

The King's College Chapel on the Strand is the venue for my potential death, on stage. The cheapest journey from Greenwich to the Strand is on the 188 bus, or right whale. A return journey will cost me £4, a tenth of my fee, leaving me with £36 to prepare for the onslaught to follow. The open consumption of alcohol on London buses is prohibited, so I try to be discreet, hiding my head under my coat. Unfortunately, my preferred spot at the back of the upper deck, with the graffiti and the chicken bones, is where the security cameras are most focused. It's not long before a pre-recorded announcement about the no-alcohol policy is deployed throughout the bus, forcing me to move further up the seats, away from the cameras, towards the tourists and other nerds. It's not like I'm a miscreant. I'm reading a book from a Pulitzer Prize winner with glowing reviews from the *New York Times*. Yes, I'm necking alcoholic substances on British public transport, but only because I have to go on stage at a supposed literary event. It's not like I'm bothering anyone. I'm hardly one of society's fringe dwellers. Now, where was I?

FP: Ah yes, 'stripped'. [*Reading aloud.*] '… stripped and blindfolded and left in the lobby of the Biltmore Hotel with bus fare taped to their genitals…'

The whisky consumption helps me with my preparations, and by the time my right whale has reached Elephant and Castle, I feel confident enough to stand at the front of the upper deck, grasping the rail, as if I were young Paikea Apirana in *Whale Rider*. If ever there were a literary event for which alcohol's calming properties were needed, it's surely this one. Pre-event drinks, as mentioned, are a slippery slope. But when faced with the prospect of competing against other authors in a performance, the success of which will grant progression to a silly game, you don't want to turn up half-cocked. What happens if I actually win? Is there a monetary prize? The producer never mentioned one. Such an incentive could well spur me on to win this godforsaken thing. Did you win, Jeffrey?

The Strand backs onto Covent Garden, thus attracting much tourist traffic, so finding a good cheap pub near King's College proves troublesome. But the Nell Gwynne is tucked away down a back-alley, offering refuge and sanctuary from the hordes. If you're in central London and you need to practise reading aloud from a book you wrote yourself, it's certainly worth considering.

Unfortunately, because it's a Friday, even the Nell Gwynne isn't immune from the part-time drunks. Society's better paid, less integral workforce seem to down tools around midday on Fridays, with the impending lure of a weekend sucking them out of stable employment into a vortex of leisure. It's not long before my own seat is uprooted and pulled away in to the melee, forcing me to stand my ground amongst lively chattering folk, drink in hand, reading aloud from my novel.

FP: Since we're in a chapel, the section I've chosen to read is from the Margaret Atwood chapter, in St James' church.
Pub Goer: What did he say?

Unlike the Morden, there's no microphone to practise with, and the competing noise from the punters and the jukebox challenges my soft, seldom-used voice, forcing me to shout. After a time my throat starts to feel dry and hoarse, so I replenish it with more wet drinks.

Bartender: A Hello Kitty purse.
FP: It's a coin pouch, actually. It's very noisy in here.

Bartender: Do you mean the general crowd chatter and music, or the solitary shoutings, by one lone individual, with a book?

FP: What were the first ones?

The Literary Death Match is part of a wider literary festival taking place at King's College. At the sign-in desk, I am allocated a nametag, which, unlike my Greenwich pass, is simply a paper inlay in a plastic sleeve. Passes and tags have become all too commonplace in this modern world of ours, defining us, confining us to certain work environments or event attendances. As a writer, you notice these sort of things. Of course, I'm no William Gibson or J.G. Ballard, or George Orwell, or Noam Chomsky, or Naomi Klein, or Michael Moore. I bet those writers would really have something to say about all the tags and passes around these days.

FP: Excuse me, where are the artist drinks?

A volunteer escorts me up an ornate staircase and along a corridor to the Festival's Green Room, or 'holding area'. To the left of the entrance is a coat rack, supporting the coats and scarves of writers. The writers themselves are seated reading magazines, or standing, talking to other writers. Before hanging my coat up, my eyes sweep the room like in some dystopian novel, electronically tracking the environment for signs of alcohol. The drinks table's outlay consists mainly of juice and water options, but red wine is also visible, thankfully, which will suffice, in the interim, for my needs. After hanging my coat up on the rack, I notice how dirty it is. It looks as though its owner rolls around in muddy puddles like a pig. The sleeve edges are frayed, and loose threads drape off it like hairs that might stick out of an ear, or a nostril. As I walk away from my coat, it barks out at me, like an untrained, flea-ridden dog, tied up outside an off-licence.

Coat: WOOF, WOOF!

Drinks Table Assistant: Can I offer you a drink?

FP: Yes, red wine, please.

Coat: WOOF, WOOF!

FP: Sorry about that.

Drinks Table Assistant: Sorry?

FP: The barking. All that noisy barking.

Drinks Table Assistant: Barking?

FP: My coat over there. The filthy, disobedient one.

Drinks Table Assistant: Your coat?

FP: Yes, it's shameful. I'd turn it inside out, except the inside is filthy also. It's been lying on mucky pub floors, and in puddles too, possibly soaking up fox wee and stale, storm-drain discharge.

Drinks Table Assistant: I wouldn't worry.

FP: You say that, but if we squeezed it out into a glass I bet you wouldn't drink it.

Drinks Table Assistant: Possibly not.

FP: And yet we drink this wine, don't we? Even though wine farmers stamp all over the grapes with their bare feet. Urgh! Could I have another one, please?

My wine glass, made from plastic, is retrieved from a towering, upside-down pile. Like my plastic pass, I fear my cup will one day find its way up a turtle's nostril. Another young helper arrives, bearing bottles of both red and white wine. Retaining my original plastic glass, I politely request a dose of the white, which I swill.

FP: I don't want to go on stage with red teeth, like a *Lord of the Flies* character, who's just eaten a small child.

Drinks Table Assistant: No…

FP: Mm, doesn't taste of feet. Could I possibly have another?

Scanning the room a second time, I seek a quiet corner where closed eyes may simply represent tiredness, as opposed to a complete unwillingness to engage. Chairs are plentiful, but there are few tables, forcing congregation with other people. It's the perfect opportunity to canvas the room, signing up recruits for the forthcoming Greenwich Book Festival. But I have my own public appearance to worry about, leading me to remain at the drinks table, propping it up. The drinks table assistant has chosen to face away and look at her phone, so I retrieve my notebook, attempting to demonstrate how the job never ends for some of us writers. The students in Greenwich could do well to learn what a modern writer's life really entails, so I jot down some useful tips, hoping to bring some on-the-spot action to their preconceived notions of French cafés and heads in stoves.

- *Don't steal things from other authors' coats, even if those coats are so much better than your own.*

- *Be aware of security cameras at all times.*

- *Even young festival helpers can double as security personnel, cradling cans of Mace.*

A woman, even shorter than my short self, approaches.

Short Woman: Francis?
FP: Yes?
Short Woman: Hi, I'm Bonnie, producer of Death Match.
FP: Has it been cancelled?
Bonnie: No, why?
FP: Just really wondering.
Bonnie: I have this for you.

Producing an envelope, she discreetly ushers it my way, spy-like. Perhaps she is aware of the surveillance team also, and the undercover agents.

FP: Thanks. That should help me break even. It's amazing how thirsty you get, when you're totally stressed to the max.
Bonnie: Oh, there's nothing to worry about. It really is quite painless. Have you met the others?
FP: Kind of. If their coats count.

As well as us four authors, there are also three judges. It's their task to rule on content, performance, and those 'intangibles'. After reading from our work for a period of seven minutes, a bell will sound. After eight minutes, two bells will sound. At nine minutes, if the author is still reading, members of the audience will be invited on stage to hug them. I suppose some people find that funny. It's interesting how some people find something funny, while others won't find it funny at all. My last book is a good case in point.

At show time, we're rounded up from the Green Room by Bonnie, with me running behind holding a full wine glass, and a larger wine glass, called a bottle. The King's College Chapel is really quite something. It's not just literature whose sanctimony will be in rags tonight. The rammed audience await in the pews as we make our entrance between them, like fictitious TV wrestlers. This theme doesn't stop there. Following an introduction by the American host, we are split into sparring partners of two. Without warning, I am selected for the first round, ding–ding, along with Australian novelist Omar Musa. Being the shorter of the pair, I am required to call on the flip, not of a coin, but of two literary quotes, each printed on either side of the same slip of paper. Already it's too much like hard work, but I manage to recall one successfully and choose to read first, to get it over with.

A microphone on a stand. All I have to do is read from my book. Except my book stinks of mouldy damp. It reeks of mouse poo, on cold concrete, in a puddle.

FP: Urk!!

The microphone is lowered to my level, like a descending periscope that I hope will continue to submerge, together with me, through the stage and beneath floor level, to an escape route/tunnel. But the blinding lights remain, collectively resembling a large truck bearing down. HONK, HONK! Although writing the words in front of me, I have no special affiliation with them, particularly on an oral level. Speaking, as I discovered at Broadcasting House, isn't something I have much connection with either. This must put me at a distinct disadvantage in a competition judged on the reading aloud of words. But surely the other authors are in the same boat too?

When the audience laughs, it's rather disconcerting. What are they laughing at? I can't even see them! My posture, perhaps? Years of leaning over spades and pints haven't been kind to me. Somewhere off to my right, the three judges are trying to think of praise for a stooped, cowering author who's reading a book. That's the long and short of it, this show. Remarkably, a warning bell signifies that seven minutes have passed. After finishing up in haste, each judge in turn delivers a positive critique of my 'performance', which is pretty much a given, seeing as the host declared upfront that they are 'not about cynicism'. Still, they could declare me the Town Wanchor and I'd cheer, knowing my seat awaited, down there, with drink. My performance summary ends with more applause, which I add to.

FP: Yay!

As well as being a novelist, Omar, my challenger, is also a performance poet. He leaves his book on the stage floor and spends the next seven + minutes reciting, off-the-cuff, a charged and powerful piece worthy of a great orator. Which makes it a bit of a Death Match mis-match. To be fair, the chair of judges, Stella Duffy, agrees, wondering how they can choose between a novelist and a performance poet in what is essentially a performance contest. But they do, and fortunately for me, I am thoroughly, and officially, outperformed. Given there are two heats and one final, if you don't win your heat you're done. Thus I find myself, in the chapel congregation, drinking an entire bottle of free wine, laughing.

FP: Ha, ha! Oh my word. Ha, ha!

The finalists are required to 'arrange' audience volunteers, who hold individual letters, into words representing the surnames of famous authors. They must physically move the audience members into position, as if it were a staff training exercise, in a hired hall. After AMIS is formed, I zone out, still riding my wave of relief, having survived my public Death Match experience without incident. Although considerably drunk, it is my fellow authors who are acting the fools. Which makes a change. Slouched in my chair, I notice the envelope poking out of my pocket. That should just about cover the pub drinks, and the bus drinks, and the fare. Forty pounds for seven minutes work. I must be the most well-paid author in Britain tonight.

Before retrieving my battered, woofing coat, I press Bonnie the producer for further details on Jeffrey Eugenides' involvement.

Bonnie: Oh yes, he was a judge for us once. In Helsinki, I think it was.
FP: A judge? So he didn't actually 'perform'?
Bonnie: No, he wasn't a contestant. He was a judge.
FP: Ahhh... stuff it.

His Dark Materials
Book One

THE GOLDEN COMPASS

To Francis —
best wishes from

Philip Pullman

PHILIP PULLMAN

ALFRED A. KNOPF · NEW YORK

A sudden burst of bright, hot light awakens me.

FP: Oh no. I've fallen asleep on the road again!

There's no roar from a large automobile, however, no sudden squeal of brakes or skidding tyres. Instead, voices can be heard, and a soft ticking sound, like the elements of an old heater warming up.

As my eyes adjust, I can just make out the edges of my university room. Beneath is camp bed and carpet, not tarmac. Perhaps it's the Armed Defenders squad, outside in the hall, with their twitchy trigger fingers. But why? I haven't even committed my terror offence yet. The massive nuclear explosion at Greenwich Power Station is still in the planning process. It's possible, of course, that I've been mouthing off down the pub, demonstrating the effects of the gigantic tidal wave with my sloshing drink. A gentle hammering comes from down in the courtyard, and more voices can be heard, in tones without urgency or threat. Holding an arm across my eyes, I cautiously approach the window, from which the light emits. Its intensity is such, I wonder if JASON, the nuclear reactor, has been clonked with a coffee mug, initiating Armageddon. And yet the voices sound too jovial for an end-of-the-world, post-existence scenario.

The stark, glaring light, it transpires, is being projected onto the building by huge lamps suspended from a crane. It's like the UFO scene in *Close Encounters*, apart from the crane, which makes it more like the behind-the-scenes making of that scene.

Dr Alex did mention some filming thing, but I haven't been keeping abreast of my emails. According to a man in a hi-vis coat down by the central steps, they're shooting sequences for a TV series called *The Royals,* based on a fictional British royal family, set in modern times. Before the actors turn up, they have to prepare the set.

FP: Are you a sailor?

Hi-Vis Man: No. Why?

FP: Well, you've got CREW written on your back.

Hi-Vis Man: I'm with the *film* crew. With this lot.

FP: Ah. So confusing. Because this is Greenwich, a maritime centre of repute.

Hi-Vis Man: Right.

FP: Perhaps, to avoid mix-ups, you should use the word TEAM, or EMPLOYEE.

Hi-Vis Man: Right.

FP: Or REPRESENTATIVE, or OFFICIAL, or WORKER. Or, what's your name?

Hi-Vis Man: Kevin.

FP: Or KEVIN.

Kevin: Right.

FP: Otherwise, if you haven't got your wits about you, you might suddenly find yourself holed up in the middle of the Pacific Ocean, covered in tattoos, with scurvy.

Kevin: Yeah, that would be unfortunate.

FP: Don't worry, I'm good with words. I can help you.

Kevin, like many of his fellows, is standing around idle. It's amazing how many people are needed to shoot a few seconds of film. To create a book only requires one person, not hundreds. Books may need editing and marketing and distributing further down the line, but so do films. At this point, they're literally just putting the words on the page. Yet it seems to require an army. Authors don't need walkie-talkies. We just listen to our inner thoughts.

FP: … five potato, six potato, seven potato, more…

Of course, it's far more glamorous being 'on set' than sitting at a desk. A fleet of white Winnebagos are parked alongside the Dreadnought building, ready to provide comfort and privacy to the 'stars'. On the doors are names of characters, rather than real actor names, so presumably, once inside, they're inside the role, in character. It's a bit of an ask, if you ask me. Someone must 'become' the Queen of England in a little cabin with two tiny tinted windows. Their 'palace', from the outside at least, is more like a prison van crossed with a horse float.

The generators that power the Winnebagos create a constant hum, and wooden supports lock the wheels in place, so they don't roll into the Thames. Separate cabins cater for hair and make-up, and it's possible to see mirrors framed with glowing bulbs, like in *The Muppets*. Above the mirrors are photos of the central characters fully made up, reminding the hairdresser/make-up artist that such and such character needs a blue Mohican, or a wart with two sprouting hairs. Wooden stands support a range of wigs, but where are the coloured foam noses? Perhaps these are kept nearby, in a drawer.

On one of the two west lawns, a huge marquee has been set up. Its designated sign reads: BACKGROUND CAST WARDROBE. A sudden procession of people emerge, all dressed in a range of modern attire. They are directed to line up along the kerb of the grass, 'shoulder to shoulder' for a costume check. While this is happening, an expensive chauffeur-driven car pulls up outside the home of the Grand Duchess Alexandra of Oxford. A rear door is opened for an older woman in sunglasses, who I recognize as Joan Collins. She is quickly bustled away into her mobile palace quarters. Why the sunglasses? Her car has tinted windows, as does her private cabin, and it is very, very cloudy.

At literary festivals, authors tend to muck in together in the Green Room, despite being the least sociable people in the entire world. But these gregarious acting types, these 'flames of society', supposedly need their 'own space'. At least, the 'stars' do. The royalty. They have their own carriages, their own private abodes, while the 'background' cast must get into line by the lawn. It would be nice to discuss this with the newly arrived Grand Duchess. Like that chap who broke into the Queen's bedroom at Buckingham Palace, finding her dressed for bed in her Liberty nightie. He didn't want jewels, or crowns and sceptres. Just a friendly chat. Same here. And maybe a nice drop of port, or a gin-mixed Dubonnet wine with a slice of lemon.

Kevin doesn't appear to have moved in my absence, or accomplished anything. He's impressed that I've written a novel. But he seems even more impressed that it's for sale on Amazon.

Kevin: Wow.
FP: Seriously? They stole their name from a rainforest, Kevin. Didn't that set your alarm bells ringing from the off?
Kevin: But… they must sell lots of your books, right?
FP: To be honest Kevin, all they do is make my publishers very angry. And my publishers are nice, reasonable people. They're like

those little rainforest creatures with monkey tails, and really massive eyes.

Kevin: Tarsiers?

FP: Possibly. Are Tarsiers monkey-like with really massive eyes?

Kevin: Yeah, kind of.

FP: Let's say they are. Well, now imagine those Tarsiers, but really angry ones. Imagine those massive eyes are red...

Kevin: Like *Gremlins*?

FP: [*Sigh.*] It always has to come back to Hollywood with you film lot, doesn't it?

Although very cloudy, Kevin is wearing sunglasses too.

Kevin: Has your book been made into a film?

FP: Not yet. Here, maybe you lot could shoot it now, off the back of this TV thing? Since so many of you are just standing around, idly chattering...

Kevin: Eh?

It's supposed to be a proper cash cow, selling the film rights for your book. Unfortunately, my previous book isn't particularly suitable as a blockbuster, given it's essentially a guidebook, for writer-types. Yawn! Mind you, there is a scene involving a giant squid, which is singing. Perhaps I could extend that bit and lose some of those boring Booker Prize winners. My new campus novel, by contrast, has 'IMAX' written all over it. Not only is it a royal fairy tale, set on the riverside grounds of a former palace, but it also involves whales and ships, and a nuclear reactor, and a massive brick power station, with four chimneys. Fable and romance, together with an underlying hint of wanton destruction and ultra-violence. Plus, for good measure, maybe I'll throw in some of that campus/fraternity element, like in *Porkies*. It's even set on a film location, for heaven's sake. Hello?

The Greenwich University environs, Dr Alex informs me, are one of the most popular filming locations in Britain. As a result, the Old Royal Naval College also offers a guided film location walk, shining a light on the grounds as a set.

It's the same drill as before, meeting in the Visitor Centre, but this time we're a crowd. Today's big stars, it seems, are more of a draw than old buildings, monarchs, and elderly sailors without limbs.

The royal family are well represented on celluloid, and it's amazing how much of this has been captured on these grounds. As well as *The Royals*, the Oscar-winning *The King's Speech* was filmed here, along with *The Madness of King George*, *The Young Victoria*, and *The Duchess*. According to our male guide, the actual Queen has been hosted here too. In 2012, Queen Elizabeth II visited the college grounds as part of an official Royal Borough ceremony. Her visit coincided with the late running of the *Les Misérables* film shoot, which only finished up the day before. Given its cast of hundreds, and shedloads of heavy film equipment, the pristine lawns were wrecked, reduced to mud. To overcome this eyesore at the eleventh hour, it was decided not to re-lay fresh grass for Her Majesty's pleasure, but to spray-paint the mucky ground green.

FP: What? Spray-paint the mud? Is that some sort of sick joke?
Tour Guide: I kid you not. This actually happened.

They say the Queen is constantly surrounded by the smell of fresh paint. In this case, it seems to have taken the form of toxic aerosol fumes. Better that, it was supposed, than expose our Queen to the sight of filthy, dirty mud. Mud, like unpainted wood, is a product of the real world, and therefore must be hidden from the royal establishment, especially its leader. As a former gardener, my tolerance and affinity for mud is higher, putting me at a great remove from Her Majesty. As a writer, this distance extends further, via chasms of wealth.

After the College lawns were turned to sludge by the *Les Misérables* crew, it appears an opportunity was missed to turn the earth over and plant some potatoes. Another chance went begging following the production of *Thor: The Dark World*. Our tour guide shows us some stills from that film, one of which depicts a low-flying alien spaceship firing a laser beam at Earth. Initially, this deathly ray is striking the Thames, churning up the water just before the college entrance. But it then proceeds across the campus itself, targeting the lawns between Queen Anne and King Charles, blasting up grass and soil, and creating a cavernous trench.

FP: Too deep perhaps for potatoes. But filled in to a certain depth, that could have been a handy furrow for a stretch of turnips.
Tour Guide: Pardon me?

Philip Pullman's book *The Golden Compass* was also filmed, in part, here at the Old Royal Naval College. Starring Nicole Kidman, the film turned the college into the headquarters of the Magisterium, a shadowy religious organization attempting to control the world. With the addition of computer-generated effects, elaborate extensions were added to Wren's existing facades. Although the tour guide, upon being pressed, doesn't think they addressed his significant interior errors.

Recently Philip Pullman resigned as patron of the Oxford Literary Festival, in protest at the author attendees not being paid. Despite the huge corporate sponsors, and the fact that everyone else involved was receiving a fee, the authors, at the literary festival, were not. As Philip Pullman said, enough's enough. The Greenwich Book Festival intends to pay their author attendees, apart from the ones I've invited, who, very probably, won't attend.

Philip Pullman didn't write my surname as part of his dedication, even though I asked him to. This, I suppose, is because he considers me a very good friend, on first-name basis, without any need for formalities.

FP: It must be my turn to come round to yours for dinner.
Philip Pullman: I beg your pardon?

For film freaks, the stone steps between the domes are a must-stop on the pilgrimage. As well as being the resting place for the death ray in *Thor*, the climatic barricade scene in *Les Misérables* was also set here. A short distance away, on the covered balustrade of Queen Mary, Javert, or Russell Crowe, rode high on horseback. Our guide shows us a photo of Jack Black from the film *Gulliver's Travels*, in which the college has become Lilliput and Jack Black towers over the twin domes and steps beneath. A funeral procession passed before these steps for the James Bond film *Skyfall*, although it was cut from the final film. They did use a scene shot in the undercroft however, in which Judy Dench and Daniel Craig inspect a large array of flag-draped coffins, following the blowing up of MI6.

FP: Have any tidal waves been filmed at the college? Or scenes of nuclear fallout?
Tour Guide: Not to my knowledge, no...
FP: Ha, ha! Just you wait! Watch this space, my friends!

Another popular filming location at the college is the Painted Hall. Today, in preparation for filming *The Royals*, all the dining tables and chairs have been moved outside, while the giant metallic grasshopper has been dissected and laid in piles. The hall is still open to the public, and devoid of furniture and scaffolding, it's even more epic in scale. Stepping into its great expanse, I feel like a sheep released into a fresh paddock of grass. Johnny Depp was dragged through here in *Pirates of the Caribbean*, and Clark Gable, together with Ingrid Bergman, danced on these black and white tiles in the 1958 film *Indiscreet*. Today they retain their polished shine, perfect for a big slippy slide.

As well as sightseers, the hall is also occupied by scruffy film types, who shuffle about with colour-coded walkie-talkies protruding from back pockets. While it's possible to avoid these people on my run-up, the element of control is lost once my slide has commenced. Wandering souls who stray into my path must be cautioned.

FP: Coming through!

There are no NO RUNNING signs, but this new rule is introduced verbally for my benefit by one of the regular guides. I feign a loss of hearing, but I'm eventually rounded up and herded from the paddock by a team of Painted Hall sheepdogs. The tour group, of which I was a part, have either departed already, or remain behind, ashamed.

A Warner Brothers truck is parked on College Way, alongside a cluster of film lights and black sturdy stands. A man wearing mirrored sunglasses sits on the steps alongside, guarding the goods. Like most CREW members, he's an older chap with long hair and earrings. Like me, he's tattooed, although his examples are well worn, as opposed to straight-off-the-shelf, unscuffed specimens.

FP: Warner Brothers? Is that who you work for?
Man: Yeah.
FP: Wow. What are they like in real life?

Man: Who?

FP: Bugs Bunny and Daffy Duck? The Roadrunner? That round-faced guy with the gun?

Man:

FP: Are you filming here too? Don't tell me… *Tom and Jerry*? In the Painted Hall? Sliding around? Hello?

Man:

FP: Have you fallen asleep?

Man:

FP: I can't tell.

August rolls around. With just five months left of my tenure, there's still so much to do. It would be sensible to start taking notes around the campus, to refer to later, when I'm moved along. Instead of stomping the beat by foot, however, notebook in hand like a laughing policeman, I decide to get some of those films out, the Greenwich ones, from the university library. Ade, one of the Creative Writing lecturers, happens to be visiting also.

Ade: Hi, Francis. What's that you've got there?

FP: These? They're just, y'know, some Russian and French arthouse films, with, y'know, subtitles.

Ade: '*Thor*'? I thought he was Nordic.

FP: Um. This is the other one. The Soviet one. The serious, high-brow one. From the Communist Bloc.

Ade: If you say so. And *Les Misérables*. That'll be…

FP: … the French version, right, right.

When you're a writer, inspiration is everywhere. Even in the words of big-muscled Nordic warriors. Although, I must say, I was expecting a bit more of Greenwich from *The Dark World*. The movie runs for one hour and fifty-two minutes, and Greenwich only features for a matter of seconds. Still, it's an impressive scene, with aliens and everything. George II's statue was directly in the firing line. No wonder his face has melted. Seeing my familiar surroundings being wantonly destroyed by laser firepower from another planet was slightly unnerving. Although, at the end of those fast-moving seconds, having seen the manicured grounds of this Royal Heritage site being ripped apart in front of my eyes, well, I must admit, it didn't half make me laugh.

To Francis Phry

Linton Kwesi Johnson

Inglan is a bitch

RACE TODAY PUBLICATIONS

In 1977, Linton Kwesi Johnson was a writer in residence too, but not just of a university. He was WIR for the entire London Borough of Lambeth. All 26.82 km² of it. What a dreamboat job. You could spend all day in a Lambeth pub, or move between various Lambeth pubs, and you'd always be in residence.

Official: Francis? Where are you?
FP: [*Sound of bottles clinking, laughing, shouting.*] Where am I? I'm in residence!

When his tenure was up, Linton Kwesi Johnson found himself unemployed. But rather than fading from view, he went on to very big things. Today he's the only living poet in the Penguin Classics series. He's received a Golden PEN award, and he's even been nominated for a Grammy. These are things I should be aspiring to also, post Greenwich. Especially the Grammy Award.

FP: Boom Shakalaka!

Tonight Linton Kwesi Johnson is part of an ensemble in conversation at Waterstones Piccadilly, including Mervyn Morris, the Poet Laureate of Jamaica. As well as chatting, the authors are reading from their work, and other people's. LKJ's hat is the colour of wet sand and his trousers are the colour of dry sand. He reads his poem 'Mi

Revalueshanary Fren', and also from the work of Martin Carter, who he rates as his favourite revolutionary poet. At one point, he removes his glasses, to see better.

Afterwards there's a signing. Two writers in residence, past and present, coming together to talk shop. It's a great photo opportunity, but no one spots the significance of the occasion. Or, perhaps like me, they haven't worked out how to use the camera function on their mobile phone.

FP: Is the Borough of Lambeth a Royal Borough?

Linton Kwesi Johnson: No, it isn't a Royal Borough.

FP: I'm currently based in the Royal Borough of Greenwich, but I'm not sure what the Royal part actually adds. There's still homeless people, with dogs, by the cashpoints. And a busy Wetherspoons pub, and a tanning shop which charges 70p a minute. Same as the Borough of Camden, my old stomping ground. That wasn't a Royal Borough either. But it did have its names printed on the rubbish bins. Once I put a Borough of Camden bin over my head and pretended to be Ned Kelly. Bloody stink!

As well as writing five collections of poetry, Linton Kwesi Johnson has recorded thirteen studio albums, plus an additional five compilations, in which his spoken word poetry is put over a thumping dub bassline.

FP: I wrote a song once.

Linton Kwesi Johnson: Oh yeah?

FP: Yes. It was inspired by a man I saw who was walking down a street with a little girl, presumably his daughter. She was trying to talk to him, but he was wearing headphones and wasn't even looking at her.

Linton Kwesi Johnson: Serious?

FP: Yes. My song was written in the hope that the girl's dad might one day listen to it in his headphones while out walking with his daughter.

Linton Kwesi Johnson: Ah. What was your song called?

FP: 'Down Here, You Dickhead'.

Linton Kwesi Johnson is going to get back to me about the festival dates, although I forgot to give him my email, or my number, or the festival dates.

There's an obstruction on the Thames Path. A uniformed man, together with a section of secure metal fencing, is blocking my thoroughfare.

Uniformed Man: The pathway's closed, I'm afraid. You'll need to go around there, through the Old Naval College grounds.

FP: What? You can't stop me walking along a public walkway.

Uniformed Man: I can actually.

FP: Yeah? You and who's army?

Uniformed Man: Ah, Her Majesty's Royal Navy.

FP: Righto. Fair enough. That should suffice.

The passage is barricaded due to the arrival of a massive navy ship. The HMS *Defender* has docked just past the *Cutty Sark*, towards Deptford, and they're using this section of the pathway as a secure embarkation point. Why do they need their own private landing base, away from the passenger jetties? Perhaps they're worried the public will point and laugh at their ridiculously flared trousers.

Naval ships used to be designed with aerodynamics and stealth in mind. But the HMS *Defender* is nothing short of flamboyant. Its mast centrepiece, with a blimmin' great ball on top, is like a huge, protruding perfume bottle. The Village People wrote a song about the navy, and now this song has manifested itself as a warship.

On board, I'm sure, it's hard as nails. I'm going to find out. Because they're opening it up to the public this weekend and I've snared one of the very last tickets. Obviously, I feel bad, taking the place of someone who might actually have a keen and genuine interest in naval ships. But since I still have a few months left in this rich maritime area, it's the sort of experience I ought to soak up. I also think, with a few drinks under my belt, it might just be a right laugh.

Being a navy event, there are loads of rules to follow. You need a valid form of photographic identity for a start. If you deface your ticket, this will invalidate it. Before leaving the jetty, you must pass through a security screening and have your bags searched. You can't smoke, you can't bring guide dogs or wheelchairs. You're not allowed any guns, firearms or other devices that discharge projectiles. Crossbows and arrows are out, as are harpoon guns, slingshots and catapults. Ice picks? No. Cleavers? Not allowed! Martial arts equipment is banned, as are blowtorches, crowbars, nail guns, baseball bats, fireworks and dynamite.

But worse is to come. As I pass through the x-ray machine, it bleeps. A naval officer leads me to one side.

Officer: Can you empty your side pocket please, sir?

FP: It's just rum. A very seaworthy drink, as you'll appreciate. Yo, ho-ho!

Officer: I'm afraid you can't take that on board, sir.

FP: What?

Officer: We'll keep it here for you, and you can collect it upon your return.

FP: You're joking! There's a bar on board though, right? Surely?

Our intermediary journey up the river, on a small vessel called the *Sarah Kathleen*, takes the best part of three minutes. In front of us, the looming warship is tautly strapped on all sides, its ropes affixed to substantial yellow weighted buoys. It's like Gulliver, captured by those wee Lilliputians. Our small boat catches the wake of a passing ferry, resulting in some minor chop. An elderly couple look at each other hesitantly. I take pains to reassure them.

FP: Don't worry. At least we're not miles off the Sicilian coast. If we get tipped into the drink, we won't exactly be stranded in the middle of the ocean, half dead, with all our possessions in the entire world. Because look, there's a blimmin' great naval ship, right there. That'll save us. Or, worst case scenario, we swim that very small stretch back to shore. To that Nandos, just there...

There is a Nandos chicken restaurant on the prominent riverside spot of the central Greenwich square. It stands between the free-flowing river water and the grounded *Cutty Sark*, preventing the great ship's escape. Recently, an American family approached me on that square, for directions.

American Dad: We're looking for a chicken restaurant called... Nandos?

I sighed, loudly.

FP: Forget Nandos. Look at *that*. It's a hugely significant, historical tea clipper ship, from 1869. Look at it, it's right there.
American Dad: Yes, we saw it.
FP: Look again! Look at those masts, those sails, that rigging...

American Dad: Right.

FP: Rigging! There's a song about that, an English song. Have you heard it?

The American Dad shook his head.

FP: It's by an English band called the Sex Pistols. I won't sing it to you because there are children present. But the basic gist is that the sailors are friggin in the riggin...

The American Mum gathered up her children.

American Mum: Let's go.

We arrive safely alongside HMS *Defender* at a small floating jetty. A lowered staircase provides able-bodied access to the starboard. On deck, we meet our guide, First Officer Richard someone.

My boots aren't as shiny as First Officer Richard's, but at least I've put them to good use. What's the point of wearing boots on a ship? It's like driving an SUV in the city. There are no rocks or earth aboard a ship. No tree trunks, or buried bones. Dead people are simply chucked over the side. They should be wearing flip-flops, these navy people. Or slippers. Equally out of place are the flared trousers. The Village People were wearing those in the 1970s. Coolness certainly doesn't come into it for these navy folk. But to be fair, nor should it. Coolness is for people without direction in life. Sailors and writers are above all that. It's a common point we both share. We might lack a hip and trendy style, but at least we can see the bigger, more important picture. Of course, that doesn't mean us writers have to dress like total geeks.

Also prowling the deck are some tough guys with high-powered machine guns. They're dressed in more fashionable camouflage fatigues. I make plain the distinction between them and their comrades.

FP: *You* don't look like a dick.
Machine Gun Guy: What did you say?

There's no rolling, like you'd expect on a ship. We are only on the Thames. It's not the high seas. Still, there is actual water sloshing about beneath, so I suppose they have some sort of high-tech shock-absorber, stabilizer thing. Because you don't want navy folk throwing up all over the place when they're trying to aim missiles at people. You don't want sick on those polished shoes and pressed trousers, or on that swabbed deck. It might even threaten the grey camouflaged exterior, if there's bits of orange in it. Speaking of which, where's the bar? Maybe it's one of those swim-up jobs.

HMS *Defender*, First Officer Richard informs us, is a state-of-the-art Type 45 destroyer. Its mission is to shield the Fleet from air attack. It can control and coordinate multiple missiles in the air at once. He hasn't asked for questions yet, but I have one.

FP: Is it true this ship is owned by Cher?

There are some titters amongst the group. Why?

First Officer Richard: No, even a big pop star couldn't afford this.
FP: So who does own it?
First Officer Richard: Well, you do. The British taxpayer.
FP: You're having a laugh. Why couldn't we have a cheaper, boring one? Instead of this Liberace-themed model?
First Officer Richard: Liberace?

FP: Yes. Also, what does 'loaded to the gunwales' mean?

First Officer Richard: Well, the nautical term refers to when a ship is loaded right up to the rails with cargo. Fully loaded, in other words.

FP: Weird. What about 'three sheets to the wind'?

First Officer Richard: That relates to a three-masted ship. When the sheets of the three lower courses are loose, it causes the ship to meander aimlessly downwind.

FP: Really? So why do they call me those things down the pub?

First Officer Richard: The term 'loose cannon' comes from the threat of an actual loose cannon, weighing thousands of pounds, on board a ship, which could potentially crush the crew and endanger the seaworthiness of the entire vessel.

FP: Sorry, what? Did someone ask that question? Who asked that question…?

For a top secret national security defensive attack machine, it's all a bit lax. They've let me on for a start. Although navigating the lowered staircase, I wouldn't trust myself behind the wheel. Watch out, Millennium Dome! First Officer Richard is obviously using a fake name, but he hasn't covered himself up to his eyes, like proper fighting types. Everything he says I take with a massive pinch of salt. When he points out the door to the 'gymnasium', it's clearly a room filled with atomic bombs, all lined up like ten-pin bowling balls. As a published author, I'm very savvy to all that PR spin. When my book was launched, the press release called it 'A meditation on loneliness'. Do me a favour! According to First Officer Richard, the Sea Viper air-defence system is for intercepting supersonic enemy attacks. Yeah right! Producing my phone, I write a text and send it to myself. The text reads: 'Hello, First Officer "Richard". Stop reading my messages. I wasn't born yesterday.'

Apparently, when out at sea, First Officer Richard remains connected to the world via social media. As if!

FP: What updates could *you* possibly offer? 'Put on the same trousers this morning, the same shirt, the same hat, the same shoes. Polished my shoes to buggery. Looked out the porthole. It's the sea again. Sea, sea, bloody sea.' Look, you don't need to lie to me, First Officer Richard. I'm not on Facebook either, or Twitter. It's a load of cobblers, right? Just people yabbering on about themselves... 'Oh, I'm on a train! Now I'm walking! I'm wearing shoes!' Listen captain, you might live a boring, regimented life, but so do they [*gesturing*]. The only difference is, you don't whang on about it.

First Officer Richard and the un-enlisted look at their shoes, polished or otherwise, avoiding my gaze.

FP: Look, I really need the Gents. The john? The latrine? The lavatory? The water closet? The powder room? What is it you sailor guys call it...?

As I'm escorted back up the secured jetty, I pass a navy careers tent. It's right next to the university. Unbelievable. They're trying to lure in our brilliant scholars, tempt our progressive, peace-loving young folk. I wonder what the pay's like.

The Navy slogan is 'Life Without Limits'. That sounds just like me, I tell the naval careers person.

FP: It's uncanny. That's my life all over. Look, an anchor tattoo.
Naval PR Person: So you're interested in a naval career?
FP: Possibly. I'm a writer, but it's treacherous work. And it pays terribly. My plan is to write a campus novel that gets turned into

a blockbuster movie and pays out loads of cash. But if that all goes tits up, then yes, I might have to sign up with you badly dressed seafarers.

Naval PR Person: Well, we can certainly offer a stable, secure income. There are very good advancement prospects. And a secure pension.

FP: Who pays for all that? Her Majesty?

Naval PR Person: No, no. We're allocated money from the government. From the Defence budget.

FP: The taxpayer, huh? Well maybe if you didn't spend so much on shoe polish and haircuts… if you actually let your hair grow a bit, there'd be some money left in the pot for housing… and hospitals…

Naval PR Person: Hmm, I… don't know…

FP: I wish authors were looked after by the state, with secure, protected incomes. But our job isn't to be compliant, you see, to follow orders. It's not up to us to serve the government, to protect their interests. It's our job to attack them! Blam, blam! That's why the government keeps us poor, you see. That's why they close down our libraries and curb our speech. That's why we don't get invited to Downing Street, like… Oasis! Because, Jeffrey Archer aside, we're not luvvy-duvvy with politicians. We don't do press-ups, and we refuse to wear flared trousers!!

Naval PR Person: [*Pause.*] Are you okay there?

FP: Yes, sorry. Have you got my rum? Where's my rum, who's got my rum…?

UPSTAIRS
AT THE PARTY

LINDA GRANT

To Francis Plug
nice to meet you
in real life
but miss

Linda Grant

virago

Dr Alex and I are seated in our office, our respective brains processing huge conceptual thoughts and monumental ideas.

Dr Alex: Oh. Ruth Rendell's died.
FP: Yeah right!

All of a sudden we're side-winded by a colossal booming blast. Fearing attack from North Korea, or the early onset of a power station meltdown, I rush outside, only to witness tugboats spouting fountains of water, with further blasts of ship horn announcing the arrival of a mega-sized cruise ship. Instead of utter disaster, there's a celebratory air, as if the Queen had accomplished a special milestone, such as staying alive. The general public line the riverside path, waving out to the tourists on the monster ship, as if applauding them for consuming many buffet dinners, or lying beneath the sun like gingerbread men. The ship horns continue to blast, causing paper signs around the university to flutter. Printed on these signs are the words:

QUIET PLEASE EXAMS IN PROGRESS.

FP: [*To ship.*] Quiet please.

The absurdly large vessel manages to dwarf the riverside buildings it passes, before coming to rest slightly upstream, in the navy's parking space. Once secured, it continues to emit a loud generator-type hum. Upon my return to the office, Dr Alex recounts the concerns of unhappy Greenwich residents worried about the pollutants spewing out from these 'ocean-going towns', now mooring frequently along-side their village. Objectors claim that the larger ships can emit diesel fumes equivalent to 2,000 lorries a day, exceeding legal EU limits on deadly nitrogen oxide emissions. Even a very old power station runs cleaner than that. Perhaps, when Greenwich Power Station unleashes its massive gas/nuclear explosions, setting off the envisaged Thames tidal wave, it can be timed with a cruise liner visit, such as this one, sending it ploughing headlong into the towers of Canary Wharf.

Later, while treading the river path, I encounter a long line of people, older to elderly in age, who are queuing in front of the Trafalgar Tavern. Curious, I approach one of the old boys for the inside scoop.

FP: What gives? Are they dishing out free drinks?

The old boy is American, as are his companions, who chip in.

Old Boy: Well, they are to us.
Old Girl: We're with the cruise ship. It's part of the package.
FP: Really? You're all on that massive cruise liner thing?
Old Boy: Yes, sir.
FP: Wow. That's weird. In the adverts, the cruise ship passengers are always so much younger.
Old Girl: Well, we're young in spirit.
Old Boy: Yes, sir.
FP: Fair enough. You're trying to cash in on free drinks – I do that myself, now, at my age.

Another Old Boy: We're in London. It's worth celebrating!

FP: I guess. But what's with all those fountains and all that friggin' loud hooting? That was a bit much, yeah?

Old Boy: It's part of the naming ceremony, for the ship. There's a big bash tonight, with a fireworks display.

Another Old Boy: Yes, sir.

FP: Seriously? They're putting on a fireworks display? Because a cruise ship is getting a name?

Old Girl: It's a big ship!

FP: What's its name going to be? *Thunderbird 6*?

Chorus of Passengers: No!

FP: Can I make a suggestion?

Old Boy: Sure!

FP: What about *Boaty McBoat-Face*? How does that grab you?

Old Girl: Hmm. Not sure about that one...

FP: No? It's a very British name. It comes, in fact, from a very fine tradition of British boat naming. Although I wouldn't include the *QE2* in that tradition. Boring!

Old Girl: Thanks, but...

FP: Fine. Try not to make too much noise tonight. I have a book to write.

Old Boy: Oh, you're a writer?

FP: Yes, I am. Have you ever read *A Supposedly Fun Thing I'll Never Do Again* by David Foster Wallace, your countryman?

Old Boy: I have not.

FP: Let me write it down for you...

Old Boy: Okay, sure. Thank you.

FP: Do you have any spare drink vouchers?

Old Boy: No.

Another Old Boy: No.

FP: Who would I speak to about getting some of them free drinks vouchers?

They weren't kidding about the fireworks display. It is altogether epic, as if a New Year were being celebrated, for an entire culture, rather than just some stupid boat-naming stunt. Personally, I would have put that fireworks money into a gigantic bottle of champagne and smashed it against the side of that boat, with a proper big smash. SMASH! And the rest of it towards more of them drinks vouchers.

Boaty McBoat-Face doesn't stick around. It sets sail the very next day on the dot of high tide. Due to its abominably large size, so out of character with its surroundings, the general public are attracted in droves to bear witness to the spectacle.

FP: How does that monstrosity actually float?
Public: Hooray!

It is given a hero's send off, as if filled with brave soldiers on their way to war, to risk life and limb for their country. Yet beneath those blasting horns, there are, most likely, the gentle strains of light entertainment, accompanying the oiling and rubbing of wrinkly feet, and the squeezing of rich food between false teeth.

FP: Hooray! Hooray for you!

When I get back to my desk, I write a letter to the captain of *Boaty McBoat-Face*, asking if he/she requires the services of an on-board Writer in Residence.

As well as residencies, published authors can also earn money through literary prizes and awards. The Booker Prize is one of the biggest British examples, although my book clearly didn't get a look-in. A more niche award is the PG Wodehouse Prize for Comic Fiction. Elly and Sam, for some reason, have decided to put me in the running.

FP: But my novel is a serious work of high literary worth.
Elly: Um…
FP: Having said that, Ian McEwan won it one year, didn't he? So perhaps the 'comic' element is very, very broad.

The winner gets a case of champagne, so I suppose it's worth a shot. Another literary prize, exclusively for women, is the Baileys, formerly known as the Orange Prize. Campus novelist Linda Grant has won it once, and now she's up for it again. Hoping to convince this prize-winning campus novelist to visit *my* campus, I head to Sloane Square for the Baileys Prize Shortlist Readings.

The interior of Cadogan Hall, an early twentieth-century concert hall venue, could easily pass for a cruise ship concourse. Its curving roof struts, balcony rails, and art deco lighting would fit right in at sea, together with resident band, the Royal Philharmonic Orchestra, doling out the tunes at sunset. In Linda Grant's campus novel *Upstairs at the Party*, Adele, the central character, says: 'Like all art deco buildings, it reminded me of a cruise ship.' Freda in Beryl Bainbridge's *The Bottle Factory Outing* also likens architecture to ships: 'the block of flats, moored in concrete like an ocean liner… the rigging of the television aerials.' In Greenwich, there's plenty of real ships to contend with, although I tend to see the *Cutty Sark* as a bottle of whisky.

While at university, Adele misses her home port of Liverpool: 'there had always been a ship to sail away on when life became too constricting.' That's a benefit of living in Greenwich too. It's nice to think, if it all goes wrong, I can escape by sea. According to Ishmael, ports are too safe. For true adventure, one needs to cast off. However, he also believes, despite man's vast academic and scientific knowledge, that the sea will insult and murder him. What a dilemma!

The prize readings are sponsored by an alcohol brand, but they don't come with a free bar, or even a complimentary drink. My pricey pint comes in a plastic glass, even though I'm remaining inside, on the carpet. They'll have lids on them next, with emergency whistles, for attracting attention.

Seven overly plush chairs are arranged on stage, bookended by two large displays of traditional, boring flowers. It may be a Women's Fiction award, but it's not exactly Pussy Riot. Even the alcohol sponsor is sweet and prissy. Why don't they use a chainsaw brand, like Stihl?

In her opening address, prize founder Kate Mosse mentions there 'are even one or two men here'. That's about the size of it. I've counted five of us, one of who's behind the sound desk, and another who's an editor, replacing an absent author on stage. As a regular author event attendee however, I'm used to it. Most literary crowds are dominated by women, and because women are statistically shorter than men, as a short man I get to see more. Although sometimes, with all that perfume, it doesn't half pong.

Linda Grant is scheduled to read third, and while she waits she appears to examine the hall, as if thinking: 'Bloody hell. I'm on a ship.' Her water glass is reached for often, although only for the most minuscule of sips. A glass can be quite reassuring, I find, giving one confidence and comfort, even when it's made of plastic and you're surrounded by members of a completely different gender.

Upstairs at the Party is set in a Yorkshire university in the 1970s. Adele sees it as 'a tiny oasis of unreality', a 'playpen of student ideas'. The students are on full grants (not Linda Grants), with free medical care, and nothing to revolt against. The dishevelled lecturers resemble janitors, and if you invite the Head of English to your birthday party, he actually shows up. Some forty years later, as an older woman, Adele reflects back on those days, clocking the resentment of a younger generation against her era with its 'way of life suited to Renaissance philosopher kings'. At least modern students have access to counselling and support services, which Adele's era lacked. The Greenwich Student Union posters attest to those services today, and with good reason. Given all the pressures they're under, it's no wonder many Greenwich Creative Writing students have immersed themselves in the fantasy genre. It makes all the sense in the world.

The stage flowers, I now realize, are funereal. They are symbols of sympathy, usually to be found bookending an altar, in a crematorium chapel. I imagine them bobbing on the surface of the sea as Cadogan Hall slowly goes under, the steadfast, unflinching authors talking on stage until the very end.

At the event's conclusion, I visit the loos and give my hands a thorough wash. Even so, I'm right near the front of the signing queue. This is because there were no queues in the Gents, and, in fact, no other gents at all.

Linda Grant: Francis Plug?

FP: Yes. Not Dora Dickie.

Linda Grant: No. I recognize your name from somewhere. Are you an author?

FP: Yes! Ha, ha! Have you read my work?

Linda Grant: No, I haven't. Perhaps we're friends on Twitter?

FP: I really don't think so.

Linda Grant: Ah. Well, nice to meet you for real.

FP: Yes, I'm real. For real.

Linda Grant: Okay.

FP: I really liked that bit in *Upstairs at the Party* when Gillian's crucifix Jesus is bouncing on her bosoms, as if on a trampoline.

Linda Grant: Good. I'm glad you...

FP: Which *Wind in the Willows* character would you be?

Linda Grant: Which *Wind in the Willows* character would I be? Oh. Do you know Sea-Going Rat? He has a minor role. Mainly him, with a bit of Mole. Definitely not Badger.

FP: A sea-going rat? Of course! You and me both. I'm hoping to be the resident writer on the *Boaty McBoat-Face* cruise liner. Maybe you could be too. We could be like Gilbert and George, on the high seas.

Linda Grant: Um...

FP: Here, maybe we could set sail straight after your event, in a couple of months, at the Greenwich Book Festival...

While loitering around Sloane Square, puffing on a Players No. 6, a message arrives from Elly. I didn't win the PG Wodehouse Prize, or even make the list. I call her back.

FP: So, who bagged my champagne?

Elly: It was Alexander McCall Smith.

FP: *Dr* Alexander McCall Smith? You have *got* to be shitting me.

Elly: Never mind, you...

FP: He can't win champagne! He thinks alcohol is poison!

In his co-authored book, *All About Drinking*, Dr Alexander McCall Smith writes:

> *If you do drink, always remember that alcohol can be very dangerous. Drink only a small amount, and you will be all right. Never drink too much as*

you may make a fool of yourself and you may cause harm to yourself and
to others.

This from a man who's just bagged a case of the stuff! Because, apparently, he's a right laugh!

Boarding the number 360 bus to Elephant and Castle, I ask a special favour of the driver, befitting my troubled state.

FP: Excuse me. When you get a bit of speed up, would you mind pulling a 360, in the 360? Go on…

Richard Russo

STRAIGHT MAN

To Francis Plug —

Richard Russo

V

VINTAGE

Although not accomplished at winning awards, I'm quite adept at attending their ceremonies. As respected publishers, Sam and Elly have been invited to the Booker Prize shortlist party. Elly, however, is unable to attend. After much pleading and friendly coercion, Sam finally agrees to take me as his date. Apparently, the drinks at this do *are* free.

FP: Yes, so I've been invited to the Booker Prize shortlist party.
Dr Alex: You? Really? Are you sure it's an invite and not a bill for damages?

Producing the actual invite, I casually extend it to Dr Alex.

Dr Alex: Well, well.
FP: I don't suppose you could mention this, in passing, to Dr Zoë? And to the rest of the department, in an all-staff email, including the Chancellor, and all of the students...?

Dr Alex, it turns out, has just had a novel of his own published. It's doing very well by all accounts, with positive reviews in the *Literary Review*, the *Guardian*, and the *Irish Times*. I suppose I should be pleased for him, but it's come as a bit of a shock.

FP: What's this? A published novel? Ha, ha! I thought *I* was the writer around here. Ha, ha! What gives?

Dr Alex: It's my second novel, actually. I thought you knew. A lot of the department have published works.

FP: Have they? Good for them. No one told me. Ha, ha.

Dr Alex: How's your new one coming along?

FP: Wow. It's really something else this new one. Yes sir. It's hot. Damn hot.

Dr Alex: Good to hear. Is it still called *Moby Dick*?

FP: *Moby Dick*? No, no. No, the current working title is… *Dirty Dancer*.

Dr Alex: *Dirty Dancer*?

FP: Yes sir. It's *damn* hot.

Dr Alex: Well… good. I don't suppose you've had any joy roping in authors for the festival?

FP: Um, well… interesting you should ask that. Do you know of Dr Seuss? He's a popular author, and also, supposedly, a doctor. But, like yourself, he appears to have no justification for this title…

While my attempts to attract authors have been nothing short of a disaster, it hasn't been an unmitigated one. It turns out our festival committee have connections in publishing and the media, and while I've been tripping over my tongue and grovelling on all fours, they've been steadily accruing talent and building up the programme.

Dr Alex: So don't worry. It's not all on your shoulders.

FP: Thank frick for that. Because weirdly, all my close author friends have chosen that particular weekend to wash their hair.

While relieved for the festival's sake, it doesn't get *me* off the hook. The staff all think I'm rounding up the A-listers. The students too. If I end up empty-handed, I'll be exposed as a total sham. Of course, there's always Richard Russo. Oh yes. Richard Russo. He'll be keen as biscuits for the Greenwich Book Fair. Absolutely. It's beyond question. Phew.

As well as the shortlist party, Pulitzer Prize-winning campus novelist Richard Russo is also on my calendar. *Straight Man* contains many insights into broad academic life, specifically in the humanities and English departments. Like many other campus novels, it features academics bringing shame upon themselves, something I've been at pains to steer clear of myself. *Straight Man* is set in West Central Pennsylvania University, in a small town called Railton. William Henry Devereaux Jr is a forty-nine-year-old tenured senior professor and chair of department. He's been at the same university for over twenty years and has a very nice house in the hills. When he wets himself in his office, it runs down one leg, soaking a sock and a shoe. Subsequent visitors to his office equate this smell with cats.

As well as weeing in non-designated areas, we also share confusing building layouts. Their social sciences building sounds remarkably similar to our King William labyrinth.

A series of pods, it's all zigzagging corridors and abrupt mezzanines that make it impossible to walk from one end of the building to another. At one point, if you're on the first floor, either you have to go up two floors, over, and down again or you have to go outside the building and then in again in order to arrive at an office you can see from where you're standing.

Yep. Sounds just like one of Wren's.

American universities probably don't name their buildings after kings, unless, perhaps, it's the Lion King. American princesses live in frozen worlds and tend to sing the same song over and over again. English princesses don't talk to snowmen. They sunbathe topless and get divorced and die in car crashes. In the popularity stakes, I'd say it's even-stevens.

Richard Russo's event is at Waterstones' Tottenham Court Road branch. The basement has an exposed concrete ceiling, exposed ventilation pipes, and now an exposed public author. Things haven't even kicked off yet, and already he's ringed by keen admirers and industry insiders. A café-bar provides the impetus for the social interaction, or in Richard Russo's case, the ambush. A reasonable £5 ticket price also includes a complimentary beer or wine. My beer comes in a bottle, and on its label is an ad for Richard Russo's new book. Richard Russo has a beer too, with a label mentioning himself. Chances are he's not even listening to all those people. He's thinking, I'm on a beer bottle. Job done.

Richard Russo has also found cinematic success. Tonight, before his talk, there's to be a screening of *Nobody's Fool*, the film of his 1993 book. A large screen has been pulled down in readiness, obscuring the non-fiction shelves behind. Not wanting to add to the scrum around him, I take a seat in the arranged chairs, knocking back a Richard Russo.

Richard Russo is seated in the front row, directly in front of my chair. Fortunately, like me, he's a short fellow. If we were watching a Paul Auster film, I'd be watching nothing but back. The back of Richard Russo's neck is noticeably red, in a rustic, Mediterranean shade. His black leather jacket is draped over his chair, and despite leaning on it, his pockets are loose at the sides. I wonder what Pulitzer Prize winners have in their pockets? Magic beans, perhaps? Marmalade sandwiches?

The film of Richard Russo's novel stars Paul Newman, Melanie Griffith and Bruce Willis. In the opening credits it reads: *Based on the novel by Richard Russo.*

FP: Yay! [*Clapping vigorously.*]

As films go, it's not seat-of-the-pants. Although there is a scene where Paul Newman's character's landlady has to go to hospital. The hospital is called Saint Francis hospital.

FP: Yay! [*Clapping vigorously.*]

Richard Russo's face has a silver coating of stubble. Although short, he's a stockier man than me, with larger hands to boot. After the film screening, there's a talk. Richard Russo has put his leather jacket back on, not because the temperature has dropped, but as protection, against his crowd. He and interviewer Stuart Evers are sitting on high barstool-like chairs, which, in a stage context, is like being stuck on a flagpole.

Richard Russo attended Arizona University as a student, which was larger than the upstate New York town he came from. Later he would teach at Southern Illinois University Carbondale, and then Colby College, encountering much material for *Straight Man*. His eyes have a constant squint, as if he were looking at the world through shuttered eyelids. As if we, his view, were too overpowering. Maybe this is something he's evolved as an author, a shield of sorts, to combat the limelight. When out of the general literary world, I bet his eyes are much wider. There's bound to be photos on the Internet of Richard Russo, in his former life, with wide, all-seeing eyes. Before his fame, before they receded and constricted like firing slots in a World War II bunker. Earlier, standing within that ring of people, I bet his eyes were closed completely.

Because of my second row seat, I'm first up in the signing queue. Richard Russo remains high in his barstool perch. Perhaps he likes to pretend he's in a bar, to make his author events somehow bearable. Maybe that's *his* barstool, which he ships around the world. Perhaps it also aids his teaching duties, allowing him to lecture his classes as if addressing a bar room. I must text Elly and Sam, with urgency.

Need barstool for author events and lectures. With footrest. Please action.

Richard Russo is searching through the pockets of his jacket.

Richard Russo: This is embarrassing. I can't find my pen.
FP: Oh dear. Here, use mine.
Richard Russo: Thank you. Wow. This pen is identical to mine.
FP: [*Nervous laugh.*] Really? What are the chances?

It's good that Sam is accompanying me to the Booker Prize do. At least I'll know *someone*. But he's also my publisher, so I'll have to keep my nose clean. I'll have to keep well away from the fire extinguishers, for instance. The party is taking place in the Serpentine Gallery's exhibition area in Hyde Park. Whenever I think of the Serpentine, I think of that song 'British People in Hot Weather' by the Fall. There's a bit where Mark E. Smith says the word 'Serpentine' then laughs, then repeats the word, making a cat-like growl. He is referring, I believe, to the Serpentine lake or lido, also in Hyde Park, which is popular with swimmers in the summer months. But I think it's possible for his cat-like growl to encompass the Serpentine Gallery, and the exhibition area outside, and this specific Booker Prize event also.

Sam and I have arranged to meet at the Queen's Arms pub beforehand, which is somewhere near the Royal Albert Hall, where my bus driver drops me off.

FP: Don't wait for me, okay?
Bus Driver: Eh?

Finding the pub isn't simple because my phone isn't quite as smart as it might like to think it is. The Queen's Arms is on some back street mews, but apparently not the one called Hyde Park Gate. According to a blue plaque, Winston Churchill lived and died on this short, exclusive street. These days it's home to super-expensive black cars with blacked-out windows and their drivers who stand round talking, except when I walk past, waving out.

FP: Say, any of you fellas free later? I've got a Booker Prize do at the Serpentine and I'll need to get back to Greenwich.
Drivers: [*Stony silence.*]
FP: I'll probably be a bit worse for wear. Munted, even.
Drivers: [*Stony silence.*]
FP: Okay, well you fellas take care now, y'hear?

On a large road called Queen's Gate, just around the corner from the Royal Albert Hall, I pass a row of immensely swanky terraced homes. A blue plaque denotes that one of these was the former home of Benny Hill. What? Benny Hill? How the heck does that work? I broach this disparity with my publisher, Sam, when I eventually find him, in the Queen's Arms.

FP: Seriously, how did he get to live in a huge place like that, at the gates to Hyde Park?
Sam: He was a big TV star, I suppose.
FP: But he stared at women's bosoms, with his tongue out. And he had a yakety sax theme tune.
Sam: Entertainment's moved on quite a lot since then.

FP: Yes, but he also hit bald men's heads with spoons. Is that still appropriate? With Roddy Doyle, say?

Sam: I doubt it, Francis. So if you see Roddy Doyle tonight...

FP: Do you think the people at tonight's bash will live in grand terraced mansions too?

Sam: Maybe. A few of them.

FP: It makes sense to take advantage of their free drinks then, don't you think? Seeing as we don't live in grand terraced mansions.

Sam: To a point, Francis. To a certain point...

It's a strange name for a pub, the Queen's Arms. Okay, she waves a lot and carries large quantities of flowers. But flowers don't weigh that much. Try carrying bricks, Your Majesty. Then you might earn the right to befit a pub name, and my own fair custom.

Sam kindly pays for the drinks and we walk past Benny Hill's old house, not laughing. As we enter Hyde Park, we pass the showy and preposterous memorial to Prince Albert, commissioned by Queen Victoria, laughing.

FP: Seriously, Sam. That royal family. They're on planet Moo Cow!

Security guards are in place to ensure the Serpentine art gallery is not bothered by tourists or genuine art enthusiasts. Tonight is not about aesthetic works or deep, contemplative thoughts. It's all about the natter, the social blinkety-blink. How do you do, sir? Good day to you, madam!

On a table in the foyer of the gallery are many nametags, arranged like the mausoleum plaques in Highgate cemetery.

Woman Behind Table: Ah, Francis Plug. Here's trouble.

FP: Pardon me?

Woman Behind Table: Try not to climb the walls tonight, if poss.

FP: Um...

Woman Behind Table: The drinks table is that way. Please leave some for our other guests.

The last Booker Prize event I attended, with Camilla, Princess of Wales, ended badly. But now, as a published author. I'm hoping to put my former life behind me.

FP: She must be confusing me with another Francis Plug, Sam. We're a dime-a-dozen, us Francis Plugs.

Sam knows quite a few people because he and Elly have published some important books. Each time I'm introduced to one of his publishing and media acquaintances, I mention how the over-sized champagne flutes resemble the Olympic torches of London 2012. Ben Okri, a former Booker winner, is wearing a beret.

FP: Hi, Ben Okri. Guess who.

Ben Okri: Sorry, remind me?

FP: Francis Plug. Bloomsbury Oxfam? You were doing a talk, despite being totally sick. And you forgot your reading glasses.

Ben Okri: Ah, yes. I remember. I hope I didn't infect you.

FP: No, no. I think all the wine kept the bugs at bay. Have you seen how big these champagne flutes are? They're like Olympic torches, from London 2012.

Ben Okri: Yes, I suppose. A little.

FP: Are you going to join us for a swim in the lido later? A splash about?

Ben Okri: Who's 'us'?

FP: Well, you, me, Sam, all the shortlisted authors, the judges…

Ben Okri: A splash about?

FP: Yes. You're the first person I've asked so far, but if word gets out that you're going, a former winner, getting their bits out in the lido, well, I'm sure there'll be other takers.

Ben Okri: I see. What was your name again?

FP: Francis. Francis Plug.

Ben Okri: Okay.

FP: Yes, I'm a published author myself now. Although I missed the Booker nod. Which was *idiotic,* in my opinion.

Ben Okri: Well, if you want to air your displeasure, you're in the right place.

FP: You think I should fire up some of these Olympic torches, Ben Okri?

Ben Okri: Nice to meet you again.

Ben Okri quickly cuts a path through the swathes of guests.

FP: I'LL COME AND FIND YOU LATER, BEN OKRI. FOR THE SKINNY-DIP…

Standing on my tippy-toes, hands raised like meerkat paws, I look about for Sam. If you end up by yourself at these events, smiling and nodding, you risk looking like a total bell-end. But who to talk to? Most people are dressed in smart suits or fancy dresses. Are they big publishers or financial highflyers? It's impossible to tell. The sponsor's logo is plastered across a fake wall behind a lectern, like your parents reminding you who paid for this room and those drinks. Honestly, these people. First they associate their dull profession with the literary world, and now they're throwing a party at a modern art gallery. It's a bit desperate. Next they'll be having their Christmas do in the Brixton Academy mosh pit.

Ah, that's Hans Ulrich Obrist, the Artistic Director of the Serpentine Gallery…

FP: Hans? Francis Plug. Look, you're Swiss, so you'll be up for a nudie-splash-about, right?

When Sam finds me, after the speeches, I'm wandering through the crowd with the lectern microphone singing 'British People in Hot Weather'. I add extra emphasis to the word 'Serpentine', and also to the cat-like growl. Sam needs to catch the last train, and suggests that I share a bus with him to the station. I can't, I tell him, into the microphone, because I have to go skinny-dipping with Ben Okri and Hans Ulrich Obrist. As someone at the coalface of literature, Sam is reliant on public transport. But I try and raise his spirits as he enters the darkness of Hyde Park by singing even louder, with ever more gusto.

DEVIL ON THE CROSS

Ngũgĩ wa Thiong'o

Translated from the Gĩkũyũ
by the author

To Frances Ploug

Peace

Ngũgĩ wa Thiong'o

LONDON

HEINEMANN

IBADAN · NAIROBI

A text arrives from Sam, checking to see I made it home okay. Not yet, I reply. I'm still here, in Hyde Park. In fact, I'm feeling a bit like *Mr Hyde*, in Hyde Park, or an American werewolf, but in London. When pressed for further details of my evening, I have nothing concrete to report, except to say that my pants are presently drying on Lady Diana's fountain.

The clothes-drying facilities at the university are a bit hit and miss. After washing my laundry by hand, with hand soap, I wring out what suds I can, in the toilet sink. Next, I slap the sodden items hard against the walls, as if attempting to put out a burning inferno in the Old Royal Naval College, which I started. This fire dousing is harder to achieve when performing the action with an individual sock, or some little pair of pants.

Saturday tends to be laundry day, giving me an extra day of drying, with less chance of my flagellations being seen or heard. Drying clothes on radiators is supposed to be bad for the health, because it encourages mould, causing aspergillosis, which plays havoc with your respiratory system. During the summer months, this is less of an issue. But now, in September, the sun's natural warming is on the wane, and I must resort once more to my methods, honed in winter, involving heated radiators and sizzling pants, emitting steam.

I feel bad about leaving damp bus seats on my journey home from Hyde Park. But that's not just any water. It's from the Serpentine Lido, commuters.

FP: Serpentine, growl.

In Nairobi, buses are known as matatus. If Ngugi wa Thiong'o's novel *Devil on the Cross* is to be believed, matatus are very social places, where even total strangers engage. By contrast, London bus passengers don't tend to engage much at all, especially with persons of an unknown persuasion. This usually suits me well, unless I'm feeling particularly talkative and wish to share my deepest troubles with a new best friend. The 188 is uniformly unchatty as I ride in today, in dry clothing, towards Bloomsbury. From what I can ascertain, the only person with a high level of alcohol in their bloodstream is myself, and even that's only high when compared with the other passengers, rather than peaking on some personal best chart.

Devil on the Cross isn't a campus novel, but it does allude to the power students can wield when the system is against them and they choose to stand against it. Near the end of the book, the students join the workers and peasants in their just struggle against the system of modern theft and robbery. The thieves in question are big business magnates, who oppress and steal the heritage bequeathed to all. One of them, addressing his fellows, says: 'When university students made a bit of noise, we could deny them air!' This nasty piece of work is Rottenborough Groundflesh Shitland Narrow Isthmus Joint Stock Brown. Who makes 'Francis Plug' sound like Plain Jane.

In signalling their solidarity with the workers and the poor, the students ask, 'What greater thing can our education do for the nation?' They call upon all educated people 'to choose the side on which they would use their education'. For self-progression in big business, or for the good of all? As a university type, it certainly makes you think.

And:

Crawl but arrive safely.

But in London, the buses presently contain very unhelpful messages such as:

Compare the meerkat.

Perhaps the University of Greenwich should get a bus, a yellow school bus, and I could wear a cap and headphones and drive it. A small supplementary income wouldn't go amiss. Of course, I could only drive it early in the mornings, due to the restrictions imposed by law intended to prevent one getting behind the wheel when cross-eyed, etc.

A Tusker beer bottle has started rolling around the floor of the 188's upper deck. I imagine myself inside that bottle, and finding, to my distress, that it's also filled with bees.

TRANSIT
Rachel Cusk

To Francis Plug —

JONATHAN CAPE
LONDON

OUTLINE
Rachel Cusk

To Francis Plug

ff
faber and faber

You need a thick skin to be a published author. Once your book leaves your hands and arrives in the unwashed hands of the great unwashed, chances are people out there ain't gonna like it. And people can be harsh, especially in today's cynic-driven, post-truth, pull-down-the-shutters climate. Sitting here in the Jeremy Bentham pub, I'm attempting to understand the latest critical response to my own work. Weirdly, it has a London bus dimension to it.

> *After forcing myself to finish Francis Plug's silly and stupid book, I posted it out the top-deck window slot of my moving London bus. I sent it to the road, hopefully instigating its delivery to a more deserved destination – beneath the wheels of a fucking big truck.* —Jim Taylor

As a piece of criticism, it's not entirely useful. Does my narrative flow need work, for instance? Jim doesn't say. One thing *is* for sure: no one's immune from the invisible critics. Even proper writers, acclaimed in literary circles, are liable to get dunked in dirt. Criticism is supposed to be a very good thing, to be defended at all costs. Particularly when the high and mighty start taking themselves a bit too seriously by far. It's when criticism turns personal, nasty and hate-filled that it becomes a wholly different kettle of fish.

No wonder writers are driven to drink. Today I attempt to drown my critics in alcoholic beverages, purchased from this very academic of Bloomsbury pubs. Jeremy Bentham (1748–1832) is seen by some as the 'spiritual founder' of University College London. He was a prolific writer, criticizing many laws of the day, and advocating very progressive views, including universal suffrage and the decriminalization of homosexuality. The last time I came to this pub, Jeremy Bentham's head was in a box upstairs. I think it was.

'Academic' or 'higher education' pubs are rather scant in London, at least to my knowledge. There are loads of Shakespeare pubs, and all manner of Charles Dickens-related taverns and inns. But campus bars, from my experience, are a bit light on the ground. Today's drink of choice seems to be coffee. Even university types appear determined to earn their coffee-buying 'rewards', via stamps, on cards. When you're little, stamps are earned for being imaginative, or polite, or skilful. But today's grown up stamps simply reward you for spending money, which any boring shite can do.

Not that I'm going to tell the students what to drink. They're at university. They're supposed to think for themselves. Instead, I simply intend to set forth a positive example, through my cheery good nature. Starting right here, in the Jeremy Bentham pub.

Barmaid: Another two?

FP: Yes, please. May I just say that the golden-ness of this ale really is quite exquisite.

Barmaid: Is it?

FP: Yes, it is. It's like some wonderful dream-like scenario, involving sunrises and spoons of delicious honey.

Barmaid: I'm glad you find it to your liking.

FP: You know, Wordsworth once wrote about a crowd of golden daffodils, next to a lake. Dancing, sparkling daffodils, they were. Golden ones. Upon reflection, you could almost imagine he was writing about this very ale.

Barmaid: Aww. That's beautiful. Thank you.

FP: No, thank *you*.

Barmaid: [*Pause.*] Although, perhaps the reason you think your ale resembles Wordsworth's dancing daffodils is because you've been drinking so many of them.

FP: You're like an angel, you are. Two angels…

After leaving the Jeremy Bentham, I walk a little unsteadily in the direction of the British Museum. After checking the time on my phone, I attempt to walk faster. In Rachel Cusk's book *Transit*, Faye is differentiated from other authors by virtue of being a fast walker, while other authors are not. I'm an author, but I'm only walking fast to see Rachel Cusk. *Comprende?*

Frustratingly, my urgent progress is halted by a befuddled tourist, one of Britain's former allies, close friends, and immediate trading partners. He is requesting directions.

European Man: Yes, I am looking for the British Museum.

FP: The Binyaki Museum? That's in Athens.

European Man: Eh?

FP: Athens! That way! [*Pointing.*]

Rachel Cusk is being interviewed at the London Review Bookshop, which isn't ideal. It's unfortunate, but I've managed to cultivate a certain reputation there. This is simply the result of some silly misunderstanding after I smashed through their rear glass door during a John Banville talk, before running away, into the night. This evening, I'm hoping to avoid any such fuss. Because now I'm an author myself, and I stand to financially benefit from the LRB, via sales of my acclaimed and heavily criticized novel. Also, I don't want to rock the boat with my contemporary author fellows, Rachel Cusk and her interviewer Adam Foulds.

My late arrival proves fortuitous. A small number of fold-out chairs have been set aside near the door for latecomers. A tray, also near the door, contains glasses filled with wine. At previous LRB events, the drinks table was right around the back, which meant passing directly in front of the featured speakers every time you needed a top-up. This, I think, helped lead to my bad rap. Tonight, however, there's a good half-dozen wines right there. Maybe the LRB have learnt from my own mistakes. When I lean across for a second, my fold-out chair creaks like hell. It's a very noisy chair for a bookshop. But I obviously can't let good wine go to waste.

Outline features a writer who doesn't seem to write, or talk, and her creative writing students who don't write but *do* talk. Rachel Cusk teaches creative writing in the real world. Perhaps her students are actually in attendance this evening. In a way, we the audience are all students, hoping to learn. Maybe that's my problem. I don't want to teach. I just want to learn.

Author events get a mention in Rachel Cusk's book *Transit*. Faye, the same narrator from *Outline*, is attending a literary festival somewhere out of London. Her interviewer and the other participants debate whether drinking before one's author talk can be likened to a jumbo jet crew drinking before take-off. After much research on this matter, I can emphatically announce that no, it's not. It's more akin to adding jet fuel to the jet, before take-off. On their way to their event marquee, Faye and company get soaked to the skin, due to poor festival organization. There's a lesson there for Dr Alex, in the lead-up to the inaugural Greenwich Book Festival. There's also a lesson for creative writing students, both in Greenwich and beyond. If you go along with all this author PR nonsense, you may end up like a drowned rat.

Some of the answers reached by Rachel Cusk in her work are taken by certain readers as provocations. Rachel Cusk herself is completely unable to understand this. On the strength of these perceived provocations, she has been on the receiving end of numerous personal insults.

Rachel Cusk: I write for an individual, who benefits from it. So the criticism is annoying. And the critics are anonymous. I'm not. I think I've possibly offered myself up as a sacrifice to the rude, hate-filled, post-Brexit, post-truth, pre-Trump world.

D.H. Lawrence, who Rachel Cusk greatly admires, came in for a fair amount of stick also. Many of his books were reviled for challenging sexual norms and using language deemed unsuitable and inappropriate. Lawrence faced sustained abuse, not just from people claiming to be offended by his work, but from official institutions too.

Outline and *Transit* are the first two books in a trilogy Rachel Cusk is writing, centred round a creative writing teacher, very much like herself. They aren't campus novels in the traditional sense, lacking a defined 'campus' for one thing. But as David Lodge recently suggested, the modern campus novel is more likely to revolve around a creative writing class than a traditional university environment.

In *Outline*, the first book, Faye spends much of her time in Athens at a two-day summer school. Her teaching topic is *How to Write*. During one of her classes, a student tells her she's a lousy teacher and they intend to seek a refund. In *Transit*, she teaches an adult fiction writing class in London. But her eye is constantly drawn to the strange cloudscapes that appear outside the classroom window. As a result, her students increasingly talk to each other, rather than to her, and end up running the class themselves. It's possible, I think, to discern very strong teaching similarities between Faye and myself. The only difference being that Faye isn't real, while I, of course, am.

Rachel Cusk's books aren't banned. She's not about to be thrown in prison, forced to write secretly on toilet paper, like Ngugi wa Thiong'o was. But she is getting a lot of flak. These days, it's not just religious extremists preaching hate. Ordinary, anonymous trolls are at it too.

Rachel Cusk is signing books, and a queue begins to form. But given all that wine, and the lovely golden ale, I must first descend to the London Review Bookshop's basement toilet, where a separate queue exists. Beside the loo is an open storeroom where staff are storing the fold-up chairs. On a shelf inside sits a massive plastic tub of Swarfega. This is rather puzzling, and a bit suspicious. Why would a bookshop need loads of Swarfega? There is also an abundance of light bulb boxes, a mop, and many cases of WD-40. Huh? WD-40? But my chair was really squeaky...?

I don't want to sound alarmist, in this age of heightened and critical terror, but I think the London Review Bookshop may be creating a bomb, right next to their basement toilet.

Rachel Cusk: A bomb?

FP: Yes. Is nowhere safe, in this day and age?

Rachel Cusk: You tell me.

FP: What's your favourite hand soap variant?

Rachel Cusk: Oh god. Really?

FP: Mine's Milk and Honey. They have it right here, in the basement loo.

Rachel Cusk: How wonderful for you.

FP: There's also a sign above the toilet that reads: PLEASE FLUSH TOILET PAPER ONLY. So at least those trolls of ours won't be flushing our book pages in here...

Rachel Cusk: God.

FP: Ed, the landlord of my old local in West Hampstead, told me they'd been using my book as toilet paper. For wiping their arses.

Rachel Cusk: [*Shaking head.*]

FP: Have *you* read my book?

Rachel Cusk: Your book? What book? Francis Plug? No, I haven't read your book.

FP: Your dark hair. It's like daffodils, sunrises...

Rachel Cusk: Next!

FP: Wait, wait, wait. There was something else, something else. Something important. Um... Nope.

OLD SCHOOL

a novel

For Francis Plug —

Tobias Wolff

Tobias Wolff (signature)

Alfred A. Knopf
New York
2003

Tobias Wolff's novel *Old School* is set in a boy's high school, rather than a university, but it still features in prominent lists of the campus genre. Class and privilege are much in evidence, with certain boys 'earning' Jaguar cars from their parents simply for turning sixteen. The narrator, however, is on scholarship, and one of the many students wishing to be writers. Writers, he believes, escape the problems of blood and class:

Writers formed a society of their own outside the common hierarchy. This gave a power not conferred by privilege – the power to create images of the system they stood apart from, and thereby to judge it.

But he also acknowledges:

Yet even in the act of kicking against it [their privilege] *they were defined by it, and protected by it, and to some extent unconscious of it.*

Tobias Wolff is yet another American campus novelist scheduled to visit London. Unfortunately, because the tickets to his talk are £50 each, it's an occasion only the privileged can enjoy.

As a creative writing academic, Dr Alex is familiar with Tobias Wolff's work. Yet he and other scholars are excluded from attending his event due to its restrictive cost. Some lecturers at the University of Greenwich are excluded from living in London for the same reason.

It goes without saying that many writers such as myself, also familiar with Tobias Wolff's work, are excluded from his London talk as well. So who is attending? Ferrari drivers, that's who.

Ferrari Driver: Brrmm, brrmm! Watch out! I'm going to see Tobias Wolff! Out of my way! Honk, honk!!

Tobias Wolff has a moustache of some significance, similar to that of Magnum P.I., a Ferrari driver. Does Tobias Wolff drive a Ferrari? Unlikely. Although perhaps he'll be in a position to, in the future, after his talk. It would have been useful to learn from him, about campus life, because as well as being a lauded writer, he also teaches at Stanford University. Not only that, I'm now up against the clock in terms of securing speakers for the Greenwich Book Festival. Of course, that would rely on the staff and students, and general public at large, actually being able to afford such a ticket.

The high school in *Old School* hosts author events with real authors, so the parallels with the Greenwich Festival are uncanny. Robert Frost, Ayn Rand, and Ernest Hemingway all get a mention in this regard. There are also examples of emerging authors being given a leg-up by older, established authors.

> *I knew that Maupassant... had been taken up when young by Flaubert and Turgenev; Faulkner by Sherwood Anderson; Hemingway by Fitzgerald and Pound and Gertrude Stein. All these writers were welcomed by other writers. It seemed to follow that you needed such a welcome, yet before this could happen you somehow, anyhow, had to meet the writer who was to welcome you.*

The narrator is hoping to gain a leg-up from the famous authors who visit his privileged school. In order to get Tobias Wolff to be my leg-up, I'll need to gatecrash a £50 event, full of privileged folk. Still, unlike most, I now have the added advantage of my esteemed position at Greenwich and my minor publishing success. I still have much to learn, especially in the befuddling non-literary, literary world, but at least I've got a base. If you're planning on a leg-up in the privileged literary world, it really helps if you're in a privileged world already.

The venue for Tobias Wolff's talk is the basement bar in Waterstones Piccadilly, as opposed to the nearby Ritz. It's not a Waterstones event, however, having been organized by some mysterious outside party, possibly involving a consortium headed up by the Sultan of Brunei. The basement bar has been shielded from public view by a set of tall Waterstones dividers, like the sort you might get dressed behind, if you were changing into a Paul Auster costume. The talk is underway already, and I find myself on the wrong side of the dividers. However, by peering around them, Tobias Wolff is clearly visible, in profile, delivering amusing anecdotes to the laughing, moneyed-up crowd. If I had the money for a ticket, I'd be laughing too, even if the bar room was completely empty, save for my laughing self.

As I peek, fists raised, muttering curses, I'm suddenly brought to earth by a light cough. It's a bearded member of the bookshop staff, standing behind me. The same gent who supplied Mick Herron and myself with our numerous festive drinks at the store's Christmas event. But he offers no acknowledgement of this previous comradery, which I appreciate. Because it's really not the done thing for a published author to be found lurking outside another author's event with a reddened, angry face.

Staff Member: Everything all right?

FP: Yes, great thanks!

Although not a water cannon approach, it's clearly a hint to move on.

FP: Excuse me. See that book protruding right out of the shelf?

Bookshop Customer: Yes?

FP: Well, it suddenly shot out of there, by itself.

Bookshop Customer: Did it?

FP: Yes. There was this mist, and a flash, and out it shot. Whiz!

Bookshop Customer: Wow.

FP: Do you think we should investigate?

Bookshop Customer: Possibly…

FP: Just in case there's a secret passage or something.

We approach slowly, with caution.

Bookshop Customer: It doesn't seem to be moving now.

FP: What is the book, exactly?

Bookshop Customer: It's… *How to Be a Public Author*, by Francis Plug. Nothing special, I don't think.

FP: Really? I heard that book was quite something.

Bookshop Customer: No, nothing to see here, me thinks.

FP: Wait. Aren't you going to remove it fully? Maybe take it up to the Payments counter?

Bookshop Customer: [*Shrugs.*] No.

FP: But… the magical wonder…

Bookshop Customer: Bye.

The bar on the fifth floor used to be called the Studio Lounge, but they've changed it to 5th View Bar & Food. It still isn't Keats or Yeats, but it does manage to cram four facts into five words.

FP: Do you have any salted bear meat, from Kamchatka?
Bartender: Sorry?
FP: Do you have any salted bear meat, from Kamchatka?
Bartender: Kam *what*?
FP: Kam*chatka*. You know, the peninsula on the remote far east of the Soviet Union. On the Bering Sea?
Bartender: [*Shrugs.*]
FP: With the salted bear meat?
Bartender: [*Shakes head.*]
FP: No?
Bartender: [*Shrugs.*]
FP: [*Sigh.*] Just the two large drinks then, please.

Since it's a Friday night, 5th View Bar & Food is doing a brisk trade in views, drinks and food. A waitress brings the drinks to my table, which is a worry, given I haven't been asked to pay yet. What do these drinks even cost? I have no idea. My corner table is very tall, requiring a barstool seat, like Richard Russo's. Near me are large office groups, excitedly reacquainting themselves with alcohol, following a week's break.

FP: [*Whispering behind my hand.*] Sshh! This is a bookshop, you know!

At an adjacent table, a late arrival removes her coat, causing a thin bangle to escape her wrist and roll upon the lined carpet floor. She and her colleagues are oblivious to its loss, so I climb down from my barstool like the Marlboro man and retrieve it, presenting it to its hapless owner.

Woman: Oh yes, that's mine. Thank you.

Rather than returning to my barstool, I linger for a reward. Although my book is for sale in this very shop, I'm not exactly rolling in it. My daily outgoings, for personal stability, regrettably exceed my daily incomings. Not being blessed with an accountant, financial advisor, or life coach, I take the more amateur 'every little helps' approach. At least I'm not dishonest. Not entirely dishonest. An entirely dishonest person might have kicked the bangle under an armchair, returning for it later, to pawn for a tidy sum. Instead, I hand it back, first gripping an end, like a Christmas cracker, to contest the outright victor, before conceding. After a protracted, uncomfortable silence, I turn and slowly climb atop my bar stool, where I sit, as if on a coin-operated supermarket horse, rocking forwards and backwards.

Having smoked the last of my Gitanes, I search for stubs outside Waterstones. The only butt on offer contains traces of lipstick, and it's been smoked to a stump. A more lucrative place to find stubs is at bus stops, or outside betting shops. While many betting shop butts are remnants of losers, spent of all puff, others have been discarded in a rush, just prior to a race. Sometimes losers will come out looking for these, but they lose again, because I'm there, smoking them. Winners' smokes are good too, because usually their owners are in a hurry to get back inside, to place more bets, in order to become losers.

Smoking is an expellable offence in *Old School*. The narrator, a smoker, keeps a store of spearmint Life Savers and uses a cigarette holder so his fingers don't stain. He wants his unblemished fingers to touch the hands of authors who have written real stories and poetry, and who have, in turn, touched the hands of other famous authors. 'I wanted to be anointed.' His obsession with famous authors is somewhat unhealthy, me thinks. Although I've met every living Booker Prize winner, with the exception of Keri Hulme, I wouldn't call myself an obsessive. Unlike *Old School*'s narrator, I'm not fixated by 'the blessed and blessing presence of literature itself', nor do I wish to speak with famous authors 'of deep matters and receive counsel'. Well, maybe just that last bit.

Tobias Wolff, now seventy-one, is scheduled to talk for two hours. If I stay in 5th View Bar & Food for two hours, I'll soon eclipse his extortionate ticket price in drinks and service. Slowly descending the six staircase levels to the basement, I try to kill time by clapping the appropriate number of times for the step I happen to be on. For instance, clapping seventeen times on step 17, before moving onto step 18 and clapping eighteen times. By the time I reach the basement, I've descended 180 steps and clapped, I think, a total of 16,139 times.

Tobias Wolff, now seated, is being interviewed by someone I can't see. My previous spot by the dividers has been taken by a tall young man in a black coat, who is making notes in a ringbinder. It's possible he's a student of literature or creative writing, and like the narrator in *Old School*, who attends an elite boarding school on scholarship, this young chap is hoping to get a special education on the cheap.

In the distance, beyond the dividers, Tobias Wolff is answering questions. His event has already over-run by seven minutes, and a woman's voice has just said, 'We'll take two more.' Those people really are getting their vast sums of money's worth. There aren't any laughs now because Tobias Wolff has gone beyond the joking stage. His entertaining has been done, the tank's in the red.

Tobias Wolff: The question was about bird imagery...

Applause finally comes after two and a quarter hours. The young studious fellow slinks off with his notes. Unlike the narrator of *Old School*, he isn't interested in touching the hand of the famous author, which has, in turn, touched the hands of other famous authors. But I am.

Inside, beyond the divider wall, a signing queue snakes past a bar counter where fancy canapés are exquisitely arranged. That's a new development in author events. Avocado. Salmon, even. But they're not being snapped up. In fact, they appear to be going to waste. It's tempting to put them to good use, to add some health and diversity to my intermittent, bargain-bin diet. But I'm not hungry, thank you. And I don't wish to coat Tobias Wolff's book, or his palm, with fishy oil.

The man in front of me is stroking the Ferrari key in his pocket. He is young and immaculately groomed. His casualwear makes my smart clothing look positively trampish. He has also donned a strong coat of aftershave, which, I can't help suspecting, contains ingredients extracted from harpooned whales.

Tobias Wolff's moustache really is quite something. It's even more impressive than David Lodge's. It resembles a furry moth, which, wings spread, has become trapped, head-first, beneath Tobias Wolff's nose. A woman two-ahead in the queue is talking to him about his university work. She's stealing my thunder.

Tobias Wolff: Actually, I finished up teaching just two weeks ago.

Darn it! That's scuppered my teaching exchange programme idea. As the man in front goes forward, smothering the author with his charms and manly fragrance, I feel decidedly nervous. Tobias Wolff might be my leg-up. This could be my big break. My palms are sweating oils secreted from my own glands, or blubber. Focus, focus. The festival. Confirm his attendance for the festival…

Tobias Wolff: Can I explain 'sexless hydrogen'? I'm not sure I can, sorry.

FP: Really? Oh well. At least I didn't fork out £50. Do you want to get your leg up?

Tobias Wolff: I beg your pardon?

FP: My leg, your hands.

Tobias Wolff: Ah…?

FP: Sorry, what I meant was, could you possibly offer me a leg-up?

Tobias Wolff: A leg-up… in what sense?

FP: For my writing career? My university status?

Tobias Wolff: Oh…

FP: Look, if you could just come to our event in a few weeks, around 7 p.m., only for an hour, one little hour. Can't promise any salmon. But a lovely riverside setting, with sea horses…

Tobias Wolff: Sorry, where is this?

FP: Greenwich, lovely Greenwich, the Royal Borough of Greenwich, by the Thames.

Tobias Wolff: Oh. I'm afraid I'm flying back to the US tomorrow.

FP: No. Don't go. Don't leave…

Tobias Wolff: Are you okay?

FP: A little drunk with spring, perhaps. Or autumn, rather. Fall, yes? Fancy one of those canapés? Nyum, nyum!

When Tobias Wolff shakes my hand, I yelp. My palms, as well as being wet with sweat, are also very tender. From all that clapping.

As if the pressure to sign up festival authors wasn't bad enough, I am needed for further tasks. The Greenwich Book Festival, it transpires, is part of a wider collection of events known as the Greenwich Festivals, all occurring around the same time in our local royal borough. An official launch is being held to kick this season off, featuring local councillors, MPs, and other dignitaries. As Writer in Residence, I have been asked to represent the university and its inaugural Book Festival.

FP: Thanks a lot!

The launch is to be held on a historic clipper ship near the Woolwich docks. The wider news media will be covering the event, so there's a sense of this being an important PR opportunity. Since I'm supposedly writing a book on campus, it's been decided that I should read a section of my novel-in-progress.

FP: Whoah. What? You… what?

In addition to the dignitaries and news reporters, both Dr Zoë and Dr Alex will be attending the launch, but only as observers. They will act as adult sheep, while I shall be the lamb, offered up for slaughter. Because it's a lunchtime event, Dr Alex, in reply to my carefully worded question, doesn't think there'll be any 'drinks'. Turns out he's right. Just as well I brought my own.

The *Morgenster* is a 'tall ship' and part of the Tall Ships Festival. But it doesn't offer much in the way of hiding places. It's also difficult to surreptitiously swig from a bottle, because whenever another river-faring vessel passes, the very floor rocks and sways like hell. For some reason, out of all the different Greenwich festivals, they have chosen the Book Festival representative to talk first. Perhaps they want to get the boring books out of the way so they can move swiftly on to the sexy ships. Still, being first up at the Death Match was a blessing. Perhaps today I will benefit in a similar way. Except, before this, I'm needed for a photo opportunity, with Kipper the dog. Kipper is a children's book character who actually *has* signed up for our festival. Today he is represented, six foot tall, in costumed fur, bringing back vague memories of my *Snowman* experience, as if these memories were dug up, by Kipper. A multitude of photographers have appeared, to snap the glittery face of the Greenwich Book Festival, which is a massive grinning dog face, and a hairy little horse, in gnashing bridle. We're asked to pose behind the ship's wheel. It's a chance to be Captain Ahab, flashing my anchor tattoo. Except I'm standing, wincing, next to a dog, also standing, waving. Once our controlled media image has been sufficiently fabricated, we're ushered to the back of the ship, or the stern I tell Kipper, for speeches. A microphone stand has been set up.

FP: [*To Kipper, pointing.*] Stand. Sit.

After an introductory speech, Cllr Denise Scott-McDonald, Cabinet Member for Culture, Creative Industries, and Community Wellbeing welcomes me, by my name.

FP: Thank you, Cllr Denise. Hello everyone. Fancy being on board a tall ship, on the Thames, in this day and age.

No reaction whatsoever.

FP: With that twenty-first-century *War of the Worlds*-type Millennium Dome just down the river there.

No reaction whatsoever.

FP: Have you met Kipper? Kipper is a dog, despite having a name like a fish. But trust me, at the Greenwich Book Festival, kids will go mad for dogs who sound like fish.

No reaction whatsoever.

FP: Anyone here read books?

A few shrugs.

FP: What about… Anyone here watch *EastEnders*?

Plenty of nods and general human movement.

FP: It's a no-brainer, right? Do you like how, at the start, in the opening credits, the camera spirals down onto the Thames?

Plenty of nods and general human movement.

FP: Me too. So, given that my new novel is in a state of flux, I'd like to read you a passage, which has some relevance, I think, to today's setting. It's called 'The Camera Spirals Down'.

Looking at each other, uncertain.

FP: So! Ahem. The camera spirals down. Down, down, down. Towards the Thames, in London's East End. But where's Greenwich? It's there. There it is. Quick, get close to the screen and jab your finger at Greenwich. Have you got it? Jab at it. Jab around the spiralling, vortex path. Jab! Jab at Greenwich! Jab, jab! Try not to become hypnotized. It's not like your TV is mounted on a rotatable axis that can be turned in the same direction as the spiralling *EastEnders* opening sequence. That's why you need to jab. Or you might go cross-eyed. Because it's like watching a washing machine cycle, right? Except, instead of sudsy water, mixed with food stains, mud, and lint, it's the Thames.

They've gone all stiff again. Maybe they're just concentrating, on the prose.

FP: Jab, jab. Hey, what's that noise? Is it a washing machine? No, it's a helicopter. Maybe it's a BBC helicopter. Perhaps they're filming the latest opening credits RIGHT NOW. Wave everybody, wave! Get on the telly! Get on *EastEnders*! [*Humming* EastEnders *theme tune, waving arms in time.*] Thank you! See you at the Greenwich Book Festival!

It's hard to fathom what Dr Zoë and Dr Alex thought of my reading. They clearly don't want to disrupt the next speaker by talking, not even mouthed words of encouragement, or a gesture, such as a thumbs-up.

GILEAD

To Francis Plug,

Marilynne Robinson

Farrar • Straus • Giroux / New York

Room KW340
King William Building
University of Greenwich
Old Royal Naval College
30 Park Row
London SE10 9LS

Dear Philip Roth,

In your campus novel The Human Stain, *Coleman Silk gets the shove from his university post as the result of an alleged slur. If I don't sign up a quality author, such as yourself, for our university book festival, I'll likely get the shove myself, for being a fraud and a bullshitter.*

Here are the details:
   Greenwich Book Festival
   University of Greenwich
   XX XX 2015.

You may have to cover your own flights, but I can set you up on a camp bed in a building designed by Sir Christopher Wren of St Paul's fame.

If you can't make it, I'd really appreciate your response, in the manner of a dear old friend, expressing profound regret and deep disappointment at your inability to move mountains, but trusting the festival will be a huge success regardless because you know me very well and rate me very highly.

Thanking you in advance, with keen anticipation.

Yours sincerely,
   Francis Plug.

Philip Roth didn't respond to my letter, which was frustrating. The time I spent writing it could have been utilized writing my novel instead. Maybe, even, a really good bit. Admittedly, by responding to my letter, he would be diverting his own writing time, and unlike me, he has a reputation to live up to. Still, it doesn't take long to write what Billy Bragg calls 'the short answer'.

It's now too late for my 'sure-thing' authors to be included in the festival programme because the printing deadline has passed, and none have confirmed, or even expressed mild interest. Perhaps separate inserts could be added to the programme later, I tell Dr Alex, or my literary giant friends could just turn up as surprise guests on the day.

FP: Like Gary Numan did that time, on stage, with Nine Inch Nails. Except it's Donna Tartt, or Tom Wolfe. With Kipper.

With days to go, I shelve the campus novel stipulation and throw myself at the feet of every big-name author I can find.

FP: I know you've won the Pulitzer Prize, but if you're not at the inaugural Greenwich Book Festival, I fear history may judge you poorly.
Marilynne Robinson: Is that so? Well, I'll just have to take that risk, I'm afraid.
FP: There'll be sandwiches. Free ones…

1 9 8 2 JANINE

BY

ALASDAIR GRAY

FOR BETHSY

and for Francis Plug,

by  *thunder!*

says Alasdair

JONATHAN CAPE
THIRTY BEDFORD SQUARE LONDON

FP: But…

Alasdair Gray: No, no, no. I'm getting too old for that festival raz-matazz. Go and find some spritely young author full of beans and smiles and what-have-you.

FP: But…

Alasdair Gray: Good luck, Francis Plug!

Interpreter
of
Maladies

STORIES

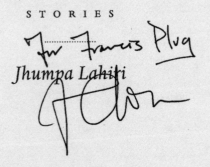

Jhumpa Lahiri

Houghton Mifflin Company
Boston · New York

FP: Please.

Jhumpa Lahiri: Sorry.

FP: [*Sigh.*] ... Rock, paper, scissors?

A Lover Sings
Selected Lyrics

BILLY BRAGG

to Francis Plug

Bill Bragg

ff

FABER & FABER

Billy Bragg: No.

FP: So, 'the short answer'?

Billy Bragg: Yes.

FP: Ha! The *long* answer! To a question about the short answer!

To Francis Plug.

JEFFREY ARCHER

THE CLIFTON CHRONICLES

VOLUME FIVE

MIGHTIER THAN
THE SWORD

Jeffrey Archer

MACMILLAN

Jeffrey Archer: You're lucky I'm even signing your book, the way you were carrying on. Understand? I really didn't appreciate all that childish laughing and stupid sword-fighting nonsense. It was most off-putting, and downright rude, actually. I can't believe I'm even signing this for you, but there you are. Honestly, just childish...

FP: So that's a no?

MANDY CHARLIE &
MARY-JANE

STEWART
HOME

For Francis Pluy

Hope your campus
novel is a slasher
too

[signature: Stewart Home]

PENNY-ANTE | EDITIONS

It's Day One of the Greenwich Book Festival, and the sun's swirling gases have graced us, providing more than adequate light for reading by. Volunteers have gathered, marquees stand erect, and authors, booked and scheduled, arrive without a hint of a hand from me. One job was all I had, a straightforward task, seemingly attuned to my role and personal interests and general place in the world. Still, abject failings aside, my university position, it appears, remains intact. As yet there's been no hint of a shove. I should therefore be striding around, welcoming my fellow writers, greeting visitors, and shaking the Chancellor's hand. Instead, I'm hiding away in the back streets, drinking with an urgent thirst.

The Morden Arms has become a great refuge these past weeks and months. Here I'm like a stray dog who always gets a pat, even with my unwashed coat and strong prospect of fleas. Today, Hannah is behind the bar, exhuming the remains of my Hello Kitty pouch.

Hannah: Here, isn't it your Book Festival today? Shouldn't you be cavorting with the bigwigs of the literary world?

FP: Yes. I'm just getting myself mentally prepared.

Ray Chipps: I trust you're going to bring all those famous authors of yours back here, Francis. We need more photos for the wall. Some friends for Mr Winkler.

The corner doors are opened inwards, to welcome the unseasonal warmth, and Ray and I sit at our usual table, washed with outside air.

357

Ray Chipps: Do they not miss you at the university when you're camped out here?

FP: Ray, as George Orwell once said, 'The imagination, like certain wild animals, will not breed in captivity.'

Ray Chipps: Am I to take that to mean that this pub is like some feral, untamed wilderness?

FP: In a manner of speaking.

Through the open doors comes a deafening and never-ending car alarm, drowning out the sounds of Beyoncé from a builder's radio. Or is it, rather, a house alarm? Is someone trying to make off with a colossal Greenwich house? Ray the Buddhist remains calm in the car/house alarm crisis. But my nerves, already frayed by prospective commitments, are further severed. Farewelling Ray and Hannah, I wander off towards the university, hands over my ears, eyes tightly shut.

The first events began at 11 a.m., but my own talk is not until early evening. So much for quick-smart, in-out, done and dusted. Normally by 7 p.m. I'm pretty trolleyed.

Large, impressive toilet facilities have been installed by the Old Brewery. A stinky, dug-out trough would be more in keeping with a festival scene, but this is, after all, a UNESCO site. Thankfully, I haven't been asked to conduct any official festival duties, such as open it. The Queen should be here to do that really, at her borough's inaugural literary celebration, but her entire family's done a no-show. They're probably at the horse races again. Maybe if they spent less time having flutters on the fillies, they could help get more folk into libraries and fewer into betting shops.

Dr Alex is careering around the campus like a racetrack rabbit. He's not stressed, he insists, just tuckered out, having been lugging large containers of water around, and carting many chairs. On top of that, he also has to manage volunteers, authors, and the authors' crotchety publicists. Prior to the festival, he was advised by a publishing source to 'Forget the authors, just keep the publicists happy'. Who exactly are these publicists? *What* are they? As a minor-league writer, I wouldn't know. Earlier, when Dr Alex tried speaking to the publicist of a well-known children's book illustrator, she apparently put her palm up to his face and began speaking into a phone. During that illustrator's event, which attracted over one hundred kids, some of the children were falling asleep, heads over arms, because the illustrator was telling them about his problems with his publisher.

There has already been one author go AWOL. A certain fantasy writer went missing after wandering along the Thames Path and 'getting lost'. He was fifteen minutes late for his event, with a near-capacity tent awaiting him, and when he finally showed, he immediately requested a double soya caffeinated latte. The public have been getting lost too. Apparently the hired help responsible for directing them, via large foam fingers, have yet to show. On top of everything else, Dr Alex tells me, there's been a 'bunting incident'. A length of festival bunting was hung on the fence railings between the King William and Queen Mary buildings, before an unnamed official deemed it would obscure the view from the Queen's House through to the river. This despite no queen or royalty being resident in said house for hundreds of years.

FP: [*Cross-eyed expression.*]
Dr Alex: Yes. [*Cross-eyed expression.*]
FP: Or this. [*Cross-eyed expression, with tongue sticking out.*]
Dr Alex: That too.
FP: Your turn.

Dr Alex: Oh. Um... [*Cross-eyed expression, with tongue sticking out, and ears pulled out by hands.*]
FP: Ha, ha!

While the flags have been unceremoniously lowered, a huge tent marquee has been raised on the King William lawn. This is my venue, for the talk I must give. A stage has been set up inside, along with microphones and a lectern, and speakers are in place throughout. According to Dr Alex, the tent even has lighting, with dimmer switches. More important to me are all the backs. There are lots of backs in there, a damn lot of backs.

Jon Ronson, the author presently engaged on the stage, is answering interviewer questions. An audio engineer is positioned near the entrance, behind a sound desk. Audio engineers, I've heard, are paid more than most authors at book festivals. Just for plugging in cords and making authors talk louder. Authors are up on stage, under the spotlight, while audio engineers stay hidden behind desks, in the shadows. This one, I notice, is looking at his phone. Maybe he's online, booking a cruise on *Boaty McBoat-Face*. Or maybe he's buying a full head-and-body lycra suit, in black. I tap on the window, to alert him to his task, but the 'windows' are made of plastic and he fails to hear. Unbelievable. How do I go about becoming an audio engineer? What a brilliant job.

The ever-present helicopters are causing their normal racket, and from the corner rooms of the Trinity music school come boisterous trumpets and drums. Young volunteers, predominantly female, are being helpful and efficient in their blue festival T-shirts. Emblazoned on the front, in big bold type, are the words BOOKS ARE GREAT. Offered a free T-shirt myself, as a recognized member of department staff, I politely refuse, citing professional standards.

FP: BOOKS ARE GREAT? Are you taking the piss? People might think the Writer in Residence wrote that. Honestly.

Dr Zoë, meanwhile, is looking with trepidation at the skies to the east.

Dr Zoë: Oh, hello Francis. Those clouds look a bit iffy, don't they?

As the department head, Dr Zoë is someone I need to impress. She has, it would seem, chosen to overlook my complete failure to fill this festival with A-listers, and has probably heard about the stinky tyre incident also, and perhaps the accompanying breath. Maybe the Painted Hall gripes have reached her to boot.

FP: Don't you worry about a thing, Dr Zoë. Leave it to me.
Dr Zoë: Sorry?

I run off.

FP: Is the manager handy?
Fan Museum Woman: That'll be me. Can I help you?
FP: Yes, you can. It's an emergency. There are rainclouds threatening the inaugural Greenwich Book Festival. Only you and your fans can save us all. It's action stations, chop, chop!

The perplexed woman stands there like a cardboard cut-out of a fan museum manager, made from something stronger than cardboard, like plywood.

Fam Museum Woman: You want us to, what, fan away the clouds? With our little fans?

FP: [*Pause.*] Ah… That's not going to work, is it?

The manager folds her arms.

FP: Ha, ha. No. That's just bloody stupid, isn't it? My word. Sorry about that.

I back backwards out of the Fan Museum, fanning my arms downwards in submission to the manager.

FP: A thousand apologies…

Back on campus, the clouds appear to be lifting. Dr Zoë isn't around, so I'm unable to try and claim credit for this new development.

Jon Ronson's event has just ended, and a queue is forming on the grass in front of the book sales marquee. Jon Ronson has chosen to stand in front of the queue, like a small bus his readers are waiting to board. It's a bit unnerving having these other authors on my turf, swanning about. For all I know, they're sizing up the lie of the land, clocking the power station chimneys and formulating their own nuclear reactor meets nuclear power station campus novels. Well, I won't have it. Not after all the time and effort I've invested in marking this out as my territory. These wannabe challengers need to know who's top cat.

FP: Hi, Francis Plug. I'm the Writer in Residence at this place.
Jon Ronson: Okay. Hi.
FP: Look, it's fine you're here. I'm cool with it.
Jon Ronson: Good…
FP: Yes, good, it's all good. I'm not going to get all territorial or anything. I'm not going to sniff your bottom, for instance.

Jon Ronson: Pardon me?

FP: I'm *not* going to do that, is what I said. I'm *not* going to sniff your bottom. Why would I? I'm top cat around here.

Did that come out right? It's hard to say. *He's* the one pretending to be a bus. Who the heck invited *him*?

Dr Alex is talking with some of the volunteers. When I pass by, waving out, he breaks off his conversation and half-jogs across.

Dr Alex: Francis. Just the man I need to speak to.

FP: Has my event sold out? Don't tell me I need an even larger venue, such as the Painted Hall?

Dr Alex: Ha, ha. No, that is most certainly *not* the case. No, no, no. But… I have been hearing reports of some very strange things you've been saying to the festival authors. Complaints, actually, rather than reports.

FP: Really?

Dr Alex: Yes. Something about 'sniffing bottoms'?

FP: Sniffing bottoms? Dear me. Quite the opposite. That's just what I said I *wouldn't* do.

Dr Alex: Francis…

FP: Sniff their bottoms!

Jon Ronson isn't in the Green Room, fortunately, so it's a good place to lie low for a bit. Also, there's a side table laden with free drinks, making it a good place to lie low for a very long time. The Green Room is made up of three large conjoined rooms on the east wing of Queen Mary. It's filled with many comfy chairs upholstered in a soft woollen fabric resembling fur, perhaps from a llama, or lots of tarsiers, or heaps of little squirrels. Large archways link the rooms, and the ceilings are also arched, curving in a grandiose style. There's at least two microwaves, along with a sizeable fridge and other conveniences. It's not a part of the university I've ever had reason to visit before, and I ask a student volunteer about its general use.

Student Volunteer: These rooms? Oh, they make up the university staff room.
FP: What? The university has a *staff* room? No one ever told me there was a *staff* room. Why did no one tell me there was a staff room?
Student Volunteer: [*Shrugs.*]
FP: *I'm* a member of staff. I *am*.

After a while, Dr Alex arrives with an author and publicist. I don't recognize the author, so the publicist is clearly doing a terrible job. But I know it's an author and a publicist because one is wearing high-end fashion labels and the other really isn't. Dr Alex offers me a brief, hurried nod. I call after him.

FP: Dr Alex. Dr Alex. This is the university *staff* room, apparently. Fancy that. Did you know this was the university staff room? I didn't. I didn't even know the university *had* a staff room. It's all news to me. I had no clue at all.
Dr Alex: We'll talk later, shall we?

Although unhappy at leaving the free drinks selection, it's probably best if I don't prepare for my tent event, in the usual manner, in the presence of my immediate superior. Some students are milling near the West Gate entrance. As I pass, I overhear the words 'bottom sniffing'.

Looking away, I encounter two further students with large blue foam hands, each with a pointing finger, pointing at me.

Ray Chipps: Where are all your author friends?
FP: I think they're… maybe… buying flowers. Yes, they'll be rammed into the florist, I suspect, buying bouquets of celebratory flowers. For the great success of the Greenwich Book Festival. No doubt they'll be here very soon. You're not hyper-allergenic to the pollen of many flowers are you Ray?

I may not have roped in Robert Frost, Mary McCarthy, or Vladimir Nabokov, but my pleading wasn't all in vain. Stewart Home, an English artist, filmmaker, writer, pamphleteer, art historian and activist, has very kindly agreed to join me on stage to talk about his campus novel *Mandy, Charlie and Mary-Jane*. As campus novels go, it's really quite something. In fact, I wouldn't hesitate to call it a pinnacle of the genre. The narrator, Charles Templeton, lectures in cultural studies at the City University of Newcastle-upon-Tyne, a place usually referenced by its acronym. Like other campus novels, the university also has a lake. Unlike the lake in Nell Zink's *Mislaid*, it doesn't end up with a car in it. There are no geese in the lake, like in Richard Russo's *Straight Man*. But, like the lake in Linda Grant's *Upstairs at the Party*, it does end up with dead people in it. Anyway, without wanting to give too much away, Stewart Home's book contains multiple murders, drug abuse, and varying strands of art criticism.

Because Stewart Home was a very last-minute addition to the line-up, our modest audience cannot be attributed to him. The Writer in Residence title may be useful for accessing power stations, but it's not much of a draw at book festivals, especially at events for yourself, in the place of your own residence.

The audio engineer is made to work hard for his money tonight. Due to a lack of power sockets, Stewart Home has him running around for an extension lead. It's not clear why Stewart Home would *need* a power supply, and I don't ask. Most of the people in the sparsely populated seats are known to me because I work with them, or they publish me. Clocking each in turn with a wave, to politely acknowledge their attendance, probably only highlights my narrow appeal further.

In my left hand is an A4 page with some questions to ask Stewart Home. In my right hand is a microphone. As soon as I ask a question, the plan is to lay the microphone in my lap and pick up a glass of wine. Behind my chair are two further bottles. I hope Stewart is someone who draws out his answers.

FP: So, Stewart Home, where's *your* home?

Stewart Home: London.

FP: Oh. [*Gulp, clonk.*] Excuse me. London. Great. Marilynne Robinson wrote a book called *Home*. And Deborah Levy wrote a book called *Swimming Home*. But they weren't about you. Swimming or otherwise. Were they?

Stewart Home: No.

FP: Oh. [*Gulp, clonk.*] Excuse me. So. Um, can you tell us a bit about your campus novel, *Mandy, Charlie and Mary-Jane*?

Stewart Home: *Mandy* is a novel set in a campus because it functions as a microcosm of the hell that is capitalist society. The unreliable narrator is a frustrated and abusive academic who totally loses the plot.

FP: Right. Yes, I really liked that bit when the university staff get brutally murdered.

Stewart Home: Okay.

FP: Right. So… read any good books lately?

Stewart Home: A couple: *Grimoires: A History of Magic Books* by Owen Adams and *Atheist Yoga* by Anton Drake. But the best one was my own last novel, *The 9 Lives of Ray the Cat Jones*.

FP: Ha, great. Um… let's see… um…

Stewart Home: Shall I read from *Mandy*?

FP: Yes, great, great idea, that's a great idea.

Instead of standing before the lectern, Stewart Home, back to the audience, crouches down on the stage, touching it with his forehead, before swinging his legs in the air and balancing on his head. In this position, upside down, now facing the audience, he begins reciting from his book. His forearms rest on his jumper, in front of which, on the floor, is the loose microphone. Stewart's black T-shirt has slipped down towards his chest, revealing his naked belly button. Jon Ronson didn't do this, at least not while I was watching.

The audience, including Dr Zoë, are watching intently. What must they think? Stewart Home is my invited guest, the one literary name I managed to snare, and he's standing on his head. For all I know, the Chancellor is out there too, one of the sparse scattering. He or she might have to write me a reference soon. Will this now compromise my respectable standing? At least I got to drink lots of wine. Also, it's funny, an author standing on his head. Booker Prize winners don't do this. I should probably stop laughing, nervous laughing.

When Stewart Home's finished and righted himself, he produces an appliance from his bag and proceeds to plug it into the extension socket. This done, he begins ripping pages out of his book and feeding them into the appliance, which, although resembling a fax machine, turns out to be a paper shredder. He continues this process, ripping pages from his book and feeding them into the shredder. It sounds like the campus gardeners, with a mower, inside the tent. But it's Stewart Home, my author guest, mowing through his book. As he does, he talks off the cuff about all manner of subjects, which, to be honest, I don't really catch, because he's feeding his book through a shredder.

Not wishing to appear too enthusiastic, my clapping is somewhat hesitant, like Morse code. But Stewart Home receives a hearty reception from our small crowd, so I start to clap a lot. His shredding talk really saved me a lot of unnecessary questions, not to mention limelight. The students, I believe, would have found much to like, but they've mostly failed to show. Despite Stewart's excellent performance, our attendance figures are poor. Compared with *The Dinosaur That Pooped A Planet!*, we aren't even on the radar.

Afterwards, Stewart Home agrees to join me for a drink in the Morden.

FP: Henry Winkler's great, isn't he?
Stewart Home: No.
FP: No, right. He's a dick. [*Pause.*] Do you have any spare rooms at your home, Stewart Home?

It's Sunday, Day Two of the inaugural Greenwich Book Festival. I sift around the Green Room/staff room, looking for free wine. Dr Alex is tucked away in a corner, eating curled-up sandwiches. Between chews, he recounts more organizational horrors, such as the hunt for square batteries. Besides Kipper, other book characters have been represented in costume form too, such as Hugless Douglas, and the Dinosaur That Pooped A Planet. Each costume contains an in-built fan, so the humans basting within the furry ovens won't die. Square batteries are necessary to operate the fans, thus the hunt.

Hugless Douglas proved a particular hit with the kids, to the point where they literally wouldn't leave him alone. Or rather *her*, the pestered second-year creative writing student inside the bear's body. On the plus side, the kids' events were all sold out, although the poets were the best acts, Dr Alex thought. They didn't care if they had an audience or not. In fact, their audience, for the most part, was the other poets.

To top the day off, a live band in the Brewery managed to drown out the authors doing the later slots, after mine, in the outside tents. Dr Alex shakes his head.

Dr Alex: And that was only Day One.
FP: So, are you all pumped for today?
Dr Alex: I'm bloody sick of this.

To Francis Plug

A
BRIEF
HISTORY
of
SEVEN
KILLINGS

Marlon James

"Dead people
never stop talking"

ONEWORLD

In the days after the festival, I collect all the Blu-Tack from the station-ery cupboard and set about creating my own death mask.

Dr Alex: Francis? What are you doing?
FP: I caa bweeve.

It's a period of self-reflection and personal soul-searching. Attempt-ing to learn just where I sit in this complex and confusing world of letters. It's not like book festivals are a new field for me. I've been kicked out of the biggest ones going. But having rubbed shoulders with the literary who's who, attending their events and shaking hands, this goodwill and support hasn't been reciprocated in kind. At my time of need, nothing but closed doors. You think you know a National Book Awardee like the back of your hand, and they leave you out in the rain like a cake.

Although there's been no direct fallout from the festival, it has been suggested I do more teaching. This translates, I believe, as 'earn your keep', or 'pull your finger out'. As weird as it may sound, I'm actually up for the task. To date, I've been more of a recluse in residence than a writer. What little student contact I've had has been overshadowed by bad smells, involving rubber, fish, and petrol. It would be a real shame if I were to finish my post without forming some sort of bond with the Creative Writing students. Instead of forming the shape of eye sockets, with blue adhesive putty.

Dr Alex confirms my teaching slot date. I'm to present a two-hour lecture on publishing. Setting aside my novel writing, I focus on inspiring and uplifting ideas for my paper, to be delivered, not entirely sober, but at least with masked breath, in dry clothing.

Two hours is a long time to wang on. Having been to dozens of author events, there's nothing more boring than a writer reading great swathes of their work. Some authors certainly like the sound of their own voice. When shouting in alleyways, or caves, my own voice always strikes me as rather nasally. Imagine listening to that for two hours. My slot at the Literary Death Match was only seven minutes, and it very nearly did me in. Some distractions will clearly be needed, and lots of opportunities for student interaction. Hopefully with stutters, some of them.

Marlon James teaches English too. He has just emerged triumphant from the Booker shortlist to take the prize. Although Booker Prize winners are less on my radar these days, Marlon James is currently here, in London, and may have some useful teaching advice to impart. He teaches at Macalester College in Saint Paul, Minnesota. Who knows, maybe they need a Writer in Residence, without prizes or credible accolades, who doesn't know how to teach, and frankly shouldn't.

Claire Armitstead, the Guardian's Literary Editor, is interviewing Marlon James in her newspaper's Scott Room. She introduces him as 'someone most people wouldn't have heard of until a few months ago. Now he's man of the moment'. Marlon James wears his long dreadlocked hair out and loose over his smart black suit top, which has only been buttoned once, revealing a white T-shirt beneath. Before winning the Booker Prize, his first novel, *John Crow's Devil*, was rejected seventy-eight times by literary professionals working in the literary profession. One publisher went as far as to say: 'The Caribbean's not in.' Marlon James has written a blog that details certain expectations held by people in the literary world, which exclude people of black and ethnic minority backgrounds. 'Cultural ventriloquism' is how he describes it. Now, as a Booker Prize winner, he is rubbing shoulders with these people. Is he flicking their ears? What about karate slices behind the knees? Knuckles on the scalp, like a mixing bowl? Or is he, perhaps, simply blowing gently in their faces, causing eyes to close, sending wayward eyebrow hairs askew? I don't know. I'll have to ask.

Since winning the Booker Prize, Marlon James has found it interesting that people who would never normally consider his work are now actively reading it. People like Camilla, the Duchess of Cornwall. When she met Marlon James at the award ceremony, Camilla claimed she'd once shaken hands with Bob Marley.

FP: [*Cough.*] Bullshit.

In *Moby Dick*, Herman Melville suggests the sea is a university. In *A Brief History of Seven Killings*, Marlon James refers to prison as a university of sorts. In my case, *home* is a university, although I don't always make it back there, after big shortlist parties, for instance.

Marlon James' microphone is still affixed to his lapel when seated behind the signing desk, but at least he's remembered to switch it off. Perhaps he read that tip in my book.

Marlon James: Francis Plug?
FP: Yes. Have you read my book?
Marlon James: No.
FP: Darn. Um… congratulations on your Booker Prize win.
Marlon James: Thanks.
FP: I was actually at the shortlist party, at the Serpentine.
Marlon James: Ah, yes. I thought you looked familiar.

FP: Really? Did we talk? Wait… did you resuscitate me?

Marlon James: Resuscitate you? No, I didn't do that. But I did hear you singing. You were doing a lot of singing.

FP: Singing?

Marlon James: Oh yes. With the microphone. You don't remember?

FP: Not all the finer points, exactly…

Marlon James: You were walking around singing something about British people when the weather is hot. And you were growling.

FP: Ah. Well, at least I wasn't singing an Eric Clapton song. Especially one of them Jamaican ones.

Eric Clapton gets a brief roasting in Marlon James' book. This is a reference to Eric Clapton's well-documented concert outburst when he told his audience that Britain should 'get the foreigners out, get the wogs out, get the coons out', before shouting the National Front slogan, 'Keep Britain white'. All of which came after 'his' hit 'I Shot the Sheriff', courtesy of Bob Marley, a Jamaican.

Marlon James: Hmm. Yes.

FP: So you didn't come for a swim in the lido?

Marlon James: No, I can't say I did.

FP: Just as well. Trying to get a lift home was a nightmare. I ended up sleeping in the park.

Marlon James: That does not surprise me.

FP: What advice would you give someone about to teach creative writing students?

Marlon James: Oh. Just get them to question what they're writing and why they're writing it. I ask my students, why are screams always ear-shattering or blood-curdling? How much is a myriad? Why does nothing ever happen at 2 p.m.? That sort of thing.

FP: Interesting. I'll give that a whirl. Thanks, Marlon James.

Marlon James: Good luck.

FP: Cheers. Say, do you know anyone who can teach me how to use C-4 explosives?

Marlon James: Come again?

FP: C-4 explosives. I need to blow up a power station.

Marlon James: Um…

FP: Also, does Macalester College need a Writer in Residence? I'd like to put my hat in the ring, as it were. Singing isn't my strong point, granted, but I'd like to think I was warm, gentle, sensitive and kind.

Marlon James: Sorry, what was that about blowing up a power station…?

The Acknowledgements page of Marlon James' prize-winning novel is cheering. On it, he concedes the book took four years to write, and was helped by a one-year sabbatical and a travel and research grant from Macalester College. This allowed him to conduct his own research on top of that being conducted already by his three or four researchers. That's worth sharing with the Greenwich students. If you're studying full-time and also pulling pints at a cheerful pub, relax. There's no rush. Even Booker Prize winners have to take time off work to write, and those that don't probably need to get out more.

In *Dead Poets Society*, John Keating, played by Robin Williams, is an English teacher at an all-boys school, like the one in Tobias Wolff's *Old School*. Mr Keating kicks off his first lesson by leading his students out of the classroom, down a staircase, and into a foyer area. Here the wall is adorned with black and white photos of the school's 'old boys', now long dead. The point of this, he explains, is that you, the modern-day students, will be dead one day too. Just as Robin

Williams himself is, proving his character's point. So live *now*, is the message. Seize the day.

Taking the students for a walk is a masterstroke. It's a brilliant way to kill time, and I really need to kill some of that class time, so I can seize the day.

FP: Peow, peow!

In *Nice Work*, the final part of David Lodge's campus trilogy, lecturer Robyn Penrose offers some comforting advice: 'a good teacher, like a good actress, should not be immune from stage fright.' This is something Janet Frame might have benefited from. And it's relevant to me, right now, as I see a queue of students loitering outside KW202, ten minutes before we're scheduled to start. Adele, who works in the department office, has arrived to unlock the door and switch on the lights. But the presence of the over-keen students means I'm unable to do my limbering up exercises, such as horizontal punches, in private. With ten minutes still to kill, and an ever-building audience, I set the alarm on my old phone, and with hands over my face, lower my arms and head to the table.

Ten minutes later, springing up, I rub my eyes, then my hands.

FP: Right! Let's learn!

More students have seated themselves during my nap. Their bench desks contain computer monitors, which some of them hide behind. My table is in its own broad space, exposed, with a modern office chair behind. Although upholstered, the chair, for the most part, is plastic. It's the sort of modern chair that's an affront to sustainability and environmental protection. Perversely, it's just the sort of chair I'd love to heave into the river with the fishes. Wheels, also made from plastic, lessen any further claims to sturdiness. Standing on it therefore is a task laden with threat. Hoping to use it as a step, to reach the table, I instead swivel around, on one foot, with my back to the class. Stepping down, I make a second ascent, this time with one hand gripping the table itself. The frisky chair, now more contained, permits an ungainly, though successful, approach. Standing upright on the table, I survey the classroom scene.

FP: Hello, everyone.

Many of the students are recognizable from the previous sessions. Most of them probably have pre-formed dispositions towards me, which are likely negative. But this lecture is going to change all that. Less tyre. More inspire.

FP: I'm standing on top of this table because as a writer, it's good to get a different perspective on things.

Some of the students look at each other, their eyes still lacking that requisite glint.

FP: Who wants to come up here and get a fresh perspective? Go on.

There are no takers, so I gently prod further.

FP: Go on.

About three quarters of the class are women, and it is a member of this majority who finally takes the initiative.

FP: Yay! Oh, mind yourself there. That chair's bloody mental.

Using a hand to help hoist her up, I move to one side, proffering space, before calling for new recruits.

FP: Come on, the rest of you. Change your perspective, why don't you?

There's a sense of hesitation from the others, possibly due to the wobbly table, and the mental chair. *Dead Poets Society* was filmed way back in 1989, when accident liability claims were still light years away. Also, the chairs were probably the tried and tested models, with four straight legs, that didn't move. As for the students, well. They've probably never even climbed trees before, this lot.

The brave volunteer is more successful at coaxing her fellows up, possibly because, as the canary in the mine, she has thus far survived unscathed. Soon there's a small party of us, like an emperor penguin egg-hatching ceremony. It dawns on me that the *Dead Poets* version was done in an orderly, one-person-on-one-person-off fashion, whereas we appear to be attempting a Guinness record. Like the table, I'm starting to feel less grounded, unhelped by insides filled with wine.

FP: Look at the new perspective… whoahh!

Stepping onto A4 pages containing pre-prepared notes, my foot slips forward and I go arse about face. It's an all-too familiar situation, although this time, after my head cracks the table edge, there's more of a drop.

Certain thoughtful students attend to my wellbeing, and I hope we can now call it a day. But we're barely ten minutes in. They've paid good money for two hours of me.

FP: I'm fine. That little slip was nothing. In my old life, I used to fall out of trees all the time.

Taking another leaf from John Keating's book, I suggest we ditch this hazard-filled classroom and escape to safety.

FP: Come on everyone. We're going to seize the day. Follow me. *Carpe diem!*

With no route in mind, I start by taking advantage of Wren's architectural limitations, directing the students on a pointless journey around the King William building, up one staircase, down another, up another. Like Maureen, my tour guide of repute, I impart useful info along the way.

FP: Jonathan Franzen kicked a book up those stairs. The college ghosts did a wee just there…

Outside I stop for a cigarette break. The smoke, I explain, is purely for atmosphere.

FP: Like Dickens' fog, right? In the pensioners' throats, yeah?

The Painted Hall has tables. Much longer and sturdier than the classroom's. Thinking we could stand on these, I lead the student contingent hither, as if in breeches, with a flute. Unfortunately, the restoration work has moved up a notch. The hall's ground level is effectively closed. A temporary floor has been built right up near the ceiling itself, and special guided tours offer visitors the chance to see the lauded art up close. You're supposed to book for these tours, which costs money. But, I explain, we're a class from the university, learning about new perspectives.

FP: This would be perfect for their studies. The university will pay. Don't you worry about a thing.

Marlon James once questioned why nothing in fiction ever happens at 2 p.m. Well, it's 2:34 p.m., Marlon, and we're about to ascend sixty feet to stare at a friggin' ceiling.

Our guide, fortunately, is new. At least, I think she is. We're told to don hard hats and blue visibility vests, which, being blue, aren't very visible at all. After climbing the scaffold steps to the vast false floor, we encounter another tour group, who are kitted out in red. It almost makes sense to suggest a game of footie, especially since we have more players. But there's no ball, and I'm still feeling a bit woozy after falling off the table.

Our guide, although a quietly spoken older woman, is easy to hear thanks to our headphones, which amplify her commentary. Quietly spoken or not, at least *she's* doing the talking. The last time the Painted Hall ceiling got a touch up, she says, was in the 1950s. The young women engaged in this work today are different from the ones I spoke to on the scaffold. Although wearing similar overalls, they're equipped with small vacuum cleaners and soft cloths. In the old days, this work was mostly carried out by artists, but today it's far more methodical and less art based. Interestingly, past conservatoires have left their signatures on the ceiling, which our guide highlights with her torch. The cheekiest scribe by far has penned their name on the exposed chest of Queen Mary, in the ceiling centre.

FP: Unbelievable. That wasn't Benny Hill, was it?

If I leapt up, arm outstretched, I could touch the Painted Ceiling, no doubt adding to its regressed state. However, upon landing, I'd probably go right through the makeshift floor, falling sixty feet to my death. So when the students and guide are absorbed in some detail or other, I instead lean through some bars at the far end and touch the gilded nose of Mars. Together with Athena, his bust relief sits above the Proscenium Arch. In years to come, when all this scaffolding and fake floor have been packed away, I shall point some sixty feet up at Mars and laugh and say, 'Hey, big guy. I've touched your friggin' nose!'

Of all the many characters depicted on the ceiling, my favourite is the old naval pensioner John Worley. John Worley spent seventy years at sea and lived to the grand old age of ninety-six. According to the Seaman Hospital records, he was a real troublemaker, due to his drunken antics. But even drunken antics couldn't deny him the honour of a painted portrait by Sir James Thornhill, and a permanent place in this most hallowed of sites. Which is kind of reassuring. Perhaps one day, drunken pensioners will again be housed in these buildings, with the more lenient criteria of one year's service.

Well, *I* certainly learnt a thing or two. As far as sticking with my 'New Perspectives' topic, this class has been a total winner. The students appear enthused and altogether positive. Except, perhaps, for the student bearing down on me now.

Student: Out of interest, what was the relevance of that lesson to our Publishing stream?
FP: Publishing? Oh… yeah…

I'm reminded of a very old *Taxi* episode where Jim tries to earn extra money through door-to-door selling. Attempting to convince a customer of his vacuum cleaner's superior qualities, he coats their carpet in all manner of filth, before remembering he's selling encyclopaedias.

FP: The thing is…
Student: Not that I'm complaining. It was really good.
FP: Oh. Good. Thanks.

Bloody hell. Maybe I'm finally getting a grip on this teaching lark after all.

Student: Oh, is that blood on your head? From your desk fall?
FP: What? This? No! It's jam!

Teaching is exhausting stuff, and I return to King William in need of a lie down. During the day, my camp bed is stored upright, out of sight, behind the door. On rare occasions, when especially tired, I'll shunt the extended bed towards the corner, sinking into it like freshly boiled vegetables in a strainer, draining. But approaching my room today, I see someone from maintenance carrying my bed out into the hallway, together with my towel, which previously straddled the radiator. From inside comes the sound of bottles being gathered together in a bag. June, a department secretary, stands in the doorway, flicking through a book from my pile, signed and dedicated to Francis Plug. As she catches my tarsier eyes, I'm reminded of those film scenes where supposed criminals return home to find their personal stuff being carried out in sealed boxes by folk in white jumpsuits, while uniformed staff stand guard, with rifles. The dome clock would do well to toll at this point, but after a protracted wait, it doesn't.

DEAR COMMITTEE MEMBERS

Julie Schumacher

For Francis Glug, with all best wishes from Julie

THE FRIDAY PROJECT

Although feeling like the faded figure of King Louis XIV, sword broken, crown askew, beneath the foot of William III, I'm well prepared for my disgrace. Disgrace is a running theme in campus novels. *Disgrace*, by J.M. Coetzee, is one example that springs to mind. There've been many others. *Blue Angel*, *Straight Man*, *The War Between the Tates*, *The Human Stain*, and *Lucky Jim*, to name but a few. And it's not just works of fiction I can learn from. Jeffrey Archer is a master in real life.

Although I've been mired in scandals before, I don't claim to be any sort of authority. Jeffrey Archer, however, has scaled new heights of the genre. As a Conservative politician, he resigned twice in disgrace. One occasion almost left him bankrupt. Another led to him being convicted and imprisoned for perjury and perverting the course of justice. But, thanks to his writing and authorship, he bounced back. These days, he's apparently sold around 330 million copies of his books.

FP: To who? Who are you people? *What* are you?

My sales are decidedly smaller. In fact, this was a matter I had hoped to discuss with Jeffrey Archer at his signing. The question of whether he could buy millions of copies of my book.

Despite being a national disgrace, Jeffrey Archer is supported by the publishing industry. Mass murderers are known to get book deals too. Hitler's manifesto, for instance, sells very well. It's a funny old business. After supposedly wrecking a Booker Prize ceremony, I was allowed to attend another one, presumably because I was a 'published' author. Just like Jeffrey Archer, and Hitler.

Jeffrey Archer hasn't won the Booker Prize, not because he's a jailbird but because his work, though popular, is not of the prerequisite standard. But neither is mine, and I've fallen on my arse. My new book should meet required literary levels, given its campus setting. Then again, literary books don't tend to sell well, and I need money because I'm rather hand-to-mouth. With any luck, the action/adventure sections of my campus novel should broaden its appeal, especially the cataclysmic blasts. And, of course, there's the sperm scenes.

A meeting has been scheduled with Dr Zoë in regards to my 'other' residency. A smart suit and tie are in order, but failing that, I make do with my former work clothes, for the garden.

At the end of our corridor, between the coffee area and the toilet, are two blue chairs, which face back along the hallway like thrones. These are for people waiting to see Dr Zoë, the Head of Department, Dr Alex in the opposite office, or other faculty members in adjoining rooms. The staff, from my limited experience, are good, caring people. But the students waiting on these blue chairs often look strung out. Sometimes they're crying. It isn't easy being a student in this day and age. Not only do you need to choose the right subjects, concentrate on your studies, complete the required coursework, meet your deadlines, study for your exams, and pass them, but you also have to survive in the outside world too. Some of the Greenwich students, Dr Alex tells me, have young children to raise, older family to support, and paid jobs, beyond academia, in order to live. London has become a city which even their lecturers can't afford. Yet our students must pay £9,000 every year for the privilege of studying. Successive prime ministers, despite not having to pay for the educations that helped them become prime ministers, have done nothing to correct this. As a system it is deeply unfair, favouring only the moneyed and privileged, while keeping the less fortunate down and without opportunity for ascension. Even a dumb-arse can understand that.

Those lucky enough to find the money aren't exactly guaranteed a windfall either. £9,000 is more than I'm earning, as Writer in Residence. So any students studying hard in the hope of being a Writer in Residence might want to hang onto that Wetherspoons job.

As a member of university staff, you must be ready to provide advice and guidance, both on a curriculum and a personal level. You should be prepared to offer sympathy, positive encouragement, and a firm steer. As an influential figure in the department, this should have been my remit too: offering support, and a voice of limited, questionable experience. But if that was my duty, then I regret to say I have failed. Instead, I've been like that singer who couldn't tell someone he loved them and had to put it in a song instead. As the saying goes, those who can't, write.

Dr Zoë: Francis, how are you?

FP: Not too shabby, thank you.

Dr Zoë: Good. Thanks for meeting up. So… I understand you've been sleeping in one of the rooms here.

FP: Yes. Apart from when I was woken by the film crews. And by those blasting horns and fireworks. And by the pensioner ghosts, with their rattly chains.

Dr Zoë: So… how long have you actually been sleeping here?

FP: Um, it must have been since the time of the bottle factory outing.

Dr Zoë: Sorry? *The Bottle Factory Outing*? Isn't that a novel?

FP: The staff outing I mean. From the department.

Dr Zoë: The staff outing? Which one was that?

FP: The Christmas one.

Dr Zoë: Oh. You've been sleeping in here since *last year*?

FP: Living here, yes. This has been my home. In a spare, unused room. Much warmer than the garage. And I've saved a blimmin' packet on bus fares.

Dr Zoë: You were living in a garage previously?

FP: Correct. Like a car, but with short, hairy legs.

Dr Zoë: Oh, Francis.

Dr Zoë holds her pen horizontally in front of her face, with two hands, as if twiddling the ends of a blue moustache.

Dr Zoë: I can't let you sleep in the building, Francis. It's a security issue, ultimately. They're really clamping down on things. I'm amazed you've managed to go undetected.

FP: I'm quiet as a mouse. Apart from when I sing. Sing and clap and cha-cha-cha.

Dr Zoë: Francis…

FP: I don't want to cause a fuss. It's just… I'm worried this is turning into a re-enactment of my first book.

When it comes to getting kicked out of places and moved along, I have a past. It really doesn't help to cement my position as a respected writer of repute. In the old days, a 'reputation' was a good thing. Think Burroughs, Parker, Voltaire, Wilde. Most contemporary authors, it seems to me, are pretty safe bets. I'm not suggesting they all start living on opioids and absinthe, in garages. But now and then can't hurt. Not the *student* writers, of course. They need to get their homework done!

Like schools, universities have rules. And rules are rules. It would be unfair for me to use my position to try and sway favour with the powers that be. Because, next thing you know, all the staff and students will want to save on transport and rent by living in a Christopher Wren pad, sending money back to family and loved ones, and ultimately forging a better life. In the Royal Borough of Kensington and Chelsea, all manner of palatial homes lie barren and empty because the top 1% have bought them as investments, rather than as homes. In Doris Lessing's *The Good Terrorist*, Alice and comrades legally squat in an unoccupied house. The current government, however, has declared this illegal, despite billing us, the taxpayers, for homes with moats, for their ducks. Jeffrey Archer, a national disgrace, now lives in a multi-million pound apartment on the Thames, near the Houses of Parliament, which, despite their name, no one actually lives in either.

They've started filming on campus again. It's yet another TV series focused on the royal family. This one is called *The Crown* and is based around the life of Elizabeth II. The first season is currently being shot, with Claire Foy playing the young Queen. It's astonishing how these film folk just take over the place. So many people. Here I was thinking it was all done on computers these days. They've even got a massive fan machine, to generate wind.

FP: Does it blow away clouds, that thing?
Crew Member: Not to my knowledge, no.
FP: I bet it does. I really could have used that at our Book Festival. Seriously, you'll put the blimmin' Fan Museum out of business with that bastard.

The crew have set up on Upper Grand Square, and they're shooting in the direction of King William Court and our office. Every time they start rolling, I hold my book up to the window and wave it frantically about. Given everyone has TVs the size of fridge-freezers these days, I'm hopeful it will really jump out.

The college gardeners are going to have their work cut out after this lot's gone. Spray paint won't solve that mess, caused, one could argue, by the Queen herself. They might need an extra pair of hands. With the tide going out on my residency, I need to try and stay afloat. Going from a titled position in a cushy office to a role tending grounds may take some adjusting. Blowing wet leaves into piles on cold, muddy mud, is not exactly my blockbuster movie tie-in. Still, needs must. A Hungarian advance might get me some good boots and a few necessary tools, but it won't afford me a charmed life. It's been nice existing within these stately grounds, but soon I'll need to up sticks and resume life on the outside. Perhaps, there's a small room, going for free, in the Queen's House…

The college gardeners work into the Buildings Manager, who has an office in Queen Anne. Although it would be quicker and more direct to drop by in person, I instead pen a long letter, using my honed craft to outline a keen interest in gardening opportunities. The Buildings Manager is a chap by the name of Denis. His office is Room 059 in Queen Anne Court. Letter written, I drop by his door, hoping to get in, get out, quick as a flash.

Unfortunately, a man, possibly Denis, is sitting inside Room 059, ready to take delivery of my letter.

Man: What's this?
FP: This? It's for Denis.
Denis: That's me.
FP: Well. It's for you, then.
Denis: What is it?
FP: What is it? Maybe you should read it and find out.
Denis: Is it from you?

FP: What do you mean?

Denis: What do I mean? I mean, is *this* from *you*?

FP: I really don't want to talk about that.

Denis: You don't want to talk about it? Why not?

FP: Because. I spent a lot of time writing it. For you to *read*.

Denis: So it *is* from you. Why don't you just tell me what it's about?

FP: I have. In words. It's right there. In there. With your name on it.

Denis: Okay. Well, what's the general gist?

FP: Read with your eyes! Honestly! Make an effort!

Denis: Make an effort? You want *me* to make an effort? You can't even be arsed speaking with your own mouth.

FP: There's no need for that. It's a perfectly straightforward letter.

Denis: Then why won't you tell me what it's about?

FP: Because it took me ages to write it! You nonk!

Denis: Nonk? What the hell is a nonk?

FP: You! You're one! You're a nonk!

Anyway, he's got my contact details and a list of references, with phone numbers and what-have-you. So, y'know, fingers crossed.

At the Morden Arms, I make a point of assessing the sleeping opportunities. It could be a mutually beneficial arrangement, I explain to Judith and David, the landlords.

Judith: You? Sleeping in here? Alone? Overnight?

FP: Another way of looking at it, you see, is that I'll be like a guard dog, protecting the bar from intruders.

David: Ha, ha. Yes. I think what worries us, Francis, is... who will protect the bar from you?

While waiting for Ray Chipps to arrive, I allow myself a shot of Prairie Vodka and set about reading Julie Schumacher's campus novel *Dear Committee Members*. Despite all the worry, anxiety and panic currently clouding my world, I have to laugh. It really is a very funny book. Jason T. Fitger (Jay), a Creative Writing and English professor, is endorsing his students, via a series of letters and emails, for employment in the big wide world. Unlike my discouraging sober truths, *Dear Committee Members* highlights the many benefits of a bookish education, deftly landing the wonderful pin-points of creative writing, the study of books, and the humanity of it all.

> *I thoroughly urge you to offer her a job. Why? Because, as a student of literature and creative writing, Ms Newcomb honed crucial traits that will be of use to you: imagination, patience, resourcefulness, and empathy. The reading and writing of fiction both requires and instils empathy – the insertion of oneself into the life of another.*

And:

> *Let me suggest that, no matter the variety of employment, there is nothing more relevant or crucial than an aptitude for original thought and imaginative expression.*

Julie Schumacher is herself a faculty member of the Creative Writing Program and the Department of English at the University of Minnesota. I could really use some of her positive reinforcement in my own campus novel. Although I'd need to cite my sources. Otherwise, as the Student Union posters warn, I 'will be caught'. Do I have to cite that source too, the poster source that tells me to cite my sources? Perhaps if I alter it slightly, I could pass it off as my own. Otherwise, as the Student Union posters warn, I 'will be tipped, arse-end first, down a deep, dark well'.

Ray always refuses to be bought a drink, but today I insist. On my way to the bar, coins fall out of my pocket onto the Morden's hard wooden floor.

FP: Oh no!
Ray: What is it?
FP: My Hello Kitty coin pouch has a hole in it!

There's been no correspondence from Denis, the Buildings Manager, in regards to my letter. This despite outlining my very keen interest in simple, plainer than plain English. Also, unlike Jason T. Fitger, none of the students have asked me for letters of recommendation. Not a sausage. Still, as Jay himself writes, 'I shall wish her well and be the first to welcome her to "the writing life", which, despite its horrors, is possibly one of the few sorts of lives worth living at all.'

A number of university staff have offered me a temporary bed, with accompanying roof, in the comfort of their own homes. It's extremely kind of them, and a bit embarrassing. Due to London rents, they all tend to live miles away, in other places. The train fares are a fright, and the prospect of timetabled car journeys, involving chat, followed by evenings of good behaviour and more chat, is, as a prospect, completely unfeasible. Claiming to be lodging with a 'friend', I quickly find my fold-out bed in one of the basement storage rooms. Rather than carting it away somewhere, I leave it where it is, in my new bedroom. Accessing this level after hours is much easier than climbing three flights of stairs. A colleague's house might be cosier and more comfortable, but here I can drink to my heart's content, and when I laugh for long periods, seemingly without reason, the general vibe doesn't die. Also, being windowless, it's perfect for sleeping soundly. Or, as Hans Fallada writes, 'that pitch-black sleep that alcohol induces, in which one is, so to speak, extinguished, one dies a modified death. There are no dreams, no notions of light and life – off into nothingness!'

The Painted Hall is accessible after hours too, simply by creeping up the stairwell beneath the King William dome. From my new basement room, armed with a bottle of Cutty Sark, I can be there in less than a minute. Normally, tonight's full moon would illuminate the many characters on the walls and ceiling, via refracted light from the tiles. But for now, the ceiling is a floor, made of wood. Up there, near the ceiling, it's very dark indeed. Procuring a ladder from the current renovation site, I plop it down somewhere near the ceiling's centre. Leaning on its upper step, back contorted, I reach up with my pen to write:

> *To Greenwich,*
> *All the best.*
> *Kind regards,*
> *Francis Plug.*

The next morning, when the Old Royal Naval College staff arrive, Francis Plug is lying prone, in state, in the Painted Hall.

J. G. BALLARD

THE
UNLIMITED
DREAM
COMPANY

To Francis Plug

JG Ballard

JONATHAN CAPE
THIRTY BEDFORD SQUARE LONDON

The automatic doors of Broadcasting House may have ushered me in with a sweep, but I depart my university home through a heavy old side door, which needs a really good yank. Perhaps the BBC has some openings. The best writers today, it's said, are writing TV programmes.

BBC Interviewer: What TV experience do you have?
FP: Well, I've written for David Attenborough. And I wrote the opening titles for *EastEnders*.

As of this morning, my tenure is officially over. My life as a paid-up writer finished, without ceremony. No fireworks, no blasting ship horns. After some sympathetic words from Dr Zoë, I returned my keys to Dr Alex, who shook my hand and wished me the best.

Dr Alex: We're looking forward to reading your book. Is it still a campus novel? I can't keep up.
FP: Partially. And also a guidebook, for the students.
Dr Alex: The Creative Writing students?
FP: Yes. It's a crash-course, pedal to the metal, like a Parisian toilet flusher.
Dr Alex: Well. Sounds like something I should read myself.
FP: I hope so. I'll need a cover endorsement, to prove that it's hot stuff.

Vacating the office, I bid farewell to my good friend and fellow author, Dr Alex.

FP: Don't forget to write!

My bedding and books, I realize, are still in the basement, which I can now no longer access. Parking this problem for later, I decide to take a final look at Greenwich from the lofty perch on the hill. There's no sign of any squirrels in Greenwich Park, or anarchists, for that matter. The squirrels have successfully completed their task of collecting and putting aside for later, and now they're kicking back somewhere, having a nap. Some of us had rather less foresight. The plan to invest my university pay in gardening equipment, to continue my trade beyond academia, has long ago withered and died. While the sun was shining I wasn't making hay. I was weeing hops and barley.

Rather than taking the windy public path to the observatory, I march straight up the steep grassy incline, side-stepping discarded bottles of London Pride. The cold hasn't dissuaded the tour groups, nor the threat of being blown to smithereens. A group of Oriental folk are being led up the spirally hill path by a young man in a hi-vis vest. He is holding a blue flag on a protruding pole, as if planning to plant it in the hill's summit. Their happy tourist chatter is drowned out by two helicopters hovering overhead. Perhaps they're BBC helicopters. Waving with two criss-crossing arms, I perform a climbing action, requesting a rope ladder.

To the north-east, planes take off from City Airport, heading for short haul business stops, or early Christmas destinations. Waterstones haven't invited me back to their Christmas evening, possibly because my book is 'last year', or because the red wine still hasn't come out of the Snowman. With a bit of imagination, however, they could adopt the costume for another book character. One of Stephen King's victims, for instance, or Stevie from *The Secret Agent*.

My aerial view of the Old Royal Naval College is blurred by watery eyes, as if I were strapped inside a burning, smoke-filled cockpit. The college buildings have barely changed in hundreds of years, but today they are cast in a brilliant, unreal glow, with strange crane appendages jabbing out amongst them. It's the film company, hoping to coat Greenwich with impossible dreams. That was supposed to be my job. I had the official imaginary role, not them. Unfortunately, circumstances have intervened. Rather than ferrying the students away, via rope ladder, or splashing enlightenment about like Blake in J.G. Ballard's *The Unlimited Dream Company*, I've been grounded. Ballard's book has been called 'above all a book about the fertility of the imagination'. It's a book I should have shouted about to the students, from the table tops. Although, from experience, it's probably the real world they're going to struggle with.

The wintry sun is shining on the Millennium Dome's dome, melting its ice cream peak. In the foreground are the power station's chimneys, protruding like the upended legs of a Keith Haring dog. Further back, behind the Isle of Dogs, the Canary Wharf skyscrapers are nothing short of hotch-potch. Compared with the carefully aligned Queen's House and Old Royal Naval College, they're a bloody shambles. A pigeon with very pink feet patters past, its back to the bird's-eye view. Peck, peck, peck, picking at the cigarette ends, in case they're made from cake. A small boy runs up behind, clapping his hands, giving it a hurry-on.

Kid: Shoo, shoo! Fly away, fly away!

Down in the Visitor Centre, it's very quiet. For some reason, people seem less drawn to costumed dress when it's blinkin' cold. Having the pick of the crop, I opt for a pilot's attire, in the spirit of Ballard's Blake. In *The Unlimited Dream Company*, Blake crashes his plane into the Thames, next to Shepperton. But my own contraption, I tell the film guy, fell spiralling into King William.

FP: [*Brushing myself off.*] It's all right, I'm okay.
Film Security Guy: Sorry?
FP: No drama. It's only a plane crash. I'm fine.

There's no sign of Kevin, the previous film security guy. Still, there's enough 'CREW' here to sail an armada.

Film Security Guy: I didn't realize there were pirates in this. Being about the Queen and all.
FP: Pirates? I'm sure there aren't.
Film Security Guy: Well, *you're* supposed to be one, right?
FP: Me? No, you're mistaken. I'm a pilot, a pioneer of aviation, a master of the skies.
Film Security Guy: So why are you dressed like a pirate? And I don't think you should be drinking that on set.
FP: London Pride? It's not my usual tipple, granted. But it was a special at the off-licence. And I like to show my support for the LGBTI community.

This security guard's called Bill. Bill has no idea when or where the wrap party for *The Crown* is. Nor can he promise that Queen Elizabeth II will receive my makeshift business card, for gardening services.

Bill: Does wardrobe know you're supposed to be a pilot? 'Pilot' does sound a lot like 'Pirate'. Seriously, all you're missing is a parrot on your shoulder…
FP: I saw a parrot earlier, flying about the college. Did you see it? There were also some condors, pelicans, scarlet macaws, scarlet

ibises, flamingoes, kites, petrels, cormorants, fulmars, cockatoos, frigate birds, deep water albatrosses, vultures, peacocks, and emperor penguins. Whooper swans, secretary birds, golden eagles, waxwings, lyre birds, falcons, and flying fish. Just earlier. Flying about here they were, except the penguins.

Bill: I must have missed them.

FP: Francis of Assisi used to talk to birds. They would line up along his arms, perching on it.

Bill: Is that right?

FP: Yes. Ray Chipps told me. I'm a Francis too, but I'm not Assisi.

An elaborate façade has been added to the side entrance of the Queen Anne building, and a vintage car is being filmed driving up to this. Queen Anne, Bill informs me, is now Buckingham Palace. The camera is dangling on the end of a moveable black crane, like a piece of bait on the end of a huge fishing rod. A number of cast members in period dress mill around nearby. Behind the waist-high alloy fencing stand the curious public, comprised of the day-to-day tourist crowd, students, and university staff. A woman emerges from Buckingham Palace talking into a walkie-talkie. Unlike the actors in their drab period costume, she is wearing a bright-orange bomber jacket and blue jeans. I hear her talking through Bill's walkie-talkie.

Bomber Jacket Woman: Okay, wrap for lunch, wrap for lunch.

The cast begin to wander off towards the west lawns.

Bill: You better go get something to soak up your Pride.

FP: One of those wraps, you mean?

Bill: Ha. Nice one.

FP: Eh?

The cast form a long queue for food, donning thin white plastic aprons to protect their costumes. This makes a lot of sense. After my Snowman episode, it's all too easy to see how food and drink disasters can occur. One wayward ketchup squirt and viewers will ask, 'Who shot the lady-in-waiting?' Food is being served out the side of a truck, while converted double-decker buses, with tables, double as canteens. The big stars are no doubt eating privately in their Winnebagos, still parked along the tree-lined grove. There is a choice of meals, which are free, but I'm not hungry.

FP: I'm not a food sort of person. Big meals tend to wipe me out. They drain my energy, rather than boost it. Maybe because they soak up the alcohol, which is my lifeblood. Could I just grab a cheeky pint or two, to save me queuing up?

The catering crew don't serve alcoholic drinks, they tell me. That's very strange, I tell them.

FP: I thought this whole film/TV thing was supposed to be a journey into an unreality. Alcohol is perfect in that regard, surely?

Catering Chap: Well, no. As an actor you're supposed to 'act' drunk, aren't you? Isn't that how it all works?

FP: Yes, but it's never very convincing. Why bother acting when you can do it for real?

Catering Chap: But then it wouldn't be, as you say, '*un*real'.

FP: So confusing!

Catering Chap: I can't imagine there's much call for 'drunk' roles in this production anyway. The last thing they'll want is some inebriated twats stumbling around.

FP: Of course, right you are. I'll be sure to keep an eye out for any.

My protective apron is covering my replete tummy when I pay a return visit to the off-licence. It's not for everyone, the drink. As J.G. Ballard said, unless you're disciplined, all you end up with is a lot of empty wine bottles. Despite starting early on the whisky, he used to write 1,000 words a day, hangover or no hangover. That's the sort of food I could use. Food for thought.

FP: Look, it's the Queen!

Claire Foy has emerged from a winnebago, chaperoned by 'her people'. Even off-set she's like royalty, sheltered from the real world, elevated to some ethereal place where the light is filtered and the landscape freshly painted. It can't be good for your head, all those paint fumes.

At least she's not a national treasure. Not yet. It must be a nightmare for the likes of David Attenborough, and Mr Blobby. All the smiling, and the handshakes, and those sad people, desperate to be your mate. The real Queen would know all about that. As national treasures go, she's probably top of the rung, despite not holding any particular talent, except reigning. Even when mixing with her subjects, she seems to lack a necessary gregariousness, or the outgoing qualities useful for social interaction. You get the feeling, given the preference, she'd sooner keep her distance entirely. Perhaps she's secretly a writer. Maybe her Christmas speech is just the tip of the iceberg.

After sitting drinking under one of the large plane trees, I take my cue from the other cast members to return to the set. Bill has pulled the metal fence back to let us through, and I give him a wink and a big thumbs-up. One of the other extras is dressed like Andy Capp.

FP: What part are you playing?

403

Actor: I play the role of Hodgkins, the journalist.

FP: A writer? OMG. I've just played that role myself.

Actor: Have you? Any advice?

FP: Well, you should appear terrified of other people, eyes diverted, head lowered, subservient, running away.

Actor: Really?

FP: Yes. It also helps if you can hide inside a costume, like a snowman or a dog. If not, pulling strange and funny faces is good.

Actor: Blimey. And how does a pirate fit into all this?

FP: Sorry, enough of the chit-chat. I need to get into character.

The woman in the bomber jacket ushers us urgently into position with her walkie-talkie. Presumably, we need to mill around in the foreground, while the vintage car drives up to the Palace behind. But I could be wrong. I totally missed rehearsals.

Bomber Jacket Woman: Positions, please!

FP: You bet!

Bomber Jacket Woman: Whoah. Hang on, hang on. Who the hell are you?

FP: Me? I'm the pilot.

Bomber Jacket Woman: Pirate? What fucking pirate?

FP: No, not 'pirate'; *pilot*. I'm the *pilot*. The *pilot*.

Bomber Jacket Woman: Pilot?

FP: Yes. *Pilot*. Normally I'm at home in the skies, soaring majestically. But my home crashed and burned, just over there. So now it's a walk-on role.

Bomber Jacket Woman: No, look at you. You're a fucking pirate. And we don't have any fucking pirates. Bill?

FP: But... my plane, it crashes, yeah? And me, I live, yeah? And walk? Yeah?

Bomber Jacket Woman: If you walk anywhere near that camera, you most certainly will not walk, *or* live. Yeah? Bill? Get rid of this fucking pirate. And *don't* let him back in!

Bill isn't well pleased. His displeasure is signalled by his violent repositioning of the fence gate. And by his sarcastic farewell.

Bill: Thanks for that. Thanks a fucking lot.

Because it's now Buckingham Palace, the Queen Anne building has presumably been outfitted with the prerequisite number of toilets. That being seventy-eight, all up. With fifty-two royal and guest bedrooms, and one hundred and eighty-eight staff bedrooms. Since my access to King William has been revoked, I'm in need of a bedroom myself.

There's no chance of waltzing through the main Palace entrance, so I pop round the back where a different guard holds fort. It's off-limits, he says, due to the filming. But producing my staff pass, now a worthless, unsustainable chunk of plastic, I explain that I have urgent business with the Queen.

FP: Don't shoot the messenger!

The guard hesitates before letting me through. He continues watching as I fumble with my pass, trying to find the pocket in my pilot suit.

The courtyard is populated with many film folk in civilian attire. Apart from talking to each other, they don't seem engaged in any meaningful employment. Seeing me, dressed in uniform for a reputable job, they stop and stare. So I dash up a nearby stairwell, seeking bedroom opportunities in Buckingham Palace.

Although formerly housing hundreds of students, and hundreds of navy staff before them, I suspect there aren't anywhere near enough toilets for Buckingham Palace's needs. My initial check, indeed, suggests they fall well short. The first floor is very quiet, and all the lecture rooms, yet to be gilded and upholstered with the finest Persian fabrics, are bare. My phone ringtone, in comparison, is very noisy.

FP: Hello?

Man: Is that Francis Plug?

FP: Yes?

Man: Hi, it's Richard here from the Inland Revenue. Is now a good time to talk?

FP: No. I'm actually in Buckingham Palace at the moment, one of the Queen's houses.

Man: Oh, really?

FP: Yes. I have a private audience, so this call is most inopportune.

Richard: I understand.

FP: Her Majesty really isn't interested in the trifling payment of taxes.

Richard: Um...

FP: We'll talk soon then, shall we?

Richard: When would be...?

Beep, beep, beep.

The second floor, like the first, is devoid of life, unbefitting the home of a Majesty. The river-facing cornets would make good homes for a queen, but these are locked, and my persistent knocking is to no avail. On the west side of the Palace, I find a large study room overlooking the film façade. It's a very good vantage point to view the action, especially when you stand atop the window ledge. The fishing rod camera is moving towards the entrance, tracking the progress of the vintage car pulling up below. Waving madly to the car, I pretend it's the King of Tonga come for a visit. But I suppose, on reflection, the Queen doesn't normally wave in this fashion. In a mad way.

Shortly after the car's arrival, the bomber jacket woman runs out from beneath the entrance, turning to stare up at me. She says something into her walkie-talkie, but this time I don't catch it. Because I don't have my ears on, breaker, breaker, fat buddy.

Bill marches me out through the entrance to Buckingham Palace. There's no sign of the Tongan party, nor my carriage. As I pass the cast members, they stare at me as if they were playing the role of bored models in fashion advertisements for very old clothes. The bomber jacket woman, by contrast, looks as if she's been inflated with red helium.

Bomber Jacket Woman: Get that fucking lunatic off set now! Off the fucking grounds!

FP: Lunatic? I'm Writer in Residence. Well, *formally known as*. But the blood hasn't even cooled…

Bomber Jacket Woman: Next time it'll be the police marching you off! Understand?

FP: Wait… does this mean I'm excommunicated? From *The Crown*?

Bomber Jacket Woman: YES!

FP: It's like Diana, all over again…

En route through the college, Bill doesn't speak, but maintains his right hand on my left shoulder. It's like a scene in a film where a death-row prisoner is being lead to the gallows, or the chair. Except I'm smiling and waving out to people I recognize.

FP: Dr Alex! Spare me the lethal injection!

Dr Alex: What's going on?

Shrugging just the one shoulder, I march on stoically, recalling many similar scenes, of a much shorter distance, through pub doors. I wonder if this ever happened to John Worley, the immortalized naval pensioner? His legacy lives on, in high art, while my mark on the university consists only of carpet indentations, from a fold-out bed.

Dr Zoë: Hello Francis. Still here?

FP: Hi, Dr Zoë. Yes, I'm like J.G. Ballard's Blake, trapped in Shepperton, unable to escape.

Dr Zoë: Are you involved in the film?

FP: Yes, as it happens. I've just been coating Greenwich with impossible dreams.

Dr Zoë: Really? Which part are you playing?

FP: I'm the pilot, the stunt pilot.

Dr Zoë: The pirate?

FP: No, the *pilot*. *Pilot*. Master of the skies.

Dr Zoë: Oh. It's just, you're dressed like…

Bill cuts in.

Bill: Sorry to interrupt, but I need to escort this little twat off the grounds.

Dr Zoë: Oh…

FP: Ha, ha! Yes, it's this scene we're doing. Where the grounded pilot finally takes flight.

Dr Zoë: I thought it was all about the Queen?

FP: Um…

Bill: Come on, move it. You piece of shit.

Dr Zoë, looking troubled, half waves. Further along College Way, numerous Creative Writing students stop and silently point. Other staff members are lined up too, on either side of my path, like sightseers at a royal walkabout.

FP: Hi Harry! Jillian, Emily, John, Heather…

But there are no flowers, no babies to kiss. Helicopters continue to hover overhead, as Bill ejects me out of the West Gate, onto King William Walk.

Bill: Pilot, my arse. Dickhead more like. And don't come back!

Shuffling past the *Cutty Sark* and the Visitor Centre, I join the river path, peering back through the railings at the campus. In Linda Grant's novel *Upstairs at the Party*, Adele is invited to return to her old university some forty years later. The chance of me being invited back to this university in the coming forty years is, I would think, a fat one.

The tide's out, so I wander down to the beach, looking for leaping narwhals and glistening swordfish. Blake's Cessna, which crashed into Shepperton's Thames in west London, may have washed downstream by now. I'll keep my eye out. It might just be my ticket out of here. Ceramic pipe handles are scattered on the shoreline, along with a pongy fish fin, but there's no tail fins from a 70s Cessna. Approaching a metal detectorist, I ask if he's detected an aeroplane. But he seems to recognize me and refuses to remove his headphones. When I mime wings with arms, he bats me off, using oaths. That's what you get, standing around in the cold, listening to bleeps.

Although I should be swimming towards the Morden, for nourishment and safety, I've veered off course. For some inexplicable reason, it makes more sense to stay right here.

Lying on the wet, tidal sand of Greenwich shoreline, I sink swiftly and deeply. Above are helicopters, but their whirring is muffled by sand clogging my ears. In the drifting, frost-edged clouds, I can see pensioner John Worley and his big, fluffy, old man beard. He doesn't wink, which would have been a nice touch. Instead, he begins to dissipate, like cracked flakes of paint, blown by a wind machine.

Before long, like a confused and misguided northern bottlenose, I am altogether beached. Closing my eyes, I feel my body sinking further, becoming one with the silt. As a final resting place, it certainly beats the Painted Hall, St Paul's, or the Palace of Westminster. And the funeral arrangements should be very straightforward, because I'm burying myself. I feel ready to join the layers of Greenwich past: the kings and queens, the naval pensioners, the pipes and pipe makers, the trinkets, the tyres, the Roman fragments of old. Perfectly preserved, like a Vesuvius victim, a peat man, smartly presented in an immaculate flying suit.

Sinking further, into the abyss, I await the angels' whispered calls and the harpsichords, and the rapid flutter of doves' wings, like the flapping of sails. Instead, my descent into never-ending peace is rudely disturbed by the sound of insistent little handclaps. Opening my eyes a snippet, I see that darned kid, the pigeon chaser, from up the hill.

Kid: Shoo, shoo! Fly away, fly away!
FP: Why, you little Henry Prick!

With wet sand clogging up my earholes, I am driven from my solemn Greenwich grave, not to a stirring Moby anthem, but to the silly parp of a Benny Hill yakety sax.

ACKNOWLEDGEMENTS

Sections of this book first appeared in the Society of Authors' *The Author* magazine, and in speech form at the Greenwich Festival and the Dulwich Festival.

The description of the book being 'posted' out of the bus window was first written, in abbreviated form, by Jim Taylor in relation to my earlier book, London Pub Reviews.

Special thanks to Neal Jones, Craig Taylor, Dan Rhodes, Dave Le Fleming, Will Ashon, Steve Finbow, and Pablo Videla.

Thanks also to Samira Ahmed, Sarah Johnson, Stewart Home, James McConnachie, Yves Capelle, Kriston Ware, Peter Hobbs, Andy Miller, Trefor (Tom) Thomas, Lucy Oliver, Andy Daley, Ant Judkins, Dan Bankowski, Emma Barry-Pheby, Grant Welch, Johnny Leathers, Jim Taylor, Liz Boyd & Mark Arn, Ruth Driscoll & Myles Bradshaw, Karen Lane & Tom Horton, and Ann-Marie & Anthony Miller.

Big cheers to my fellow Galley Beggar authors for their huge support and friendship. Cheers also to Kit Caless and Gary Budden at Influx Press, Andrew Gallix at 3:AM, Geery Feehily, and to Creative New Zealand.

Thanks to Shakespeare & Company, Paris (Sylvia Whitman, Adam Biles and staff), Bookseller Crow, Crystal Palace (Justine Crow, Jonathan Main and staff), and everyone at Turnaround.

To the staff and patrons of the Morden Arms, Greenwich, especially Ray Chipps and Judith & John. Thanks also to the staff at John the Unicorn, Peckham, and Hermits Cave, Camberwell.

A huge thanks to the staff and students of the University of Greenwich, particularly legends Alex Pheby and Zoë Pettit.

A bloody massive thanks to Elly and Sam, my brilliant and brave publishers at Galley Beggar Press. Please continue to give them your support.

Most of all, a very special thanks to Linda, Violet & Vincent, my UK family, and all my family back in New Zealand.

In memory of Steve MacDonald.

GALLEY BEGGAR PRESS

We hope that you've enjoyed *Francis Plug: Writer in Residence*. If you'd like to find out more about Paul, along with some of his fellow authors, head to www.galleybeggar.co.uk.

There, you'll also find information about our subscription scheme, 'Galley Buddies', which is there to ensure we can continue to put out ambitious and unusual books like *Francis Plug: Writer in Residence*.

Subscribers to Galley Beggar Press:

· Receive limited editions (printed in a run of 500) of our four next titles.

· Have their name included in a special acknowledgements section at the back of our books.

· Are sent regular invitations to our launches, talks, and annual summer and GBP Short Story Prize parties.

· Enjoy a 20% discount code for the purchase of any of our backlist (as well as for general use throughout our online shop).

WHY BE A GALLEY BUDDY?

At Galley Beggar Press we don't want to compromise on the excellence of the writing we put out, or the physical quality of our books. We've also enjoyed numerous successes and prize nominations since we set up, in 2012. Almost all of our authors have gone on to be longlisted, shortlisted, or the winners of over twenty of the world's most prestigious literary awards.

But publishing for the sake of art and for love is a risky commercial strategy. In order to keep putting out the very best books that we can, and to continue to support new and talented writers, we ourselves need some help. The money we receive from our Galley Buddy subscription scheme is an essential part of keeping us going.

By becoming a Galley Buddy, you help us to launch and foster a new generation of writers.

To join today, head to:
https://www.galleybeggar.co.uk/subscribe

FRIENDS OF GALLEY BEGGAR PRESS

Galley Beggar Press would like to thank the following individuals, without the generous support of whom our books would not be possible:

Jo Ayoubi · Alan Baban · Linda Bailey · Edward Baines · Shenu Barclay · Deborah Barker · Rachel Barnes · Paul Bassett Davies · Jaimie Batchan · Tim Benson · Mark Blackburn · Jessica Bonder · Naomi Booth · Hilary Botten · Edwina Bowen · Greg Bowman · Ben Brooks · Justine Bundenz · Alisa Caine · Suzy Camp · Stuart Carter · Leigh Chambers · Lina Christopoulou · Enrico Cioni · Andrew Cowan · Alan Crilly · Toby Day · Paul Dettman · Janet Dowling · Ann Eve · Allyson Fisher · Simon Fraser · Gerry Feehily · Hayley Flockhart · Graham Fulcher · Paul Fulcher · Neil George · Phil Gibby · Ashley Goldberg · Carl Gosling · Simon Goudie · Neil Griffiths · Robbie Guillory · Drew Gummerson · Greg Harrowing · Luisa Hausleithner · America Hart · John Harvey · David Hebblethwaite · Penelope Hewett Brown · Hugh Hudson · Bex Hughes · Ruth Hunt · Maggie Humm · Agri Ismail · Hayley James · Alice Jolly · Diana Jordison · Riona Judge McCormack · Dani Kaye · Brian Kirk · Jacqueline Knott · Phillip Lane · Jackie Law · Noel Lawn · Thomas Legendre · Joyce Lille-Robinson · Serena Locksmith · Jerome Love · Sean Lusk · Benjamin Lyons-Grose · Philip Makatrewicz · Anil Malhotra · Robert Mason · Adrian Masters · Victor Meadowcroft · Leona Medlin · C.S. Mee · Marilyn Messenger · Tina Meyer · Ian Mond · Linda Nathan · Catherine Nicholson · Seb Ohsan-Berthelsen · John O'Donnell · Liz O'Sullivan · Eliza O'Toole · Chris Parker · Victoria Parsons · Roland Pascoe · Nicola Paterson · Jonathan Pool · Alex Preston · Richard Price · Polly Randall · Barbara Renel · Pete Renton · Ian Rimell · Clive Rixson · Jack Gwilym Roberts · Angela Rose · David Rose · Libby Ruffle · Seb Ohsan-Berthelsen · Richard Sheehan · Ben Smith · Chris Smith · Hazel Smith · John Steciuk · Nicholas Stone · Juliet Sutcliffe · Helen Swain · Ewan Tant · Sam Thorp · James Torrence · Eloise Touni · Margaret Tongue · Anthony Trevelyan · Edward Valiente · David Varley · Stephen Walker · Steve Walsh · Tom Whatmore · Wendy Whidden · Emma Woolerton · Bianca Winter · Lucie Winter · Ian Young · Rupert Ziziros · Sara Zo · Carsten Zwaaneveld